Mulberry Lane
Babies

ROSIE CLARKE was born in Swindon, but moved to Ely in Cambridgeshire at the age of nine. She started writing in 1976, combining this with helping her husband run his antiques shop. In 2004, Rosie was the well-deserved winner of the RNA Romance Award and the Betty Neels Trophy. Rosie also writes as Anne Herries and Cathy Sharp. Find out more at her website: www.rosieclarke.co.uk

ROSIE CLARKE
Mulberry Lane
Babies

First published in 2018 by Aria, an imprint of Head of Zeus Ltd
This paperback edition published in 2019 by Aria

9 7 5 3 1 2 4 6 8

A catalogue record for this book is available from
the British Library.

ISBN (PBO): 9781788549929
ISBN (E): 9781786693006

Typeset by Divaddict Publishing Solutions Ltd.

Printed and bound in Great Britain by
CPI Group (UK) Ltd, Croydon CR0 4YY

Head of Zeus Ltd
First Floor East
5–8 Hardwick Street
London EC1R 4RG

WWW.HEADOFZEUS.COM

Chapter 1

The lane was bitterly cold that morning in December 1941. Clusters of frost clung to drainpipes and rooftops making lacy patterns on the windows of the houses and shops, and the pavements were icy underfoot, forcing the woman to tread carefully as she crossed the road. Somewhere in the lanes, chestnuts were roasting over an open-air fire and the smell made her hungry. She pulled up her coat collar and shivered as she looked up and down the lane. No lights shone in the shop windows and very few had bothered with decorations, except for Mrs Tandy, at the wool shop, who put the same things out every year. Winter was bleak enough in these lanes at the best of times, but the bombing earlier in the year had made things so much worse. Someone had pulled down enough of the damaged building, where the lawyer's office had once been, to make it safe. But the blackened ruins looked dismal and forlorn, the pavements dirty, much the same as bombsites all over the city as they awaited clearance. Yet it wasn't the cold weather or the ruins that brought a frown to the woman's face.

'Oh, hello,' Anne said as she met Ellie Morris coming from the cobbler's shop, just down from the Pig & Whistle in Mulberry Lane. She smiled at the pretty young girl, who was a talented hairdresser. 'I was going to come and see you later today. I wanted a trim and a shampoo and set on Friday – after school finishes. It takes me a while to see the children off – so about four-thirty?'

'Yes, I'm sure I can fit you in,' Ellie said and smiled. 'You might have to wait a few minutes but I shan't keep you long. I'll book you in as soon as I get back to the shop.'

'Thanks.' Anne shivered. 'It's cold today, isn't it?'

'I hate the winter and dark nights.' Ellie pulled a wry face. 'I'd better get back or the door will be locked when my next customer arrives…'

Anne nodded and went into Bob Hall's shop. She had two pairs of shoes that had worn very thin in the soles, but she didn't like the thick rubber that was being used for repairs these days. The last time her shoes had needed repairing, Bob had used nice thin leather soles, which didn't spoil the shape of the uppers.

He was sitting behind the counter of his rather dark little shop, which smelled of glue and leather and polish, hammering away at a pair of what looked like Army boots. As Anne entered, he glanced up and got to his feet at once.

'Good morning, Miss Riley.' He greeted her with a smile of welcome. 'It's nice to see you back – are you here in London for good now?'

'I'm not sure, Mr Hall,' Anne flicked back her light brown hair as she replied. Her nose felt as if it might be red from the icy cold of the air outside. 'We're opening up some of the schools again – at least, we've opened a temporary school to accommodate the children who have returned to London.

Some of them just couldn't settle in the country and their mothers wanted them back now the bombing has calmed down a lot, but I intend to stay in teaching if I can.'

'Well, I'm sure Mrs Ashley will be glad to have you back helping in the bar of the Pig & Whistle at night – and all your friends, too.'

'Thank you.' Anne smiled because Peggy Ashley was the landlady of the pub next door, and one of Anne's best friends. She took her shoes from the wicker basket she carried and placed them on the counter: a pair of smart grey suede courts and a black patent pair of lace-ups that had seen better days. 'I wondered if you could give me leather soles and heels?'

'Well, I might manage leather for the suede courts,' he said after looking at them. 'But I think rubber would be better for the black shoes, Miss Riley. They need a good thick sole to pull them back into shape.'

'I don't like the rubber ones much; they're so heavy,' Anne confessed with a sigh, 'but I suppose...'

'I do have some thinner rubber...' He was about to show her an example when the door to the back room opened and a man entered dressed in Army trousers with braces over a string vest, his arms and shoulders bare.

'Bob, are the boots ready...' the words died on his lips and a faint flush spread up his neck. He was clean-shaven, good-looking, with high cheekbones, dark curly hair and blue eyes, with lashes so thick any girl would envy them, and Anne could smell the fresh clean scent of his soap. 'I do beg your pardon, miss. I didn't realise there was a lady here...'

'You should think before you walk about like that, Kirk,' Bob reproved. Older, with some grey at his temples, there was a noticeable resemblance between Bob and the younger man. 'I'm so sorry, Miss Riley. Kirk is my sister's boy and he's staying with me for a couple of days.'

'Kirk Ross,' the soldier said and moved towards the counter, offering to shake hands. Anne noticed that his nails were broken but clean, his fingers long and shapely, but calloused as if his hands had seen hard work. 'I'm sorry for embarrassing you, Miss Riley.'

'That is perfectly all right,' Anne replied, though her heart was pumping a little faster than normal, because he was rather a magnificent specimen. Obviously, he was fit and strong, with muscles any weightlifter would be proud of. 'I've seen a man in a vest before, Mr Ross.' She averted her eyes, deliberately looking at the shopkeeper. 'Very well, leather on the grey and rubber on the black; they're on their last legs and I should probably have bought new if I could find anything I liked.'

'Thank you, Miss Riley. I'll use the thinnest rubber I have,' Bob Hall promised. 'They will be ready on Friday afternoon.'

'Thank you, good afternoon, Mr Hall – Mr Ross…'

Anne went out into the cool fresh air. It had startled her a little when Bob's nephew had walked in half-dressed, but she couldn't help noticing how well he looked. You didn't often see a man with a body like that and she couldn't wait to tell Peggy about the small incident. She'd been going to call in and tell her friend that she'd moved into her room at Mavis Basset's house, at the other end of Mulberry Lane. It had been Peggy's idea and it meant that she wouldn't have far to go at night after helping out in the bar, as she was this evening. In fact, she now had plenty of time for a little gossip before she went home to change for the evening. Kirk Ross was going to cause a little stir in the lane with those eyes and muscles! She wondered if he would make the Pig & Whistle his local while he was staying with his uncle… and found herself hoping he might be in that evening.

Anne was smiling to herself when she left Peggy half an hour later. They'd had a laugh and a chat and Anne had left believing life was at last taking a turn for the better. She'd been feeling listless and bored for ages after her affair with a married man had come to an end, and then she'd been shifted about all over the country for her job. It was good to be settled in London again and living near to friends.

Peggy was always ready with the teapot and a piece of cake, even though she had her own troubles with her husband estranged and living somewhere in Scotland. Anne thought of her almost as a sister and admired her. Peggy was in her early forties and heavily pregnant; already a grandmother to her daughter Janet's child, Maggie, she seemed to make nothing of having another child, although her son and daughter were now adults.

Maureen Hart, another of Anne's close friends, lived just round the corner in her grandmother's house now. She'd been married for just over a month and seemed very happy with her nursing and looking after her new husband's daughter, Shirley, because he was away serving in the Army – and of course, she was pregnant herself, rather more than a month. She'd told Anne the truth, asking her to keep it private, because she and Gordon wanted people to think the baby was his when it came. Gordon was a decent man and Anne had never seen Maureen as happy as she was when she married him. He'd been patient, carrying a torch for her when she'd thought the father of her baby, Rory Mackness, was the man she loved, and when he'd let her down again, Gordon had asked her to marry him, promising to care for the new baby as his own.

Maureen was really lucky to have found love, Anne thought and sighed. She suspected it was pretty much the same for Peggy. She'd never told Anne about her affair with the young American, but working in the bar Anne had seen the way Able looked at Peggy and envied his adoration. It must be wonderful to be loved so much.

Poor Able Ronoscki had gone missing when the light plane he'd been travelling in had disappeared over the English Channel. Peggy had been recorded as his next of kin and that told Anne of his love for her. Although Peggy hadn't chosen to talk about it, Anne understood the temptation that her friend must have felt to snatch at the chance for love and happiness when any of them could die at any moment. After the devastation of the Blitz, when London had been bombed night after night, the shortages of all the small luxuries they'd once taken for granted and the strict rationing, life was precious and everyone must take what they could when the opportunity arose.

Anne wished she might have the chance to find love again. In her heart, she'd known that the affair with the headmaster of her old school wouldn't last. She'd been foolish to listen to his stories of loneliness and needing her. If he'd truly been willing to leave his wife, it might have been different – but he wasn't, when it came to it, and since then Anne hadn't really met anyone she cared for. She'd thought she might have earlier in the year, but in the end, it hadn't worked out. It meant she was on her own again with no one to take her dancing or buy her flowers for her birthday, and despite a job she loved and lots of friends, she was often lonely. With most of the younger men away fighting this awful war, there wasn't much chance of her finding anyone young and single.

Sighing, Anne walked into the house at the end of the lane. Mavis Basset was putting the kettle on and smiled at her as she entered the kitchen. She was a woman in her sixties, grey-haired, small and slightly bent over; she had on a blue and white pinafore over her dress and blue slippers on her feet. She wore a fine grey hairnet over tight curls and a pair of pink-rimmed glasses on the end of her nose, and she smelled of lavender water.

'Here you are then, Miss Riley,' she said. 'I'm making a cup of tea if you'd care for one – and I could cook you a couple of veggie sausages and some mashed potato, if you would like it. I'm going to have some myself.'

'Thank you very much for the offer, but I'm not hungry,' Anne said. 'I ate my lunch at school and I have some marking to do before I go to Peggy's this evening.'

'Oh, well, if you're busy,' Mavis Basset said and looked disappointed. 'You'll have a cup of tea?'

Anne felt obliged. She'd just had one with Peggy, and she would have something light to eat at the pub later with a drink, but she couldn't refuse the elderly lady, who, she suspected, had been rather lonely for quite some time. 'Yes, I'd love a cup of tea,' she said. 'I'll buy a packet of tea leaves and some sugar tomorrow and that will make it more fair. I usually just have toast and marmalade or a muffin in the mornings, if I can get them, so I shan't be much trouble to you, Mrs Basset.'

'No...' Mavis looked regretful. 'Well, you must do just as you like, Miss Riley – or may I call you Anne?'

'Of course you may, and I'll call you Mavis,' Anne said and sat down at the table. 'After all, we're going to be friends, aren't we?'

Anne wasn't sure why she'd put on her best grey box-pleated skirt with a pretty white blouse that evening; at least, she wasn't willing to admit that she'd worn them in the hope that Kirk Ross would come in. However, she was glad that she had and that she'd chosen a wide red leather belt and her newest red suede shoes – they were her only smart ones and she wore her old ones until she changed them in the pub. She wore her hair fluffed out and waved on her collar when she didn't pull it into a severe bun at her nape. She was lucky enough to have a natural wave in her hair and only needed to get it trimmed occasionally. She'd worn lipstick and a little powder on her nose, which she didn't bother with too often, preferring a plain no-nonsense look for work since it was almost impossible to purchase her favourite Coty face powder these days.

As the evening wore on, Anne felt her sense of anticipation ebbing as customers came and went and there was no sign of the man she'd hoped might visit. They'd been busy all evening but trade was just slowing down when the door opened and two soldiers walked in, laughing and talking as they made their way to the bar. Anne was clearing tables and Peggy went to serve them, but Kirk turned and noticed her as she brought a tray filled with used glasses back to the bar.

'Ah, Miss Riley,' he said and those piercing blue eyes went over her, registering approval. 'Uncle Bob told me you sometimes worked here in the evenings…'

'Yes, I help Peggy out when I can. We've all had to do our bit for the war effort. It isn't easy to find staff these days – everyone has at least one job and sometimes two.'

'Like you?' He raised his brows. His friend touched his arm, indicating that he had their drinks. 'Take them to the table, Mac. I'll be with you in a minute...'

The other soldier carried the tray to the only empty table. He set the tray down and looked about him, and then noticed the girl sitting alone at the next table. In an instant, he moved across, glass in hand, and sat next to her, leaving Kirk's drink behind.

'That's Mac for you,' Kirk said and laughed. 'No pretty girl is safe when he's around.'

'And are they when you are?' Anne asked, smiling as she teased him. It wasn't her nature to be so forward when she hardly knew someone, but she'd taken to Kirk the moment she'd seen him.

'Depends,' he replied and winked. 'I prefer my ladies to be ladies – and I like a little bit of intelligent conversation. Bob said you were a teacher before the war?'

'I still am, but I've had to do all sorts of things recently. I had a go at driving an ambulance part-time, but I didn't want to join the volunteer services and be sent off goodness knows where. At least with my job, I'm free to come and go as I please... and I like working here with my friends.'

'It's a nice place, warm and friendly...' His eyes dwelled on her face. 'Can I buy you a drink?'

'Thank you for the offer, but I don't drink while I'm working – I'd soon start spilling the beer,' she said and laughed, but the look in his eyes was making her heart beat faster. What was it about him that had appealed so swiftly?

'I suppose you get half the customers asking?' He arched his brows knowingly.

'Quite a few, but most know I don't accept. Everyone knows everyone in the lanes, of course.'

'I'm sure you've got lots of friends?'

'Some…' she said, realising that he was fishing and then she turned away as another soldier asked for a pint of bitter.

After she'd served the other customer, Anne looked across the room and saw that Kirk's friend had got up and was leaving with the girl from the next table. 'It looks as if your friend is going.'

Kirk frowned. 'He's had rather a lot to drink this evening. I ought to have warned her.'

'Someone should,' Anne remarked. 'Ellie Morris is married… silly girl. She comes in quite often and I've seen her drinking with strangers, mostly soldiers. Her husband would be furious. If she keeps doing it she will have everyone gossiping about her.'

'Yes.' Kirk turned, watching as his friend left. Several more of the customers were leaving and he glanced at his watch, noticing that it was late. 'Can you come and sit with me while I drink my beer? Or shall I bring my glass to the bar?'

'Well, I've got a few tables to clear. I'll come and talk to you for a minute,' Anne said. 'You'd better drink up or it will be last orders.'

'I'm not too bothered about another one,' he said. 'Are you off soon?'

'Yes, when I've finished clearing up.'

'Where do you live?'

'At the other end of Mulberry Lane.'

'Can I walk you home when you've finished – perhaps make a date for another evening? I'd like to go dancing or to the flicks, if you're interested?'

Anne hesitated and then nodded. 'Yes, I think that would be very pleasant – is it Sergeant Ross?'

'Yes, just got my stripes, but call me Kirk,' he said. 'My promotion is the reason we were celebrating. Look, you get on with your work and then I'll walk you home and we'll have a chat.'

'Yes, all right, see you later…'

Anne smiled and went off to catch up with her jobs. Peggy had called time and everyone was finishing their drink. She was feeling the thrill of anticipation as she took the last tray of glasses to the kitchen and then fetched her coat. Kirk was as interesting to talk to as he'd first appeared and she was looking forward to getting to know him a little better.

Kirk was waiting for her when she came back with her coat on. He smiled at her and nodded as she took his arm.

'You said you lodge at the end of the lane?'

'I've just moved in,' Anne said. 'It's nearer to where I work – and my friends are here.'

'It was lucky for me,' Kirk said. 'We might not have met if you hadn't come into Uncle Bob's shop this afternoon…'

'No, I suppose not,' Anne said, glancing at him curiously. He was so good-looking and she liked his smile and his way of saying what he meant straight out; in fact, she liked everything about him.

They said goodnight to Peggy, who was getting ready to lock up, and left the pub together, walking side by side up the lane.

'I'd really like to see you again, Anne. Do you have to work every night – or could we go out some nights?'

'It's up to me when I work,' Anne said. 'Peggy doesn't mind – she is a good friend.'

'So will you?' he asked, catching her arm and swinging her round to look at him. 'I like you a lot – and I'm sure you get that all the time, but I mean it…'

'As it happens I don't…'

'Really? Are all the men around here mad or blind?' he asked and smiled in a way that made her heart flip. 'I think you're lovely, Anne. Not just to look at but inside, I think.'

'Flattery will get you everywhere,' she said, laughing, but his words touched a lonely spot inside her and made her heart sing.

Although there were a few others making their way home, it was dark because of the blackout, and it felt like they were almost alone. They had passed the disused bakery when they heard the girl scream just ahead of them.

'What the hell – I bet that's Mac and that girl,' Kirk said. 'I'd better sort him out, Anne…' He went off at a run, leaving Anne to follow more slowly in his wake.

It wasn't easy to see what was happening, but as Anne's eyes became accustomed to the gloom of the blackout, she saw a soldier had a girl pushed up against the wall and she was screaming and hitting out at him. Kirk arrived and jerked his friend back, gave him a hard slap around the face and then caught his arm as he tried to punch him.

'Stop it, you stupid fool, or I'll have you on a charge.'

'Bugger you, Kirk. I wasn't doin' no 'arm…'

'You're drunk, Mac. The lady said no – and no means no.'

'She's no lady just a cheap little tart…' his friend claimed drunkenly and Kirk gave him a shake. 'She asked for it…'

'I didn't…' said the girl Anne had called Ellie Morris, and burst into tears. 'He said I looked lonely and offered to walk me to my bus – he didn't even buy me a drink…'

'You'd best get off while you can,' Kirk said. 'Can you get home all right?'

'I haven't got any money for my fare…'

Kirk stared at her hard, and then put his hand in his pocket, pulled out some silver and gave it to her. 'Get home and be more careful in future,' he warned. 'Soldiers on leave are after a good time and if they're drunk they don't always behave right so just remember that…'

'Thanks for helpin' me,' she said, then threw a shamed look at Anne and ran off into the shadows.

Kirk turned to Anne with a rueful look. 'I'd better get Mac home. I'm sorry, Anne. I'll come in and see you tomorrow. We'll arrange something, I promise.'

'Yes, all right,' she agreed and watched as he walked back down the lane towards his uncle's shop. No doubt Mac would be spending the night on the sofa, sleeping off the drinks that had made him rude and abusive to the girl he'd tried to molest.

Anne watched for a moment and then walked off in the direction of her lodgings. It was a pity that the incident had happened, because she'd been looking forward to talking with Kirk, but she was glad that they'd been there in time to save Ellie from a worse ordeal. She really was a silly girl, because if her husband found out what she'd been doing while he was away there would be trouble. Anne was certain she wasn't a bad girl, just lonely and fed up because her husband was away. It was a difficult time for everyone just now.

Chapter 2

'I've got plenty of knitting patterns so I shan't need these back for a while,' Maureen Hart said when she popped in to have a chat with Peggy Ashley that Monday. There were only a couple of weeks or so until Christmas and it was very cold, and she'd brought some of her first size baby coat patterns in for Peggy, who wanted to borrow them. 'I was passing Mrs Tandy's shop this mornin' and there's a notice in the window about rationin'. It's not just coupons; she is havin' to limit what customers buy – particularly certain colours. I think she has plenty of white, pale lemon, blue and pink, though.'

'All the colours mothers choose to knit for their babies,' Peggy said. 'This make-do-and-mend the government is on about is all right in its way. I don't mind pulling old woollies undone to make a jumper for me or Janet, but I think babies should have a few new things, don't you?'

'Mine will have to be new because I don't have anythin' put aside,' Maureen said. 'I think Mum gave all my baby clothes away years ago. People were collectin' for the church jumble sale and other things – and she didn't know we were goin' to have another wretched war…'

'How could she?' Peggy said and stopped as her daughter Janet burst into the kitchen with her little girl Maggie in her arms.

'Mum, put the wireless on…' Janet said breathlessly. 'I can't believe it…'

'What has happened?' Maureen felt a cold shiver down her spine. 'Is it somethin' to do with the war?'

Peggy snapped the wireless on and they heard the chilling words: 'The United States is now at war with Japan after the terrible raid on Pearl Harbor yesterday…'

'Good gracious…' Peggy looked at her daughter and then at Maureen as they listened in horror to details of the devastation the Japanese planes had inflicted without warning on the US naval base. 'War with Japan… America is in at last. Do you realise what this means for all of us? We've been struggling for months and this will make all the difference.'

'I caught somethin' last night, but the news of the attack was only just comin' in then and I didn't realise how serious it was,' Janet said, rocking Maggie in her arms as she started to grizzle. 'I can't believe the Americans have actually declared war at last…'

'I saw somethin' about an attack on Pearl Harbor on a newspaper stand when I was on the bus making my way home,' Maureen said, 'but I didn't realise it was an American military base or how serious it was. I'd never heard of it…'

'I don't think any of us had really,' Peggy said. 'This must be devastatin' for the Americans… so many people killed and so many ships lost, but if it shortens the war…'

'It must have been hellish,' Janet said and put Maggie into her playpen so that she could play with her new bricks and a little wooden truck. 'They were completely unprepared and those ships were like sittin' ducks – all those men killed and injured...'

'It should help to balance things out for the Allies – if America takes on Japan in the Pacific area...'

'We'll be at war with Japan too now,' Maureen said and shook her head. 'Every time you think perhaps things may start to get better, somethin' awful like this happens.'

'Well, I suppose it had to happen,' Janet said. 'America has been warnin' Japan to back off and they had no intention of doing so... it's really horrible.'

'Yes...' Peggy looked from one to the other. 'Able would've been in it now. I shouldn't have known where he was...' Tears hovered on her lashes as she spoke of the young American captain whose child she was carrying.

'Don't upset yourself, Mum,' Janet said looking anxious, because although Peggy was only in her early forties it was late enough for childbearing. 'I think it's a cause for celebration in a way. Someone has to stop Hitler before he destroys the whole world. I know it's awful about the ships and the men who were hurt and killed, but we can do with some help and it should shorten the war with America fully committed – shouldn't it?'

'We can only hope so,' Peggy said and stood up to put the kettle on. She looked at her daughter's anxious face. 'Don't worry about me, love. I think it's my hormones goin' wild. I feel weepy over everythin' these days.'

'Yes, I know. I got a bit like that when I was havin' Maggie...' Janet glanced at the knitting patterns. 'Some of these look nice – but they're a bit small for Maggie; she will be two in March, but I'm sure she needs that size already.'

Peggy picked one up to look at it. 'Maureen is lending them to me. She has loads of patterns, because she's been knittin' for friends for years. It's just a case of whether we can get enough wool. I've got a few of your things and Pip's put away. I should've kept them for Maggie, but you had so many lovely things given you.'

'I was lucky,' Janet said. 'My friend Ryan gave me far too much stuff for her after everything was lost in the cottage in Portsmouth, when the plane crashed on it. Ryan was tryin' to make up for what I'd lost, but he was too generous. Some of Maggie's things have hardly been worn.'

'Mrs Tandy was tellin' me she's thinkin' about sellin' baby clothes in her shop,' Maureen said. 'She says she's goin' to take in good clothes and sell them for the mothers and keep a shillin' in every pound for herself.'

'That is a good idea,' Peggy said. 'You could take some of Maggie's things and offer them for sale, Janet.'

'I think I'd rather give them to you – or Maureen,' Janet said and looked at Maureen. 'The dresses are very fancy and will only be used for best, but some of the bonnets and coats are lovely. If either of you has a girl they could be useful.'

'Maggie had some lovely things,' Maureen said. 'I was just tellin' Peggy that I don't have anythin' much yet. I've made a few things, but I still need most of it. I'd be happy to buy anythin' you don't want, Janet.'

'It's all for a girl – pink with flower embroidery.' Janet laughed at Maureen's eagerness. 'If you have a boy there are two white outfits. I didn't even use them for Maggie because they weren't as pretty.'

'Are you sure you shouldn't keep them in case you need them in the future?' Maureen asked and then wished she hadn't as she saw Janet's smile fade.

'It will be a long time before Mike and I have another baby,' Janet said and her eyes were heavy with the sorrow she normally hid so well, because although Mike was now recovering from his terrible wounds, he still couldn't remember her or their marriage. She turned away to prepare some rosehip syrup for Maggie. The government had recently raised the allowance of cod liver oil for children to help make up for what they lacked in their diets, because of the dearth of fruit and other necessary vitamins, but Maggie preferred rosehip syrup which was more widely available and was just as good for her. 'Mike isn't up to that kind of thing for now. Besides, the hospital won't let him home for good yet…'

'I'm sorry. I didn't mean to pry.'

'Of course you didn't.' Janet shook her head, cradling Maggie's special mug in her hands. 'We're lucky we've got our Maggie. A lot of women may never have their husband's child because they've lost them to the war through death or terrible injury.'

'I know. We saw hopeless cases on the ward all the time at the military hospital in Portsmouth,' Maureen said, 'but Mike isn't hopeless, Jan. I'm certain he will get better in time. He didn't get wounded… well, down there, did he?'

'No, of course not!' Janet managed a laugh, though it didn't reach her eyes and Maureen guessed there was some private sorrow Janet wasn't sharing. 'It's more a mental thing with him I think – anyway, let's talk about the babies we do have. I want some cardigans for Maggie in her size – why don't we have some sort of swap? You make me two cardigans and I'll give you some of Maggie's baby things.'

'Yes, all right. I asked Mrs Tandy to put aside several bundles of wool for me and she did, even though she wouldn't for anyone she didn't know. What colour would you like?'

'I thought I'd like somethin' in pink and white – if that's not too much trouble?'

'No, that's ideal. I can use bits and pieces to do stripes or patterns,' Maureen said and stood up. 'Well, I'm sorry there was such dreadful news for the Americans, but now they know how we feel. I'd better go and get ready. I'm on duty at the hospital this evenin'…'

'How long are you goin' to stay on?' Janet asked. 'Do they know you're married?'

'I haven't told anyone anythin' yet,' Maureen said. 'I've had a bit of sickness in the mornings the past couple of days, but by evenin' I'm fine, so I shall carry on workin' for as long as I can.'

'Good…' Janet smiled. 'I'll sort some things out for you then.'

'And I'll call in on Mrs Tandy tomorrow and get some of the pink wool I've reserved.' Maureen kissed her cheek and then Peggy's. 'Your hair looks nice, Janet. Did Ellie Morris cut it for you?'

'No, I went to that hairdresser up past the market,' Janet frowned as she answered. 'Ellie is a good hairdresser but…' She shook her head. 'The least said the soonest mended. It isn't my business what Ellie chooses to do.'

'No…' Maureen nodded in agreement. 'I do know what you mean. I saw her walkin' home with a soldier the other night. He had his arm around her waist and was kissing her neck – in the lane…'

'Yes, well, you shouldn't gossip about her, you two,' Peggy said. 'None of us can throw stones. We've all got our own secrets.'

'Yes, I know,' Maureen agreed ruefully, because goodness knows she couldn't take the moral high ground when she was carrying a former boyfriend's child. At least she hadn't tried to deceive anyone; she'd told Gordon the truth and he'd still wanted to marry her. 'It isn't my business, but if someone tells Peter Morris – he's got a violent temper. I wouldn't want to be in Ellie's shoes if he discovers she's been carryin' on…'

'As long as he doesn't hear it from us,' Peggy said and smiled at them. 'Let the girl do what she likes. It's her life and she's only eighteen. She got married too young in my opinion – and, anyway, who knows whether Peter will come home or not…'

'We none of us know,' Maureen agreed and a shiver went down her spine, because she hadn't had a letter from Gordon since he'd returned to his unit after their wedding and she was a little worried. 'I hope the poor man does return, for his own sake – just as I pray for Gordon every night for me and Shirley.' Shirley was Gordon's daughter by his first wife and one of the reasons that Maureen and Gordon had become close and married just a few weeks earlier.

'Well, I'll sort those things out for you,' Janet said. 'I've got a couple of maternity tops you can borrow if you like…'

'Thanks,' Maureen said. 'I'm goin' to make my own things when the time comes, but I can use yours as a pattern. I've got a lot of Mum's dresses and the material is good, so I'll cut them up when mine get too tight. I'm sure she'd be thrilled if she knew.' Maureen felt a pang of sadness that her mother hadn't lived to see her married and carrying her first child. At least her father had pulled through his latest illness and the doctors were promising that if he continued to improve he could come home for Christmas, though he would still be an invalid.

Maureen bent down to touch Maggie's golden curls and then took leave of her friends. It was tempting to sit in Peggy's warm kitchen and chat with both her and her daughter, but Maureen had some shopping to do before she went home to change for her shift at the hospital. She would have lots more time for chatting when she gave up work, but for now she was determined to work for as long as she could get away with. Even though she now received some of Gordon's pay, the extra money would come in useful.

Leaving the pub, she walked the length of Mulberry Lane, past Mrs Tandy's wool shop, which had a 'Back Soon' notice in the window and entered the grocery shop, where she'd worked and lived most of her life until she'd taken up nursing at the start of the war. Jack Barton was serving a customer with a packet of Player's cigarettes and a bar of Fry's dark chocolate. Jack's house was across the road, he'd just got out of prison after making the biggest mistake of his life by robbing a post office. He'd regretted it and Maureen knew he wasn't a habitual criminal, just a man driven to desperation by his situation and his wife's nagging. It was his wife's illness and the death of his youngest son, Sam that had got him out on parole.

He looked up and smiled as Maureen entered.

'It must seem strange,' he said as the customer paid and left. 'After years of standin' behind this counter to come in and see a stranger in yer place.'

'You're not a stranger, Jack,' she said. 'Dad is glad to have you here. I wish you could stay for longer.' Henry Jackson, Maureen's father owned the business and had recently married Violet, a lady some years younger than himself who ran her own little business making bespoke corsets from the living quarters above the shop.

'I've got another month and then they want me in the Army,' he told her. 'This is a good job and I'd 'ave liked to stay on and look after the business for yer dad and Violet – but I don't 'ave a choice. It's either the Army or back to prison.'

'I know,' Maureen gave him the list of goods her grandmother wanted. 'You would've gone in the forces anyway, Jack. You couldn't have stopped home once the war started if you hadn't been in prison.'

'You're right,' Jack agreed. 'It's just that Tilly still isn't well enough to come home. I've left Tom sitting twiddlin' his thumbs in the parlour and he's bored stiff I can tell yer.'

'He was always doin' small jobs,' Maureen agreed. It was unfortunate that Jack's wife, Tilly, had suffered an nerves after her youngest son was killed on a bombsite the previous year and was now in hospital, having suffered a nervous breakdown. 'Have the doctors said how long it will be before Tom's shoulder is right again?' Tom had been trying to get his brother away from the bombsite when the explosion happened, killing Sam and injuring Tom. However, he'd been lucky and was out of hospital and home again.

'I think about three months, if he does the exercises they gave him,' Jack said and totted up the bill. 'There you are, Maureen – fifteen shillings, sixpence-ha'penny.'

'Thank you,' Maureen said and counted out the change from her zipped purse. 'I haven't time this afternoon, but I'll pop round tomorrow and have a chat to Tom. I think I might know of somethin' he can help with while he waits for his shoulder to heal.'

'I should bless yer for that,' Jack said and smiled. 'You Mulberry Lane ladies are lovely people, Maureen. With my son and wife both in different hospitals, I don't know what I'd 'ave done stuck in prison. Peggy got up that petition to get me home for a while on parole and it made the world of difference – especially now we've got Tom 'ome again. If I was stuck in prison they'd 'ave put my boy in a 'ome, 'cos 'e's only fourteen.'

'Peggy helps everyone,' Maureen said. 'I'll talk to Tom tomorrow – I must fly now or I'll be late for work.'

Seeing the notice was still in Mrs Tandy's window, Maureen crossed the street. She would go for the wool tomorrow after she popped in to have a little chat with Tom Barton...

Ellie combed through her customer's hair, looking at her in the mirror. Mrs Tandy's hair was thick and a nice silvery-grey, which she sometimes allowed Ellie to blue rinse if she was going to one of her meetings at the Women's Royal Voluntary Service or the Women's Institute. She was a great jam maker and her local branch had borrowed a canning machine so that they could use it to preserve as much jam and fruit as possible; the Women's Institute was playing a large part in helping the women of Britain to adapt and keep their spirits up despite the hardships of war.

'Did you want a blue rinse today, Mrs Tandy, or perhaps you would prefer a friction? We've got some lovely new ones in this week.'

'Oh, I do like a friction,' Mrs Tandy said, smiling at her in the wall mirror. 'What perfumes do you have this time?'

'Black Gardenia, Midnight in Paris and Lily of the Valley,' Ellie said, showing her the small bottles of friction. Sprinkled on the hair, rubbed into the scalp and then combed through the hair, they were refreshing for the customer, making the scalp tingle pleasantly and smelling lovely for days.

'I've had Black Gardenia before,' Mrs Tandy said. 'It is very sophisticated. I think I'll have the Lily of the Valley please...' She sniffed as Ellie undid the little bottle and held it under her nose. 'Oh yes, that is lovely and reminds me of spring. It is a real treat. I didn't think you could get these now.'

'We can't very often,' Ellie said as she sprinkled the friction and rubbed it gently into the scalp. 'I don't know where Mrs Stimpson gets her stock, but this week she managed to get some waving lotions as well as shampoo and hair lacquer. I've been told to use it all sparingly, because she may not be able to get fresh supplies for a while.'

'Oh, don't tell me,' Mrs Tandy made a wry face at her in the mirror. 'I'm findin' it more and more difficult to replenish my stock. I crammed my shelves and stockroom as full as I could before the war started so I can just about manage to keep goin', but unless things improve I'm not sure for how long.'

'I think a lot of shops are in difficulties,' Ellie sympathised as she began to finger wave Mrs Tandy's hair. She made deep waves at either side of her head and fastened them with special pronged clips, and then she began to select small sections of hair and make pin curls, a tidy row one way and then the other, right down to the nape. The neat flat curls would brush out into a fluffy mass of waves and curls once dry.

'Well, I'm considerin' takin' in second-hand baby clothes and resellin' them for a small commission for the mothers – and I may have to take on a lodger.' Mrs Tandy sighed. 'I'm reluctant to do that, but one cannot always choose...'

Ellie paused in the act of tying the pink hairnet over her curls. 'If you do decide to take on a lodger – would you consider me, Mrs Tandy?'

'You, my dear?' Mrs Tandy looked puzzled. 'I thought you were livin' with your mother-in-law?'

'I am...' Ellie sighed deeply. 'Peter thought it would be best while he was away in the Army; he thought it was too expensive to run a home on what I would get from his wages. He wanted me to save what I earned so we could have nice things when he gets out.'

'But you're not happy with the arrangement?' Mrs Tandy's brows rose.

'Doris doesn't like me much,' Ellie said. 'She's told me I've got to pay more for my keep and be in when she says – and she's forever goin' into my room and readin' my letters…'

'Oh dear, that doesn't sound ideal,' Mrs Tandy said sympathetically. She hesitated and looked thoughtful as Ellie wheeled the hairdryer into place and switched it on, tipping the hood to place it over her head.

'Is that comfortable?' she asked. 'Would you like a magazine and a cup of tea?'

'Yes, thank you, Ellie,' she said and accepted the magazine. 'We'll talk about your little problem later, dear.'

Ellie's next customer arrived at that moment. It was a young woman for a Marcel wave and a shampoo. Ellie put a fresh gown on her and asked her to wait while she went out the back and brought a cup of tea for Mrs Tandy.

She spent at least three quarters of an hour on the Marcel wave and apologised to Mrs Tandy when she rescued her from under the dryer, because she was looking hot and bothered, her cheeks very pink.

'I'm sorry to keep you so long. My apprentice left last week. She decided they pay better in the munitions factory, but Mrs Stimpson has employed another girl straight out of school and she'll be here when you come next time.'

'I could see you were busy,' Mrs Tandy said as Ellie deftly removed the pins, gave her hair a light brush and then fluffed up the curls at the bottom. 'That looks beautiful, as always, Ellie…' She stood up as the gown was whisked away and followed Ellie to the desk to pay. 'Is that four and sixpence as usual?'

'Oh, I'm afraid the friction has gone up to one and sixpence – it's five shillings altogether.'

'Everything goes up,' Mrs Tandy grumbled. 'But that isn't your fault, Ellie – and here's six shillings; the shillin' is for you.' She put her purse back into her bag and snapped it shut, then, 'If you like, I'll show you my spare room. You can pop round this evening when you finish here and we'll discuss terms then.'

'Oh, thank you,' Ellie said delighted at the prospect. 'I've been looking for a room for ages, but the only one I could find was awful – and it meant an even longer bus ride in the mornings. If I lived next door it would be so much easier for me, and I'd save three shillings a week on fares.'

'Yes, well, I think it would suit me too,' Mrs Tandy said. 'I shall expect you at about six this evening then.'

'Half-past. I've got a perm this afternoon at four...'

Ellie watched as Mrs Tandy left and went next door, feeling elated. She was sick and tired of Peter's mother going on at her when she returned late at night. They'd had several rows over it and Doris had threatened to write to Peter and tell him that his wife was carrying on with soldiers. The old misery guts didn't see why Ellie should have fun when her precious son was out there fighting for his life.

'Yer an ungrateful girl,' Doris had told her sourly. 'If my Peter knew what you've been up to behind his back he would give yer a good hidin'!'

'If he did, I'd walk out on 'im,' Ellie shouted back at her. 'If I'd known what it would be like to live 'ere with you, I'd never 'ave got married. My aunt warned me how it would be when she signed for me to get married. She said you were a sourpuss... and I can't stand being 'ere wiv you!'

'How dare you, you little cat!' Doris yelled at her. 'If it weren't for my Peter, I'd throw you out now. What he saw in you I'll never know...'

'He loves me,' Ellie said defiantly. 'And don't worry, the minute I can find a room somewhere else I'm orf...'

She smiled as she saw her customer for a permanent wave coming. If Mrs Tandy didn't change her mind, Ellie could move in straight away. She would have more freedom away from her mother-in-law's prying eyes and she knew Mrs Tandy's home wouldn't smell of stale cabbage or drains. It was a wonderful chance for her and she could hardly wait.

Chapter 3

Tom Barton grimaced as he lifted the heavy coal bucket and carried it into the kitchen. His left shoulder was still stiff and sore; he'd broken it in two places as well as receiving deep gashes to his lower arm, and he couldn't carry anything much with that hand yet. They'd told him the broken shoulder would heal and if he worked at his exercises he would be able to use it almost as freely as he once had; it was the cuts to his lower arm that had worried the doctors most. They'd been afraid of blood poisoning, because of the rusty metal on the bombsite that had sliced through his flesh, but fortunately he'd been so much luckier than Sam, who had died instantly, and now he was back at home.

It was good having his dad here, even if it was only for a short time. Tom was a little ashamed that he didn't miss his mother much, but he knew that when he saw her again she would blame him for Sam's death. Even if she didn't say the words, she would look at him in a way that told him she hated him. He'd known that since he was quite small, though he'd never had any idea why his mother disliked him so much. Sam was her favourite and Tom had been aware that his mother seemed to take against him even more as he grew older. He'd never said anything to her and he never cheeked her or refused to do whatever she asked, the way Sam did, and yet Sam could do no wrong – and now she would hate him even more because Sam was dead. Tom knew he'd been on the way when his parents had got wed, so did his mother blame him for being born, trapping her in marriage to a man she didn't love? He couldn't ask his father a question like that and his mother would just turn away if he asked her why she didn't like him.

Tom's throat tightened with grief, because he'd cared about his brother even though he was always causing him bother. He wished it had been him that had died when the unexploded shell went off, and he'd said as much to his father during one of his visits to the hospital.

'Don't be daft, son,' his father had replied gruffly. 'You're a good son to your ma and me – and I'm glad you didn't die.'

'But Sam did and that's my fault,' Tom said. 'I should 'ave done somethin' – stopped 'im goin' on those ruins...'

'You told him enough times, I've no doubt,' his father said and looked sad. 'I'm the one that should bear the guilt, Tom. If I'd been 'ome instead of banged up in prison, Sam would 'ave done as 'e was told. And you wouldn't 'ave been hurt bad. It's my fault, not yours.'

'I knew what he was doin'. I should've gone to the coppers – they would've stopped him going to the bombsites. I wish I had; he might still be alive now...' Tom sucked in his breath because it still hurt that his brother had been killed for nothing.

'Yer couldn't 'ave seen your brother sent off to a remand

home, Tom. It's what might 'ave 'appened if you'd told the police.'

'Yes, but...' Tom had stopped short of telling his father about the man he'd seen up on the bombsite talking to the boys. Sam had told him there were people looking after him, and Tom guessed there were criminals running the gangs of boys, black marketers and fences for stolen goods. They let the youths risk their lives for a few bob and took anythin' of real value for themselves. Those shadowy men were the real thieves and the cause of Sam's death, because without them he would've given up long ago. A few bits of scrap metal for Bert round at Three Farthings Court was one thing, but digging on the ruins of a jeweller's shop for gold and silver was a crime, far more risky. Tom knew that Sam probably couldn't have got out of it if he'd tried. Once that sort got their claws into you, you couldn't break free without a struggle.

'Is there somethin' you want to tell me, son?'

Tom hadn't been able to meet his father's eyes as he shook his head. His father would want to get to the bottom of it if he told him and Tom knew that he couldn't let him get involved. Jack Barton had gone to prison for robbing a post office up the West End and Tom knew one wrong move and he would be back behind bars with extra years to serve. If he behaved himself, he would be permitted to join the Army instead of returning to prison and Tom knew how much his dad wanted that... to hold up his head again, to wear the uniform of a soldier, instead of the badge of shame he'd earned by one stupid act.

Tom made up the range in the kitchen so that it would be hot when his father returned from work in Mr Jackson's shop. They were managing with fry-ups and toast most of the time; pie and mash with gravy from the shop twice a week when Jack went to the hospital to visit Tilly, and a shepherd's pie on Sundays, courtesy of Peggy Ashley. She'd sent them an apple pie one day and some rock buns another – and she'd told them they could go over for a meal whenever they liked, but his dad was too proud to take advantage. He accepted what Peggy sent over, but to have expected a meal every day was too much and neither of them wanted charity.

Tom had helped his father finish papering Peggy's bedroom the previous Sunday morning. He couldn't do much, but he'd held the paper straight for his dad to cut and he'd helped brush the paste in, but hanging it was beyond him yet because of his injured shoulder. Peggy had been delighted with the result and wanted to pay, but Tom's father had shaken his head.

'Not this time, Peggy. You've done too much for us. When Tom gets back to work properly, he'll be on a regular basis, but this one is on us.'

Tom worried that he might not be able to manage all the jobs that he'd been doing before the accident. He was working on the stretching and pushing exercises that the hospital doctors had shown him, but they made his shoulder sore if he did too many and he still couldn't lift anything heavy with that arm; in fact, he'd been warned not to. He made himself useful about the house, managing the washing up, even though he couldn't dry the dishes very well and had to let them just drain; it took ages to straighten the bedclothes with one good hand, but he managed and was teaching himself to flex his fingers again.

He was setting the kitchen table for their tea that afternoon when the doorbell rang. He went to answer it warily and then grinned as he saw who had come to visit him. Opening the door wide, he invited her in and led the way through to the kitchen.

'We're not as tidy as we could be,' Tom said and gestured to Maureen to sit down. 'Would yer like a cup of tea?'

'Yes, please, if it's no trouble,' Maureen said. She hesitated for a moment as he hung the kettle over the cold tap and turned it on, letting it fill nearly to the top. 'Do you need any help, Tom?'

'Nah, I can do easy jobs like this,' Tom replied without turning his head. 'It takes a bit longer. My left 'and is all right as support but I can't 'old anythin' 'eavy yet and if I try it just drops through me fingers.'

Maureen sat down at the kitchen table, watching as he fetched cups and saucers from the dresser and a jug of milk from the pantry. He didn't put a sugar bowl out, but like most people, the Barton men had given up bothering with it, because there wasn't much in the shops these days.

An open newspaper was on the table. It was a few days old and Maureen's eye fell on an article saying that all unmarried women between the ages of twenty and thirty were to be called up for war work. The factories were already filled with young women, but now it seemed they were needed for other jobs, like anti-aircraft defence and more important work that would once have been the prerogative of men. Men previously needed in office jobs were to be called up for service and women were to take their place. Maureen wondered if Anne would have to give up teaching – or was that a reserved job?

'Do you want saccharin?' Tom asked as he put a little packet on the table. 'Me and Dad prefer tea without, but we put it in coffee – not that we drink that often. Yer can only get that chicory stuff in a bottle round 'ere.'

'No, I mostly drink my tea without,' Maureen said. She accepted the cup of tea from him and sipped it, a little surprised to discover that it was good. 'How are you feelin' now, Tom?'

'My shoulder hurts like hell sometimes, especially after I've been doin' me exercises,' he said and massaged it with his right hand. 'But otherwise I'm all right. The 'eadaches went weeks ago and I was lucky not to get blood poisonin'. I'll be all right soon, so they tell me.'

'What are you goin' to do with yourself now?' Maureen asked. 'Are you stayin' on at school to take your certificate at sixteen?'

'I don't want to,' Tom said and looked thoughtful. 'Dad says I needn't if I can find payin' work to do after Christmas. The hospital said I could come 'ome but I was to take it easy for a few weeks – after that I should be as good as I will be...'

'You can manage light jobs, though, can't you?'

'Yes, I reckon. I keep the fire goin', make the tea and wash up... beds too, and bring in the coal, but I can't chop the wood properly yet.'

'I was wonderin' what you would think of helpin' out at the shop when your dad goes into the Army...' Maureen hesitated as he looked at her. 'For now, I thought stocktakin', helpin' sort the papers – and maybe a few deliveries in the lanes. Violet was sayin' a lot of people want deliveries, because they're busy these days; even married women with older kids are signin' on for a bit of war work part-time. I've bought a second-hand bike with a basket. Do you think you could ride or push a bike? Or would it be too hard?'

'I'll learn to ride again,' Tom said, looking at her uncertainly. 'But who is goin' ter keep the shop open?'

'Well, my father is comin' home for Christmas,' Maureen said. 'He won't be able to do much and he'll need help. You wouldn't mind workin' with him, would you? He doesn't always get his words out very well and he can't walk more than a few steps – but he'll tell you what wants doin' – and we're goin' to advertise for a girl to come in part-time. I thought you might manage it between you. After all, you'll be fifteen next spring.'

'Yer don't need a girl an' all, Maureen,' Tom said. 'I could do deliveries last thing after the shop shuts, or in me lunch break – and all yer dad needs to do is sit in 'is chair and tell me what 'e wants.'

'I'm not sure if he will be able to come downstairs at all for a start,' Maureen said and hesitated, then, 'Are you sure that you can manage it all, Tom? You'll need to stock the shelves and unpack when it all comes in.'

'What about the wholesaler?' Tom asked, looking thoughtful. 'I don't reckon I could do that yet.'

'I've been orderin' what we need by telephone,' Maureen said. 'I went in and had a good talk with Mr Bennett at the wholesaler. He's the new manager and he was very sympathetic – told me I could phone my orders in and his son would deliver everythin' to the shop. He promised to let me know about any special offers and seemed keen on keeping our business.'

'That sounds all right then,' Tom said, feeling excited now. He narrowed his gaze. 'You're sure you ain't just bein' kind?'

'We need someone we can trust, Tom,' Maureen assured him. 'The wages aren't as much as you could earn in some of the factories, but in time – if we can get the business goin' again – it will go up. Your dad is gettin' two pounds and fifteen shillings, but you would only get thirty-seven shillings and sixpence at first. I tried to persuade Violet that you were worth as much as your dad, but she won't budge – she'll have to put the wage up once you've proved you can do it, Tom. Otherwise, we'll threaten her with you leavin'.'

'Nah, I shan't do that,' Tom grinned, looking as pleased as punch. 'Once I've got me shoulder right I can earn a few bob extra somewhere. I wouldn't leave 'er in the lurch when she's been good enough to give me a job.'

'Well, she needed a little persuadin',' Maureen said. 'I managed to make her realise that Dad is never goin' to be well enough to manage on his own – and I've no intention of standin' behind that counter all day. Between you and me, I might help out a bit once I've given up nursin', and then you'd be able to take the deliveries out sooner – but I'm not goin' back full-time.'

'Well, you won't be able to when you get the baby, will you?' He grinned at her. 'I bet Shirley will love havin' a brother or sister to play with.'

Maureen looked surprised. 'How did you know I was havin' a baby?'

'I've seen yer goin' in and out of Mrs Tandy's shop regular,' Tom told her with a grin. ''Sides, you and Janet were talkin' about babies in the lane the other day, and the way you looked, I sort of guessed.'

'Well, you're a sharp one and no mistake,' Maureen said, looking as though she'd had the wind taken out of her sails for a moment, and then she laughed. 'Well, I don't suppose I shall hide it for much longer.'

'You'll be about to keep an eye on things fer yer dad,' Tom said. 'I reckon he didn't know how much you did fer 'im until yer went off to be a nurse. 'E'll be glad you're back in London fer good.'

'Yes, I know. He's already told me,' Maureen smiled. 'You can tell your dad about the job then, Tom – and if you want to start practisin' with the bike it's at Gran's. Pop round and get it when you like and then your dad can see who would like their orders delivered; maybe just wheel it for a start? Just until your shoulder is better.'

'I could manage that all right,' Tom said and the excitement was in his eyes. 'When can I start?'

'As soon as you feel able, I think. We're goin' to make a small charge for deliveries – I'm not sure whether to charge sixpence or a shillin'.'

'If you make it too dear they won't use the service,' Tom said. 'Try sixpence fer a start and see how yer go on.'

'We shall make a businessman of you yet,' Maureen said and stood up. 'That was a nice cup of tea, Tom. I'm glad I came. I wanted to offer you the job if you thought you could manage it.'

'I'll manage it,' Tom said. 'Me shoulder will get better and stronger – and I'll show you how grateful I am, Maureen. I shan't let yer dad down and I shan't pinch from 'im – and nor will Dad.'

'I know that, Tom. Your dad isn't a thief by nature. He made a mistake because he was desperate, but he's learned his lesson.'

'Yeah, I know. 'E give me 'is word 'e'd never do it again,' Tom said and looked thoughtful. 'I reckon it was Ma what drove 'im to it. She kept on at 'im because 'e wasn't earnin' enough and 'e got muddled up in 'is 'ead. I ain't makin' excuses fer 'im – but that's 'ow it was. 'E was just tryin' to please me ma.'

'Yes, I'm sure he was,' Maureen said. 'Well, I must go because I have to get ready for work.'

'Thank yer fer comin'.'

'That's all right. I'm glad you've agreed to help us out.'

Tom walked to the door with her and then returned to the kitchen. He was grinning as he started to wash the cups they'd used. The wage wasn't as good as he could've got at the munitions factory, but they wouldn't have taken him on at his age, especially with his arm the way it was. An apprenticeship as a mechanic or a carpenter was out of the question, because he couldn't afford to pay the fee to be taken on, and until his arm was fully recovered he would find it hard to get any sort of manual work, so shop keeping was a good job. If his arm got back to normal, he might start his own business up one day, but not until he'd saved some money. His dad would be sending money home in future and Tom would be able to keep some of his wage. He would go to night school and learn various skills and then, when the time came, he could set up as his own boss, as he'd always planned. He wasn't going to work for an employer all his life; he had ambitions.

Maureen was thoughtful as she walked back to Gran's to change into her uniform. The pavements were damp and greasy underfoot because it had rained overnight. It wasn't much like Christmas, because the shops couldn't light their displays the way they normally did, and there was very little to see or buy these days, even though the government had increased the supply of essential goods a little just for Christmas.

Tom was happy and she felt pleased with herself. It had taken a lot of persuading to make Violet agree to giving Tom a chance in the shop. Both Violet and Maureen's dad wanted her to take over the shop and she'd had to make them believe that she was never going to give up her hospital work for the shop, and she hadn't told them yet that she was pregnant. Tom probably wouldn't want to work behind a counter for years on end, but once Maureen's father was well again – *if* he was well again – he could take over some of the work and perhaps take on a girl part-time if Tom left. Maureen had already decided she might lend a hand when necessary once she was forced to give up at the hospital to have the baby, but she wasn't going to be a full-time shop assistant again. She would have her hands full caring for her child and Shirley.

Shirley was sitting at the kitchen table eating bread and butter and strawberry jam when Maureen got in. She jumped up and ran to her, throwing her arms about her and telling her all about her day at school.

'You've been making a scrapbook of the king and queen?' Maureen said, going to the sink to wash her hands. 'That sounds interestin', darling. Have you got lots of pictures to paste in?'

'Gran gave me some papers she'd saved with pictures of Queen Elizabeth when she married King George,' Shirley said, her eyes sparkling. She was nine now but she'd had to grow up fast during the time she was evacuated to the farm where she had been very unhappy. 'No one else had got any so that makes my project special, doesn't it?'

'Yes, I should think so,' Maureen said and looked at her grandmother. 'That was good of you, Gran. Was it your special souvenir magazine?'

'Yes,' Hilda Jackson looked up from the old jumper she was unravelling in order to make a new cardigan for Shirley.

'I kept it for years, but I thought Shirley would make better use of it so I gave it to her.'

'I hope she isn't too much for you, Gran?' Maureen asked softly.

'Shirley is never any trouble to me. I love havin' her here.' Gran smiled at the child fondly. 'We've also made a few decorations for Christmas, but we shan't show you yet, because it is a surprise.'

'You have been busy…'

'It's fun living with Gran,' Shirley ran to give her a hug. 'We've got lots of surprises for Christmas.'

'Well, that's lovely, and I'd like to see your scrapbook, Shirley.'

'I shall keep my scrapbook forever,' Shirley said and went back to the table to finish her tea. 'This jam is lovely, Mummy. Are you goin' to have some?'

'Yes, why not?' Maureen said. She smiled, because Shirley was so loving and always called her Mummy now. When Gordon first brought her to tea she'd been missing her dead mother and was sulky, and spoiled by her grandmother, but her experiences as an evacuee had taught her a hard lesson. 'I have to leave in half an hour. What are you goin' to do this evenin', Shirley?'

'Gran says she's got lots of old newspapers in a trunk upstairs, so we're goin' to look for other pictures to put in my book.'

'You mustn't wear Gran out, love.'

'The child is no bother to me,' Gran said. 'She'll be huntin' for them, not me.'

'There's a letter from Daddy for you,' Shirley said. 'It's on the table in the hall. It came by second post this afternoon, when you were out.'

'A letter from Gordon?' Maureen left the table and went to find it, tearing it open with a sense of relief as she saw her husband's writing.

It's been a while since I've had time to write. We've been busy –

The next few lines were scored out with blue pencil. Maureen frowned because the censor had been strict and almost a third of what Gordon had written had been obliterated.

I miss you and Shirley very much and when I'm standing down I plan where we're all going for our holiday next time I'm home. I love you so much, my darling, and I think of you all the time. I hope Hitler is giving you a rest at home. I pray you and the baby are keeping well. Please don't do too much, for my sake, because I couldn't bear to lose you or the little one. I'm so lucky, Maureen, and I wonder if one of these days –

The next sentence had been scored out again and Maureen made a sound of annoyance in her throat. It really was too bad of the censor to scribble out something she was sure was personal, just because it might sound defeatist if a soldier spoke of death.

Gordon had finished his letter with more words of love and begged her to write. He told her that her letters meant the world to him and repeated that he was thinking of her constantly. Maureen sighed as she replaced it in the envelope and slipped it into her pocket as she went upstairs to change. Because of the censor she had no idea where he was or how hard things were where he was stationed, but she guessed he was in the thick of it somewhere. She was lucky to get a letter at all, and relieved, because it meant that he was still alive – or he had been when he wrote these few lines.

'Please come home to us,' Maureen said fervently as she changed into her nurse's uniform. 'We need you, Gordon. Please keep safe for us.' Yet she knew that he'd been sent out to fight and that was what he must do, whatever the cost. He was just one of thousands of men fighting to keep her and all the women and children at home safe. And now the news from the Far East wasn't good. Two of Britain's battleships had been sunk in the past month and the Japanese were invading both British and US territory.

Feeling a little faint, Maureen sat down on the edge of the bed. She hadn't experienced faintness for a while and had hoped that she was over it. It soon passed, but it would be very awkward if it happened at work when she was looking after a patient.

Maureen brushed her hair and went back down to the kitchen. She had time to talk to Shirley for a few minutes and then she would have to leave for work.

Chapter 4

Anne looked at her reflection in the mirror and sighed. She was over thirty and tiny lines were beginning to show at the corners of her eyes, but with her hair freshly cut and set she didn't look too bad. Kirk was taking her dancing that evening. They'd been to the pictures together to see a Charlie Chaplin picture midweek, which had made them laugh; the alternatives had been gangster films or Westerns and they'd decided on a comedy because the newsreels were dire enough.

'I get enough fightin' without watchin' more,' Kirk had told Anne. He'd given her a small parcel wrapped in brown paper. 'I wanted you to have this…' he said, looking a little shy. 'I saw it in the Portobello this morning and thought of you…'

'What is it?' She'd looked at him in surprise. He laughed and told her to open it and she did, staring at the small amethyst pendant on a gold chain in shock. 'Kirk, it's beautiful – but you really shouldn't have spent so much money on me.'

'Why not?' he'd asked and smiled as she touched it with one finger. The look in his eyes had sent shivers down her spine, because she knew he wanted to kiss her. 'If you like it that's all that matters…'

'I love it, but you hardly know me… No one has ever given me presents like this…'

'Well, I shall…' Kirk had said. 'I don't have much time to court you. We've got two weeks, Anne – and I have to squeeze such a lot into that time…'

'You're really nice,' she said and put the box in her pocket. 'Thank you so much.'

'You're welcome,' he'd said and grinned. 'Next time I might make it a ring…'

'Kirk, stop teasing me…' she'd gasped, feeling as if she couldn't breathe.

'I thought we might go to a dance on Friday,' he'd suggested as he'd walked her home later that evening. 'A dinner dance at a nice hotel. It will give us a chance to talk more than the flicks, really get to know each other.'

'Sounds lovely. I enjoy dancing,' Anne had replied. 'It's quite a while since I've been anywhere like that…'

'I should've thought you would have willin' escorts queuin' up to take you out?' Kirk had said with a lift of one eyebrow. 'No one special around at the moment?'

'There hasn't been for some time,' Anne had said, then: 'There was someone, but it's been over for a while…'

'You've been honest and so shall I. I'm thirty; an accountant before the war, now in the Army for the duration, and single. My mother is a widow and she worked hard to give me a decent education, so when I have a choice I'll go back to a boring job in an office that pays well. I intend to buy my own house when that sort of thing is feasible again, and when I get married I want two kids and a wife who can cook…' He gave her a cheeky grin. 'How are you with apple pie?'

Anne had laughed, because she liked the direct approach. 'I'm a little older than you. I should like to marry and have children before it's too late for me, but it has to be to the right man.'

'You're an independent woman and you think for yourself,' Kirk had replied with a faint smile. 'I think that's what appealed to me from the first. A lot of women would have made a fuss or been covered in embarrassment when I walked into Uncle Bob's shop half-dressed.'

Anne's eyes had teased him. 'I dare say quite a few men might walk around without a shirt if they had your physique.'

'You noticed then?' Kirk's eyes had glinted with amusement.

'Oh yes, I noticed,' Anne said. 'I think half the women in the lanes are already drooling over you – or they would be had they walked in to Bob's shop at that moment.'

'Thank you, kind lady,' he'd mocked, eyes bright with mischief. 'However, I would rather be admired for my mind.'

'Ah, I see – the intellectual type,' Anne had said, giving him back in kind. 'You think it's an insult if women want you for your body?'

'Do you want me for my body, Anne?'

'I think you have a fine physique and that's all I'm sayin',' she'd teased. 'However, it doesn't hurt to be as beautiful as you are – beautiful in a masculine way, of course.'

'So I should hope.' Kirk had given a throaty chuckle. 'I like it that you have a sense of humour, Anne. My parents used to tease one another. They were very happy until my father died. He was such a strong man, a docker and out in all weathers – but then he got a soakin' at a football match; stood about in wet clothes and had a drink with his mates. He developed a chill a couple of days later and it turned to a putrid chest and pneumonia. He died so quickly, Mum and I didn't have time to say goodbye.'

'Oh, I'm so very sorry. How old were you at the time?'

'I was just eleven and I'd won a place at the grammar school. They'd planned for my education so that I would rise above the kind of life they'd had and my mother took a job so that she could support me through college. I had an aptitude for figures, so I went in for accountancy, which is a solid job and normally lasts for life.'

'That's what I thought about teaching,' Anne had said. 'I was eighteen when my parents died. I'd just started my college course and my father had banked the money for me so there was no threat to my education. My uncle and aunt gave me a home – and then my aunt died a few years ago.'

'So, you only have your uncle?'

'And my friends. Peggy is like a sister, and Maureen too is a good friend, as is Janet Rowan, Peggy's daughter – and a girl named Sarah Milner; she's another teacher and we go on holiday together sometimes, but Peggy and Maureen are like family. All the people in the lane are casual friends; it's that sort of place.'

'My mother has moved out into the suburbs near to a friend of hers now that I'm in the Army. She has a job cooking cakes and serving tea in a nice little teashop, but it was a bit too much like village life for me, so I decided to visit Uncle Bob this leave – and I'm glad I did.'

'So am I,' Anne had said and hugged his arm. 'How long do you have before you go back?'

'I report back on Christmas Eve. I hope you'll come out with me as often as you can until then, Anne.'

'I'd love to,' she'd said. 'It is really nice for me to have a male friend...'

'A friend?' Kirk had stopped walking and turned her to face him, his strong hands holding her with a gentle firmness that made her tingle. 'I hope we're going to be more than that, Anne? I know I'm feeling much more – and I'm not just talking about sex.'

She'd drawn a deep breath, then, 'Yes, I should like that, Kirk. We hardly know each other but…' He'd leaned forward and kissed her softly on the lips, taking her breath. 'I do feel there is something between us,' she'd said when she could speak again. 'Something special…'

'You said you like my body,' Kirk had teased. 'Well, I like yours, Anne. In fact, I like everythin' about you – and I'm askin' you to marry me, now, before I go back out there. I want to make love to you, but I shan't insult you by askin' you to sleep me with me without a ring on your finger. And I want to know you're here, waiting for me to come home – I want love, Anne. I think it's someone to cling to and think about when life seems close to the edge. No one else has ever made me feel like this…'

'Kirk…?' Anne's mind had whirled in confusion. For a few seconds she'd thought she must have misheard; he couldn't have proposed to her – yet he had looked at her intently, waiting for her reply. To her surprise, she'd discovered that she wasn't sure how to answer. She ought to have dismissed it with a laugh and a firm refusal, but she'd found herself wanting to say yes. 'I'm not sure… I mean I like you an awful lot and…' He'd kissed her again, holding her pressed against him so that she could feel the arousal of his manhood. Her breath had come faster and she'd been aware of a throbbing need, a longing to lie with him and touch those powerful muscles and feel his strength as he loved her. She couldn't know what else she felt because it was too soon, and yet she'd

never felt anything like it before in her life. 'It is totally mad…
I'll need a few days to think…'

'You have until Friday,' he'd told her, his demanding eyes
seeming to compel and draw her in. 'I'm going to buy the
licence and book a room for us – and you can tell me your
answer at the dance. Either we go to bed and act shamelessly
or you marry me on Saturday and we'll have a few days
honeymoon somewhere…' Kirk had looked deeply into her
eyes then. 'It's wartime, Anne. I might never come back, but
I'll leave everythin' I've saved to you, so if there's a child you
will be provided for. I'm askin' you to take a chance on me, to
let us both snatch some happiness from this wretched world
before it's too late. What has either of us got to lose?'

'Oh, Kirk…' Anne had whispered, her heart racing wildly,
because he was right. What had she got to lose? 'I think I'm
going to say yes. Give me until Friday and I'll give you my
answer then…'

Looking at herself in the mirror now, Anne knew the
answer she would give. Kirk hadn't talked about love, but
he'd spoken of desire and wanting – and the need to find
happiness together. It was much too soon! She didn't know
him. Yet something was telling her to take what he offered
and worry about the consequences later. If she didn't take her
chance now it might never come again and she wouldn't be
the first girl to have a whirlwind affair because of the war.
It was happening all the time, though not every relationship
ended in marriage, and the unfortunate ones found themselves
alone and pregnant. Anne was lucky to have found a man
who really cared and wasn't just looking for sex. Perhaps
she was a fool, but she knew in that moment that she was
going to say yes and grab the chance for happiness now
before it disappeared. She was over thirty and men like Kirk

didn't come into her life that often. If she let this opportunity slip through her fingers it might not happen again. Anne didn't know if she loved Kirk or if he loved her, but she did know that she enjoyed being with him and she wanted to be loved.

She'd seen the way Kirk had handled the drunken Mac and knew other men respected him. Anne liked him, felt drawn to him, and she was so tired of being alone. She'd almost given up on marriage and a family and now Kirk was offering her all the things she'd imagined had passed her by.

Seeing Peggy and Maureen planning for their babies had made her feel broody, a little out of it. She wouldn't mind a bit if she fell pregnant with Kirk's child immediately – even though what she was doing was totally mad. Anne had believed she wouldn't risk her heart again unless she was sure, but Kirk's proposal had taken the wind out of her sails. It had to be now or never and so there really wasn't a choice. She was going to grab him now with both hands and hope that he wasn't killed and that when he eventually returned to her, she would be able to make a happy life for them both...

Ellie was aware that she'd had too much to drink again. She hadn't meant to have that last gin and orange because Mrs Tandy wouldn't like it if she was tipsy now that she was living in her spare room. They'd arranged five shillings a week for the room, and five shillings for breakfast and a sandwich lunch. Ellie hadn't wanted an evening meal, because she preferred to buy something out. Quite often she was offered free drinks by the men she met in various pubs, and sometimes something to eat from the bar, a piece of pie or toast and scrambled egg or a tomato sandwich. She wasn't that bothered about food, but she'd discovered that she needed her few drinks in the evening. It had grown on her, the desire for a boost of alcohol and she needed more to give her that warm safe feeling these days.

She went to various pubs in and around the lanes. At first, she'd always gone to the Pig & Whistle, but she'd seen Janet looking at her oddly a few times when she'd been flirting with soldiers, and so she'd decided to vary her drinking habits. She knew she was being foolish, accepting free drinks all the time because one of these evenings it was going to get her into trouble. Most of the soldiers she drank with were happy to walk her part of the way home and get a few kisses and a fumble in a dark alley somewhere, but one of them had turned nasty when she stopped him going further.

'You're a cheatin' whore,' he'd said furiously when she fought off his attempts to get her knickers down. 'I've paid fer yer drinks all night and now I want me money's worth.'

'I'm not a whore,' Ellie had said and when he'd pushed her back against the wall she'd kneed him where it hurts. He'd gasped in pain, swearing and hitting her round the face before she escaped and ran off, leaving him winded.

'You wait, you little bitch,' he'd called after her. 'Next time, you won't get off so lightly. You'll get what's comin' ter yer one of these nights.'

Ellie had run and run until she was out of breath and had had to lean against the wall gasping for breath. She knew she'd been lucky to escape and it slowed her down for a while. Afraid of bumping into the soldier again, she'd avoided the pub, which was at the end of Commercial Road. She'd refused free drinks for a while and gone home sober, because her wage wouldn't run to more than a shandy or two, and she certainly couldn't afford her favourite gin and orange. She'd decided to stick to somewhere in the lanes, but after a while she'd started going to Peggy Ashley's pub for her snack and a shandy.

It was then that she'd had her second unpleasant encounter. His name was Mac and he was a little drunk, but he'd seemed so nice and she'd agreed to let him walk her to the bus stop. He'd tried to force himself on her, just like that other one, but this time she'd been lucky and his friend had made him leave her alone. Her rescuer had been with Anne Riley and asked if she could get home and she'd lied, made out she hadn't got her bus fare. He'd given her ten bob in change. If all the men were that generous, Ellie could make a lot of extra money, but most of them would want something in return, and she wasn't a whore and didn't want to be one. But surely it wasn't so wrong to want a little bit of fun! After all, she was only eighteen.

Ellie loved Peter, at least she'd thought she did when he asked her to marry him and bought her a ring. The trouble was he'd been sent overseas soon after they were married and she hadn't seen him for months. He wrote occasionally, but only brief notes that didn't mean much. Ellie wanted a man who was here with her, someone to take her out and spoil her, take her to the pictures and dancing, and buy her flowers or chocolates for special occasions.

She wished the other soldier had picked her that night, the one that had come to her rescue: Anne's escort. He was strong and he'd got a nice face. Ellie thought she wouldn't have minded having sex with him. Not much chance of that though. He was going out with Anne Riley. Ellie wished she was single again. She might have found a bloke with a little money in his pocket. She was fed up with working for two pounds a week plus tips. Mrs Stimpson had promised more once she worked up a clientele, but every time Ellie asked, she'd made excuses about how expensive everything was.

It was such a dull life being married to a soldier who was away all the time. Ellie was too young to sit at home knitting and she didn't have friends her own age in the lanes; her school friends, who were from a different area, were all working in factories or had joined the voluntary services. When Peter had asked her to marry him, she'd been so excited, but she hadn't liked living with his mother, who was always picking on her and warning her that Peter wouldn't like her going out. She wanted some excitement, a bit of life, which was why she went to the pub every night. Most evenings a few soldiers or sailors would come into the bar and buy her a drink. This evening though, she hadn't had one drink bought for her and she'd spent all her own money. Now she couldn't afford another drink and she might as well go home. The saner part of her mind wished she hadn't had as many as she'd had already, but her loneliness made her miserable and so she drank to forget. Where was Peter when she needed him? Other people got leave, why didn't he?

She got to her feet, feeling a bit light-headed and walking a little unsteadily towards the door. Just as she was about to leave, a soldier entered the pub. Ellie didn't even look at him until he grabbed her arm as she opened the door.

'Not goin' already?' he said in a cold voice that sent shivers down her spine and triggered an unpleasant memory. It was him! The man who'd tried to rape her round the back of the pub down Commercial Road.

'I'm goin' home,' she said, aware that her head was spinning. 'Leave me alone.'

'You still owe me, Ellie,' he said. 'I don't spend money on a girl for nothin'. You and me 'ave unfinished business...'

Ellie felt a spiral of fear down her spine. She tried to pull away, but he had a firm grasp on her arm, his fingers bruising her flesh.

'Call out and ask for help and I'll make you sorry another night,' he hissed in her ear. 'Either you pay up now or they'll find you dead in the lane one mornin'…'

Ellie felt the dread and fear spreading through her body. Resistance was futile. She should never have accepted his drinks that night and knew that she had to pay. She closed her eyes and allowed him to push her out of the pub and into the lane. Her throat was closing and she wanted to cry or scream, but she was paralysed with fear. One false move and he would cut her with the knife he had pressed against her side…

Chapter 5

Maureen bent over the bed she'd just stripped and remade it with clean linen, straightening the blanket. There were twelve beds in this ward, six on each side. On this busy ward, the curtains were dark green, matching the gloss paint that reached halfway up the walls, giving the ward a dull, cheerless atmosphere, and there was the usual pervading smell of strong disinfectant. However, the patients all had get well cards pinned up above their heads and there were some vases of flowers on the windowsills making things feel a bit cheerful. The other nurses had told her that they put a few decorations up at Christmas, which would improve it for a while.

She was nearing the end of her shift and she'd been feeling tired for the past hour; so, when her head suddenly started spinning and her knees buckled, she fell on to the bed and just lay there as she fought the nausea.

'Are you all right, Maureen?' one of the other nurses came rushing up to her. 'What happened? Did you feel faint?'

'Oh… yes, just a little,' she said. 'I'll be all right in a moment, Janice.' She sat up and then felt the sickness rushing up her throat and grabbed a little sick bowl from the cabinet beside the bed, vomiting into it.

'What is all this?' Sister Morrison came bustling up to them, a look of annoyance on her face. 'Are you sickening for something, Nurse Jackson?'

'It was just a little faintness and nausea. I'll be all right in a moment.'

'I see...' Sister frowned. 'I think we need a little talk in my office, Nurse Jackson. Nurse Brown, finish off here please.'

Maureen followed behind Sister Morrison, realising that the moment of revelation had come. It would be pointless to lie, and perhaps she would be better off staying at home and looking after herself for a while.

'Well, nurse, I think you have something to tell me,' Sister said when she had seated herself at the desk. 'You may sit down. You are obviously not well – so perhaps you would like to explain.'

'I'm having a child,' Maureen said, looking proudly at the Sister as she sat in the chair opposite the large mahogany desk. She took the chain she wore under her uniform out, unfastening it and slipping off the wedding ring, which she slid on to her left hand. 'I was married a short time ago, and I'm pregnant.'

'I suspected as much,' Sister said and glared at her. 'Well, I'm very disappointed in you, Nurse Jackson – or what is your name now?'

'Hart – I'm Mrs Gordon Hart,' Maureen said and it gave her a lovely warm feeling inside to say the words. Maureen was unafraid, because her marriage was her armour against what she thought of as silly rules. 'I know I ought to have told you before, but I was hoping to work for a few months before I gave in my notice...'

'Well, I see no reason to change that,' Sister Morrison looked put out but also approving. 'You were highly recommended to us and we're still short of nursing staff. Do you feel able to continue your duties here for a bit longer, nurse?'

'Yes, I think so. I was a little faint and nauseous earlier, but it usually passes quickly and I'm all right afterwards.' Maureen felt a faint sense of relief that she wasn't to be sent off under a black cloud, because she hoped to return to nursing one day.

'Well, in that case, put your ring back on the chain inside your uniform and keep this information to yourself, Nurse Jackson. I am prepared to overlook the fact that you did not tell me the truth immediately. My personal feelings on the subject are that we should not dismiss a good nurse simply because she gets married. Goodness knows, we need all the trained nurses we can get while there's a war on. Once your condition becomes obvious you will have to leave, but perhaps another month or even two at a pinch.'

'Yes, Sister, I agree – and thank you for your tolerance. I should've told you sooner.'

'You should, but I understand why you didn't,' Sister replied calmly and then a faint smile relaxed her mouth. 'Are you feeling able to continue your work or would you like to leave now? You are due off duty in an hour.'

'I feel able to continue,' Maureen assured her. She tucked her chain and ring back out of sight and left the office.

Janice came up to her as she returned to the ward. 'Did you get a ticking-off? I could see you were ill, but my rushing up to you like that drew her attention. I'm sorry if she was awful to you.'

'She was quite sympathetic,' Maureen told her and smiled. 'I'm sorry you had to clear up after me. I would've done it myself if Sister hadn't interfered.'

'It was no bother,' Janice said. 'Do you feel rotten?'

'No, I'm all right now,' Maureen said. 'Don't tell anyone, but I'm pregnant.'

'Gosh…' Janice looked at her oddly. 'Did she hit the roof?'

'She wasn't pleased, but she needs all the nurses she can get, so I'm stoppin' on for a while.' Maureen saw the other girl look at her left hand awkwardly. 'I am married but I don't wear my ring at work for obvious reasons.'

'You are brave,' Janice said admiringly. 'My boyfriend wanted me to get married when he came home on leave, but I wouldn't. I'd have to give up my job and…' Her eyes opened wide. 'I wouldn't though, if I did what you've done…' she gave a little laugh. 'Harry is home again next week for ten days' leave – do you think I dare?'

'It depends on what you want,' Maureen said. 'If you really love him – but it's not very nice when they go back on duty, is it?'

'No, that was one of the reasons I refused last time,' Janice said. 'You can't go out much if your husband is away in the Army. Everyone thinks you're cheatin' on him if you do.'

'Yes, I suppose they would,' Maureen agreed. 'It doesn't bother me not goin' out much. I've got my husband's little girl at home; her mother died some years ago and she calls me mummy now. We live with my grandmother, and she looks after her when I'm at work. Gran loves her and she's really happy now that we're living with her. I take Shirley out at weekends when I can and I visit my friends – and when I'm at home, I knit.' She smiled. 'We all make things for the Red Cross to go to the prisoners of war. I've been making scarves and socks, as well as baby clothes.'

'I like to go dancing with my friends,' Janice said, looking thoughtful. 'We go in a group and I don't walk home with a man, just a couple of girlfriends – but I'm not sure Harry would like that if we were married.'

'Well, that's a problem you'll have to work out,' Maureen said. 'I've got some bedpans to scrub in the sluice room. I'd better get on...'

She left the other nurse to get on with her own jobs. It was better that her situation was out in the open now. Maureen hadn't liked deceiving her superior on the ward, but the rules in many hospitals forbade married nurses. It was such a foolish rule, especially when the hospitals were so busy. Anyway, she'd been given a few more weeks before she had to leave and Maureen was grateful and got on with her work with a will.

She thought about what Janice had said concerning marriage to a soldier in the present times. It did mean that a girl couldn't just go out as freely as she once had without causing gossip and in many cases living alone must be miserable. Maureen was lucky, because she had Gran, her family and friends and Shirley, but some girls had no one – like Ellie Morris.

Maureen recalled how excited the girl had been when she got married, but her husband had been away for ages and now she was always at the pub and often let soldiers and other men buy her drinks, and she'd been known to leave the pub with a soldier. People had started to gossip about her and her husband was almost bound to hear some of it when he got back.

Drying her hands and rubbing in a little cream before she left the sluice room, Maureen wondered if she ought to have a chat with Ellie. If the girl was just lonely, perhaps she could help her, arrange to have her over to tea or something...

As she fetched her coat and then left the hospital, Maureen decided that she would pop into the hairdresser's on her way home and ask Ellie if she would like to come for tea on Saturday.

Ellie stared at her face in the mirror, touching her mouth with tentative fingers because it hurt so much. She had a dark bruise on one cheek and a split lip where that soldier had hit her several times, and her body was covered in bruises. A shudder went through her as she remembered the brutal ordeal she'd endured. He'd banged her against a wall, pulled her knickers down and taken her in the most savage way imaginable, biting at her ear, thrusting into her so hard that she had screamed in pain and wept. At first she'd tried to resist, but after he'd hit her, knocked her down on the pavement and kicked her, she'd just lay and let him get on with it. Then, after he'd finished, he had started to abuse her verbally, slapping her face and calling her awful names. When at last his spite was exhausted, he'd stared down at her and spat on her.

'That's the way I treat whores,' he'd said. 'No one cheats Knocker out of his rights and gets away with it…'

Ellie had shut her eyes and prayed that he'd finished with her. Tears had slipped down her cheeks and she had been overwhelmed with shame and misery as she heard him walk away. She'd just wanted to lie there and die, but even though her body felt so sore and her mouth tasted of blood, her heart kept on beating and after a while she'd dragged herself to her feet, feeling dazed as she pulled her dress down and found a way to walk home. Ellie had known she must have looked awful, but it was so dark because of the blackout that no one noticed her or challenged her appearance.

Mrs Tandy had asked her to come in the back way at night and left the kitchen door unlocked for her. Ellie had locked up after herself, realising that the house was dark and quiet. She'd switched on the light and run some cold water, drinking straight from the tap and letting the cooling spray ease the pain of her face. Patting it dry with the small hand towel, Ellie had replaced the towel on the nail by the sink, switched out the light and gone upstairs in the dark.

She would have liked to have got in the bath and scrubbed herself all over, but the noise would have woken Mrs Tandy and she hadn't wanted her landlady to see her in that state. Entering her bedroom, she'd locked the door and staggered over to the bed and collapsed on to it. What little energy had remained after the brutal beating had left her then and she'd fallen asleep.

In the morning, Ellie heard Mrs Tandy go downstairs and she ran quickly to the bathroom to run some warm water, immersing herself in it and working the soap vigorously all over herself. Her body was stiff and ached all over, but some of the pain eased in the hot water. Not everyone in the lane had the luxury of a proper bathroom, but Mrs Tandy's husband had had it put in when they married, and Ellie had never been more thankful for the comfort. She knew that she might be able to wash away the stink of that man's body, but she would never cleanse him from her mind. His bestiality and foul language as he'd raped her would live on in her mind even when her body had healed.

After she was dressed, Ellie put on a thick layer of make-up to hide the bruises, but her mouth was swollen and there was nothing she could do about it, because it was too sore to put lipstick on. She looked pale and there were shadows under her eyes, which did not go unnoticed as she went into the kitchen for her breakfast.

Mrs Tandy looked at her sharply. 'Ellie, my dear, you look terrible – and I saw a trace of blood on the kitchen towel; what happened to you?'

'I 'ad an accident as I walked home last night,' Ellie lied. She hated lying to her generous landlady and took to concentrating on spreading marmalade on to her toast. 'I was feelin' a bit lonely and I had two gin and oranges...' She heard her landlady tut. 'Yes, it was foolish of me, but it's so long since Peter was home...'

'Yes, I know, Ellie,' Mrs Tandy's voice was sympathetic. 'It's awful for you young girls. You ought to be courtin' and be taken to the pictures and dancin'. It's the fashion to get married in a hurry before the men go off to war, but it can lead to sadness. I think you've learned your lesson, whatever happened last night, and I doubt you'll go drinkin' alone in future.'

'No...' A shudder went through Ellie. She certainly wouldn't give that brute another chance to beat her and misuse her.

'Well, I know I'm just a silly old woman, but you can talk to me and share my supper any day you wish. I like you, Ellie. Not only are you like the daughter I never had, you do my hair beautifully. We might go to the pictures once a week if you like – and we could listen to the wireless together in the evenings. I know it is a little borin' for a girl like you, but – Peter will come home again one day you know, and it would be best if he didn't hear gossip about his wife.'

Tears had welled in Ellie's eyes as she saw nothing but kindness in Mrs Tandy's face. She'd thought her landlady would read the riot act and perhaps threaten to throw her out, but instead she was understanding and trying to help. Suddenly, the tears poured out of Ellie as she sobbed out her hurt.

'There, there, my love,' Mrs Tandy comforted. 'Why don't you tell me what really happened?'

'I can't... it was so awful,' Ellie wept, but then found herself telling the older woman about what the soldier had done to her. After a while she quietened, accepting the handkerchief Mrs Tandy gave her and wiping her cheeks, covering the material with make-up. 'I'm sorry. I've ruined yer hanky.'

'Never mind that, it will wash,' Mrs Tandy said and looked angry. 'Why didn't you wake me last night, Ellie? I would've called the police. That evil man needs to be taught a lesson. He should be in prison – or better still hung.'

Ellie gave a watery smile. 'Thank you, yer've made me feel so much better. After what 'e did and said, I felt worthless...'

'No! You must never feel like that,' Mrs Tandy said firmly. 'He had no right to treat you that way, Ellie. It was his choice to spend the money on you. He should not have expected that you would let him have intercourse because of a few drinks.'

'I knew I shouldn't take drinks from strangers,' Ellie said, 'but once I started, I couldn't seem to stop – I tried stayin' away from pubs, but I got lonely and went back to sittin' in the bar just for some company. I can only afford a shandy, but I like gin and orange and I need it to pick me up sometimes.'

'It seems to me you've been gettin' into bad habits, my girl,' Mrs Tandy said. 'Well, this goin' to the pub every night stops now, do you hear? I shall buy a bottle of gin and we'll sit and have a drink in the evenings. I quite like a gin and tonic myself, but I never have more than one – and from now on, that's what you'll have.'

'Yes, thank you,' Ellie said, hiccupping as she dried her tears. 'I'd already decided I wouldn't go to the pub alone again. Whatever will Peter say to me?'

'You won't tell him,' Mrs Tandy said firmly. 'We'll keep it between us because it's too late to tell the police now. I know you've got some cuts and bruises; all over you, I imagine, but you've had a bath. Last night we might have convinced them that you'd been assaulted but now…' She shook her head. 'Did you know this man's name?'

Ellie frowned. 'I'm not sure… he said somethin' like – "no one does Knocker out of 'is rights" – but I don't know if it's 'is first name or 'is last and I don't want to. I couldn't go to the police, Mrs Tandy. I should feel too ashamed. You know that they would say it was my fault. I go to pubs alone and I let men buy me drinks and walk me home – I'm askin' for trouble. No decent girl does that sort of thing – and me with a husband away fightin'.'

'Yes, my dear.' Mrs Tandy looked sad. 'I'm afraid that is exactly what everyone would say, includin' the police. It would be their case that you gave tacit consent by acceptin' drinks and then lettin' the man take you home.'

'He had a knife in my side when he made me go with him,' Ellie said and anger sparked in her eyes. 'I was forced, believe me.'

'I do believe you, my dear – but a police officer might not and you would be made to look and sound like a bad girl in court. It is most unfair the way young women are treated in these cases.'

'They would blame me for going to a pub alone…'

'My instincts make me want to see this man behind bars

or hung – nothin' else is enough, but I fear you would suffer more than he if you went to the police now. I think all we can do is try to forget it, my dear.'

Ellie looked at her in silence and then inclined her head. 'I know you're right, Mrs Tandy. Besides, everyone would gossip and point the finger, and I want to forget if I can.'

'Are you willin' to give up the visits to the pub and spend your evenings with me?'

'Yes, I am,' there was a note of determination in Ellie's voice. 'I know I've been stupid and I think I'm lucky he didn't slit my throat.'

'Yes, perhaps,' Mrs Tandy agreed. 'Now eat your breakfast, Ellie, and get to work. You can't let him ruin your life, my dear.'

'No, I'm not goin' to. I know my face looks awful – but I'll just have to say I had an accident.'

'Say that you slipped on dog mess,' Mrs Tandy advised her. 'There has been some on the pavements recently. People can't feed their dogs now and they just turn them out to roam the streets. The government warned everyone to send them to the country or have them put down at the start of the war, but you know what folk are like. The kids want their pets, but then when food is short...' She shook her head. 'It's as good an excuse as any.'

'Yeah, it is,' Ellie said and smiled tentatively. 'You've been very kind to me, Mrs Tandy.'

'Most people are if it suits them,' Mrs Tandy replied. 'I like havin' you here, my dear. Now stick your head in the air and forget what that brute did. If you let him make you unhappy, he wins.'

'Yeah I know,' Ellie agreed, but it was easier said than done. A little doubt was lingering at the back of her mind, but surely, she couldn't have got pregnant because of that brute's attack. It never happened just like that – did it? She gave a little shiver and pushed it from her mind. She would worry about it if she had to... for now the horror of the attack was as much as she could face.

She finished her breakfast, washed her face and applied more make-up, and went to work. Maureen Hart was the first person to come into the hairdressing shop that morning and Ellie turned from the mirror to face her with some trepidation.

'Good mornin', Ellie,' Maureen said brightly and then stopped. 'What happened? You look as if you've had a nasty accident?'

'Yes, I slipped on some dog mess on the pavement last night,' Ellie said. 'I went down with a real bang and hit my face on the kerb. I've got bruises all over.'

'Oh, how awful for you,' Maureen said sympathetically. 'That was very unfortunate. The council should round up all the stray dogs, because there are several of them runnin' round now.'

'I expect they got lost or perhaps lost their homes in the Blitz,' Ellie said, and then, needing to change the subject she added, 'it's sad really. Did you want to make an appointment?'

'Yes, I'd like a trim and a shampoo and set on Saturday next week,' Maureen said. 'I'm taking Shirley to a matinee at the pictures this afternoon. I wondered if you would like to have tea with us afterwards – say at six, after you close for the night.'

'I close at five on Saturdays,' Ellie said, feeling pleased. 'It will give me a chance to wash and change. I'd like to come very much, Maureen. Thank you.'

'You're very welcome,' Maureen said and smiled at her.

'I shall see you later then, Ellie – and I hope you soon feel better.'

'Thanks, you're very kind,' Ellie said. 'I know where you live and I'll be there at six this evening.'

Maureen nodded and went out, slipping the appointment card Ellie had made out for her into her pocket. She'd only just left when Ellie's first customer arrived. She took her coat off and turned, giving an exclamation of shock when she saw Ellie's face. Explanations followed and were accepted and Ellie started her first shampoo of the morning.

She was better than she had been before her chat to Maureen, and Mrs Tandy had helped her a lot, but in her heart, Ellie knew that she would live with fear from now on – and she would live with shame. Nothing anyone could say or do would take the sense of self-disgust from her. She could bear it when she was with other people, but alone in bed at night, it would haunt her. She'd never be able to forget the humiliation of what that brute had done to her, or the humiliation he'd made her feel.

Chapter 6

Peggy glanced through the several-days-old newspaper, nodding in grim recognition of the declaration of war on the USA by Rome and Berlin after the attack on Pearl Harbor, which had caused the American President to declare that his country was now at war with Japan. It hadn't stopped the Japanese bombing Singapore, but no one ever said war was easy. She screwed the paper into crackers to make them burn longer, because she didn't have any firewood, as her usual supplier hadn't been round lately. So Peggy was still making up the fires when Anne walked in that Saturday morning. She looked at her in surprise because it was very early and she hadn't expected her until much later that day.

'Somethin' wrong?' she asked.

'Yes, and no,' Anne said a little tentatively. 'I'd like to ask a favour of you, Peggy – and I'm going to have to let you down in a way too. I shan't be able to help out for a week in the bar and I'm getting married at three this afternoon. I'd like you to be my witness if you will?'

'What?' Peggy stared at her in disbelief. 'I couldn't have heard right – did you just say you're gettin' married at three today?'

'Yes, I did…' Anne laughed awkwardly. 'You must think me utterly mad, and I think so myself – and yet it's something I want to do…'

'Who are you goin' to marry – not that soldier you went dancin' with last night?'

'Yes. He asked me on Wednesday and I asked for two days to decide. He'd already bought a licence and booked the registry office when we met last night, and he's bought the rings…' Anne sounded breathless, oddly shy, as she laughed. 'You're going to say, "You don't know him. You only met a few days ago…"'

'Love at first sight?' Peggy's brows rose mischievously. 'You came in and told me about him walkin' into Bob's shop without his shirt – we had a good laugh over it.'

'Yes, I did. Ridiculous, isn't it? We don't know anything much about each other and yet – there is something strong and meaningful between us. Kirk said we either went to bed together, and behaved shamelessly, or we got married.' Anne gave a nervous laugh. 'I felt that if I didn't take the chance I might never get another. Do you think I'm a fool, Peggy?'

'I haven't talked to him enough to judge his character,' Peggy said, looking at her friend anxiously. 'It could be taken as desperation on your part, Anne love – but I don't think it is. You've always been so independent and sure of yourself. This just isn't like you.'

'No, it isn't desperation. I wouldn't marry just anyone. I've had chances years ago but turned them down. I just feel as if he's the one… but I know it's a hell of a risk. He could be a wrong one, and yet I think I would sense it. He seems honest and sensible and decent, and he's intelligent and fun to be with. We laugh a lot and tease each other and…'

'It sounds to me as if you're smitten,' Peggy said. 'If that's how you feel – go ahead and marry him, Anne. Do you remember Able Ronoscki?'

'Yes, of course I do.' Anne smiled. 'You had a bit of a thing with him – didn't you?'

'Yes, I did…' Peggy nodded and placed her hand on her gently swelling stomach. 'I don't regret it for a moment. None of us knows what will happen next. Normally, I would urge caution, but not in this case. You've been let down in the past, Anne, and if Kirk makes you happy – take what you can while you can.'

'Yes, that's how we feel. Kirk doesn't talk about what it's like out there, but from little things he says, what he's seen has affected him a lot. We both believe that we should take a chance – but I'm sure most people will think we're mad. I phoned the school and told them I wouldn't be in until after Christmas; we break up on Tuesday anyway so it's only a couple of days and if they sack me when I get back, too bad! There's only the carol service and a party for the kids, nothing important. So I've burned all my boats in one go and I don't care…' She laughed, looking radiant. 'Be happy for me, Peggy.'

'As long as you're happy,' Peggy said. 'What about Maureen – have you asked her to the wedding?'

'We're just having one witness each,' Anne said. 'I'll explain to Maureen. We're not having any sort of reception… because we're rushing away for a week, and our train leaves an hour or so after the wedding.'

'You must come and have a drink here after the ceremony.'

'Well, if there's time...' Anne smiled at her. 'Thank you, that would be nice.'

'So – what shall you wear?'

'I shall wear my best tweed suit and the hat that goes with it...'

'That pink felt?' Peggy wrinkled her brow in thought. 'No, it's too severe for a wedding. Why don't you wear your navy dress and coat – and I'll lend you a lovely white hat I've got upstairs. I know it will suit you – and you can borrow my white shoes, bag and my blue gloves for luck.'

'I don't think I'd fit into your shoes,' Anne said ruefully. 'I've got some white shoes and a matching bag though. Let's go and look at that hat...'

The ceremony was short and sweet, almost unreal Anne thought afterwards. When it was over they went outside and Peggy sprinkled confetti over them and Bob, Kirk's uncle, gave Anne a beautiful bouquet of flowers tied up with blue ribbons, and an envelope with a cheque for fifty pounds.

'You're a lovely girl and Kirk is lucky to get yer,' he said as he kissed her cheek. 'His mother will be upset that she didn't get to the wedding, but maybe she'll forgive yer if yer give her a grandchild...'

Anne blushed and then kissed his cheek. He'd been approving from the moment Kirk told him they were getting married, welcoming her to the family and wanting to arrange a reception.

'We'll just have a drink together at Peggy's and then get off and catch our train,' Kirk told him. 'One day we'll have a big party and ask everyone we didn't ask to the weddin' and celebrate.'

'When the war is over,' Bob said and nodded wisely. 'Yes, I understand, lad. Now isn't the time for fancy weddings. Yer can give everyone a knees-up when yer 'ave the christenin'.'

'Steady on, Bob,' Kirk said with a grin. 'We've only got a week or so together. I'm not sure I can guarantee a son and heir just like that...'

'Well, yer know my feelings, my boy.'

Kirk just smiled at his uncle and said nothing, but later on, after they'd had a drink with Janet, Uncle Bob and Peggy at the pub, and were alone on the train, their cases stowed overhead, he told Anne that Bob was leaving him his business. 'Bob wants me to take over from him in a few years, but I'm not sure that's the life for me and I've told him so. He was sayin' he might sell up in that case, but now he says it's ours when he's gone. He likes you, Anne, and he wants to see me with a family, so excuse the heavy hints.'

'I don't mind what he says.' Anne smiled. 'In fact, I would be happy if we did have a child quite soon. I love the idea of being a mother, Kirk – and I'm looking forward to havin' your children and making a nice home for us when you come back after the war.'

'Good.' He smiled and kissed her softly on the mouth. 'We've agreed you will stay where you are for the time bein', but you can look round for somethin' for us if you like. I don't think there will be much to rent just now, because we've lost so many houses in the Blitz. We might have to take a prefab or something for a start, but if I can, I'll buy a house out in the suburbs when this is all over.'

'We'll think about that when it happens,' Anne said and smiled up at him. 'I'm an East End girl and I have my friends here, but once we have a home and children, I dare say I can live anywhere.'

'You won't want to give up your job until you have babies,' Kirk said, looking at her in a way that made her spine tingle. 'And I suppose one day you might want to go back to teachin'…'

'Yes, when the children are grown,' she agreed and laughed. 'We're hardly wed and we're planning for years ahead…'

'Daft, isn't it?' he said with a smile that made her heart dance, 'but I've felt a sense of urgency ever since I walked you home that first time and had to leave you when Mac attacked that girl – the idiot. He's no trouble unless he's drunk…'

'No, but he might have hurt her had you not been there.'

'He was sorry afterwards. Asked me if he should apologise, but I told him he would be best to stay away, so he went home, all the way to Devon.'

'Yes, probably best,' Anne said and settled into her seat. 'Where are we going?'

'Just down to the sea for a few days. I know it isn't beach weather but there are lovely views and I'm told it's a nice hotel. We can look out of the windows now and then – if it's too cold to go for a walk.'

Anne laughed as his brows rose mockingly. 'As long as there's a decent bed and it's warm…'

'You're a wicked woman, Anne,' he said and moved closer, intending to kiss her. 'But I like you that way…'

Kirk looked up in annoyance as the door of the carriage opened and a woman and two children entered. He'd purchased first-class tickets for them in the hope they would have the carriage to themselves, but the woman had on an expensive fur coat and her children were well dressed so he had to accept that she'd bought first-class tickets too.

'Sorry, love,' he murmured close to Anne's ear. 'We're goin' to have to wait…'

'Yes…' she murmured and reached for his hand.

The woman sitting opposite stared but Anne just smiled at her and she looked away. This was her wedding day and she wasn't going to let anything spoil it. She knew she'd been reckless, taking a chance on a man she knew nothing about, but something inside told her it was right and she had to trust her instincts and believe Kirk was the man he seemed to be.

Later that night as she snuggled in Kirk's arms in the bed they'd shared, Anne acknowledged that they fitted together beautifully in every way. Her husband was the sweetest lover a woman could ever have, taking care to please her and, even in the throes of passion, making sure that he didn't hurt her. She learned what loving between a man and woman could be that night as they came together several times. Her brief affair had been nothing like this and she was glad that fate had given her this chance to experience love.

It had been late when they finally arrived at the hotel, which was set back from the promenade overlooking the sea in Clacton. Kirk had told her that it had been recommended to him by his mother who had once stayed there with his father, and it turned out to be a quiet rather old-fashioned place, but clean with a nice view over the sea.

'I thought this was better than draggin' you all the way down to Cornwall or somewhere else when we only have a few days to ourselves – but if I'd realised what the hotel was like I would've chosen somethin' else.' Kirk frowned as he surveyed the room the next morning, obviously feeling it wasn't what he'd expected.

'Don't be disappointed for me,' Anne said and kissed him. 'It's clean and the owners are lovely, so anxious to make things nice for us. We've got the place almost to ourselves – and the food is all home-cooked. I'm happy with this, Kirk.'

'Are you?' He looked into her eyes and then a smile entered his own. 'Yes, you are, aren't you? That's all right then. It is clean and comfortable and the food is all right if a bit basic.'

'I don't think anyone expects culinary marvels these days,' Anne told him and laughed, hugging his arm. 'I couldn't care less where we stay, Kirk. I thought it was a risk when I married you, but now I'm certain I made the right decision. I do love you. I just want to make the most of our time together.'

'Good, because I knew I loved you the minute you smiled at me,' Kirk said. 'I thought you would tell me I was mad when I asked you to marry me – and I couldn't believe my luck when you said yes.'

'I'm lucky to have found you.'

'Naturally…' he grinned in that maddening way he had sometimes. 'You had a good view of the body before you made up your mind.'

'You!' Anne said and put her arms about him, giving him a warm hug.

'What shall we do after breakfast?'

'It's looking nice out there,' Anne said, gazing from the window at the pier and the almost-deserted promenade with its shops, cafés and hotels, 'bright and sunny, though I suspect the wind will be bitter, bound to be so near to Christmas.'

'Yes, it is,' Kirk said and pulled her close, gazing down into her eyes. 'Let's have our Christmas now, Anne. I shan't be here when it comes, so I'm goin' to buy you something lovely. We'll go shoppin' and choose a present and then we'll ask if we can have chicken or turkey or some sort of special dinner tomorrow and that will be like Christmas.'

'Yes, all right, but I don't want to know what you buy. I'll send you off when I see something I want to get for you and make it a surprise.'

His eyes sparkled with fun. 'All right,' he agreed. 'Come on then. I hope they've got bacon for breakfast, because I'm starvin' after last night.'

Chapter 7

'I couldn't believe it when Anne told me she was gettin' married,' Maureen said when she went to visit Peggy on Sunday morning. 'She was a little embarrassed about not asking me to the weddin', but I explained that I couldn't have gone anyway. I'd promised Shirley a visit to the pictures in the afternoon and afterwards Ellie came round to tea with me.'

'Ellie Morris?' Peggy said, looking surprised. 'I didn't realise you were that friendly with her?'

'One of the nurses said something to me the other day. It made me realise that young girls with soldier-husbands can get very lonely and that made me think about Ellie. I know she's been behavin' foolishly recently, and I thought it might be loneliness – and then when I saw the state of her face...' Maureen paused as Peggy raised her brows. 'She had a nasty fall on Friday night. She said she'd slipped on dog mess, but...'

'She was probably a bit tipsy,' Peggy said and Maureen nodded.

'Yes, she told me she'd had too many drinks and said she wasn't goin' to do it again. Mrs Tandy was very kind to her and said she would keep her company in the evenings – go out with her sometimes. I thought I'd ask her round once a week and I might invite her to a matinee at the pictures. I work nights, but I could go on a Saturday sometimes – and when I give in my notice, I could go in the evenin'…'

'Your trouble is you think too much about everyone else,' Peggy said and laughed, and then the smile faded. 'So she fell on Friday night… I seem to remember seeing Ellie that night…'

'Was she with anyone?'

'No, not for most of the evenin'…' Peggy's frown cleared and she nodded. 'Yes, now, I remember. She was a little tipsy, not drunk, but just a bit unsteady as she walked. I saw her get up to leave. She met a soldier at the door and left with him…'

Maureen looked at her in horror. 'Do you think he hurt her? Is that what you're sayin'?'

'I don't know – but there was somethin' I didn't like about the way he looked at her, Maureen. I was busy, so I didn't take too much notice, just thought he looked the nasty sort, had a sneer on his face. Not the kind I'd want my daughter to know, and she seemed a bit – well, scared…'

'Oh, Peggy. She didn't tell me anythin' like that, but she said she'd realised what it looked like – her goin' to the pub and talkin' to soldiers. And she didn't want Peter to think she was cheatin' him – but there were tears in her eyes and I wondered if somethin' else was wrong…'

'I wish I'd gone over now and asked if she was all right, but I was pullin' a pint and when I looked again, they'd both gone.'

'Did you recognise him?'

'He wasn't one of my regulars,' Peggy said. 'I think I'd know him again, because there was a tiny scar at his left temple and his nose was a bit crooked. Not much to go on, but that's all I had time to notice.' She was thoughtful, then, 'The more I think about it, the more I realise that she must have known him. But she didn't like him.'

'Yet she went with him…'

'Perhaps he forced her…'

'Oh, Peggy. I've got shivers down my spine,' Maureen said. 'If he hurt her, she should have gone to the police.'

'You know what would've happened then.' Peggy made a wry face. 'Ellie has a bit of a reputation for drinking and then goin' off with soldiers. The police would say she'd given him the opportunity and even if they arrested him, the military police would take over and he would be shipped back abroad and Ellie would just be labelled a liar and a whore.'

'Poor Ellie…' Maureen felt a rush of sympathy for the girl and was glad that she'd invited her for tea. 'It's a rotten thing to happen. I know she's been a bit silly, letting strangers chat her up, but just because a man buys a girl a few drinks it doesn't entitle him to… well, you know.'

'Yes, I do, and I know that it wouldn't be the first time it has happened.' Peggy shook her head. 'I would bet that quite a few girls fall into bad ways because some man did that to them against their will. Anne told me that Kirk had to rescue Ellie one evenin' last week. He was walkin' Anne home and they heard her scream. Kirk went and sorted the bloke out – it was a friend of his. Mac had offered to walk her to her bus, but he turned nasty when she refused to let him pull her skirt up. Kirk told Anne he was fine when sober, and he'd wanted to apologise the next day, but Kirk told him to stay away from her.'

Maureen was thoughtful. 'Do you think this Mac was the soldier she left with on Friday night?'

'I have no idea,' Peggy said. 'Kirk's friend bought their drinks from Janet the night they came here together. I probably saw Mac but I didn't notice him in particular. Janet would know. I was more interested in Kirk, because he was talkin' to Anne and they left together…'

'And now they're married,' Maureen said and smiled. 'I can't believe it – I don't even know his surname.'

'Oh, it's Ross,' Peggy said. 'He's Sergeant Kirk Ross.' She smiled. 'Let's forget about Ellie for the moment. I know you feel sorry for her, Maureen, but there's not much we can do for her, is there? If she comes in here alone, I'll keep an eye on her – but perhaps she'll be sensible in future and not go drinking alone.'

'Yes, I'm sure she will,' Maureen said and nodded. 'We're merely speculatin', Peggy. We don't know that anyone attacked her. Perhaps she did slip on some dog mess because she was a little tipsy…'

Peggy looked up as her daughter came into the kitchen after Maureen had left. Janet arched her eyebrows at her questioningly.

'You two seemed so serious that I left you to it,' she said. 'Something about poor Ellie?'

'Oh, she had a nasty fall and hurt herself,' Peggy said. 'You look happy, darling?'

'Mike will be home for Christmas,' Janet said. 'The hospital has told him that he can have two weeks this time – and then, if he gets on all right, he can come home for good in another month; probably the end of January, or February at the latest.'

'I'm so pleased.' Peggy smiled and gave her a hug. 'I know

you've had such a lot to put up with, and you've been brave and steadfast and I'm proud of you, Jan.'

'I'm lucky to have a mum like you,' Janet said. 'It's because Mike can come here that we can manage – if we just had one smelly horrid room in a lodgin' house they would make him stay in hospital for ages.'

'This is your home, Jan – yours and Mike's, for as long as I have any say in the matter.'

'Have you heard anythin' from Dad?' Janet asked.

'He hardly ever writes these days. He doesn't send money, except to buy Christmas and birthday presents, because he knows I'm all right. I've always had my own money – and he's angry with me. It's only natural.'

Janet frowned over her answer. 'You say I've been brave – but you've been through a lot, too. I think Dad could at least keep in touch, make sure you're all right...'

'Well, some of it was my own fault – though you can't help fallin' out of love with one man and into love with another,' Peggy said. 'I was so hurt when I knew your father had had an affair, but now I understand that it happens. Our marriage was good for a long time, but it faded away, just tickin' over but meaningless... and then he went away and it fell apart.'

'It's all so sad, Mum. I wish you still had Able to take you out and love you.'

'Yes, so do I,' Peggy agreed. 'I wish with all my heart that he was here now, but he isn't and I can't bring him back. I had a letter from his British solicitor tellin' me that he'd left me some money, which apparently I can have when I sign the forms. They said that normally you'd have to wait seven years after the person went missin' – unless there was proof of the death – before it's legally yours, but Able intended I should have it even if he hadn't died, and he'd already put the account into my name. I don't understand all the legal jargon, but there's about two thousand pounds available now if I claim it. I think there's more if he never comes back...'

'Mum! That's a fortune,' Janet said, looking stunned. 'What will you do?'

'I've no idea,' Peggy sighed. 'I don't want the money, Jan. I want Able to come back and smile at me, to kiss me and tell me he still loves me.'

'Of course you do – but, obviously, he wanted you to have this money, to make you independent – and perhaps he thought there might be a baby and he wanted you to have something for the child's upkeep.'

'Yes, he did say somethin' once about if I split up with Laurie then I ought to be independent... but I didn't take much notice. I thought he was talkin' about a share of the pub because of all the years I've worked here. We were drivin' back to London at the time and I spotted a place where we could have lunch so the subject was dropped... It would feel wrong to take Able's money. I know we were lovers and I'm havin' his baby but...'

'No buts about it,' Janet said. 'Able would want you to have it – and you should take it for the child, even if you don't want it for yourself. It's only sensible, Mum.'

'Yes, I see your point. Maybe I'll pop in to their office and sign that form,' Peggy said. She looked rueful as Janet put an arm about her. 'I'm getting so big. Everythin' is almost too much trouble.'

'You sign that paper, Mum,' Janet advised. 'You might need money one day. Besides, if Able ever returns, you could always give it back to him.'

'With the greatest of pleasure. I'd like to see him walk into the bar more than anythin' in this world.' Peggy stifled a sob.

'Poor old Mum...' Janet said softly.

'Not so much of the old!' Peggy lifted her head. 'I'm all right, Jan. I've got you and Maggie, and Pip – even if I've only had one postcard in months from him, but he signed it with love, so hopefully my son has forgiven me.'

Pip had taken his father's side over Peggy's affair, though when Janet told him that their father had been unfaithful to their mother first, he'd calmed down and started to think about it.

'He's enjoying life in the RAF too much, and I expect he's busy. He can't be bothered to come home for a few hours when he can meet friends where he's stationed.' Janet turned away and set up the ironing board. 'Thank goodness for electric irons! I can't think what it was like when they all had to be heated on the fire. I've got loads of Maggie's things to do.'

'Yes, I can see that...' Peggy smiled as she looked at the full basket. 'I'd give you a hand, but I'd better get on with my bakin'...'

Janet re-read the letter from Mike after she'd finished her ironing and got Maggie up from her nap. There was just time to go for a little walk before she would need to help make their lunch. Since it was just the three of them and Nellie, her friend and cleaner, they didn't always bother with a big meal. Today they were having some nice pork chops that Janet had managed to buy, with mashed potatoes and vegetables. She would mince a little of the meat from her chop with carrots and potatoes and greens, make it tasty with gravy, and feed it to Maggie. Janet was lucky in that her little girl would eat almost anything, although she loved stewed fruit and custard best, and Janet would do a few stewed apples for her afters.

Mike's letter sounded so much more confident and cheerful than the one he'd sent in October on his first visit home from the military hospital. Then, he hadn't been sure of his welcome, but he'd made friends with Peggy while he was here for a couple of days and by the time he left, they were getting on really well together. Mike hadn't made love to Janet the last time he was home, but they had kissed and he'd held her close in bed, before he turned over and seemed to go to sleep, though she wasn't sure he had. Janet missed their passionate love making and she thought he must too, even though he still couldn't remember anything. Most of his other wounds were healing now, but his memory showed no sign of returning.

It wasn't like their marriage had been at the start, when they couldn't wait to get their clothes off, but she believed there was a warmth building between them. Perhaps the love making would come soon, perhaps even at Christmas – and then she might feel more like she was married again. She couldn't wait for his arrival on Christmas Eve and her presents were all bought and wrapped. She'd been scouting round the market and shops for weeks, picking up whatever she could, though most things were poor quality. It was often better to buy second-hand goods than the rubbish being produced now. All the factories were busy keeping the nation going with essentials and there was no time to produce luxury goods.

Sighing, she tucked her letter away with the others she'd kept and put Maggie's coat and bonnet on and then her own. Going downstairs, she saw her mother busy removing scones from the oven and told her she was taking Maggie for a walk in the pushchair.

Maggie could toddle well now for short distances, but Janet used the pushchair because it was easier than the leading reins. She went out into the cool air, pulling her scarf up and tucking Maggie's blanket round her tightly. Janet was on the way to the market, hoping for a few bargains. The shops had very little extra to offer for Christmas, even though they'd dragged out their old decorations and attempted to dress the windows, but somehow, she usually found something on the market stalls. She probably wouldn't have bothered with the stalls once, but these days you had to be grateful for anything you could get, and she'd bought one of Maggie's presents from a stall selling good second-hand toys.

Some young boys were pulling a home-made trolley filled with old saucepans, rusty nails, broken tools and some fancy iron railings. The government had announced that the efforts to collect scrap metal had to be quadrupled and these boys were clearly taking it to heart, possibly because Bert at the scrapyard was offering the prize of a large bar of chocolate for the gang who brought in the most scrap.

As she walked down the street, towards the corner shop where Maureen used to live, she saw a girl emerge from the side passage of Mrs Tandy's shop.

They met halfway along the lane and Janet could clearly see that Ellie had a massive bruise on her face. Ellie ducked her head down, as if ashamed, but Janet smiled at her.

'Mum said you had a nasty fall,' she said. 'I hope you're all right?'

'Yes, thanks,' Ellie said. 'It was my own fault. I was a little tipsy and I slid on dog mess.'

'Oh, well, that's awful. I hope you will soon be feelin' better.'

'That's kind – everyone has been kind,' Ellie said but didn't look her in the eyes. 'Thank you…'

Janet walked on by, but she was thoughtful. Ellie looked as if she'd been beaten; it wasn't just the bruises, but the defeated air she wore. She didn't look like the same girl. Janet remembered watching her being pushed out of the bar on Friday night and she'd seen the man's face. In fact, he'd stared straight at her for a moment, his eyes narrowed, as if challenging her. He'd had an evil leer on his face and Janet wouldn't have trusted him as far as she could throw him. She wondered if Ellie had gone willingly – and if he was the one that had given her a nasty beating. If it had been her, she would've gone straight to the police, and damn the consequences.

Chapter 8

Peggy was up earlier than usual because it was Christmas Eve and she wanted to prepare the food for her party in the bar that evening. Cooking made her back ache now and it was awkward bending sometimes, but she was all right if she gave herself plenty of time. She'd been saving what coupons and money she could for weeks and she'd been out and bought what she needed the previous day. She would provide a decent spread that evening, even though it lacked a lot of the perennial favourites of Christmas. She couldn't make an iced fruit cake, but she'd got two jars of mincemeat, because Jack Barton had put them by for her, and she'd made a couple of fatless sponges. She'd also managed to get a jar of thick cream from the milkman; it had preservatives in it and Peggy hadn't used it before. She suspected it might be too thick to whip, because it would go buttery, so she would leave it until last thing and then spread a thin layer on top of the jam for the sponges.

'Are you working already, Mum?' Janet asked as she entered the kitchen in her pink dressing gown. Her hair was still all over the place and she was yawning. 'I'm just going to make a cup of tea for us and take it upstairs. And I'll warm some milk for Maggie. She still likes warm milk in the morning, and I'm teaching her to use her own cup.'

'Go ahead, darling, I'm preparing the food for the bar first and then I'll do most of the party stuff this afternoon.' Peggy smiled at her daughter. 'How is Mike this morning?'

'Better, I think. He was so tired when he got here last evening.' She looked at the preparations her mother had begun for the party. 'Let me help you with that, Mum. I'll be down soon.' Janet filled the kettle and began to lay a tray. 'Would you like a cup of tea before I take ours up?'

'No, thank you, Jan; I had one half an hour ago. I've got rather a lot to do today and I wanted an early start.'

'I'm not sure I'd have gone ahead with the party if I'd been you,' Janet said. 'It's just too difficult and it is a lot of work – especially for you at the moment. You really shouldn't do too much, Mum.'

'I've got plenty of energy,' Peggy said and smiled as Janet set some of the best china on her tray. 'I thought Laurie might be home for Christmas, but he sent me twelve pounds and said to buy presents for all three of us – and he's sending Pip money as well. Oh, and there's a card for you and Mike.'

'I think that's a bit mean of Dad, expecting you to buy everything and not comin' near for Christmas himself.'

'He says he's too busy,' Peggy said and shrugged. 'I'm not sure I mind, Jan. It could've been very awkward. He hasn't forgiven me for taking a lover and he's furious because I'm havin' Able's child. I know he sent me a civilised letter and wants me to allow people to think it's his child – but underneath he's resentful and angry. I don't blame him, but in the circumstances it's as well he isn't comin' home.'

'He could've helped you a bit...'

'Maureen will help me this evenin',' Peggy said. 'She's got five days off over Christmas and she's going to fetch her father from the hospital with Gran and Violet this afternoon. Then she'll come in around six and help me finish off laying tables in the bar.'

'I'll be helpin' you as much as I can all day,' Janet said, nodding.

'You've got Maggie and your husband to look after. Mike will be feeling strange for a while, so make him your number one. Besides, Nellie will do all the cleanin' this mornin'. I'm lucky to have so many good friends – and my lovely daughter.' She hesitated for a moment, then, 'I bought Maggie a pretty dress – well, I got the material from the market and had it made for her and a bead necklace. What did you manage to find after all?'

'I got her a lovely teddy bear and a second-hand doll's pram,' Janet said. 'One of Nellie's friends wanted to sell it and it's like new – she's already got several dolls that were mine and Nellie has made her some pretty covers to put in the pram...'

'Oh, that's good,' Peggy said. 'I don't suppose Mike thought of gettin' her a present, did he?'

'He's been ill for so long, but he seems to have accepted she's his now so I think he has. Anyway, he seems so much happier this mornin',' Janet said and switched on the wireless. The sound of Christmas carols floated out to them, making them both smile. 'When he arrived yesterday he looked weary, but we both slept well and he seems relaxed and at home this time. He asked if we had a Christmas tree and said he has some parcels for all of us.'

'No tree this year, I'm afraid,' Peggy said regretfully. 'I've put a few decorations up in the bar, but I just didn't get round to buying a tree.'

'I thought about getting a small one for Maggie, because we saw a silver one in a shop window and she was fascinated, but in the end, it seemed frivolous and a waste of money at such a time. I put up the paper chains in the sitting room upstairs yesterday and we can put our parcels on the sideboard. I might buy some holly and make a little decoration – if I get time to visit the market this mornin'. I do love a Christmas market.'

'You should take Mike with you,' Peggy said. 'It will do him good to get some fresh air – you and Maggie too.'

'I'll see what he thinks,' Janet agreed and picked up her tray. 'I'll get dressed when I've drunk my tea and come down and help you…'

Peggy nodded but didn't answer. She didn't want Janet giving up too much of her time to help with the work now that Mike was here. They'd had so little married life together and they needed to be together so that Mike could begin to know her again and to feel that she was his wife and Maggie his daughter. As far as Peggy knew, his memory hadn't returned and he was just doing his best to live as normal a life as possible.

Life hadn't been normal for any of them since before the war, Peggy thought as she slipped another batch of scones into the oven, cheese-flavoured this time. She would make some celery soup for lunch and that would have to do for the bar food today; she could also make some paste and tomato sandwiches if anyone wanted anything different. They would all have to make do, because it was as much as she could manage.

Pausing for a moment to think, she remembered that Anne would be back from her whirlwind honeymoon today and a smile lightened her heart. Anne had looked so happy on her wedding day. Peggy hoped that everything had gone well for her and Kirk at the seaside.

Anne finished unpacking their cases and sighed as she saw some of Kirk's things mixed in with hers. He'd told her he didn't need the casual shirts and trousers he'd worn on their honeymoon, asking if she'd keep them until he was on leave again. There were a couple of new shirts that she'd bought him as a Christmas gift and the beautiful cashmere scarf that he'd loved.

'If I take it with me, I shall either lose it or someone will pinch it,' he'd told her. 'I'll leave it with you, Anne. It's so warm and I could probably do with it out there – unless they send us somewhere hot this time – but I don't want to lose it.'

'You don't know where you're being sent?'

'We were told it would be a different tour of duty the next time,' Kirk said with a frown. 'I was in Norway for a bit early on and then France, lucky to get out in the evacuation from Dunkirk. Since then I've been stationed down South for various reasons, but when they gave us this long vacation they told us we'd be goin' overseas again next tour.'

Kirk had left her as soon as they got back to Mulberry Lane. They'd cut it fine and he'd had to go straight to his uncle's, pick up his Army kit and catch a train back down South. He hadn't let her go to the station with him.

'I hate long drawn-out goodbyes,' he'd told her, kissing her deeply as he left her outside her lodgings. 'I'll write as soon as I can, darling, let you know if it's warm or cold where I'm goin'. Try not to worry too much and remember I love you. I promise I'll be back and we'll have a good life…'

Anne had held back the tears until he was on his way to the station in a taxicab, but she'd shed a few while she was unpacking. Their brief time at the seaside seemed like a dream now that she was back in Mulberry Lane, but she would treasure the memories all her life. They'd filled every day and night, eating late breakfasts and walking for miles along the promenade and the sands. The sea had been dark green, broken by crests of yellowish brown, and the wind had blown furiously off the water, bracing and very cold at times despite some weak sunshine.

After a snack, one lunchtime, they'd played table tennis and darts in the hotel's sports room, meeting up with some elderly, all-year-round residents, who challenged them to a little darts tournament. Kirk could have won, he admitted it to her afterwards, but he'd let one of the old men have his triumph and treated him to a whisky in the bar.

Once they went to a dance at a pavilion on the pier and twice they visited the pictures to watch whatever film was showing, most of which had already been shown in London, other nights they'd just gone for a walk, had a drink at a nice pub they'd discovered and then gone back to the hotel and to bed.

Going to bed with Kirk had been wonderful. Anne knew she was going to miss him dreadfully; her bed would feel cold and empty until he was home again, and she would be lonely despite the job she loved and her friends.

Sighing, she slipped her cases into the bottom of the large, old-fashioned wardrobe and picked up her handbag and some small parcels. She would visit Maureen and then Peggy and see what had been going on since she'd been away. She must also find time to visit her uncle and take him a present. Life had to go back to normal again, even though she would feel hers was on hold until Kirk came home.

'I went round to Maureen's,' Anne told Peggy when she popped into the pub that lunchtime. 'I was going to give her my Christmas presents, but the house was empty. Is everything all right?'

'They've gone to fetch her father from the hospital,' Peggy said and smiled at her. 'I wasn't sure what time you would be back today.'

'Kirk had to report back this afternoon. We came up on the milk train, got off and dashed to his uncle's to pick up his kitbag, and then he took a taxi to the station. If he'd lingered and missed that train he would have been AWOL.'

'Goodness, he doesn't want that,' Peggy said. 'Shall you come to the party this evening – or don't you feel up to it?'

'Yes, I'll come,' Anne said. 'Kirk said he might ring the pub at about nine if he can manage it. I told him I would come and help out.'

'Well, I'll be glad of the help,' Peggy said and broke off to serve a customer with half a pint of pale ale. She handed him his glass and rang the price into the till, turning back to Anne as he moved away. 'Jan does as much as she can, and Maureen is comin' later to help me finish off, but Mike is here and I don't want Jan to feel that she has to be workin' all the time... so if you feel like givin' me a hand, that would be lovely.'

'Of course I will,' Anne said. 'I have to carry on as normal, Peggy. I've been lucky to find someone I really care about, but now I must face reality. He loves me but he may not come back. We both know it and we've accepted it in our hearts, though he swears he'll be back...' Anne smiled. 'I tend to believe him after spending a week in his company. Kirk has a way with him. You sort of feel that whatever he sets out to do, he will...'

'So you're glad you married him?'

'I thank God I was mad for once in my life,' Anne said, happiness bubbling out of her. 'Even if that holiday was all I ever had of him, I'd still be glad we found each other. I'm so lucky, Peggy. I don't know why but... it was just meant for us.'

'I couldn't be happier for you,' Peggy said. 'I had some doubts and yet I felt you should take the chance. You must get on with life and believe he's goin' to come back to you.'

'I shall – I do,' Anne said. She took some parcels out of her bag. 'Those are for you, Janet, Maggie, and a small thing for Mike. I bought a book token for Pip and sent it off with a card to the address you gave me.'

'Pip will love that, thank you, Anne. I have something for you and Kirk upstairs. I'll give it to you this evenin'.' Peggy sighed. 'I sent Pip and Laurie book tokens and some other bits in the post...'

'Aren't either of them coming home for Christmas?' Anne looked a bit disapproving. 'Surely they can get leave now and then?'

'Laurie claims he's tied up where he is. I think if it wasn't for the war, we'd probably have split by now,' Peggy said and shrugged. 'Pip sent me a card but no message other than that he loves me, so I've no idea what he's plannin'. I'll have plenty of company though. Jack and Tom Barton are comin' to lunch. Nellie, Jan, Maggie and Mike will be here – and I wondered if you would like to come, too?'

'Me?' Anne looked thoughtful. 'I should've liked that very much, Peggy, but Mavis was so pleased I was back. She said she'd managed to buy a small chicken for Christmas and was thrilled that I would be there to share it with her.'

'Ah, yes, I see, you couldn't disappoint her,' Peggy said. 'Perhaps you could come over for tea then?'

'Yes, I think I could come about six. Mavis will be settled down with the wireless and her knitting by then. Yes, I should like that, Peggy.'

'Do you want to leave Maureen's things here? She will be over later – it will save you another journey...'

'Yes, thanks,' Anne said. 'I'll get off then, because I've got to visit the headmistress this afternoon. I was lucky to get time off for my wedding and I need to find out when they'll want me back after Christmas. We should have the new school up and running by mid-January if we're lucky...'

'Well, I'll see you this evenin'.' Peggy waved as Anne walked away, and then she rang a bell to let her customers know that they had five minutes to closing time. 'Happy Christmas to you all,' she said as everyone looked at her. 'If you're comin' to the party this evenin', I'll be happy to see you, otherwise, we open again on Boxin' Day in the mornin' for two hours and in the evenin' from seven until ten...'

Several customers wished her a happy Christmas, and a few of the regulars assured her they would be in later.

'I wouldn't miss yer party for anythin',' Alice Carter said and grinned at her. 'It's the best part of me Christmas, Peggy girl. I'll be sure to put on me best bib and tucker and get ready ter sing a song fer me supper.'

'Off you go then, all of you,' Peggy said, leaving the bar to open the door. 'I've got lots to do this...' The words died on her tongue as she looked at the man in uniform about to enter the pub, and then she flung herself at him. 'Pip, Pip, my love – why didn't you let us know you were comin'?'

'Hi, Mum,' he said and gave her a quick self-conscious hug, to the amusement of the interested watchers. 'I wasn't sure until the last minute... Hope you can squeeze another one in for dinner tomorrow?'

'Oh, Pip, of course I can,' Peggy said and beamed at him, her heart spilling over with happiness. 'That is the best present I could have...'

The last customer left and Peggy locked the door, turning to look at her son in joyous disbelief.

'I didn't think you were comin'... it's just wonderful...'

'Steady on, Mum,' Pip said. 'It's just tonight and dinner tomorrow and then I'm straight back on the train on Friday morning.' He glanced at her bump, a little embarrassed. 'Are you all right – with the baby and everything?'

Peggy smiled lovingly. 'Yes, of course I am. You're here for Christmas and that's all that matters – but I sent your presents through the post...'

'I got them this morning,' Pip said. 'Sheila said I should come and bring you, Jan and Maggie your presents. I sent Dad a book token, easier and I know it's what he likes.'

'Yes, we think alike over your dad,' Peggy said, 'in his tastes and pleasures anyway.'

'I know things weren't right between you for a while,' Pip said and smiled at her.

He was so much taller than her now and she laughed, because her little boy had filled out, become a man – and a confident one. He'd grown a small moustache and it suited him, gave him an air of devil-may-care, but perhaps it was the uniform and life in the RAF that had done that?

'I wish it hadn't happened,' Pip said, 'but Sheila told me her parents split up years ago. She was shocked and blamed her dad for a long time, but then she began to understand that it's just life. People change – and sometimes they want a change too.'

'You *have* grown up,' Peggy said and tucked her arm through his. 'Come and have some lunch with us and you can tell me who this Sheila is…'

'Oh…' Pip's cheeks went a little pink. 'She's just a girl I've got to know quite well. We go out a bit and share the same tastes in most things. You'd like her, Mum, and I know she'd like you. She wants to meet you one day soon…'

'Well, of course I'd like that,' Peggy said. 'You know you're welcome to bring her with you whenever you wish.'

'I wanted to bring her this time, but she has to go to her grandmother for Christmas – and she says you need to get used to the idea before she comes here…'

'What idea is that, love?' Peggy looked at him. He was nineteen now and seemed like a man in his mid-twenties, which was due to the work he did and a consequence of war – but to her he was still very young.

'I'll tell you later, Mum.'

'Oh, I see, it's serious then?' Peggy swallowed hard, because she couldn't tell this confident man that he was too young to marry.

'Yes, I think so,' Pip said, following her into the kitchen. 'Mum, I know…' he broke off as he saw Mike and Janet setting the table and Nellie stirring something in a pot. 'Oh, hi, Mike.' He went forward and offered his hand. 'Good to see you, old chap. How are you?'

Mike took his hand and shook it briefly. 'Very much better at last, thank you – you must be Pip.'

'You've had a bit of a rough time I understand.'

'I can't remember a damned thing about it,' Mike admitted. 'Nothin' but wakin' up in a hospital where I didn't understand one word they said to me until a doctor who could speak English visited. I suppose that's a bit of luck for me.'

'How are you, Jan?' Pip turned to his sister, seeming unsure for the first time. Peggy realised he didn't know what more to say to Mike, a man who had been plucked from the sea more dead than alive, and who must live with the consequences of losing his memories. Pip had a sophisticated veneer, but underneath he was still her son. She was glad and felt bound to rescue him.

'Pip is home for Christmas Day and then he's off again,' she said. 'Isn't that lovely?'

'Yes, great that you're home,' Janet said. 'You can help us put some decorations up in the sittin' room... Mike wants a little Christmas tree if we can find one.'

Pip grinned at her. 'Sheila's mother had hers up a week ago – but Dad never did want the decorations up until the last minute, did he?'

'He's not here now, so we can do what we like,' Janet said and Pip frowned, but said nothing, simply taking the mug of tea Nellie offered him.

It wasn't until just before the party that Peggy managed a talk with her son alone. She wanted to ask him again about this Sheila, the girl he was so keen on, and Pip surprised her by being ready to talk.

'I want to marry Sheila,' he told her and smiled eagerly. 'I've bought an engagement ring for her but I've got to write and ask for Dad's permission before we get married...'

'Pip...' She looked at him in shock. 'I should like to meet her soon, whenever you can get leave to bring her home...'

'I'll do my best,' Pip said and grinned. 'You'll like her, Mum, and I know you would give us permission – but I don't want to fall out with Dad. He writes to me sometimes and, well... he is my father...'

'Yes, of course he is, love,' Peggy said. 'You go ahead and ask him – but remember I'm just as interested in your future as Laurie is, and I want you to be happy.'

'Sheila makes me happy,' Pip said. 'Sometimes, it's pretty rough on ops, you know, but she makes me want to come back...'

'Then you should marry her,' Peggy said and smiled. 'Come on, you can help me set the food out in the bar – it will be good trainin' for when you're a husband...'

Chapter 9

'What are we goin' ter give Peggy and 'er family fer Christmas?' Tom said to his father on Christmas Eve. He'd bought a few bits of holly from the market and arranged them round the mirror, but hadn't bothered with any other decorations other than cards on the mantle. 'If I'd kept up the allotment I would've taken 'er a big box of veg...'

'I've got a large box of Fry's chocolates for 'er,' Jack Barton said with a smile. 'Violet insisted on giving them to us as a Christmas box, but I thought you'd rather have other things – so we'll give Peggy the chocolates and a bottle of sherry I bought, and I think that's as much as we can manage, Tom.'

'Yes, she'll be happy with that,' Tom agreed. 'If I'd been earnin' I'd 'ave got 'er somethin' special just for herself, but that will have to be another time – perhaps on 'er birthday, whenever that is.'

'I think it's May or June, but you can find out when the time comes. You'll be takin' over at the shop after Christmas, because I leave on Boxin' Day mornin'.' He smiled at his son. 'Then you'll be earnin' a proper wage, Tom.'

'I'd rather 'ave you 'ere, Dad,' Tom said fervently.

'Yes, I know, son, but we're lucky I was given a couple of months at 'ome. I could've been stuck in prison for another two years.'

'I know – and I've got Peggy to thank for it. She was the one that got the petition up to get you parole,' Tom said and grinned at him before changing the subject. 'Mr Jackson looked better than I expected. I thought 'e managed the stairs pretty well fer a man what's been as ill as 'e 'as.'

'Yes, but I'm sure a lot of that was bravado,' Jack said. ''E would have been very tired when 'e got upstairs and sat down. I think 'e'll be leaving most of the work to you for a while, Tom.'

'The more the better,' Tom replied. 'I like to be busy and my arm is nearly back to normal.' He rubbed his shoulder. 'It aches if I use it too much, but if I don't do the exercises it goes stiff. I 'ave to put up wiv the damned pain fer now.'

'Yeah, you're doing well,' his father approved with a nod. Then he added: 'You need to watch yer language though, Tom. Serving in the shop, you'd better not drop too many "aitches" or use slang, and don't swear. Make an impression and one day you'll be ready to move on to another, better-paid job.'

'Yeah, one day,' Tom said and pulled at the old school tie his father had made him wear. 'Maybe then I'll be able to choose when I wear one of these things…'

Jack laughed. 'I'm not a fan myself, but I thought we should be respectable, Tom. Peggy is cookin' a lovely dinner for us tomorrow and I thought we ought to make an effort – this evenin' and tomorrow.'

'I suppose…' Tom made a face. 'All right, I'll wear it until we get 'ome but then it's comin' off…'

'I wouldn't expect you to wear it at 'ome.' His father hesitated, then, 'We'd better have a little chat now, Tom, because there won't be time in the mornin'. You've got to be the man of the family while I'm away. Your mother is gettin' better – at least that's what the nurses told me, but she won't look at me or speak to me. I'll be sendin' most of my Army pay 'ome and I've asked for it to come to you. I'm expectin' you to take over and see things are right. The rent needs to be paid regular or we'll lose our 'ome.'

'Yeah I know, Dad.' Tom grinned, because in his emotion his father had reverted to his normal speech; despite warning him about dropping his 'aitches', he did it himself, but Tom didn't point that out. Having his dad home had meant so much and Tom knew he was upset at the prospect of having to leave him to keep the house going on his own – and with coping with a mother who was far from being right, even if she was allowed home. 'I'll manage, don't you worry, Dad. I'll keep things goin' until yer get back, I promise.'

'Yer mum won't be easy,' his father warned. 'Sam was always her favourite and she blames us for being alive when he's gone. It's not right that you have to cope with it all, Tom. I should be 'ere to shield you from 'er temper and spite – and she *can* be spiteful.' He sighed deeply. 'She was better when we were courtin'. You were on the way before I realised what a mistake I'd made. I couldn't walk out on 'er or you, Tom. I've always done my best, but it was never enough for 'er. After Sam was born she made it clear 'e was the last and that was the end of our marriage…'

'I knew you were miserable when we were kids,' Tom said. 'I was too young to understand any of it – but I know Ma don't like me. I've never understood why – do you know?'

His father shook his head. 'No, idea, son. Perhaps yer too much like me in your ways and I know she 'ates me. Sam seemed to be 'ers from the start and she spoiled 'im – that's why no one could do anythin' with 'im. If anyone is to blame for what 'appened to 'im that day it's 'er, but I'd never tell 'er…'

'She would never accept it,' Tom said regretfully. 'I told 'im what 'e was doin' was dangerous and wrong. It was lootin', Dad. They had 'im down the station once, but when 'e came back, all she did was go on about the bloody police and 'ow it was someone else's fault.'

'Yes, I know, but it's too late now,' his father said. 'Right, let's go and show our faces at the party, Tom, but we shan't stop long. We ought to pop up the hospital and visit your mum, take 'er a card and some flowers, and a bag of fruit sweets. She won't thank us for it, but we must do it all the same…'

Tom had a lemonade shandy and ate a couple of Peggy's sausage rolls. They were delicious and he told her so when she offered him a mince pie.

'I'm glad you enjoyed them, Tom,' Peggy said 'Don't be late for dinner tomorrow, will you?'

'We're lookin' forward to it,' Tom said and stood up as his father signalled to him. 'We're off to visit Ma at the Lee Infirmary now – happy Christmas, Mrs Ashley.'

'You know it's Peggy to you,' she said and smiled. 'Happy Christmas, Tom – and I'm lookin' forward to havin' you and your dad to dinner.'

'You've got a houseful, I think,' Tom said and she nodded before turning away to speak to his father and wish him goodnight.

Alice Carter was just starting to sing one of the old songs she did so well as they went out, and Tom was sorry they couldn't stay longer. Everyone was laughing and joining in the chorus as Alice capered about the room, acting out her comic routine. It was a lovely atmosphere in the pub that evening and it was the first time Tom had ever been to a proper party. He wished they could stay, but knew his dad was right; they had to visit his mother.

On the bus, Tom noticed that everyone was getting into the party spirit. No one was looking gloomy and he hadn't heard the word 'war' mentioned once. It was as if the people of London had decided that Hitler wasn't going to spoil their fun this year. You couldn't see much sign of Christmas cheer from the bus; there were no lights, of course, and even the bus had shaded lamps, as did the vehicles they met. It was too dangerous for buses and cars to drive about with no lights so they used special shaded ones or simply painted over most of the lamp so that only a faint downward glow showed, because you couldn't be too careful, even if Hitler had stopped raining bombs on London for the moment. It seemed he was too busy trying to subdue the Russians to worry about the British for a while.

The hospital had no lights showing outside, because there was a blackout in place, but inside it was busy and the wards were all lit, though at a low level in the corridors to save energy for more important things. They were all aware that energy use had to be reduced and even water was rationed, in as much as they were exhorted to use only the minimum in the bath, and to share bathwater whenever feasible.

Tom stayed as close to his father as possible, his stomach catching with nerves as he smelled carbolic, disinfectant and stale-dinner odours, which masked an even worse underlying stench of sickness and urine. Hospitals were not the nicest places and Tom felt a surge of sympathy for those who had to be there during this special season.

The Sister in charge of the women's ward met Tom's father and spoke to him in hushed whispers. She asked how old Tom was and raised her eyebrows when she was told he was fifteen, which was a small exaggeration as he wasn't until April next year.

'Still a little young for visiting, I'm afraid…'

'It is Christmas, Sister, and I'm leavin' for the Army after Christmas. Unless Tom can visit occasionally, Tilly won't get any visits at all.'

'Well, she may be able to come home in a few weeks,' the senior nurse said. 'Perhaps he could go in just for a few minutes – but if he makes too much noise I shall ask him to leave.'

'Tom won't make a noise, I'll vouch for that,' his father said. 'Thank you very much, Sister. I'm very grateful…'

His father led the way down the ward to a bed at the far end. The curtains had been drawn round it and when Tom followed him inside them, he caught the smell of vomit immediately. His mother had clearly been sick and no one had noticed; it was all over the sheets and her nightgown.

'Just go and tell the nurse, Tom,' his father said. 'I'll clean her up if she brings a bowl of water…'

Tom left the stuffy cubicle and went up to the nearest nurse. Mindful of Sister's warning, he spoke softly remembering to watch his language like his dad had told him.

'Oh, yes, I'll bring some water at once. Mrs Barton has been sick several times today.'

'Has she picked up a bug of some kind?'

'You'll have to ask Sister,' the nurse said shortly and went off to fetch a bowl of water. She took it behind the curtain, asking both Tom and his father to wait outside while she made Mrs Barton comfortable. They went out into the corridor and sat looking at the floor and not speaking until the nurse drew back the curtains and beckoned to them.

Tom's mother looked at them sullenly as they approached. 'What're yer here fer?' she asked Tom, making no effort to accept the card or flowers. She ignored them, continuing to look at Tom angrily. She didn't even look at her husband when he asked her how she was feeling. 'You needn't bother comin' up 'ere again,' she told Tom. 'You'll 'ave ter find a job and look out fer yerself in future. I'm a sick woman. I can't be bothered with yer.'

'I'll hang on to the 'ouse until you get back, Ma,' Tom said, holding back the rush of angry tears that stung his eyes. She was so unfair, behaving as if his father wasn't there and treating Tom with her usual coldness. Yet he knew he couldn't help it. She'd had some sort of a stroke after Sam was killed and it had affected her mind. She seemed to have forgotten how to be kind or to show warmth. 'I've got a job workin' for Mr Jackson. It's not much money at first, but I'll 'ave Dad's pay as well once 'e's in the Army and I'll manage to keep the house.'

'Don't expect any 'elp from me. If I ever come out of 'ere I shan't be well enough to scrub floors. I think they're sendin' me to a nursin' 'ome and then the workhouse in the end. That's what yer father brought us down to, Tom. My boy dead, me ill and fit for nothin' but the scrap 'eap – so you're on yer own… unless they put yer in an orphanage.'

'You won't go in the workhouse as long as you've got a 'ome to come to, Tilly, so don't talk daft,' Jack said in a rallying tone. 'You only 'ave ter get better and Tom will look after yer until the war is over and I get back 'ome.'

'I don't want ter come back there if you ever step inside it again,' Tilly said bitterly and her eyes moved to his, looking at him for the first time. 'I 'ope yer get shot and die in agony – it's what yer deserve for what yer've done to me.'

'Mum, that's not fair,' Tom said, indignant for his father. He saw pain flicker in his father's eyes but Jack's tone was placid as he shook his head at Tom. The damage had been done years before and Tilly hated her husband, and her illness only made it worse.

'Well, Tilly, we wanted to wish you a happy Christmas and let you know you had a 'ome and a good son waitin' for you, but it's your life. If yer want to wallow in self-pity and die in the workhouse – or the infirmary, as they often seem to call it these days – that's up to you. Goodbye, Tilly. If I survive the war, I shan't trouble you, my dear, you can believe that…'

He signalled to Tom that they were leaving. Tom glanced at his mother. He wanted to let her see he was angry with her for the way she'd spoken to his dad but he couldn't speak. Instead, he just gave her a long look and then turned and followed his father out of the ward.

When they were outside the hospital, he pulled at Jack's sleeve. 'I want you to come back for me, Dad,' he said earnestly. 'I'll do my duty by Mum, but I don't love 'er – I love you. I'm goin' to work 'ard and I'll study at night until I can find a job that pays good money. I'll always see she is taken care of, I promise – but you're the one I care about. You're the one I'll ask God to look after…'

Tom knew there were tears in his eyes but he wasn't crying. He wouldn't let his mother's spite make him cry, because he wasn't a kid now; he was a man and he was ready to do a man's work.

His father put a hand on his shoulder, giving it a hard squeeze and when Tom looked up, he saw there were tears on his cheeks. His dad was man enough to cry and that made Tom's own tears spill over, though he didn't make a sound. They walked in silence for some time, and then Tom felt his father's arm about his shoulders; it was warm and comforting and filled the emptiness inside him.

'It's late now, Tom. Too late to go anywhere else this evenin', but we've got tomorrow ter look forward to. Shall we just go 'ome and 'ave a cup of cocoa before we go to bed? You never know what Father Christmas might bring you in the mornin'.'

Tom gave a choking laugh. 'Yeah, I've got you somethin', Dad. It ain't much – but you may need it out there… wherever you get sent.'

'Thanks, son,' his dad said and tightened his arm about his good shoulder. 'Tilly can't help being that way, Tom. She's a bitter, unhappy woman, and I must 'ave made her like it, but I can't for the life of me think 'ow…'

'She was always sharp,' Tom said. 'I don't think it was you – more somethin' inside her. Somethin' she didn't get that she wanted…?'

'Maybe. We'll never know, son. Let's just forget it now. It's Christmas… Listen, Tom. Can you hear that?'

They were passing a church and the sound of carols being sung came faintly on the air to them. By mutual consent they drew nearer, and then went into the porch, where they could hear the beautiful music clearly. For some minutes they stood there in silence, just listening and sharing the unexpected pleasure. When it finally finished, Tom's father smiled at him.

'I'm not a churchgoer, Tom, never 'ave been – but I've always believed. Just remember when I've gone and perhaps your ma... well, if you feel alone, remember you're not. I think God looks after us in His own way, even if it is mysterious at times.'

'I shan't be alone,' Tom said and grinned at him. 'I live in Mulberry Lane, remember – and you can't be alone there for long. Peggy and Maureen wouldn't let you...'

'No, you're right on that one,' Jack said and chuckled as they started walking again. 'Peggy Ashley was a real beauty when she was young, Tom. I fancied her years ago, but she never 'ad eyes for anyone but Laurence Ashley.' He shook his head. 'It seems odd to me that he's never 'ome. You'd think 'e would get back for Christmas, even if only for a couple of days...'

Laurence Ashley sat at the back of the church in a small Scottish village, but he wasn't alone. Eileen Martin was with him. It had been her idea to come to the midnight mass and Laurence had enjoyed it more than he'd expected to when he'd agreed to accompany her. They'd been lovers for three weeks now and he enjoyed Eileen's company, so when she asked if he would take her, he couldn't refuse. Now, sitting in the dimly lit rather chilly church, he felt peace steal over him.

He'd been feeling bitter and hard done by for months, ever since he'd got that wretched letter from Peggy telling him she was having another man's child. His anger had worn off gradually, but the feeling of bitterness had grown in its place, at least until he'd finally asked Eileen out and they'd ended up in bed together at the inn she owned.

Since then they'd been out often, to dinner somewhere or for a visit to the cinema, and they were lovers and friends. Laurence didn't feel the way he had for Marie, the French girl he'd met after joining the intelligence group he worked for. Marie had swept him off his feet despite him being married, making him feel young and introducing him to a kind of sex he'd never experienced before. His marriage had already been all but finished as far as he was concerned and he'd truly loved Marie. He didn't feel anywhere near as much for Eileen. She was rather jolly in bed, but there was nothing sophisticated or advanced about her love making. Laurence didn't mind, it was just having someone pretty to be with and to make love to that gave him pleasure. He wasn't in love with her and he didn't think she loved him. They were simply making the best of bad times.

'That was wonderful, wasn't it, Laurie,' Eileen said, touching his arm as the service came to an end. 'I've always loved the midnight mass at Christmas, though I don't go to church often.'

'Yes, it was lovely; the choir's voices were especially pleasant,' he said as he ushered her out into a bitterly cold night. 'Happy Christmas, my dear Eileen. Shall we go to your place tonight?'

'Yes, of course,' she said. 'It wouldn't look right if I came to your room up there...' She glanced towards the large house, which was set in secluded grounds and surrounded by a high wall and was home to Laurence and his colleagues for the duration of the war.' 'You're going to stay with me tonight and have dinner with me tomorrow, I hope. You've got the day off, haven't you?'

'Yes, I have a week off,' Laurence said and smiled at her. With Eileen he minded his P's and Q's, because she would expect it, and there was little trace of his London accent these days. Mixing with men and women who were mostly of the middle class up at the house, he'd got into the habit of speaking as they did. 'We could go somewhere together for a few days after Christmas if you wished?'

'Where would be better than my cosy warm house?' Eileen asked and laughed. 'Was that what attracted you to me, Laurie – as you're a landlord too when you're not doing whatever you do up there... my pub?'

He laughed softly. 'Well, I feel at home in a pub, and yours is a rather nice one, Eileen. I'm lucky to have found such a good local while I'm here.'

'Well, I thought you were rather handy to have around,' she teased. 'When my barman was off sick, I just couldn't manage those barrels myself. My husband always did that before he died.'

Laurie nodded. He thought Eileen might be expecting him to hang around after the war, but once they told him he could go home he would be off back to his own pub.

For a moment he thought about his home and Peggy. He was still angry with her, even though he'd accepted that her betrayal was partly his fault. It wouldn't have been so bad if she hadn't fallen pregnant with a kid – he could have accepted it then, but he wasn't sure how he felt about living with her when she had another man's child.

It was something he would have to face up to when the time came...

Chapter 10

Tom's father told him not to accompany him to the station on the morning of Boxing Day. 'It's a lot of bother for yer waitin' around and then you've got to get back to the lanes,' he told him. 'We'll say goodbye 'ere, lad. I've 'ad a really good Christmas and me only regret is that I have to leave yer to cope on your own.'

'It was a great Christmas, Dad.' Tom grinned and agreed. Peggy had done them proud and it was by far the best Christmas that Tom could recall. Everyone had been happy, laughing, giving Peggy a hand in the kitchen, clearing tables and washing up together. Afterwards, they'd played cards and a few party games. Peggy had found a box of crackers on the market and, though poor quality, the jokes inside had made them all laugh as they sipped the Christmas sherry. 'It's all right, Dad,' Tom said and offered his hand. 'I'll manage – and I've got friends to 'elp me if I need them.'

'Yes, you've got friends.' His father smiled and shook his hand. 'Well, take care of yourself, son. You will get my Army pay soon and I'll write to yer and tell yer as much as they will let me.'

'Take care of yourself,' Tom said gruffly, because his throat was dry. 'Come back when it's all over.'

'The Jerrys can't get rid of me that easy,' his father said. He picked up his kitbag and walked out, leaving Tom in the kitchen.

It was strange how silent and empty the house seemed all at once. With his father at home it had been a warm and friendly place, but now it was empty and he didn't want to be there. However, he made himself wash up their breakfast things and tidy the kitchen. Tom had promised to keep things going while his dad was away and so he had to do his best.

When he couldn't find any other small jobs to do, Tom pulled his threadbare jacket on and the warm scarf Maureen had knitted for him as a Christmas gift, and went out, making sure he had the key in his pocket as the door shut behind him. He crossed the road, going straight to the shop on the corner. He would just knock and let Mr Jackson know he was available. They weren't open until the following day, but Tom could make a start on the stocktaking; he thought there might be a lot of stuff that could be set out on the shelves that hadn't even been unpacked. He rang the bell and waited until the door was opened and Violet inclined her head and stood back to let him in.

'I'm g-glad yer've c-come, lad,' Henry Jackson said when Violet showed him into the sitting room. 'I k-know you'll b-be on y-yer own a lot n-now yer dad's gone.' He paused, taking a deep breath, because sometimes he still had to struggle to get his words out. 'I k-know I c-can trust yer, Tom. I'm goin' ter give yer a key to the b-back d-door...' Again, he gasped for breath and had a little coughing session before he could continue. 'Yer can c-come in early w-when yer w-want and m-make a start.'

'I'd rather be doin' somethin',' Tom told him with a grin, because he was probably being taken advantage of, but he knew Mr Jackson needed his help and he liked Maureen. She didn't want to be drawn back into working in the shop and the more Tom did to please his employer the less likely it was that would happen. 'If I've got nothin' else to do I can make a start on the papers – and I'll take the deliveries out in me lunch break…'

'Yer a good lad, T-Tom,' Henry said and nodded. 'We'll see h-how you go on, but more w-wages are on the cards if we suit. I'm not goin' ter be m-much use round 'ere fer a while. I shall be relyin' on you, T-Tom; m-my Maureen says she'd trust you with her life, and that's g-good enough fer m-me.'

'I think the world of your daughter, Mr Jackson,' Tom said. 'Maureen and Peggy Ashley are a couple of good'uns if you ask me.'

'Well, s-she t-thinks a l-lot of you,' Henry said. 'You c-can always come to us i-if yer n-need h-help…'

'That's enough talkin',' Violet said, returning with a cup of tea on a tray and a plate with some bread and margarine and marmalade.

Henry looked at it and shook his head. 'I'm n-not 'ungry, Violet l-love…'

'You've got to eat somethin' or you'll be back in hospital,' Violet said.

'Maybe l-later…'

'I shan't have time later,' Violet said. 'I told you, Henry. I'm off out in a few minutes. I'm meetin' a friend and I shan't be back until this afternoon, so you'll have to manage fer yerself.'

'Don't you worry, Mrs Jackson,' Tom said. 'Give me that key and I'll pop up later, after I've finished sortin' out the stockroom – and I'll make you a cup of tea and a sandwich then, Mr Jackson.'

Henry brightened. He picked up his cup and blew on the tea, sipping it loudly. Tom saw Violet pull a face of distaste and sensed a bit of atmosphere, as if they'd had a disagreement. Henry would obviously need quite a bit of help with washing and dressing, and still needed assistance to get to the toilet, though he could manage once he got there. His wife was a businesswoman and, Tom thought, might find his disability rather irritating if she had work to do.

'That's a g-good, lad. I'd be g-grateful fer yer h-help, Tom.'

'Well, that's settled,' Violet said and gave Tom a saccharine smile. 'I'll leave you to get on then. I must go or I shall be late...'

Henry winked at Tom as she went through to the bedroom. 'W-Women...' he said in a whisper. 'Violet isn't a bad'un b-but she does like to rule the r-roost – m-make sure you keep on the right side of 'er, lad.'

'Yes, o' course,' Tom said and gave him a cheeky smile. 'I'll get on then, Mr Jackson. I reckon there's a lot of boxes need unpackin' – things we could be sellin'.'

'Yeah, I k-knew it was m-mountin' up,' Henry said, 'b-but I 'adn't b-been feelin' too good fer a w-while...'

'Well, I'll make a start then,' Tom said, 'and I'll come up before I go 'ome ter see as you're all right.'

Tom took his leave and went down to the storeroom. There were lots of big cardboard boxes piled up, one on top of the other as though someone had just dumped them and couldn't be bothered to sort them out. As Tom started to go through the boxes, he found tinned condensed milk, a few tins of pink salmon, tomato soup, golden syrup, cocoa, corned beef and Spam, as well as boxes of Sunlight soap, toothpaste and toilet soaps, some of which looked as if they'd been pushed out of the way and forgotten, probably at the start of the war when Mr Jackson had been stocking up for a time when these things would be in short supply.

As he carried the boxes through to the shop and began to unpack them, Tom had a contented feeling because the empty spaces on the shelves were starting to fill, making it look almost as it always had before the war. Tooth powder was nearly impossible to buy these days and a lot of people were going to grab that, but he would have to limit it to one tin per customer. Tom's father had unpacked any new stock that Maureen ordered, but he obviously hadn't thought of rummaging in the storeroom to see what was in all the boxes stacked right at the back. Tom thought it was best to get all the older tinned stuff out and sell it before the metal started to rust and they could only sell them as damaged goods.

He had unpacked about a dozen boxes and filled his shelves when Maureen walked in. She'd come in through the back kitchen and he'd been so engrossed in his task that he hadn't heard the door go.

'How did you work that little miracle?' Maureen said, looking at shelves filled to the brim. 'I don't think the shop has looked this good since I left to take up nursin'.'

'I saw a load of boxes at the back of the stockroom and I asked your dad if I could sort it out and he said he hadn't got round to it but meant to – so all this is stuff I found, hidden behind a lot of empty boxes and new stock.'

'It must be the stuff Dad bought at the start of the war and he just kept piling bits in front of it and forgot what he'd bought earlier. If you hadn't sorted them out they might have been wasted.'

'Tinned food lasts nearly forever, I reckon, 'specially bully beef, and that soap could be there for years and it wouldn't hurt,' Tom said. 'But the tins can get damaged or go rusty, so it's best to get the old stuff sold and then use the newer stock.'

'I can see the shop is in good hands, so I can stop worryin',' Maureen gave him a brilliant smile. 'How's Dad this mornin'?'

''E looks a bit tired,' Tom said. 'Mrs Jackson went out to meet someone – and I said I'd go up and see if 'e wanted anything to eat before I go 'ome.'

'That was good of you,' Maureen said. 'I've come on the same errand…'

'Are you workin' at the hospital this evenin'?' Tom asked her. It was obvious now that she was havin' a baby because it had started to show when her coat was open. Tom knew she wouldn't want to go on nursing much longer, but he didn't think she would want to come back here either.

'Yes, I had Christmas off, so I have to work over the New Year period,' Maureen said. 'I shan't be able to work at the hospital much longer, Tom – but I've no intention of standin' behind a counter in the shop. I'll help out now and then if necessary…'

'I'll be here to see to things now,' Tom said. 'You can rely on me, Maureen.'

'I know that, Tom.' She smiled at him. 'These things work two ways. With that house to manage all on your own, you'll 'ave a lot of things to see to. If you need help with household things, just ask Peggy and me, and we'll help you sort it out if we can. It's coming up to a new year now, Tom, and we all have to stick together – get through these dark times as best we can.'

'Yeah, that's the way I feel,' Tom said. 'Dad went to see the landlord while 'e was 'ome. 'E talked to him and it's been agreed that I can stay there alone until me ma gets back from the hospital. When we visited on Christmas Eve they said she could come out soon, but she thinks they'll send her to the infirmary. Dad says he thinks she'll come 'ome, but we 'ave to wait and see.'

'It's all you can do, Tom. I'm glad your dad went to see Mr Pearson, because Peggy was afraid he might try to turn you out when he realised you were there alone.'

'He promised Dad he wouldn't try to put us out, as long as the rent was paid on time, and I've promised me dad it's the first thing I'll pay every month when I get the Army money.'

'Yes, you make sure you do,' Maureen said. 'I know you could find a room anywhere in the lanes, Tom. Alice would be only too glad to have you and so would Peggy, but it wouldn't be right for your mum to lose her home.'

'I reckon that would make her ill again,' Tom said. 'Mr Pearson gave Dad his word, so it should be all right.'

'If you were older you could put your name on the rent book, but Mr Pearson wouldn't accept that, so we'll just have to hope he sticks to his word.' Maureen glanced at the little watch she had pinned to her uniform under her coat. 'I'd better go up to Dad. I'll make him a cup of tea and somethin' to eat, Tom. I'll bring you a mug of tea and a paste sandwich if you like.'

'Thanks, Maureen,' Tom said. 'I should like that – and then I can finish up here before I leave. I shall still pop up and make sure Mr Jackson is all right afore I go, though.'

Maureen nodded and left him to finish a bit more unpacking. She'd spotted the tins of golden syrup and she would let Peggy know so that she could pop along and buy some first thing, because they were sure to sell as soon as customers saw them on the shelf. Tom had put everything out rather than keeping a few under the counter, as she would have, but she wasn't going to start interfering, because she didn't want to get drawn in too much. Tom would learn that some customers were special, and then he'd think about reserving a few of the items that were scarce for the ones who came regularly...

It was after four when Tom said goodbye to his employer and left the shop, locking the door carefully behind him. Violet still wasn't home and he was a bit uneasy about leaving Mr Jackson entirely alone, but he'd told him he was all right. Tom had helped him to the bathroom and back to his chair, leaving him a drink of water within reach.

'Y-you go, lad,' Mr Jackson told him. 'I'll b-be all r-right until my w-wife gets back. Sh-she won't b-be long.'

It was almost dark now and Tom realised how cold it was as he ran over the road. Just as he was about to dash down the alley and let himself into the house the back way, a man stepped out of the shadows and took a firm hold on his arm.

'Yer back at last,' he muttered. 'I've been waitin' fer yer, Tom Barton. You and me need a little talk...'

'Who are yer and what do yer want?' Tom demanded, trying to shake the man's hand off and failing, because his grip was too strong.

'It don't matter who I am, but what I want is what yer thievin' little bruvver kept from me. I told 'im where to dig and what to look out fer and I paid him good money, and then the silly little blighter got 'imself blown up – and now I want me goods.'

'I don't know what yer talkin' about,' Tom lied. He'd recognised the man now as the bloke who had been there with Sam and the other boys when Tom reached the bombsite that fatal day; though, with a dark trilby pulled low over his brow, it wasn't easy to see his face.

'Yer can't pull that one on me,' the man grunted. 'I know Sam found somethin' good, 'cos 'e told me 'e wanted more money – a lot more. I reckon yer know where 'e hid his stuff, 'cos 'e told me yer had found it. Get it and give it ter me or it will be the worse fer yer.'

'I don't know where he put the bits he found,' Tom said and managed to wrench his arm free. 'Sam never told me what he was doing and I haven't seen anything. Clear orf and leave me alone. I'm not gettin' drawn into yer dirty little schemes. It's thievin' from the dead or those what have lost everythin' and I want nothin' to do with it.'

The man slammed him back against the wall of the house, pushing his face close to Tom's so that he could smell the stink of his breath. 'When Knocker tells yer what to do yer do it or yer get yer throat slit, savvy?' He was so close to Tom that he could now see the tiny scar above his left eye and the way his nose was slightly crooked, as if he'd been a boxer at some time.

Tom, held so tightly about the throat that he couldn't breathe, could only nod. Knocker, as he'd named himself, released his throat and Tom gasped out the words: 'I'll look, but 'e moved his stuff after I found it and I don't know where 'e 'id whatever it is you want…'

'Well, it's got ter be in the 'ouse. Find it. I'll give yer a week and then I want what's mine or it's curtains fer Tom Barton.'

He banged Tom's head against the wall, leaving him feeling dizzy and sick and then he was gone, melting into the darkness. Tom was shaking, more frightened than he'd ever been in his life.

Managing to get himself into the house, Tom collapsed onto the chair and sat very still until his head cleared. The rotten devil who had attacked him must have waited until his father had left, and then, knowing Tom was alone, he'd struck.

What had Sam found that Knocker wanted so badly? It must be something valuable or he wouldn't have come after Tom like that. He wished his father was still here, because he needed to talk to someone – but he couldn't go to Peggy or Maureen about something like this... it was too shaming and it would be dangerous to draw them into it. He just wished he could forget the whole thing, but he knew Knocker wouldn't go away.

Chapter 11

Ellie hung over the toilet as the acrid vomit came up her throat. It tasted vile and she felt weak and dizzy as she knelt there on the floor and wondered what was wrong with her. She'd never felt this ill in her life and it was the third day in a row that she'd been sick. What on earth was wrong with her? Ellie pulled the chain and struggled to her feet, leaning against the basin for a minute until the feeling of nausea cleared.

She wiped her mouth with a wet flannel and then left the bathroom, going slowly downstairs to the kitchen, where Mrs Tandy was making toast. She turned and saw Ellie and the smile left her face.

'What's wrong, love? You look terrible.'

'I feel it,' Ellie said and sat down on a kitchen chair. 'I was sick again this mornin' – I almost passed out and everythin' just went round and round. Do you think I'm gettin' somethin' nasty?'

Mrs Tandy looked devastated and seemed to be weighing her words. 'Well, my love, I'm afraid you may think so – because I suspect you're pregnant...'

'Pregnant – I can't be!' Ellie felt the shock hit her and she might have fallen had she not been sitting down. 'Peter has been away for over a year…' She gave a little sob of despair, because she'd been gradually getting over what had happened to her and now she was caught in a trap. Tears were burning behind her eyes and spilling over. 'Oh no – that means it's his – it has to be. What can I do? Peter will hate me. He'll never believe I didn't go with that man willingly…' She sobbed and swiped at her eyes with the back of her hand.

'I'll tell him,' Mrs Tandy promised. 'I'm so sorry, love. You must go to the doctor and let him examine you to be sure, but I think – it shows in your face a little. I have wondered recently but didn't want to worry you.'

'I don't want that beast's child,' Ellie said as the panic swept through her. She couldn't face her friends and neighbours if they all thought she'd got pregnant going with other men. Maureen had been kind to her, having her to tea, but she knew some of the women in the lanes would think it served her right. It wasn't fair when she'd been raped and she hated the very idea that the child inside her was made from the seed of the man who had forced himself on her and then beaten her. 'I'll have to get rid of it – there must be a way…'

'There are women in dirty back street rooms who would murder your baby for you,' Mrs Tandy said, 'but they might kill you too. I know it's hard, Ellie, but I can't see any way out of this…'

'Peter will kill me!' Ellie remembered what his mother had said about him giving her a black eye for going with other men and shivered.

'He's more likely to kill the man who raped you,' Mrs Tandy said, looking at her sadly. 'I think we might be able to arrange for you to go away somewhere for a few months.

You could have the child at a Salvation Army home and they will have it adopted for you. Then you can come home and no one will ever know for certain, though there are bound to be whispers.'

'What about my job?'

'I'm afraid you will have to give it up. I'll tell Mrs Stimpson that you have to go and look after your grandmother, who is very ill, and we'll let everyone think the same thing – and then you can return to me and find another job. It might not be hairdressin', but there's plenty of work about.'

'You would have me back?' Ellie's eyes filled with tears. She thought that if it weren't for her friend, she might have tried to find one of those women who got rid of unwanted babies, but Ellie didn't want to die – and, when she thought about it calmly, she didn't want to kill the life that had begun inside her. The baby was innocent; it was just that it had an evil father. 'I don't want to 'ave the baby, but if I must...' She bent her head as the tears spilled over.

'There, there, my love,' Mrs Tandy said and stroked her head tenderly. 'It isn't the end of the world, Ellie. It has happened to other girls. I know you feel revolted at the thought of bearin' the child of a man you despise and hate, but the baby is innocent. You wouldn't really want to destroy a blameless baby, would you?'

'No,' Ellie admitted, though without the support of Mrs Tandy she would probably have tried some of the old-fashioned remedies, except that she knew none of them really worked. There were gruesome stories of girls sticking knitting needles up inside themselves to try and kill unwanted babies, but they either killed themselves or ended up in hospital fighting for their lives, and if they lived, they often could never have another baby. If there had been a safe, easy way, she would probably have done it quickly, but Ellie wanted to be able to have Peter's child one day – if she managed to get away with her deception. 'Do you think I can manage to hide it for long enough?' She looked at Mrs Tandy with the anxious appeal of the young girl she was, making her friend smile. 'What am I goin' to do if he finds out and disowns me?'

'We'll face that when we come to it. In the meantime, we have to let your clothes out as you get bigger, and you can buy a corset of some sort to hold you in a bit. When I think it's becoming noticeable I'll tell you and send you away. I'll go in and see the "Sally Army" people, explain what happened, and book a place for you – at least we know when to expect it. You were raped a few weeks before Christmas so it should be in September, which means you'll need to go into the home durin' May, if not before, if we're goin' to have a chance of hidin' it.'

Ellie sniffed and wiped her eyes. Her sickness had passed now, but all she fancied was a piece of toast with just a scraping of marge. As she chewed her toast, it actually helped her and she began to feel better, more able to cope. She was frightened and angry of course, but at least she had a good friend in Mrs Tandy. If it hadn't been for her, she didn't know what she would have done.

'I'd better book an appointment with the doctor for Monday mornin',' she said. 'Get it confirmed. You don't think he would arrange to get rid of it if I told him I'd been raped?'

'I know he wouldn't,' Mrs Tandy said. 'I think you have to be very brave and face up to it, Ellie. You don't have a choice.'

Ellie nodded. A part of her was still in denial and she felt terribly conflicted, but the idea of aborting the life growing inside her at one of those awful backstreet houses terrified her. She put a hand to her stomach, feeling oddly protective even though she wished with all her heart that the baby she was carrying was Peter's and not the beast who had raped her. One part of her wished she could pluck the child of that evil beast out of her body, but there was another part of her that wanted to protect the life inside her. Ellie had never known a mother's love; she'd been brought up by an aunt who couldn't have cared less about her – and she felt sad that something like that might happen to the baby she carried. Yet what else could she do but give it away?

Peggy looked at the loose top she'd put on that morning. It was pale blue with tiny silk spots and she was wearing it over a dark navy maternity skirt that she could keep letting out at the waist as she got bigger. She felt as big as a house already, even though she was just seven months gone. Her baby would be born sometime in March if everything went well, and she was eager to hold Able's son in her arms. She kept thinking it had to be a boy because she hadn't put on anywhere near this much weight when she was having Janet. She didn't think she'd got this big with Pip either, but she'd been bigger with him than with his sister and she was carrying high this time. Nellie said she was having a boy and so did Alice, who had given birth to three sons, none of whom had survived their infancy; two had died of diphtheria and the third during an outbreak of typhoid.

'I always wanted more babies,' she told Peggy as they had had a little chat that morning. 'I'd 'ave 'ad them too if me 'usband 'ad survived the Great War, but the poor bugger got gassed.'

'Yes, I know, Alice love,' Peggy said and cut her a slice of apple pie. 'It's on the house this time.'

'You'll never make a profit, Peggy Ashley,' Alice said and grinned, but she ate the pie with relish. 'You're a good cook, love. What yer gonna do in the last weeks? You can't do it all yerself.'

'I'm not goin' to try,' Peggy assured her. 'Janet will do more in the bar and Anne is goin' to help as much as she can in the evenings. Nellie does all the cleanin' now – and I'm tryin' to find someone to help a bit with the cookin'.'

'Maureen is a good little cook, though not as good as you, but she'd probably help you out – at least until she gets too big herself.' Alice cackled with laughter. 'Must 'ave been somethin' in the water in this lane... you're all havin' babies.'

'Maureen has already offered to help sometimes,' Peggy said, 'but I'd like to get more permanent help if I can. I suppose I could put an advert in...' she broke off in surprise as the door opened and a woman slightly older than she was, walked in carrying a suitcase. She knew her at once and smiled. 'Helen – you've done it at last... you've left your husband.'

'Yes, I walked out on him,' Helen Barnes said, her look something between bewilderment and pride. 'It was something he said about Sally and the way she died – I just couldn't take any more, so when he left for work, I packed my case and locked the door behind me. I came here in the hope that your offer of a temporary home still holds...'

'Yes, of course it does,' Peggy said, because she'd taken to Helen when they'd talked after her lovely daughter Sally was killed in a bomb blast. Sally had visited the pub with Maureen and Peggy had really taken to her; it had felt like losing a friend when she'd been killed and Peggy had felt sorry for her mother. She'd learnt then what a bully Helen's husband was and offered her a home if she left him. 'I'll ask Janet to take over here – and I'll show you your room. It is clean, but it hasn't been prepared. You'll need to make up the bed, but I'll show you where the sheets are kept.'

'Thank you so much…' Helen said as Peggy went to the door into the hall and shouted for Janet.

Janet nodded when her mother explained and came to talk to Alice while her mother led the way upstairs.

'Well, that's a turn-up,' Alice said after they'd gone. 'As if yer mum hasn't enough to do…'

'I think Mum would give up her own bed if someone needed it,' Janet said and shook her head. 'I knew she'd invited Mrs Barnes here – she's Sally Barnes' mother. She was a nurse with Maureen and she was killed in a bombing raid. She only came here once, but Mum took to her and she was upset when Sally died.'

'Yes, I remember Peggy bein' in tears over it,' Alice said. 'You want to make use of Sally's mother while she's 'ere, get 'er to serve in the bar – or do some of the cookin'.'

'I expect Helen will help out,' Janet said. 'Mum said she's thinkin' of becomin' a secretary, but while she's learnin' she can help here in some way or other.'

'Well, things have a way of turnin' out right,' Alice said and finished her drink. 'I'll get orf then. I've got to do me shoppin' and get me 'ousework done some time today… not that there's a lot ter do fer one.'

Janet nodded and smiled. She was serving her third customer when Peggy returned to the bar.

'Thanks, love. You can go back to whatever yer were doin' now. I'll take over.'

'I was just writin' a letter to Mike. Why don't you sit down for a while, Mum? Maggie is asleep and I'm all right on my own.'

'Well, I'll get ahead with my cookin' for tonight, if you're sure,' Peggy said and laughed as Janet shook her head, because she'd meant her to sit down and rest. 'I'm feelin' fine, Jan. When I'm not, I'll tell you – but I shall have some help now with the cookin'. Helen has some experience of caterin'. She took a cooking course in a high-class restaurant for a few months just after she got married. Her husband didn't want her to work at all, and she gave up her secretarial work, but just did a few hours three mornings a week at the restaurant – until he found out and made her give up. She says she'll be best makin' scones or fatless sponges, but she can turn her hand to anythin', so we're goin' to work out what suits us best, and it will save you tryin' to do too much when I have to put my feet up – because you'll have Mike home for good soon. He will need your help and attention.'

Janet looked at her hard. 'Are you sure you're all right with Helen movin' in, Mum?'

'It will only be for a while and she doesn't mind what she does – it's goin' to make life easier for us all, Janet. 'Sides, her husband is a cold brute and she wouldn't have left him if I hadn't told her she could come to us. Helen will move on when she's ready, but for the moment I'm glad to have her here. I couldn't stop Sally getting killed but I can give her mum a home for a while.'

'As long as you're not being taken advantage of...'

Peggy laughed. 'It would take more than Helen Barnes to put one over on me, love. I'm goin' to get on with my cookin'. Helen will come down and clear tables and whatever you need when she's changed...'

Peggy was smiling to herself as she went through to the kitchen. If Helen's cooking was reasonable, she would be a godsend for the next few months, because Peggy knew that very soon now she would start to get extremely tired and the work would become a chore rather than a pleasure. For the moment, it was just a bit of a backache if she did too much, but she would be glad to have some help.

She started measuring flour into a bowl and was just cutting a slice from the margarine block when someone knocked at the back door.

'Come in...' The door opened and Tom Barton walked in. Peggy smiled at him. 'It's nice to see you, Tom, but shouldn't you be at work?'

'I've been deliverin' groceries,' he said. 'Mr Jackson is sittin' in the shop, but I can't stop long, because he gets flustered if too many customers come in – only I have a problem and I don't know what to do...'

Peggy could see how anxious he was and knew it was serious, because Tom wouldn't come to her unless he really needed to. 'Come and sit down, Tom,' Peggy said. 'I'll have a sit-down myself. I've made a pot of tea, so I'll have a cup with you.'

'I'd rather not,' Tom said a little stiffly. 'I didn't want to come askin' for help, Peggy. It's somethin' Sam did – and I'm ashamed...'

Peggy felt coldness at the nape of her neck because she could see he was really troubled. 'We're friends, Tom. Just tell me and then I'll see what I can do to help.'

'You know what Sam was doin' the day he got killed – up there on the bombsite?' Peggy nodded. 'It wasn't just lads messin' about and hopin' ter find somethin'. That mornin' there was a bloke talkin' to them when I arrived, tellin' them what to look out for and where to dig. He went off straight away when he saw me, but I knew why he was there. Two nights ago, he grabbed me as I was on me way 'ome. He said Sam 'ad found somethin' better than usual and that it belonged to him. He told me to find it and he'd come back in a week and if I didn't give it to him, he'd kill me...'

'Oh, Tom,' Peggy said, looking at him in distress. No wonder he'd come to her; he must be at his wit's end. 'That's a wicked thing to say to you. How are you supposed to know where Sam put things?' She saw the expression in his eyes and gasped. 'Or do you?'

'I always knew Sam hid things from Ma,' Tom said. 'I found his stash of pinched stuff once before and he grabbed it and ran off. But I knew there were other hidin' places and I found one last night...' He took a deep breath, put his hand into his coat pocket and brought out a flat jeweller's box. 'I think these must be worth a lot of money...' He offered the box to Peggy. She took it, opened it and stared in shock.

'If these are diamonds they must be worth a fortune...' she breathed in awe. She touched the necklace made of large white gems that glittered and sparkled up at her. The stones were set in a white metal she thought might be platinum and they looked expensive and beautiful. 'Oh, Tom...no wonder he threatened you. They must be worth at least a thousand pounds, perhaps more...'

'They don't belong to him and they didn't belong to Sam,' Tom said, looking angry. 'They're stolen goods, Peggy, and I ain't gettin' involved with a man like that. Once I give them to him he'll be after me to do other stuff and I don't want that – I'm goin' to give them to the police, but they might think I stole them...'

'If this man doesn't get them, he'll hurt you, Tom...' Peggy looked at him anxiously. 'Are you sure you want to risk it?'

'I'm not goin' to be a thief, Peggy. If I let him bully me into givin' him that necklace, he'll just keep comin' back and I shan't be able to go to the police then, because I'll be guilty of handlin' stolen goods. I've made up my mind. I'm handin' the diamonds in to the police – but I need someone to come with me and back up my story so they don't think I stole them.'

'You've got a few days before he returns,' Peggy said and frowned. 'Why don't we think about it? Surely there's some way round this – a way to get the necklace to the police but keep you safe…'

'I've thought about it all night,' Tom said. 'I don't know what else to do, Peggy. That necklace belongs to the man that owned that jeweller's shop. He's lost so much and it could make a lot of difference to him. Don't you think he should have it back?'

'Yes, of course I do, Tom – and takin' it to the police is the right thing to do, but there might be another way. Supposin' you leave this with me for the time bein'? I know someone who might be able to help… but you'll have to trust me and it might still get you in a bit of trouble with that bloke you told me about – if you're prepared for that?'

'All right,' Tom said. 'I know I can trust you, Peggy. If you keep it hid here somewhere, it will be safe.' He looked relieved. 'I didn't want to worry you, but I didn't know who else to ask.'

'You were right to ask me, Tom. I'm goin' to talk to someone who might be able to help us…' She gave him a bright smile. 'I'll put these in a safe place and you should get on with your work. Don't worry about it, Tom. We'll sort things out…'

'Thanks, Peggy. I'm glad to get rid of that damned thing. I was frightened to leave it in the house in case someone broke in while I was out – and if I carry it around and he grabs me…'

'Leave it with me and I'll be in touch…' Peggy said and picked up the box. 'I'm goin' to put this away right now, Tom. I don't want it to go missin' while I have charge of it.'

'Right, see yer later,' Tom said. He grinned and went off whistling, relieved that one of his problems was solved, at least temporarily.

Peggy went up to her bedroom. She had a small safe built into the wall, hidden behind a framed tapestry of 'Home Sweet Home', in which she kept sums of cash from the bar when she didn't have time to visit the bank. She unlocked it and placed the diamonds inside, feeling relieved as she locked the safe again.

She sat down on the edge of the bed, picked up the telephone receiver and dialled a number she'd used a few times on Tom's behalf when he was in hospital.

It rang three times the other end before it was picked up, then, 'Yes, Doctor Blake here – how may I help?'

'Doctor Blake – it's Peggy Ashley. I don't know if you remember me…'

'Of course I do, Peggy. How could I forget? How are you?'

'Blooming,' she said and laughed. 'I do have a problem, but not with my health. I wonder if you could call and see me sometime?'

'No time like the present,' he said. 'I'll be there in half an hour – if that suits you?'

'That is so very kind,' Peggy said. 'Yes, that would be just right.'

'I'll be there soon.'

He replaced his receiver and Peggy did the same. She looked at herself in the mirror. She couldn't do much by changing her clothes, but she would put some fresh make-up on and brush her hair – and then she'd just have time to pop those scones in the oven before Doctor Blake arrived. He'd been so helpful when Tilly was ill that she knew he wouldn't mind advising her on what they ought to do about those diamonds and that wretched man.

Chapter 12

Tom was alone when Peggy entered the shop the next morning. She smiled at him as he approached the counter, looking very professional in his striped apron and white shirt, the sleeves rolled up to his elbows and held by black cuffs.

'Good mornin', Mrs Ashley,' he said in a polite manner. 'How may I help you today?'

'Maureen told me you had some golden syrup – I hope there's a tin left for me.'

'I remembered you making a delicious treacle tart, so I put two under the counter,' Tom said and grinned. He took them out for her and placed them in the basket she'd put on the counter.

'I'd also like two large tins of Spam and two jars of chicken paste, and my rations of butter, margarine and sugar. I think I've got enough coupons for eight ounces of bacon, and eight of ham. Also a box of Swan matches, three candles and a bar of Sunlight soap please.'

Tom produced all the items she'd ordered and totted up the price. 'That is two pounds eighteen shillings and seven pence – the soap is on special discount and so are the candles, as they've been in stock awhile.'

'Thank you,' Peggy said and paid him, glancing over her shoulder, before she said, 'I've got somethin' to tell you about that other business, Tom – it's bein' arranged for us by the same person that helped me get your dad out on parole. He's got a friend in the police and he's goin' to set up what he calls a little sting – and that's all I know for now.'

Tom nodded, a little frown creasing his brow. 'Are you sure you can trust him?'

'I'm quite certain,' Peggy said. 'Doctor Blake helped your mum that day at the bombsite and he's a decent bloke. I'm not sure what he'll come up with yet, but I'm sure we can work somethin' out…'

Just at that moment the door opened and Mrs Tandy entered. She nodded and smiled to Peggy and the two women exchanged pleasantries.

'I'll see you later,' Peggy promised and went out, leaving Tom to serve his customer.

'I've just popped in for some barley sugars,' Mrs Tandy said, because Tom delivered all her other goods for her on Fridays. 'Ellie has been feelin' a little under the weather and I thought they might cheer her up.'

'Yes, I'm sure they will,' Tom said. 'She's been lookin' a bit pale lately. I hope she's all right?'

'Yes, she's just a little tired,' Mrs Tandy said. 'I think she had a letter about her grandmother that upset her.'

He nodded, weighed the sweets up and added one extra, just as Maureen always had. Mrs Tandy noticed and looked pleased.

'It's pleasant to have such nice people servin' in the shop, Tom. Your dad was lovely to everyone while he was here.

I know what he did, stealin from that post office, but he made a mistake and we're all capable of doin' that, aren't we?'

'Yes, we are, and Dad would give anythin' if he could go back and undo the wrong he did.'

'Well, he's servin' his country now and we can't ask more of any man.'

Mrs Tandy picked up her bag of sweets and went out. Tom screwed the top back on the jar and replaced it. The jar was half empty. He would put barley sugars on his list of stock to reorder, ready for when Maureen came in...

'Well, I've given in my notice, even though I felt able to go on a bit longer, but Matron was starin' at me as I bent over a patient and I know I'm beginnin' to show, so I thought I'd better give up before I get thrown out,' Maureen said and laughed.

'Sister Morrison will be sorry to lose you.'

'Yes, she will.' Maureen sighed. 'I don't like leavin' when the wards are still so full, Peggy, but it can't be helped – anyway, it means I can help you now and then if you want me? Janet told me that your new lodger is helpin' with the cookin', so I thought I'd serve in the bar when you need me. Give Jan or Anne a break sometimes.'

'Helen is a lovely cook,' Peggy said. 'She has her own methods and Jan says my scones are better, but she makes a lovely light sponge and the plum crumble and custard she cooked sold out in minutes yesterday...'

'Well, she will make things easier for you,' Maureen said. 'Jan told me Mrs Barnes has enrolled in a night-school class for shorthand and typing.'

'She was a trained secretary before she got married, but her husband made her give it up – and then when she took a little job cookin' he made her give that up too. He was a bully, the controllin' sort.'

'Yes, I remember from the time I stayed there with Sally – and he was awful to her.' Maureen's eyes pricked with tears. 'I still want to cry when I remember how she died... this rotten war!'

'I know, love.' Peggy was sympathetic. 'Too many people died durin' the Blitz.' They were both silent, grateful that for the moment the Germans had turned their attention away from London.

'Sally had left home, but she told me she still cared about her mother – but she hated her father. Mr Barnes is a horrid man.'

'I'm glad Helen has left him. Jan thinks he'll come here when he knows where she is – but I'll deal with him if he does.'

Maureen nodded, smiling at the glint in Peggy's eyes. 'Well, I'd better get home and give Gran a hand with the housework. It's been a lot for her to do lookin' after Shirley. I'm glad I shall be around to help more in future, though she says she can manage fine and she told me to come and help you.'

'Hilda is a determined lady,' Peggy said. 'She's been good to you, Maureen – and to her son, though he didn't appreciate it for years.'

'I think he does now.' Maureen looked uncertain, then lowering her voice, 'I know you won't gossip, Peggy. I'm worried about the situation there... Violet is impatient with my Dad and she doesn't seem to care much about him. She goes out several days a week and she's gone hours – she says to visit clients. He's left alone. I pop in before I go to work

– and Tom goes up first thing and later if Dad doesn't go down. Some days he sits in the shop while Tom takes the deliveries out, but he can't do more than half an hour or so… and he made a mistake with the change yesterday, gave the customer two shillings too much; luckily, she gave it back, but some wouldn't.'

'I suppose he's lucky to be able to do anythin' after what he went through, Maureen.' Peggy looked concerned. 'I'm sorry Violet isn't more carin' though. He's her husband after all…'

'I half-blame his illness on her,' Maureen said, 'for giving him too much greasy food. I seldom let him have big breakfasts because I knew they didn't suit him, even though he likes them… but she cooks a huge plateful of greasy food every other day and gets cross if he doesn't eat it.'

Peggy was thoughtful. 'Does Violet still not know that your grandmother owns the shop?'

Maureen hesitated, then, 'Gran has put it into my name. She insisted on doin' it. She says she wants to make sure I don't get cheated out of it, so she's had a solicitor draw up the conveyance and I had to sign it.'

'Oh dear…' Peggy sighed. 'If Violet doesn't know, she may be expectin' to take over if the worst should happen.'

Maureen felt a little sick at the thought. 'I've wondered if that was what she was hopin' for, to own the property if he dies – she might even neglect Dad in the expectation that another stroke would almost certainly kill him.'

'You can't think she would…' Peggy looked horrified.

'Not kill him, no, I don't think she would go that far, but as far as I can see, she's not tryin' to help him recover.'

'It's a good thing he has you and Tom to look out for him,' Peggy said and sighed. 'It never rains but it pours…'

'Somethin' botherin' you, too?' Maureen asked.

'Yes…' Peggy hesitated, then, 'Tom has a spot of trouble and I'm tryin' to help him. I can't tell you it all, but there's a nasty character lurkin' and we have to sort him out.'

'Sounds a bit dangerous?' Maureen was anxious. 'Is there anythin' I can do for you or Tom?'

'I'm not sure yet,' Peggy said. 'There might be – just as a witness perhaps. I've got to talk to Doctor Blake again this evenin' and then I'll know…'

'You know where to come if you need me,' Maureen said and smiled. She kissed her friend's cheek, thinking that Peggy looked a bit tired, which was only to be expected at this late stage in her pregnancy; it must be about seven or so weeks to go now if Peggy had got the timing right.

She walked home feeling thoughtful. Had Peggy read Violet's expectations correctly – did she believe the shop would be hers if anything happened to Maureen's father? Henry was a proud man. He probably wouldn't have told her that the property belonged to his mother – no doubt he'd thought it would come to him when Gran died. It was the reason that Hilda Jackson had insisted on transferring it into Maureen's name now.

'I let him sign another lease for three years,' Maureen's gran had told her, 'because I couldn't sell it while there's a war on – no one wanted to buy anythin' durin' the Blitz, but I told him I might sell once the war was over. He got very annoyed with me, told me I had no right to sell because it ought to be his when I went – so I know if I go first they will make trouble for you, Maureen.'

Maureen hadn't wanted her grandmother to transfer the property but she'd insisted, and in the end, Maureen had given in rather than see her upset – but she wasn't looking forward to the arguments when Violet and Henry understood the situation. Maureen's father was being grateful and nice to her at the moment, but what he would think when he discovered that his mother had given the shop to her, she daren't contemplate. She wouldn't turn him and Violet out at the end of the lease, but she would ask for some rent. Maureen thought her grandmother should've had rent all these years. Gran wasn't as hard-up as some of the other widows Maureen knew, but she surely didn't have a lot to spare. She had bills and her food to pay for, even though Maureen paid her share of the expenses now. A fair rent could have made a big difference to her these past years; if Maureen's father had been a caring son he'd have insisted on giving her something, even a few bob a week might have made a difference.

If Maureen's father felt a little disgruntled over the situation, Violet would be furious when she discovered the truth. Yet if she was hoping her husband would die so that she could inherit, it might be better if she knew what was really going to happen. At the moment, there was an unspoken truce between her and Maureen, but it might be worth putting up with Violet's fury if it saved her father from more unkindness. Maureen was sometimes tempted to tell her, but she was afraid it might lead to more neglect or even cruelty towards her father. She was torn and didn't know which of the two ways would make the situation better.

No! Perhaps she was wrong to think so ill of Violet, Maureen thought. She'd seemed genuinely fond of her husband when he was in hospital, looking pleased when the nurses had told them he would be home for Christmas, but now… Maureen thought she'd noticed a difference in Violet's manner recently. Perhaps it was just that she didn't have the patience to put up with a sick husband who needed looking after. She was used to running her own bespoke corset business and because her husband was ill, she was going out to her customers instead of asking them to come to her for fittings. Her excuse was that it might put women off if they saw a man sitting around the flat all day.

Deciding she'd misjudged Violet, Maureen quickened her step. Since she didn't need to get ready for work that evening, she was going to make Shirley a strawberry blancmange. One of the things Tom had unearthed at the back of the storeroom was a box of blancmange and custard mixes and Maureen had bought two boxes of strawberry flavour, because it was Shirley's favourite.

Tom locked the shop carefully and tucked the key inside his inner jacket pocket. He was whistling as he crossed the road and went through the side alley between two houses on his way home. It would soon be his first payday and he was looking forward to having some money in his pocket. His shoulder was feeling a bit sore, because he'd washed some of the shelves down that morning and also the inside of the shop window. The customers had been slow in coming first thing, so he'd filled his time with all the little jobs he could find.

He was thinking that he ought to buy a little treat for his mother and visit her if the hospital would let him. His father hadn't written in a while, but no doubt he was busy. Tom wrote once a week and he knew his father enjoyed getting his letters, even if he didn't always reply immediately.

Reaching the back door of his home, he went to unlock it, but it swung back as he touched the handle and he saw that the lock had been broken. A chill went down his spine as he gingerly pushed it open with the toe of his boot. Going into the kitchen, he switched on the light and knew at once that the house had been ransacked. Cushions were pulled from chairs and ripped open, the upholstery on the old sofa had been cut from head to tail and most of the horsehair stuffing pulled out.

As he went through to the sitting room, Tom found similar devastation; the drawers of the sideboard had been opened and tipped on the floor, cushions from his mother's prized three-piece suite torn and discarded, china smashed and pictures taken off the wall, the glass broken on one of them.

Upstairs, it was the same story; everything had been pulled from the beds, the mattresses ripped, ornaments smashed and drawers emptied. Some of the floorboards had been prised up, and the wardrobe in his mother's room had been emptied, clothes strewn on the floor.

What a mess! Tom stared at it helplessly, too stunned at first to do anything. Someone had searched with vicious intensity and caused a lot of malicious damage. Tom's feeling of content and pleasure in the prospect of his first wage vanished in an instant. Some of the damage was repairable, some was not. He would have to try and clear up as best he could and then get someone in to repair what was too difficult for him.

He was about to start picking things up when he changed his mind. Tom knew who was responsible for the wanton damage and he ought to report it. He didn't want to disturb Peggy again, but he couldn't think of anyone else – unless he went to Maureen.

Yes, perhaps that was best. He had to talk to someone and he couldn't put all of it on Peggy, even though she'd told him to. He would walk round to Maureen first and then call in on Peggy on the way back.

★

'You must tell the police,' Maureen said when he told her what had happened. 'If your parents have some insurance they will need a police report or the firm might think you'd done it yourselves for the money.'

'If Dad had insurance, Mum wouldn't have kept it up,' Tom said with certainty. 'But I think I'll tell the police – but do I tell them the whole story?' He'd had to explain about the necklace and Maureen had looked horrified. She clearly didn't know what to advise him and Tom sighed. 'I didn't want to disturb Peggy again, but perhaps I'd better...'

'I'll come with you,' Maureen said. 'We'll see what she thinks – but I think the police ought to be told, Tom.'

Tom agreed, but still wasn't sure whether to tell them everything. Maureen fetched her coat, told her gran she wouldn't be long and then they walked round to the pub together. It was chilly, smoke drifting from the chimneys and the threat of a foggy night was descending on the lanes, which made the sound of their footsteps eerie.

When they arrived, Peggy was sitting in the pub kitchen with an attractive, well-dressed man that she introduced them to as Doctor Blake. Tom hadn't met him previously, because he'd been in hospital when he was treating Tom's mother after Sam's terrible accident, but he knew him by reputation. The doctor's work was at the London, but he often treated people who needed it in his spare time if they sent for him.

'I can see somethin' else has happened, Tom,' she said after one look at their faces. 'Doctor Bailey knows about the necklace, so you can tell him all of it.'

Tom cleared his throat and described the scene that had met him on his return from work. 'I can repair some of the damage myself, but I'll have to get help for the upholstery. Mum was real proud of her three-piece, but I'm not sure what can be done. I think it's ruined.'

'That's terrible,' Peggy said and looked angry. 'This man is ruthless and cruel. He needs to be stopped.' She looked at Doctor Blake. 'What do you think, Michael?'

'Well, Peggy, I think I'm going to take this young man to the police station and speak to my friend Maurice. He knows what is going on so we'll let him see the devastation for himself – and then he'll tell us what he thinks best.'

'I could give you a hand with clearin' up,' Maureen offered, looking at Tom with sympathy.

'I don't think Tom should stay at the house alone for the time being,' Doctor Blake said. 'I believe you have a houseful, Peggy?'

'There's always room for one more...' she said, but Maureen shook her head.

'You've got enough to do, Peggy. Alice Carter will take him in,' she suggested and Tom nodded as she looked at him. 'I know she'd love to have you with her, Tom. She told me if you found it too much to look after the house she would give you a home.' Maureen turned to the others, 'I'll go round and talk to her while Tom is with the police.' She explained to the doctor that Alice lived only a couple of doors away from the Barton family and he nodded his approval.

'What a good idea,' Doctor Blake said. 'We don't really want Tom on the premises here at the pub if we're goin' to trap our nasty little thief, Peggy. If he is living nearby, he'll take the same journey home every night.' He looked at Tom. 'I'll explain what we have in mind on the way to the police station. I have my car outside – if you're willing to trust me, Tom?'

'Yeah…' Tom's feeling of oppression lifted as he saw the expression in the doctor's eyes. He wished his dad was here, because this would never have happened if Jack Barton was around, but it had and he would be glad of a man's perspective. Doctor Blake had helped his mother and he was grateful for the offer of help now. He didn't want to keep worrying Peggy and Maureen, both of whom were pregnant. Peggy getting very near her time by the look of things; she could do without his troubles, but this man looked to be made of sterner stuff and if he was willing to take a hand it would suit Tom down to the ground. 'I'd be glad of your help, sir.'

Doctor Blake smiled in approval and Tom followed him out to his car, sitting up front with him in the comfortable 1930s Morris, and admiring the old leather seats and the beautiful wood on the dashboard. As the doctor drove through darkened streets, he explained what his friend in the police force had thought they might do and Tom looked at him in awe and respect. Here was a man who believed in fighting back against the criminals and Tom liked it that he was being asked to play his part. Most men would have just said leave it to the police, but not this one.

'I reckon that's clever,' he said. 'Knocker will be desperate to get his hands on them diamonds, and frustrated because he didn't find anythin' at the house when he trashed it.'

'Yes, I'm sure he will – and you're happy to go along with our plan? You know that he may knock you about if you don't tell him where the necklace is straight away?'

'Yeah,' Tom said, 'but if your friend gets 'im, it's worth it – and if I told 'im straight off that Peggy has it, he'd smell a rat.'

'Good lad,' Doctor Blake smiled at him. 'Peggy didn't want you involved, but if it's going to work, you have to be.'

'Yeah,' Tom grinned at him. 'Peggy is great, but she's too soft-hearted. I don't mind a few bruises if that bugger ends up behind bars – sorry, sir. I didn't mean to swear.' He flushed, mindful of his father's warning to watch his speech. He'd been trying very hard not to swear or drop his 'aitches', but sometimes emotion made him careless.

'That's all right, Tom, I think you're entitled after all that has happened to you. You're a brave lad – and remember, if you need any help with repairing your mother's home, changing the locks and things, I'll give you a hand...'

Chapter 13

Maureen couldn't help feeling a little nervous as she went down the lane to Alice's house and knocked on the door. People round here were mostly honest and looked out for each other, but it wasn't a nice feeling to know that a violent and evil man was lurking in the shadows.

Alice answered the door and invited her in, offering her a cup of tea. Maureen went into the hall but refused the tea, wasting no time in telling Alice the reason she'd come. The elderly woman looked upset as she heard that Tom's home had been virtually destroyed by a vicious thief and said yes immediately when she was asked if Tom could stay with her for a while.

'Of course he can.' She nodded vigorously. 'I'll be glad of the company until that beggar is in jail.'

'Yes, I kept lookin' over my shoulder as I walked from the pub,' Maureen agreed. 'I'm sure you needn't worry too much, Alice. We think this burglar, whoever he is, believes there is somethin' valuable in Tom's house – somethin' his brother found on the bombsites.'

'A bit of jewellery, I reckon,' Alice said. 'Well, he'll have found it now if it was there, so perhaps he'll be satisfied and leave the rest of us alone.'

'Are you worried about takin' Tom in – are you thinkin' it might bring the thief here?'

'I wasn't thinkin' that, though it might if 'e didn't find what 'e was after. I don't have anythin' of value, but I shouldn't like my bits and pieces damaged...' Alice said, 'but I wouldn't dream of turnin' Tom down. If that beggar comes here, I'll hit 'im with me copper warmin' pan. By the time I finish wiv 'im', 'e'll wish 'e'd never been born.'

'Oh Alice...' Maureen laughed with her. 'Shall I help you make up a bed for Tom? Have you got a spare bed for him?'

'Course I 'ave,' Alice said, 'and it's made up ready just in case. I didn't like to think of the lad livin' there alone...'

'Doctor Blake has taken him to the police to let them know what's goin' on – and they'll probably come and have a look, so if you see lights and hear things, you'll know it's them.'

Alice nodded, and then cocked her head on one side. 'That Doctor Blake was the one what looked after Tilly when Sam was killed. He visited 'er a few times and I've seen 'im goin' round the back at the pub... Do yer think he's a bit sweet on our Peggy?'

'Surely not,' Maureen said and frowned. 'I hadn't thought about it. I haven't seen any signs of anything...'

'Well, what was 'e doin' at the pub when Tom went there?' Alice asked. 'I know she's fell out with that 'usband of hers. 'E ain't been 'ome in ages, and I don't think 'e's fightin' 'cos 'e's too old. So why ain't 'e comin' ter visit? And that baby she's 'avin' ain't Laurence Ashley's.'

'Alice! You shouldn't say such things. I thought you liked Peggy?' Maureen was a little shocked.

'I love 'er like she was my own,' Alice said, 'I shouldn't say it to anyone I didn't trust, Maureen, but I reckon it's that American serviceman she was sweet on – and don't tell me she didn't go away with 'im last summer, because I know she did.' Alice gave a little cackle of triumph as she saw Maureen's face. 'Knew I was right, but I shan't tell. I'd never 'urt Peggy. It's just between us.'

'You'd be sorry if you did tell, Alice,' Maureen said. 'If a rumour like that got around, I think Peggy might leave and there would be someone new at the pub.'

'Lord, save us from that!' Alice said and grinned. 'I shan't tell a soul, I give yer my word, but I still think that Doctor Blake's got his eye on her. Unless 'e fancies bein' landlord of the Pig & Whistle.'

'You're a wicked woman,' Maureen laughed with her now. 'He's very attractive and you can see he admires her – but Peggy is married and I'm not sure she's interested. Besides, she's havin' a baby, her husband's baby as far as anyone knows. Laurence came home last summer so it could easily be his…'

'He ain't got it in him, if yer ask me,' Alice said coarsely. 'Had the mumps just after Pip was born and that often does for a man's chances of more kids.'

'Oh, I didn't know that about Laurence…'

'Well, yer weren't much more than a twinkle in yer dad's eye then; yer couldn't have been more than six or so at the time,' Alice said. 'How is yer dad now, love? I see that wife of 'is goin' out all the time – and she were in a café with a man down Commercial Road the other day. Eating coffee cake and drinking tea she was, and all dressed up like a dog's dinner…'

Maureen's nape prickled. Alice didn't miss much; she knew everything that was going on in the lanes. If she'd noticed

Violet behaving oddly, then perhaps Maureen wasn't wrong to be suspicious of her stepmother.

'What are you hintin' at now, Alice?'

'I ain't sayin' anythin' – yet,' Alice told her with a little frown. ''E looked a bit too young fer Violet, if yer ask me – but yer never know. Some women like 'em young and some blokes like older women. I might get a young lover one of these days...' She went off in a cackle of laughter.

'Alice, you're dreadful,' Maureen said, but she smiled as she walked away from the house. She was so caught by the things Alice came out with that she might have walked right past Ellie if she hadn't darted out at her and clutched her arm.

'Maureen! Thank God,' she said. 'I saw him leavin' Tom's house and I was so frightened I couldn't move – 'E's coming after me again...' Ellie sobbed, her words tumbling over themselves. 'I couldn't bear him to touch me again. I'd die first...'

'I don't understand...' Maureen looked at her, her thoughts tumbling over each other as she tried to make sense of what Ellie was saying. 'You saw a man leavin' Tom's house – do you know what he did there?' Ellie shook her head. She was trembling so much that Maureen put her arms round her. 'Look, shall I take you home – and then we can talk?'

'Yes, please,' Ellie sobbed and held on to her arm for dear life.

Maureen put an arm about her, guiding her back to Mrs Tandy's house and following her into the kitchen behind the shop. Mrs Tandy was sitting there looking anxious and she jumped up as they entered.

'Ellie! Thank goodness you're back. I was afraid somethin' had happened to you...'

'Oh, Mrs Tandy,' Ellie said and ran to her, sobbing as Mrs Tandy took her into her arms and held her. 'I couldn't move. I hid until Maureen came up the lane and she brought me home. I was so frightened… because he's 'ere again. I saw 'im come out of Tom Barton's house.'

Mrs Tandy held her back so she could look into her face. 'Do you mean *that man*?'

'Yes. I saw 'im as he came from round the back of the house just as I was on my way home and I've been hidin' ever since…'

Mrs Tandy looked directly at Maureen. 'Ellie was attacked in the lane last year, just before Christmas…'

'Yes, I thought that was what must have happened when I saw those bruises. I'm so sorry, Ellie.' Maureen hesitated, then: 'You saw him come from the back of Tom's house – and you knew him. Do you know his name?'

'He called himself Knocker…'

'It sounds like it's the same man…' Maureen said thoughtfully and her gaze went from Mrs Tandy to Ellie, because obviously they didn't know what else had happened. 'Tom's house was ransacked this evenin'. Everythin' has been torn apart, upholstery ripped and things smashed. Tom thinks he might know who did it – and it sounds as if Ellie knows him too…' She hesitated, then: 'Would you be willin' to tell the police about this man, Ellie?'

'No, I couldn't!' Ellie shrank back against Mrs Tandy. 'Please don't ask me to, Maureen. I know it's right, but I know I can't face it…'

'Ellie was assaulted, badly beaten and threatened with what would happen if she told anyone,' Mrs Tandy said and Ellie gasped. 'You mustn't expect her to come forward, Maureen – and I must ask you not to tell anyone what you've heard here tonight.'

'I understand why you didn't go to the police, Ellie, and I give you my word that I shan't tell anyone what you've told me – but if you're frightened of him, you ought to tell someone who can help,' Maureen said.

'No, I can't… he had a knife…' Ellie raised her head, looking at her with eyes that carried too much pain. 'You don't know what he did – people would blame me, say it was my fault, but I couldn't stop him.'

'Your friends wouldn't think it was your fault, Ellie.' It was clear to Maureen that Ellie had been raped and she understood why she wouldn't talk; too many people would blame her simply because she'd let men buy her drinks. 'But if there's anything you know that might help the police catch him – could you tell me? I might be able to pass the details on without bringin' your name into it.'

'He was a soldier, wasn't he, Ellie?' Mrs Tandy answered for her.

Ellie nodded. ''E 'ad a scar here…' she pointed to her temple. 'And 'is nose was a bit bent, as if it 'ad been broken. I didn't encourage him, believe me – I hated his every touch…'

'Thank you. I will pass those details on to someone who might be able to help,' Maureen promised. 'I shan't tell anyone it was you he attacked – but the information you've given might be important. He's an evil man, Ellie. It's because of him and men like him that those kids got killed on the bombsite last year. I can't tell you anythin' more, but the police will be lookin' for him soon and when they get him, he'll be in prison for a long time – he might even be hanged, because what he's done is lootin' on a large scale. Only he gets kids to do his dirty work and I think that is despicable.'

'Well, I hope he is hanged; he deserves it,' Mrs Tandy said and put her arm around Ellie, who was shivering. 'I think I'd better get you to bed, my girl – unless you'd like a nice warm bath first?'

'I went round your house to ask you to bring Shirley for tea on Saturday,' Ellie told Maureen. 'It was only half-past five when I saw 'im come from that house. I thought I'd be safe if I didn't go out late at nights...' Tears were trickling down her cheeks.

'Don't let him frighten you,' Maureen said. 'Sooner or later the police are goin' to catch up with him. And Shirley would love to come to tea – especially if you make a strawberry blancmange.' She went over to Ellie and kissed her on the cheek. 'We're your friends, Ellie. We'll look out for you...'

Maureen was angry as she left Mrs Tandy's house. The man that had hurt and raped Ellie had also ransacked Tom's house, caused the death of three young boys by encouraging them to dig in dangerous bombsites – and was even now planning to steal a valuable necklace. They had to do something about it! At the very least, he should be behind bars for a long time, though like Mrs Tandy, Maureen thought he deserved to hang for what had happened to those kids. It was certainly time this Knocker – or whatever his real name was – had his wings cut. She just hoped Doctor Blake's plan to catch him red-handed would work...

As Maureen hurried home she met her friend Anne walking towards the lanes. A little girl was walking with her, talking and looking up at her with a kind of reverence as she hung on to her hand. Anne smiled and answered the child's questions and then gave her a little tap before sending her off to her home nearby. Maureen thought how good Anne was with children. She was born to be a mother and perhaps now that she was married to a man she loved it would happen.

'Anne,' she cried. 'How are you? I haven't seen much of you lately.'

'I've been busy setting up the school and one thing and another,' Anne said. 'I've got time for a cup of tea and a chat... if you have?'

'Yes, come home with me now and stay to tea. Shirley would love to see you.'

Maureen pushed Ellie's problems to the back of her mind; it was a treat to have Anne to herself for an hour or two.

Maureen picked up the post when she went into the hall one morning later that week and smiled when she saw there was a letter from Gordon. She'd only had a brief postcard since Christmas and it was hard not knowing where her husband was and if he was all right. Her feelings for Gordon were deeper than she'd thought they would be when she'd agreed to marry him. He was a kind, gentle man, and a good father, and she truly cared for him, even if it wasn't the passionate love she'd known as a young girl for a man who didn't deserve it. Maureen hadn't thought of Rory in weeks now. Her life was too busy, too caught up with her work, her friends and life in the lanes.

She opened her letter eagerly and began to read:

My darling Maureen,

Just to let you know I'm all right, love. I've been slightly wounded in my left leg. I hoped it might be a Blighty and I'd get home to you and Shirley, but no such luck. I'm in what they call a field hospital and they're looking after me very well.

Maureen gave a little gasp, because Gordon had broken the news of his injury so casually. He was making light of it but he had to be in pain and for a moment her eyes filled with tears, because he was so far away and she couldn't reach him, couldn't comfort him.

She resumed reading her letter:

I have a nurse called Rita changing my dressings and she said to give you her love. She applied for overseas duty after you left the hospital in Portsmouth. She wrote but doesn't know if you got her letter, because she's never had a reply.

Anyway, I'm feeling a bit sore still and it will be a while before they send me back to work, so I'm reading old magazines and feeling sorry for myself. I wouldn't mind some more socks and some fruit sweets if you can get hold of any, but it doesn't matter if you can't. I hope you're taking care of yourself, my darling, and it's time you gave up work if you haven't already. I think of you all the time and I'm so glad Shirley is with you. I know she's happy and I hope you are too. I'm longing to see you all – including the baby, when it comes – but I know it will be ages until I get leave again. In the meantime, think of me, go on loving us all – but I know you will, because that's you.

I love you, Maureen. Love to Shirley and Gran and lots of kisses.

Maureen smiled mistily and folded her letter, putting it into her jacket pocket. Gordon was all right, coping with his pain as he always did.

It seemed that her friend from Portsmouth was out there nursing and somehow that made her feel a little better. Rita would take good care of him. Maureen hadn't received Rita's letter, but the post sometimes got lost these days. She could write to Gordon and enclose a letter for Rita, which he could pass on.

For the moment she had chores to finish here and then she ought to go round to the shop, see how her father was and also Tom. It must have been awful for him discovering his house had been trashed like that. She didn't know what they could do about the furniture, unless it could be reupholstered?

Tom could mend locks and tidy up the house himself, but he would need help to pay for new furniture or the restoration of the pieces that had been ruined. Yet furniture was just wood and material – Ellie had suffered far worse and Maureen's heart ached for her. She hadn't been able to get the girl's fear and distress out of her mind.

She'd promised Ellie she wouldn't tell anyone but she was tempted to talk to Peggy about it. If the women of Mulberry Lane put their heads together, they might be able to come up with something. Maureen, like many others in her part of the world, didn't have a great deal of faith in the police sorting things out. If they'd done their job properly, Sam and those other lads would have been kept clear of dangerous bombsites in the first place – and if it was the same man, Ellie's attacker might have been in prison already and she wouldn't have been hurt.

An able-bodied man, capable of trashing Tom's house and attacking a girl like Ellie ought to be in the Army – why wasn't he?

Maureen frowned as she recalled something that Mrs Tandy had said. Ellie had told her that her attacker was a soldier, but Tom said he was a thief and a fence. Something didn't add up – unless it was two different men after all? Yet Ellie had seen him and been so frightened she'd hid in the shadows and couldn't move… it had to be the same man.

So was he in the Army or not? Could he possibly be a deserter?

Chapter 14

Anne was at the counter buying her groceries when Maureen went into the shop. She paid for her bits and pieces but stopped to chat for a few minutes, her basket over her arm.

'I've just heard from Kirk,' she said and smiled. 'I got my first letter this morning. He's fine but says he's longing to come home already.'

'Snap!' Maureen laughed. 'I got a letter from Gordon yesterday. He says he has a slight wound to his leg but not bad enough to get sent home; he's in a field hospital, whatever that is... but he's bein' well looked after. It sounds as if a nurse I know is out there and she's seeing to his dressings. I think he's gettin' made a fuss of by the sound of it.'

Anne touched her arm sympathetically. 'I'm sorry Gordon was hurt. I hope he will soon feel better.'

'I think he was lucky and it was just a flesh wound. I hope so anyway, because there's nothin' I can do to help him. If it had been a Blighty he would've been sent home, but he would've have been in a lot of pain. I can put up with the separation, as long as he gets home safe one day.'

'Kirk was in a field hospital earlier in the war,' Anne said. 'He said it was pretty basic, but I suppose they have to be if they're near the action...' She sighed. 'Oh dear, I do wish it was all over. I don't know how you feel, but it seems endless. I'm fed up with ration cards and making do; now they've said we can't have more than three pairs of shoes a year.' Anne made a wry face. 'Most women round here are lucky if they can afford one new pair a year. I don't think that lot at the War Office know what they're doing half the time; they just make laws to make us all miserable. It's all so drab and dull, nothing but bad news in the papers... Did you read about the actress Carole Lombard last month?' Maureen shook her head. 'She and her mother were found dead in the wreckage of a plane in Las Vegas. I liked her, she was a lovely actress.' Anne flicked her hair back from her face. 'I'm thoroughly fed up.'

'I feel the same,' Maureen agreed. 'What we need is a night out somewhere – go to the flicks or somethin'...'

'Yes, I'd like that,' Anne said eagerly. 'What about Friday night? Peggy has extra help now, so we could go with an easy conscience...'

'Yes, I'd love to.' Maureen smiled at her. 'I've no idea what's on – but I'm sure we'll find somethin'.'

'I think *The Thirty-Nine Steps* is on – or there's Fred Astaire in *Top Hat,* I've heard it's wonderful.'

'I like a love story best' Maureen said, 'but I don't mind either and it will be lovely to go out for a change – and afterwards we'll go back and have a drink at the pub, make sure Peggy is okay.'

'Yes, all right,' Anne said. 'I'd better get these things back. Mavis is always giving me cake and nice meals. I need to replace some of the stock in her store cupboard. She's very partial to these barley sugars…' She popped them in her basket, smiled to Maureen and left.

'We need some more of those sweets,' Tom remarked after Anne had left. 'I've put it on the stock list for you, Maureen.'

'Yes, thank you, Tom.' She looked at him. He seemed normal and cheerful, but she suspected he might be hiding his feelings. 'How did you get on with the police?'

'It was just Doctor Blake's friend. He came out and had a look – and both he and the doc were disgusted at the mess. After he'd been, the doc and I cleared up a bit. He says he knows someone who can recover the three-piece and make some cushion covers. I'll sew the old sofa back together myself and get a rug or somethin' to cover it up, but I'll have the suite covered for Ma as soon as I can afford it.'

'Doctor Blake seems a very helpful and pleasant man.' Maureen made a mental note to find a way of helping Tom pay for the repair to his mother's three-piece suite. 'I thought so anyway.'

'Yes, he is,' Tom agreed. 'After he left, I secured the door and went round to Alice's. She gave me a huge breakfast this mornin', but I've got me ration book and I'll take her some bacon and sugar back tonight.'

'Yes, you must look after her. Alice says some funny things, but she has a good heart.'

'I like Alice,' Tom said and smiled. 'I've been up to see yer dad, Maureen. He seems a little better this mornin' I think – but Mrs Jackson went out early.'

'Has she returned yet?'

'Not that I've seen or heard.'

'I'd better go up and see how Dad is then,' Maureen said. 'If you've got that stock list ready, Tom, I'll take it before I leave…'

Maureen went through the back and then up the stairs to her father's living accommodation. He was sitting in his chair by an electric fire reading his paper, a blanket round his shoulders, but looked up with a smile as she entered. It felt a bit chilly in the room and she went to check the range, which was almost out.

'Didn't Violet make up the range this mornin'?' she asked and looked in the coal box. 'There's no coke – have you got any left in the shed or shall I order it for you?'

'Violet told me to get T-Tom to fill the sc-cuttle and bring it up, but I f-forgot,' her father said. 'She'll be f-furious with me if it goes out, b-because she doesn't have the k-knack of lighting it like you d-did, M-Maureen.'

'I'll fetch some coke and get it goin',' Maureen told him and picked up the coal box. Seeing him so helpless had made her realise that despite all his faults and his selfish ways, she did care for him, and oddly, she wanted to protect him. 'It's cold in here, Dad. That electric fire doesn't keep this place warm and it's wasteful.'

'Be c-careful out in the yard, Maureen love,' her father said. 'I think it might b-be a bit icy this m-mornin'.'

'Yes, some of the pavements were slippery in places. Don't worry, I'll be careful...'

At the foot of the stairs, she met Tom. He was carrying a box of tins, which he stood down when he saw her. 'You give that to me, Maureen. We can't have you luggin' heavy coal scuttles in your condition. Listen out for the shop door while I fetch the coke and take it upstairs.'

'All right, I'll go through until you come back...' Maureen smiled as she went into the shop, because it might have been his father talking. Tom was so grown-up and responsible these days. He was more than an asset, he was a treasure and her father was lucky he'd come along at a time when he was most needed, and so was she, because although she could still do most things at the moment, she might not be able to in a few weeks.

'Good mornin', Maureen, don't tell me you're back behind the counter,' a woman said as she entered the shop. Maureen recognised her as one of her old customers.

'Just standin' in for Tom while he fetches some coke for my father,' Maureen said. 'How are you, Mrs Bean?'

'Oh, me bunions are playing me up somethin' cruel,' the woman grumbled. 'My Josh 'as lost the little job 'e 'ad down the munitions factory – said he was too clumsy and might set somethin' orf. Don't suppose you've got a job fer 'im?'

'I'm sorry, I don't think so, not at the moment – but I did hear they want workers at the boot factory.'

'Right, I'll tell 'im ter get his lazy backside down there,' Mrs Bean said. 'I'll 'ave a small tin of corned beef and me butter ration, and some marge, 'ave ter mix it these days or it don't go round... Oh, and a quarter pound of tea.'

'I try to use the butter sparingly if it's just bread and butter and put marge in sandwiches and cakes. Shirley won't eat bread and marge unless I disguise the taste with jam or paste.'

'Right little madam, I suppose? If I 'ad 'er fer a few days she'd eat everythin' she was given or go without.'

Maureen made no comment. She didn't much like Mrs Bean, who was always complaining about something.

Tom came back from washing his hands just as she left. He set down a box containing packets of dried peas and smiled at Maureen, nodding at the retreating figure. 'Did Mrs Bean ask you for credit?'

'No – has she asked you?'

'Several times; I told her I wasn't allowed to give it, but she said you used to let her have things on tick when she was short.'

'Don't fall for that one,' Maureen said and laughed. 'She won't be the only one to try it on – but the best thing is just to say Mr Jackson would sack you if you did; they won't ask again.'

'Right, thanks for tellin' me. Your dad wouldn't let me make up the range – he says you do it best. Sorry, I'd have done it if he let me…'

'That's all right, Tom, I know how to handle it – apparently, Violet doesn't get on with it very well.'

Tom hesitated, then, 'I don't know if I ought to say… but is she unkind to Mr Jackson?'

'What do you mean?' Maureen looked at him steadily.

'Well, he was sittin' there cold when I went up. He looked a bit blue in the face, so I put the electric fire on, stuck a florin in the meter, and fetched him a blanket, and then made him a hot cup of cocoa – he likes that sometimes better than tea.' Tom looked awkward. 'I noticed a bruise on his neck when I put the blanket round him – and there was another on his hand. I'm not suggestin' anythin' but… sometimes she says nasty things to him.'

Maureen went cold all over. She'd thought she was imagining things, but now she knew it wasn't just her noticing these little incidents. Alice had observed how often Violet went out alone and now Tom was concerned about the way she treated her husband. 'Thank you for tellin' me, but don't mention it to anyone else, will you? I don't want to upset Violet until I'm sure of my facts.'

'Course not. I'll keep me eyes peeled though,' Tom grinned

wickedly. 'He's an old devil at times, but he's your dad, Maureen, so I'll do me best to see he's all right.'

Maureen laughed as she left him and went up to the flat to get the range going. Tom was right, her father was an old curmudgeon, but he was her dad and she wouldn't let Violet make him suffer – whatever her reasons for doing it. She still had an uncomfortable feeling that Violet wanted him out of the way so that she could take over the shop – either to use it for her own business or to sell it.

It was hard for Maureen to believe that a woman who seemed pleasant – at least when she wanted to be – could actively harm a man she'd married only a few months previously. Clearly, she found him a nuisance but surely she must want him to recover? It didn't make sense, unless she thought he owned the shop and she needed the money.

No, Maureen must be wrong to harbour such suspicions against her father's wife, despite what Alice had said. Violet had been nasty to her on a few occasions, but having a sharp tongue didn't make her capable of harming her husband.

Maureen knew she couldn't talk about this openly. Peggy had been immediately suspicious when she'd mentioned the greasy food Violet was giving her husband, but it was mere speculation. Violet was just thoughtless. She didn't really want Henry to die, of course she didn't. If Maureen told her what Tom had said, Peggy would probably say she ought to have it out with her – and yet her father thought a lot of Violet. He would think Maureen was just being spiteful if she hinted at her suspicions.

For the moment there was little she could do, except visit and keep an eye on things. She was so thankful that Tom was on the premises, because if he hadn't switched that electric fire on and fetched a blanket, her father might have taken a chill and perhaps developed pneumonia. The doctors had told Maureen to watch out for that.

'Your father has made an excellent recovery, Mrs Hart,' they'd told her when she'd fetched him home. 'But he isn't strong yet. Make sure he doesn't do too much. He needs to keep warm – and to eat sensibly. No fried food, or not very much – minced beef if you can get it, rice pudding or a sandwich with salad, a thin layer of cheese and tomatoes is best, home-made soup – or perhaps some bread and milk with a little sugar at first if he can't digest more solid foods.'

Violet had heard the advice and yet she still cooked huge fried breakfasts at least three times a week, giving her husband all their bacon rations, with fried bread or potatoes, because she didn't eat bacon herself. Maureen had warned her against it and been told that, 'Henry likes it. Just because you were too lazy to cook him a breakfast, it doesn't mean I shouldn't.'

'It isn't good for him,' Maureen had told her but Violet just glared at her.

'Your trouble is you think you know best and you don't.'

Maureen hadn't bothered to answer her. She was trying to keep the peace for her father's sake – but she couldn't just stand by and see him suffer. If she knew for certain that Violet was mistreating him she would say something, but her father never complained about his wife. How was she supposed to sort Violet out if her father wouldn't tell her what was going on?

Shaking her head, Maureen made a paste and tomato sandwich for her father, using just a scraping of butter and making it tasty with a little salt and pepper on the tomato. She gave him a cup of tea and asked if he wanted to use the bathroom.

'I've got me s-stick there,' he said, pointing out an old broom with half a handle. 'I can g-get there usin' that without bein' a n-nuisance to anyone n-now.'

'You are not a nuisance,' Maureen told him. 'I know we fell out in the past, Dad, but you're not well and I don't mind helpin' you as much as I can.'

'It's Violet's job to h-help me m-most of the time,' he said. 'I'm a n-nuisance to 'er s-sometimes, but at least I can get there on me own n-now. I shall be back to me old s-self afore long, you'll s-see.'

'I hope you are,' Maureen said. 'Just remember I'm here, Dad.'

'I know and I'm g-grateful,' he said. 'You get off home and don't worry, Maureen. I can f-fend for meself and I'm not daft...'

Maureen nodded, said goodbye and left. She wasn't quite sure about the look he'd given her. Did he know what Violet was up to? Or was she making too much of it all?

'I have to get back or he'll be wondering where I've got to,' Violet said to the attractive young man sitting opposite her in the café. Coffee cups were on the table in front of them and a plate that had once contained an omelette and chips. 'And I need to do some work this evenin'. I mustn't neglect me clients.'

'You shouldn't 'ave to keep slavin' away fer 'im,' the man said, giving her a dark look. 'I thought you said he had a good business?'

'Henry has the shop, but it doesn't bring in as much as I expected...' Violet fidgeted with her gloves. 'I've given you all I can, Bryan. You will just have to be patient – there's nothin' in the flat I can sell. That selfish bitch took it all with her...'

'You should demand your share of it...'

'How can I? It belonged to 'er mother. I've asked Henry, but he won't ask for it back – says it was left to her and I don't need it.'

'Well, you'd better think of somethin' fast,' Bryan reached out and took hold of her wrist, his fingers bruising her flesh so that she winced and pulled back. 'I need another thousand pounds quick, and if I don't get it, I'll come round and help myself to whatever I can...'

'There's never above a few pounds in the kitty. Maureen banks any extra money in the till twice a week – and she pays for the stock by drawing from the bank. Henry used to keep a couple of hundred in the stockroom, but she says it's silly and draws what she needs when she needs it. She knows just what is in the till and so does the boy...'

'Hoity-toity bitch! She wants puttin' in 'er place. It ain't like you not to get yer own way, Violet.'

'She takes no notice of anythin' I say.' Violet hesitated. 'Henry promised me that everythin' he's got would be mine once he's gone... The hospital told me 'e probably wouldn't survive another stroke. I could sell the place and give you the money when he's dead...'

'What the hell is the good of that to me? I need that money now, Violet. I told yer, I'm in trouble – if I don't get the money I'll be dead meat...' He made a cutting sign across his throat. 'You promised me it would be easy.'

'You said a few hundred...' Violet said, eyes brimming with unshed tears. 'I've given you my savings. I can't do any more until... he's gone.'

'Then get rid of 'im,' Bryan said viciously. 'If yer let me down, yer've seen the last of me...'

'Bryan, please...' Violet made a grab for his arm as he left the table and walked out, expecting her to pay the bill for his meal.

Tears stung her eyes. She hadn't heard from her son for years and now that he'd finally made contact again all he did was threaten her. She'd given him five hundred pounds, which was all the money she'd saved since she'd begun her own corset-fitting business, plus a few pounds from Henry's money tin, snatched before Maureen started banking the takings. Violet had no idea how much the shop was worth and she didn't want to push her husband into an early grave. She'd been quite fond of him at the start, but Henry hadn't been as well off as she'd expected and he wasn't particularly generous with his money. Since his return from the hospital, he'd been a lot of trouble, wetting himself a few times because he couldn't get to the toilet in time

What was she going to do now? Violet didn't want to cause her husband's death; it would give her nightmares if she did that, but she certainly wasn't going to put herself out looking after him. With all her savings gone and Bryan demanding more, she would need to work hard just to get back to what she'd had before he turned up.

Violet was comfortable at the flat above the shop, and her business brought in a bit of money that she'd looked forward to having for extras – if she gave way to Bryan, he would take the lot and leave her with nothing.

A look of anger entered her eyes. It was that bitch Maureen's fault. If she'd left a few bits of silver in the flat, Violet could've sold them, and she was entitled to a few pounds from the shop takings over and above her housekeeping allowance. What right had Maureen to just waltz in and start laying down the law, telling her – Henry's wife – not to feed him greasy food?

Violet wasn't sure she was ready to give Bryan the money from the shop when she sold it, but if he thought she intended to, it would keep him sweet for a while, and she was a little frightened of him, because he could be mean, like his father had been, at times. Perhaps if she could get him a few pounds now and then, it might keep him quiet – and, of course, when she had a few thousand in her pocket, she could simply disappear. After all, it wasn't as if he cared for her. The only reason he'd made contact was for the money…

Chapter 15

'You don't mind if I go to the pictures with Anne on Friday night, Gran?' Maureen asked later that day. 'I might ask Ellie to come too if Anne doesn't mind. I think she gets bored with her husband away all the time.'

'Why should I mind, my girl?' Gran said. 'You do as much as you can 'ere and the child is never any trouble to me. She's as good as gold, even if she is a little faddy with 'er food.'

'I don't like bread and marge either, do you?' Gran shook her head. 'I use it for all my cookin' and try to use our butter ration thinly so we all get a little taste of luxury. I never used to think butter was a luxury – but I suppose it always has been to some folk.'

'In my day there were a lot of homes that couldn't afford it. Most families saved their drippin' from the meat they cooked at the weekend and spread that on their bread. I never took to drippin', because it made me feel sick – far too greasy. Your grandfather loved it, and so did your dad when he was young. He always was one for the fatty things…'

'Violet says he likes a big cooked breakfast several times a week, but I think he should have toast or a boiled egg in the mornings, when we can get them.'

'It's mostly that awful powdered stuff these days,' Gran agreed, 'but I managed to buy a few last week and I took him two for his tea. I cooked them myself and he enjoyed them.'

'Violet says I'm jealous and don't know what's good for him, but I'd rather he didn't become ill again just yet…'

'After the way he treated you?' Gran looked at her hard, because Maureen's father had used her for his own convenience for years, never wanting her to go out and paying her a pittance. He'd played on his weak chest, using emotional blackmail to keep her tied to the shop. 'He won't be around for ever, love and when the time comes you can run it as you please – let it to someone else or sell…' Her words seemed to hold a question and Maureen knew what her grandmother was asking.

'I know,' Maureen agreed, 'but I don't want to do any of those things. You gave him another three years' lease and there's still more than a year to run, so I'm not sure I could tell Violet to go even if it did happen, and I hope it won't – I'd much rather he had a few more years himself. I don't want Dad to die, even if he didn't treat me as he should have, Gran. One day I suppose I might do something with it – but it belongs to Dad while he wants it… after all what else would he do?'

'Henry must have money put by for his retirement; his father had nearly a thousand pounds when he went, most of it in stock, which Henry inherited.'

'Violet has her own business, of course… I suppose he might be relying on that… She's always worked and not just because of the war like most women…'

'I doubt if many women will want to go back to the old ways when the war is over,' Gran said. 'They've had to work in the factories and look after the kids as well as the house – so why should they give all that up?'

'I don't know.' Maureen smiled. 'I know I liked being a nurse and helping others... but I wouldn't stand in the way of a man gettin' his job back, and once they come home a lot of women will have to step aside – besides, it's right in a way. The men have sacrificed more than we have, even if we've had it hard...'

'You're a lovely girl,' Gran smiled at her. 'No wonder that husband of yours is potty about you. You go for your night out with Anne. You haven't had a lot of time to enjoy yourself, apart from the few days Gordon was home, and don't worry about me – or your dad.'

'No, but I don't want to go out much. Anne was feeling down, so I suggested we go to the flicks together, but mostly I'm happy with my knittin' or a good book.'

'I like my wireless,' Gran said. 'I enjoy the music, the afternoon play, and that Tommy Handley makes me laugh. I can do a bit of mendin' or sewin' while I listen – and it's lovely havin' you and Shirley for company. I don't mind an evenin' round the pub now and then, but I'll miss you two when you get yer own house.'

'That won't happen until the war is over and Gordon gets his house back. I know I could afford to rent a place for the time bein', but he's here so seldom – and Shirley loves you. I wouldn't want her to come home to an empty house if I was out for some reason. So I shall stay here for now.'

'It works very well as it is.' Gran nodded her satisfaction. 'You know the house will be yours one day, Maureen. It's not much and you might want to sell it and get somethin' better, especially if Gordon sells 'is too – but that's for the future.'

'Oh don't talk about things like that,' Maureen cried. 'I don't want to lose you, Gran. You're worth more to me than a dozen houses.'

'Get on with yer, girl!' Gran said but gave a shout of pleased laughter. 'You tell Anne she's to come and have her tea with us on Sundays. She's a nice lady...'

'Yes, I will. I think it will be good for her to get out more often. Mavis likes havin' her there a bit too much and poor Anne will find herself tied if she isn't careful. Her uncle had her runnin' round after him for ages, and now she's half afraid to go out and leave Mavis alone...'

It was Friday night and Tom had been paid. Mr Jackson had given him his wage packet himself, and put an extra half a crown in it for him.

'You're a decent lad, Tom,' he'd said. 'I'm very p-pleased with you and I w-want to m-make sure you're s-satisfied workin' 'ere.'

'I love it, sir,' Tom said respectfully. 'It's even better than I thought it would be. I'm glad you're satisfied with me.'

'More than,' Mr Jackson said. 'Y-You can go at half-past six t-tonight if you like.'

'I've got some jobs in the stockroom, sir. I want to stack everythin' so I use it in date. I'll go at seven as usual, but perhaps another Friday if I want to go somewhere special, I'll leave at half-six.'

'All right,' Mr Jackson said and his eyes gleamed. 'It's a p-pity a f-few more aren't like you, T-Tom. There would be less p-poverty about if they were all willin' ter work like y-you.'

Tom glowed with pride. He tucked his wage packet into his inner jacket pocket and then thought better of it. It was a week since Knocker had grabbed him and threatened him and he didn't want to lose the money he'd just been paid. He slipped it into his apron pocket and hung it up in the shop. If his assailant roughed him up, there was a chance he'd take whatever Tom was carrying.

He worked until just after seven. The job in the stockroom could have waited, but he wanted to go home at the same time as he had the previous week, because if their trap was to work, Knocker had to walk into it.

He walked across the road whistling, just as he had a week earlier, trying not to listen for sounds behind him or to glance back. A large hand went over his mouth as he entered the passageway between his house and the next, and a strong arm pressed against his throat, cutting off his air.

'Have yer got what I asked fer?' a voice growled in his ear. Smelling the beer on his breath and the odour of stale sweat, he knew it was Knocker who had grabbed him. Tom shook his head and his assailant turned him round, keeping an arm pressed hard across his chest and shoulder as he glared down at him. 'You'd better have it somewhere or you'll be sorry... I warned yer about what I'd do if yer tried ter cheat me.'

Tom could feel pain in his injured shoulder; it hurt like hell, but he didn't cry out.

'You should know – it isn't in the house. You tore the place apart – ruined my mother's things,' Tom said, looking at him accusingly. 'What did yer want to do that for?'

'It's the least I'll do if yer don't come up with what I want...'

'I ain't got it...'

'You little runt! I'll thrash yer until yer beg fer mercy.'

'I can't give yer what I ain't got – they weren't yours or Sam's...' Tom gasped in horror as he let the information slip.

Knocker's eyes gleamed with avarice. 'So yer found the diamonds, did yer? I thought Sam were 'avin me on fer a start when he told me about them, then I heard there were some valuable things missin' from that jeweller's place when they cleared the rubble – so the little bugger really found somethin' good...' He grinned, but then his eyes narrowed. 'You'd better give them to me or I'll knock yer brains out – not that yer've got any...'

'I told yer I ain't got them anymore...'

'But yer did 'ave, so where are they? If yer've pawned 'em, yer can give me whatever yer got...'

'I ain't pawned them. They weren't mine. I would've taken them to the police only she said...' Tom broke off and shook his head. 'No, I ain't tellin' – they're goin' back where they belong...'

'You've given 'em to someone to keep 'em safe...' Knocker stared at him suspiciously for a few minutes and Tom's stomach churned. 'I bet it was that bloody woman at the pub...'

'No, it wasn't,' Tom sounded worried and afraid. 'Peggy is a friend of mine and if you 'urt 'er I'll tell the police...' He wrenched himself from the other man's hold and tried to dodge the punch aimed at his face.

A heavy hand hit him so hard that he felt his lip split and tasted blood. He kicked Knocker in the shin and tried to break free, but he held him tight, hurting him so much it was all he could do to resist and not scream out. Tom wriggled and then managed to turn his head enough to bite the brute's hand. Knocker yelled, grabbed him by the throat and shook him, making him gasp as he struggled to breathe, and then he released his hold, pushing Tom against the wall.

'Go and tell that bitch that I'll be in later tonight, afore closin', and she'd better 'ave them bloody diamonds ready – if she tries anythin' stupid, I'll kick that kid out of 'er and I'll slit yer throat...'

Tom felt himself pushed forward. He fell to his knees, his head reeling from the blows Knocker had imposed, and by the time he got up again his assailant had gone, disappeared into the darkness of the wartime streets. This blackout was perfect cover for men like that, Tom thought ruefully as he set off across the road to the pub, a little smile on his face because that bully had fallen into his trap, hook, line and sinker...

'That was a real treat,' Anne said as she and Maureen left the bus and started to walk the last few yards to Mulberry Lane. 'We had a good giggle and it has made me feel much better...'

'Me too,' Maureen said. 'It was fun. Even though the Pathé News was dire; what with our troops in Malaya havin' a wretched time of it, and the bloody Panzers pushin' back the 8th Army, it doesn't look good for the Allies.'

'No, but the film was good and it made a break from reality.'

'Yes,' Maureen smiled at her. 'I enjoyed myself.'

'We must do it again. Perhaps Peggy will come with us, and Ellie if she wants. She was busy late in the shop tonight, but I know she doesn't get out much. I thought Janet and Helen could've managed the pub this evening so that Peggy could have a night off, but she said she had to be there tonight.'

'Yes, it would've been nice if Peggy could come too,' Maureen said. 'We'll have to go soon, or Peggy and me will get too big to fit in those seats – mind you, she'll be back to normal sooner than me. I've got at least two months longer than she has…'

They were laughing as they walked into the pub. Heading up to the bar together, they asked Janet for two glasses of orangeade. She told them to sit down and she would bring their order over.

'Did you enjoy the film?' Janet asked when she brought the drinks. 'I told Mum she should go with you, but she said she had to be here this evenin'…'

'We were just sayin' Peggy would've loved the film,' Maureen agreed. Peggy was looking fixedly at the door, as if expecting someone. Maureen wondered if the anxious look on her face had anything to do with the necklace Tom had found and was about to get up and ask her friend if she was all right when a man walked into the pub and went straight up to the bar. He said something to Peggy and Maureen watched as Peggy replied and then shook her head. Maureen hesitated, remembering that Peggy and her friend, Doctor Blake, had been planning something. She saw the man grab hold of Peggy's wrist and exert pressure, and the next moment she seemed to give in and reached beneath the counter, handing him something in a brown paper bag, which he hastily tucked inside his shirt.

Janet had noticed and she made as if to go back to the bar, but Maureen caught her arm. 'Leave it, Jan. Your mum knows what she's doin'…'

'What do you mean?' Janet stared hard at the man as he walked away. 'I remember him – he was the one that forced Ellie to leave with him…'

'Just let him go...' Maureen said and Janet nodded, but returned to the bar as the man left, and then spoke to her mother. She was obviously asking about the man. Peggy shook her head and said something in her ear.

'What was all that about?' Anne asked, frowning.

'Peggy will tell you when you see her privately,' Maureen said.

'But you know something?'

'I suspect, but I don't know...'

At that moment, they heard the sound of police whistles outside the pub and then shouting and what sounded like a fight. A couple of the customers rushed to the door and looked out. Anne jumped up and followed. Maureen went over to the bar and spoke to Peggy.

'Was that it?' she asked and Peggy nodded.

'He grabbed Tom this evenin' and gave him a good slappin'. Tom let slip that I had the diamonds, as we'd planned, and then came to give me a message. I let Michael know and by the sound of it, everythin' went to plan.'

'The police have arrested that man who was just in here,' Anne returned to the counter as several customers went to watch. 'There were at least a dozen of them and they've got one of their big vans – a Black Maria, I think they call them.'

'Yes, I expect so,' Peggy said. 'Come through to the kitchen, you two. I can't explain here.'

She lifted the bar flap and they followed her into the big warm kitchen, which was redolent with the smell of herbs and baking.

'I haven't had a chance to tell you, Anne – but Maureen knows that Tom Barton was threatened last week. That man you saw me give a package to, knocked Tom about and said Sam had somethin' that belonged to him – a diamond necklace that Sam found in the rubble of the bombed-out jeweller's shop. The man told Tom he would kill him if he didn't find it – and meanwhile, he trashed Tom's home searchin' for it, but Tom had already given it to me for safekeepin'.'

'How did he know you'd got it?' Anne asked and Maureen nodded, because she wanted to know too.

'We set it up with a police officer who is a friend of Doctor Blake. You remember I got to know him when Tom's brother Sam was killed in that bomb explosion? He suggested that Tom allowed this villain to knock him about a bit and then gradually let it slip that he'd given me the necklace to keep safe. We hoped he would take the bait and demand it from me, which he did – the rest you know...'

'So it was a set-up,' Anne said. 'He was arrested with the necklace on him – which means he should end up in prison for quite a time...'

'Yes – unless they send him out to the Front,' Peggy said. 'Michael Blake told me that it's what they sometimes do with looters. This man didn't do the lootin' himself, he got young boys to do it for him – and caused the deaths of three that we know about...'

'They should hang him,' Anne said and looked disgusted. 'He's a murderer and worse.'

'I hope they do,' Maureen said. 'Aren't you worried that he may come after you, Peggy? He won't be in prison forever – unless they do hang him...'

'If they send him out to the front line he could be killed...' Peggy shrugged. 'If he goes to prison it will be years before they let him out – we none of us know where we'll be in ten years' time.'

A knock sounded at the back door. Peggy went to answer it, and Anne seized the poker, following behind her, just in case it was the thief having escaped from custody.

'May we come in, Peggy?' Doctor Blake's voice asked as she opened the top half of the door. He smiled at her and Peggy's cheeks tinged with pink. 'We just wanted you to know that everything went well.'

Peggy unlocked the door and allowed him in. He was accompanied by a police officer, who took his helmet off respectfully.

'You've got him safely behind bars?' Peggy asked.

'Yes, and we found the diamonds on him. He's denying all knowledge of them, of course, but he was in possession of stolen property when arrested and that will go hard with him – especially if the owner confirms they were taken from the ruins of his shop. We don't much care for looters.'

'He may be guilty of more crimes,' Maureen said. 'Someone – a young local woman – told me that he raped her. It was before Christmas and she didn't report it because she was afraid that she wouldn't be believed. I promised I wouldn't tell anyone her name – but she saw him coming from the back of Tom Barton's house the night it was ransacked. She was terrified he'd returned to hurt her again and told me her story...'

Peggy and Anne looked at her in surprise, because Maureen hadn't told either of them about what Ellie had confided.

'We can't take a case based on hearsay to court,' the police officer said. 'It happens too often in rape cases – the girl thinks she will lose her reputation and so she doesn't tell us and the bastards get away with it. Excuse my language, ladies.'

'But if you know what he is, you may find more evidence against him...'

'We already have the evidence we need to see he pays for his crimes,' the officer looked grim, 'but I'm not doubting your word, ma'am. These nasty types are up for all that sort of thing. If I had my way, he would hang for what he did – because it was nothing short of murder sending those boys on to that bombsite.'

'Well, I'm glad your idea worked, Michael,' Peggy smiled at Doctor Blake. They had become friends these past months. She sometimes thought he might have more in mind than friendship, but as yet she wasn't ready to think about that; her heart still belonged to Able. 'I can't thank you enough for what you've done.'

'We all have to thank Tom,' he replied with a smile. 'He played his part to perfection and got a beating in the process – but it wouldn't have worked any other way.'

'He's very brave,' Peggy said. 'Can I get you gentlemen a cup of tea or a drink?'

'Thank you very much but we have work to do at the station. Doctor Blake is our main witness to the arrest and his possession of the diamonds. I need to take his statement – and Tom's. We're going to collect him now and with both statements I don't think there is any doubt that our suspect will go to prison for a long time, and we might even get a charge of manslaughter to stick with Tom's help – unless Knocker chooses the alternative of enlisting immediately into the Army.'

'That's another thing…' Maureen said. 'When he attacked this girl, he was wearing a soldier's uniform; he's either been impersonatin' a soldier or he's on permanent leave…'

'Without permission, you mean?' The officer nodded grimly. 'A deserter maybe – in which case they may well shoot him when we hand him over. A very satisfactory outcome if it should be the case… but for the moment we'll concentrate on the charge of looting and possession of stolen goods.'

Maureen was silent as the two men left.

Peggy turned to her immediately, her brows raised. 'You didn't tell me about the rape?'

'I gave my word I wouldn't tell anyone. I was goin' to tell you part of it – but this happened before I had a chance.'

'Poor girl,' Peggy said and shook her head. 'I know who you mean, of course. Don't worry, Maureen, I shan't let on.'

'Would anyone like to tell me?' Anne said plaintively.

Peggy laughed in spite of herself. 'She used to come in several times a week but hasn't been for ages – and we all saw those bruises on her face before Christmas. Not you, Anne, because you were on honeymoon, but everyone else saw them. She said she'd had a fall, but I always thought that was an excuse.'

'We mustn't let her know you've guessed,' Maureen said. 'I think there's worse to come, but it's only a guess…'

'Not pregnant?' Peggy saw the truth in Maureen's face. 'Now that is awful – her husband has been away more than a year. No one would believe it was his.'

'You're talking about Ellie,' Anne said, looking upset. 'That is truly awful. I know her husband Peter a little and he has a terrible temper.'

'It wasn't her fault. She was raped.'

'But if she hadn't been to pubs on her own it probably wouldn't have happened,' Anne said and looked grave. 'Whatever will she do?'

'I don't think she will have it here,' Maureen said. 'The Sally Army gives girls a home for a few months if they agree to have the child adopted. I should guess that is what Ellie will choose to do.'

'Yes, that is one option, but she has to hide it well or people will talk – and it is bound to get to Peter's ears one way or the other.'

'She would be better to tell him about the rape herself...' Anne suggested.

'I'll tell her Knocker has been arrested and suggest that she should write to Peter about the rape,' Maureen said. 'I feel so sorry for her. I'm sure she's at her wit's end over all this...'

'It's all very sad,' Peggy said. 'I don't normally wish anyone harm – but it would be a good thing if that wicked man did get shot...'

Chapter 16

Ellie looked at the words on the page and started to tremble. She'd been pleased when the letter arrived, because Peter seldom wrote letters, although it didn't look like his writing. She normally just got a postcard to say he loved her and was thinking of her, but this time he'd written quite a long letter. She'd torn it open in haste and read his message and now she was feeling sick and afraid.

My dearest Ellie,

I've got good news and bad, my love. I was wounded in the arm a week ago, but it isn't bad enough to get a Blighty home as a rule. However, I've been told that as I'm due some leave they're going to send me back. I'm good and ready for it, I can tell you. My arm is still a bit weak, but it won't stop me kissing you. I'll be home soon and we can make up for lost time.

I can't tell you exactly when I'll be back, but it shouldn't be long before I can hold you in my arms.

*You've no idea how much I've been hoping for leave.
It's worth getting a bullet in the arm to come home to
the girl I adore. We didn't have much time together, and
I'm going to make up for months of missing you, my
darling.*

*My captain is writing this, Ellie, because my hand
won't hold a pen at the moment. Don't worry, I'll soon
mend when I get home to you.*

All my love, Peter.

Ellie blushed to think that Peter's captain had written such
an intimate letter for him, and in a way Peter could never
have done himself, but her embarrassment was far less of a
problem than her fear of him coming home. She didn't show
much in her clothes, in fact hardly at all, but naked she could
just see the little curve of her stomach. If she was careful, she
might hide it from him – and yet it was a risk. If she managed
to deceive Peter, her problems were over. She could pretend
the child was his. If he was back at the Front, she could delay
the letter about the birth and not register it until six weeks
later… all manner of ideas ran through her mind, as she tried
to think about her problem.

She decided to ask Mrs Tandy for advice that evening, and
slipped the letter into her pocket. Ellie would ask if Peter could
stay with her and she was sure her kind landlady would agree…

'Henry, I need some money,' Violet said that morning. 'I'm a
bit short and I have to pay a bill at my suppliers. Maureen
banks all the shop money and I haven't had a penny more
than my housekeeping for months. I want you to tell her to
leave a few pounds extra in the till.'

Henry looked at her for a few moments in silence. 'W-what's happened to the m-money you m-make?' he asked, frowning at her. 'I t-thought you w-were doin' w-well?'

'I'm doin' all right, but I've had a lot of expenses recently,' Violet glared at him. 'I haven't asked you for a penny over me housekeepin' since we were wed – why are you questionin' me now? I'm your wife. Surely I'm entitled to fifty quid now and then if I need it?'

For a moment he was silent and then he inclined his head. 'You'd best ask M-Maureen,' he said clearly. 'I don't k-know what s-she has in the bank. You didn't want n-nothin' to do wiv me sh-shop, Violet. If yer n-need money, yer entitled, I s-suppose.'

'Why can't you just tell Maureen to give it to me?'

'Sh-she's lookin' after things 'cos I can't,' Henry said. 'Just tell her what you need. Sh-she'll give yer what she can…'

'I don't see why I should have to ask your daughter,' Violet said, furious now. 'I'm your wife, Henry. I'm entitled to know about the shop and how much it makes.'

'Just ask h-her,' Henry said and closed his eyes wearily. 'I ain't up to this, Violet. M-Maureen's the boss now… you'll have to ask her if yer want money.'

Violet glared at him and left the room with a flounce. A few minutes later he heard her leaving the flat and a single tear trickled down his cheek. Somehow, it had all gone wrong. He'd thought marriage would be comfortable and easy for him, but Violet wasn't like his first wife. She wanted her own way and made demands he found hard to satisfy. Violet had been angry with him over the money, but it wasn't his fault. He'd thought she had plenty of money coming in from her business – what had happened to it all…? Unless she was lying to him? Henry didn't mind giving her money, though he wasn't sure the business could spare fifty pounds. Of course, there was always his secret hoard; Henry had been putting a pound or two by over the years, hiding it just in case it was needed, but he didn't want anyone to know about that yet, especially Violet. Yet Violet was his wife and if she needed fifty pounds, she ought to have it, if there was enough in the bank. Maureen would know. She was a good girl.

A few more tears flowed down his cheeks and then he brushed them away. He'd never been one for feeling sorry for himself, even though he'd often made out he was suffering more than he had been to get his own way with Maureen, but he'd always been in control of his emotions and tears were a weakness. It was time he pulled himself together and started to get on top of things again. He didn't begrudge Violet money, even if she hadn't been a good wife to him. He'd made his will, leaving everything he had to her when they married, but recently he'd felt a bit mean over that – not that he had very much. Besides, he knew that his mother would leave the shop to Maureen. Violet would get what belonged to Henry, but it wasn't a great deal – the stock in the shop might be worth a couple of hundred or so and whatever was in the bank, plus the furniture. However, he ought to let someone know about his little secret – someone he could trust... he should have told Maureen when she was here, because it was for her. He hadn't treated her well and that little bit he'd got hidden should be hers by rights...

Shaking his head, Henry negotiated the first step down towards the hall below; time to let Tom have a break, he thought just as the little explosion in his head made everything go wild. Fear raced through him, and for a moment he seemed to see the important decisions of his life playing on the wall like a film and it was then he knew regret. Maureen... he wanted his daughter, wanted to tell her that he knew how good she'd always been to him. The pain in the side of his head was worse than he'd ever experienced and suddenly he felt dizzy and sick; everything had gone dark and then he was falling – falling into a bottomless pit.

Maureen opened the door to Alice, staring at her in astonishment as she saw that she was out of breath and looked white with shock; her hairnet had fallen off and her stockings were halfway down her legs.

'Alice, whatever is the matter, love? Has somethin' happened – are you hurt or Tom?'

'Gawd bless you, love, it ain't me or Tom,' Alice said and looked at her sadly. 'It's yer dad, Maureen. He fell down the steps and Tom found him straight away – heard his cry; he's hurt... you've got to come quick, love. Tom told me to come fer you...'

'Dad fell down the stairs?' Maureen's throat tightened and she gave a cry of distress, putting a hand to her face. She'd become protective of him of late and it hurt to know that he'd fallen and hurt himself when she wasn't there. She grabbed her coat. 'I was just about to go round to him...'

'You'd best come now,' Alice said. 'Tom's upset and they've carted yer dad off somewhere...'

'To the hospital...' Maureen said and caught back a sob as she followed Alice into the street and slammed the house door. 'I'll come straight away. Gran is down the market. I'd better sort out what I can before I see her, because this will upset her too.'

'We all thought he was gettin' better?'

Maureen shook her head. 'He managed to get down to the shop some days for an hour or so, but he wasn't really up to it. The doctors at the hospital said if he had another stroke it could happen suddenly, but I hoped it wouldn't be for another year or two... Oh, God!'

She started to run, leaving Alice to follow at her own pace. Maureen's thoughts were going round and round in her head as they headed back to Mulberry Lane. Tom had put the 'Closed' notice on the shop door, but he opened up to her, looking anxious as Maureen entered, followed a few moments later by a breathless Alice.

'I didn't leave him there for more than a minute,' he told her. 'I heard him fall so I put the lock on the shop door, went and found him and then rang the doctor quick... but it was too late...'

'What do you mean?' She stared at him in distress, because Alice had just told her he'd had a fall. 'What are you sayin' exactly, Tom?'

'His eyelids flickered and I thought I heard him speak your name, Maureen, but it wasn't clear. I'm so sorry. I was about to go up and see if he needed anythin', but then I heard his cry and the sound of a fall...but, it was quick; he couldn't have suffered much.'

'He's dead?' Maureen was shaking and feeling sick. She didn't want to believe it had happened. 'What did the doctor say?'

'He thought Henry must have had a massive stroke at the top of the stairs. He said it was the kindest thing because if he'd lived...' Tom caught back a sob. 'I thought he was gettin' better, Maureen. I saw him first thing and we had a bit of a laugh...'

'Yes, he had seemed better,' she agreed and blinked back the tears. Inside, she was hurting so much but she couldn't let him see, couldn't let him blame himself. 'Don't be upset, Tom. None of this is your fault.'

'No, but I feel as if I should've gone up to see he was all right after she went out…'

'When did Violet leave?'

'Just a few minutes before he started to come down – couldn't have been more than five. She slammed the door. I think she was angry…'

'Well, someone ought to tell her,' Maureen said, holding back the tears, because if she started she wouldn't be able to stop. 'I don't suppose you know where she went?'

'She never says…' Tom hesitated, then, 'I could go and look for her…'

'I've seen her in the Roundabout Café,' Alice said. 'It's on Commercial Road – near the end.…'

'I know it,' Tom said. 'Dad took us all there once for a treat on Mum's birthday, years ago…'

'I'm going to make a few phone calls,' Maureen said, looking thoughtful. 'If you wouldn't mind lookin' for Violet please, Tom? We can't open the shop today – not until after the funeral – and Violet needs to be told what has happened.'

'I'll go now,' Tom said. He moved towards her suddenly and gave her a hug, his eyes sparkling with unshed tears. 'I'm really sorry…'

'I know…' Maureen swallowed hard; she mustn't give into emotion. She needed to keep strong for everyone's sake. 'I'd better stay here and make those calls – and if you see my gran tell her to come here, Tom, but don't say why. I'd rather tell her myself.'

'Right,' he agreed and left the shop.

Maureen locked the door after him. She sighed and went through to the back kitchen, Alice following silently until Maureen asked her to sit down.

'Shall I put the kettle on for you, girl – while you make them calls? You need a drop of brandy or summat for the shock, girl. It ain't right fer yer to have all this trouble on yer shoulders in your condition.'

'Alice, would you? Thank you...' Maureen smiled at her. 'Come upstairs and we'll have our tea there. I want to see if Dad left any messages... Not that he would've known to.'

'A stroke like that would be sudden,' Alice agreed and looked at her in sympathy. 'I've seen it 'appen afore, love. He didn't know much about it if you ask me.'

Alice filled the kettle while Maureen looked round the small sitting room. She could hardly believe her father was dead. When the hospital had sent him home for Christmas she'd thought he would make a good recovery, perhaps even manage the banking and ordering again one day, but now he was gone – and only yesterday he'd been thanking her for all she'd done to help him.

She telephoned Peggy first and asked her to tell Anne and Janet. Peggy wanted to come round, but Maureen told her to wait.

'I'll come and talk to you later, when I've finished up here,' she said. 'I've got to ring the doctor and find out where they took dad and then the undertaker – though perhaps that's Violet's job...'

'She ought to have been at home lookin' after him...'

Maureen sighed. 'Don't get me started on that, Peggy. I know there's goin' to be a huge row when she finds out Dad didn't own the shop. Still, it has to happen sometime, but not until after the funeral if I can help it.'

'No, best to wait if you can,' Peggy said. 'I'm here if you want me, love, and if you want a little do for your dad, I'll be happy to arrange it for you.'

'Thanks, Peggy. I'll see what Violet wants – after all, she's his wife.' Maureen replaced the receiver.

'Not that you'd notice that she's his wife,' Alice said, coming in with a tray of tea. 'Drink this up, Maureen. It ain't fair on you, love. You 'ad all them years lookin' after things 'ere and now she'll take over...'

'I almost wish she would,' Maureen said. 'Gran owned the shop, Alice. It didn't belong to Dad and it doesn't belong to Violet – all she owns is the stock and the furniture, oh, and a few pounds in the bank...'

'What will 'appen to the shop then?'

'Perhaps Violet will keep it open; Dad had another year's lease to go, so she's got it if she wants it,' Maureen said. 'I know it will be awkward for people in the lane if she closes it down. You'll get used to goin' elsewhere – but Tom is the one that will suffer most. He was proud of earnin' a few bob and I don't know where else he would get a job he can do, at least until his shoulder is properly healed.'

'Poor bugger,' Alice said. 'As if 'e ain't 'ad enough to put up wiv. His mother stuck in the infirmary and his father in the Army... and Sam dead an' all.'

'Yes, I know. I would've kept the business goin' somehow, but I'm not sure what Violet will do. She complained that it was hardly worth opening for what it earns only a few days ago...and I'd keep the shop open if I could, but I don't have the money to buy the stock from her.'

'No one earns a fortune out of a shop like this,' Alice said, 'but you and your dad kept it goin'. It's a shame if it closes down now.'

'The stock must be worth a hundred or two, because I've been puttin' most of the money back into it recently. Dad told me to pay the bills and put the rest into stock; he thought Violet had her own money, all of which she kept. He never asked her what she earned but she seemed to have a few bob when they married...'

'Well, maybe she'll keep it open,' Alice said optimistically.

'I wish I could think so,' Maureen said, but she knew what Alice didn't. Once Violet knew that the property wasn't hers, she would be furious.

Chapter 17

Every house on the lane had its curtains closed as the funeral cortège passed by. Violet had wanted black horses and a carriage with glass windows so that the coffin could be seen. It was covered with flowers: an elaborate wreath from Violet, a smaller one from Maureen and Gran, and quite a few bunches of flowers from the community. Henry Jackson might not have been universally popular, but he was respected.

The funeral procession had been slow, because all those attending had walked behind the carriage and horses. The church wasn't too far and the people of the lanes were tough; a cold frosty morning in late February wasn't going to put them off. Every business in Mulberry Lane had closed for the morning, and most of the residents either followed or were already assembled in the church.

Violet took the first place in the pew, as was her right as Henry's wife. Gran sat beside her and Maureen was next with Peggy and Janet, Maggie on her lap. In the next row, Tom, Alice, Mrs Tandy, Ellie, Anne, and her husband's uncle, Bob

Hall, were seated, behind them other residents of the lanes. Hymns were sung, prayers and the address followed and then most people trooped outside to the pleasant churchyard, where the coffin was interred.

Violet had dabbed at her eyes throughout the service, although Maureen hadn't seen any signs of tears. She thought it was all a sham on her stepmother's part, but she kept her mouth shut, just as she had ever since Violet came back home that day and started dictating what she wanted for the funeral. Maureen hadn't tried to change anything. She really couldn't interfere, though she didn't think her father would've wanted all the fuss and expense of the funeral; he would have preferred to keep it simple.

Peggy had offered to put on a little do in the Pig & Whistle but Violet had refused the offer and chosen another pub in Commercial Road. She spent the whole time playing the grieving widow, ignoring Maureen and Gran, as if they were irrelevant and had played no part in the life of Henry Jackson.

Maureen and Gran stayed to greet all Henry's friends and then left Violet to her role of the dutiful wife.

'I'll expect you tomorrow,' Violet said to Maureen as she took her leave. 'We've got some sortin' out to do…'

'Yes, I'm afraid we have,' Maureen said. 'I'm sorry you didn't have longer to enjoy being Dad's wife. I just hope you can find happiness in your new life.'

'What is that supposed to mean?' Violet's eyes narrowed.

'We'll tell you in the mornin',' Gran said and took Maureen's arm. 'Ten o'clock sharp – don't be late.'

'You can't tell me what to do…' Violet muttered angrily.

'Everythin' comes out in the wash Violet, so they say…' Gran said and smiled.

She walked away, her hand guiding Maureen firmly into the street. Peggy, Anne and Janet followed, Maggie bawling her head off as they turned towards home.

'She's goin' to be so angry...' Maureen said. 'I'm just glad I didn't tell her while Dad was alive.'

'Daft fool should never have wed her,' Gran said and shook her head. 'We shall have a fine mess to clear up, Maureen. I doubt she's got the money to pay for all this lot and that means we'll have to contribute – no doubt she thinks she's in for a fortune...'

'There's a couple of hundred pounds or so in the bank, which should pay for the funeral and more,' Maureen said, 'but of course the stock is worth double that... if she can find someone to buy it.'

'That shop is stayin' open,' Gran said with a determined look. 'It's your birth right not hers and I shan't let her ruin a good business. You'll make about twenty pounds a week once the bills are paid, and that's decent money for anyone. What's left of the lease is hers if she wants it, but she'll have to keep the shop open and she'll need to pay you rent. If she's sensible, she can keep goin' and earn a livin' from it – if not, she can clear orf and good riddance to her.'

'Are we being too hard on her?' Maureen asked doubtfully. 'Dad married her and I think he was happy...'

'Not for long. He soon discovered what a selfish bitch she was, didn't he?' Gran said and scowled. 'Ideas above her station – look at this funeral. Henry would've hated it. Don't be fooled by that show of grief, Maureen. She didn't shed a single real tear. She married him for the shop and it will be my pleasure to tell her she doesn't own it...'

'She will insist on stayin' in the flat,' Maureen said. 'After all, it's her home – and we can't put her out...'

'You're too soft,' Gran said. 'She can stay if she's willin' to be reasonable. If she wants a home and a small business that will bring in a few pounds she can stay until the end of the lease – but you'd be a fool to let her stay longer, Maureen. You want to make that property pay for you.'

'I'm going to ask for rent when the lease is up,' Maureen said. 'But I shan't tell her she has to leave. Violet can stay in the flat and if she doesn't want the shop perhaps I can let it to someone else…'

'Most folk who want to run a business prefer to live over it,' Gran said and looked at Peggy. 'You're a businesswoman, what do you think Maureen should do?'

'Well, it depends on how Violet behaves,' Peggy said. 'Her husband had the lease to the flat and shop and she does have the right to stay on if she wants – but I think she'll make trouble for Maureen. She's goin' to kick up a fuss – and she will need some convincin' that Henry didn't own the shop. Everyone thought he did… and that's your fault, Hilda. You ought to have made him pay a proper rent.'

'I let him have his way there for years,' Gran said and grimaced. 'I didn't need or want the money, but I don't feel obliged to her. I can't see her wantin' to stay once she knows the truth…'

'I hope for both your sakes she goes quietly,' Peggy said and paused to press both hands to her back. 'I'll be glad to put my feet up with a nice cup of tea – but if you need my help with Violet tomorrow…'

'Don't you worry,' Gran said and laughed. 'I can handle her sort and I'll have Maureen with me. We're more than a match for that woman…'

★

Ellie listened to the conversation between the others but heard very little of it. All she could think of since she'd had Peter's letter was what would happen when he came home and saw her without her clothes on. If he guessed she was having another man's child, he would half-kill her!

They had reached the end of Mulberry Lane now. Peggy, Anne and Janet smiled at the others and went into the pub, Maureen and her gran followed. Mrs Tandy shook her head when Ellie looked at her.

'Best to stay out of pubs, Ellie love,' she said. 'I could do with a cup of tea though...'

They walked down the lane. Alice and Tom were standing outside Alice's house talking seriously. They waved to Ellie, and Alice called out something. Ellie wasn't sure what they were trying to tell her and then she saw a man in uniform standing outside the hairdressing shop. Her heart caught, first with fright because he was home, and then when he saw her and smiled at her, an overwhelming surge of love and delight.

She ran to him and he opened his arms, taking her in and holding her pressed close to his body as he kissed her deeply. Ellie clung to him, returning his kiss with fervour, her happiness flowing out as she realised that she still liked being kissed by Peter. She'd been afraid that she would not be able to respond because of what had happened to her, but now that his arms were around her all she felt was love – and safety. She felt safe at last and it made the tears run down her cheeks.

'Where have you been, Ellie?' Peter asked. 'Mum told me you moved out, so I came lookin' and the shop was closed... all the shops are closed.'

'We've been to Mr Jackson's funeral,' Ellie said. 'Maureen Jackson's father used to run the grocery shop but he was ill – and then he fell down the stairs and died.'

'Poor bugger,' Peter said and his eyes were shadowed by recent memories she couldn't share. 'Too many people dyin' these days...'

'Does your arm hurt?' Ellie said, noticing that he'd dropped one arm and seemed to be holding it awkwardly. 'Is it very painful?'

'It hurt like hell at the time,' Peter said. 'I had it in a sling until a couple of days ago, but it's gettin' better now – and much better now you're here.' He looked into her face. 'Why did you move out of Mum's? She was upset over it.' There was a hint of something in his eyes now that sent shivers down her spine and she remembered that he'd practically forced her to live at his mother's house when he was called up. She realised now that he'd bullied her into it. She hadn't wanted to, but she'd been so excited over the wedding and all the things he'd lavished on her that she'd agreed.

'We didn't get on,' Ellie said and smiled at him. 'I've got a nice room at Mrs Tandy's house and it's next door to my job. I save what she charges me on bus fare and I like it better... Don't be cross, Pete...'

'I'm not cross,' he said, but she thought he was annoyed; his eyes glittered for a moment and she guessed he'd have more to say when they were alone. 'I didn't have much choice but to leave you there, love – but I'm glad you've found somewhere you like better... though I think you might have tried to stay on for my sake. She's very hurt...' He was trying to make out she was in the wrong, not his overbearing mother, but Ellie didn't want to make a scene.

'How long a leave have you got?' she asked, clinging to his arm and looking up at him. She'd been frightened of him coming home but now she was glad. If he had a few drinks at night, he wouldn't notice she'd put on a bit of weight and with any luck she would get away with it – after all she was only just over two months gone and it didn't really show, just a faint curve and slightly fuller breasts that she was aware of but he might not notice. She would just have to make sure he didn't get too close a look in daylight.

'Three whole weeks,' Peter said and grinned. 'I might get some more trainin' before I go back overseas – they're talkin' about makin' me a sergeant 'cos I've got leadership qualities.'

'Oh Pete, that's wonderful,' she said and clung to him. 'I'm so glad you're home.'

'You've missed me then?' he said and looked her in the eyes. 'I thought you might have got tired of waitin' and gone off with another bloke after Mum said you'd moved out.' Again, his expression hardened and she caught her breath.

'I wouldn't do that…' Ellie said, her throat feeling tight. 'I love you, Pete…'

'You'd better… I wouldn't like it if I thought you'd been playing around.' There was menace in his voice and Ellie felt cold with fear. What would he do if he discovered the truth?

'Of course I do! I was miserable a lot of the time after you left, especially when your mum got on to me.'

'She's like that, but you don't have to go there if you don't want to,' he said. 'We'll find somewhere we can make a home – but it's not easy in London. I think we might stand more chance out in the suburbs…'

'Not until you're home for good,' Ellie said. 'I get on well with Mrs Tandy. She's like a mother to me – and I'd be all alone in the suburbs. Let me stay here where my job and friends are – until the war is over and we can be together. I don't mind where we go then.'

'All right.' Peter grinned and was suddenly more like the man she loved. 'Have you got to work today – or are you closed for the whole day?'

'I start at half-past two,' Ellie said. 'We've got time for a drink and a sandwich somewhere...'

'We'll go to the Pig & Whistle then,' he said. 'I'll go and get my things from Mum's afterwards – if Mrs Tandy will let me stay with you for my leave?'

'Yes, of course she will, I've already asked her – and I've booked a week's holiday for when you came home,' Ellie said. 'We could go away for a few days or just go out somewhere for the day...'

'I think I'd rather stay round here,' Peter said. 'We can go up the West End for a few treats – I'll buy you some clothes and take you for meals and to the flicks. Payin' for a hotel would be expensive. Better to spend the money on you and havin' some fun...'

'Yes, all right, whatever you want,' Ellie said, smiling at him as they walked up the lane. 'I'm just so glad you're back...'

If only he didn't notice anything different about her – and surely it wasn't truly noticeable yet? Ellie didn't want anything to spoil this visit home for her husband. She'd forgotten how handsome he was and how much she'd loved him, still loved him – and she would give anything for that awful man never to have attacked her. It meant she had to deceive Peter and to go on doing so all their lives. If he believed that the child was his he would love it, but Ellie would carry the guilt of deception all her life.

★

'Morning, Ellie,' Maureen said as she and Gran paused outside the shop the following morning. 'I'm afraid we're not open yet if you were lookin' for somethin'…'

'No, I've been round the corner and fetched some milk and some fresh bread from the bakery. We bought our rations here last week just before… But we'll have to go somewhere else now Peter is home, because he eats more than the pair of us…'

'You're glowin',' Maureen said and smiled. 'You must be happy to have Peter home?'

'Yes, very happy,' Ellie said. 'It's lovely… Bye for now…' she said and walked hastily on.

Maureen inserted her key and opened the shop door. She went in and closed it, locking it after them, because people kept coming to the door and trying it in the hope that they were open.

'Well, this is it,' Maureen said. 'You've got all the documents from the lawyer, Gran?'

'Yes, I have,' Gran said and set her mouth. 'It's a copy of Henry's latest will, and the lease he signed – and a copy of my deeds that I've signed over to you. Your original deeds are in the bank.'

'Yes, and that's where they're stoppin',' Maureen said. 'I want this shop open for the people who live here – and I just hope Violet sees sense…'

Violet was sitting at the table waiting for them when they walked into the sitting room. It was evident that she'd been sorting through the sideboard drawers, hunting for papers. A copy of what looked like a previous will lying on the table with a bank book.

'You might have knocked before you came in – this is my home not yours, Maureen.'

'Yes, it is your home, at least for the time bein',' Gran said, going straight in for the kill. 'However, the property does not belong to you – and if you want to live here you can pay some rent... say seven bob a week. That's fair in my opinion.'

'Henry made a new will makin' over all he owned to me,' Violet said. 'I've rung the solicitor this mornin' and he's sendin' me a copy.'

'No need for that – I've got one here,' Gran said and handed it to her. 'My son changed his will when he married you and left you what he owned – which is the furniture here, the stock in the shop and, as you already know, two hundred and five pounds in the bank as well as whatever is in the till...'

'And this property,' Violet said with a smirk. 'I've had it valued and they say I might get six hundred or so if I can find a buyer...'

'You could... if it was yours,' Gran said calmly. 'Unfortunately for you, Violet, this shop and flat never belonged to Henry or his father. My maternal grandfather left it to me and I let it to my husband and then my son for a peppercorn rent. It was all done legally and two years ago, I granted Henry a further three years – so you can stay here for a year, but I shall want rent from you.'

'Liar! I don't believe you...' Violet cried, but the colour drained from her face as her mother-in-law placed some documents on the table in front of her. She looked at them hastily and saw a lease signed by Henry Jackson and also what were obviously copies of old conveyances, stating that the property at number 12 Mulberry Lane belonged to Hilda Jackson, bequeathed to her by a Mr Thomas Benson in 1918. 'You're tryin' to cheat me of what is legally mine... and I shan't let you get away with it.'

'It is all perfectly legal. You are entitled to stay here for another year, should you choose to, and carry on the business – but in the last lease, it states that if Henry married, I should be entitled to ask for rent on his death. And I think in the circumstances, I must do so. To be perfectly honest, Violet, I don't trust you. I think you would try to get the property away from us if there was any way of doin' it – so I'm not prepared to let you stay for a peppercorn rent. If you want the flat and the shop it will be a pound a week and that's still cheap.'

'I have no intention of runnin' this stupid little shop!' Violet said furiously. 'I'm going to sell the stock for as much as I can get and close the bank account… and I'm goin' to a lawyer, because I don't believe this shop belongs to you. You wicked old witch…' Violet jumped up and made a violent movement towards Gran.

Maureen moved in front of her. Putting up her arm to fend off the blow. 'As a matter of fact, it belongs to me now, Violet – so attackin' an elderly woman isn't goin' to get you anywhere. We are prepared to let you stay here if you keep the shop open, otherwise I shall take it that you've given notice and let it to someone else…'

'Damn you! I might have known it was your doin',' Violet said. 'You little bitch. You've had it in for me the whole time and now you've got your way…' She glared at them both and snatched up the documents. 'I'm goin' to take these to the lawyers – and I'll make you pay compensation for turnin' me out of my home.'

'But we haven't,' Gran said calmly. 'You may stay here and carry on your business if you wish for a year – and Maureen will let the shop to someone else if you're sure you don't want it?'

'What I want is the money for the stock…' Violet stared at them belligerently. 'It's worth two hundred pounds at least.'

'Yes, if you bought it from the wholesaler,' Gran said, 'but I don't think you'll find anyone will pay you that. I, however, know someone who might give you a hundred pounds…'

'A hundred and fifty or I'll take it with me…'

'I think you would find that difficult… and with the rationin', any sale of a significant amount of food outside of a shop would be thought of as black market trading. I think the law might take a dim view of that…'

Violet snatched up her coat from where it lay over the back of a chair. 'I'm goin' to the lawyer's – and when I get back I want you out of here. This is still my home and I'll have the locks changed if I need to.'

'Have new locks on the flat by all means, as long as you give your landlady a key – and don't forget you'll be payin' twenty shillings a week in future – or just seven bob if you only need the flat.'

Violet sent Gran a look that would have killed a lesser person and stormed out.

'Well, that went better than I expected,' Maureen said and looked at Gran for a long moment.

'She was a mite upset,' Gran said, 'but I expected it. She'll find both the lease and the deeds watertight – and if she thinks about tryin' any funny business she'll discover every page is stamped copy and my lawyer has the originals in his safe. Violet will rant and rave and hate us, Maureen – but there's nothin' she can do.'

'Yes…' Maureen sighed. 'I wish she'd been sensible. I feel a bit guilty over all this, Gran. She was Dad's wife – why couldn't she just be content to stay here and run both businesses? She would earn a nice little bit that way – more than most widows get from their pensions, I'll bet – and it would've been better to be friends.'

'Yes, I'm sure she could've earned a nice income for herself, but it's her choice,' Gran said. 'I wonder if she will let us have the stock for a hundred and fifty pounds when she calms down…'

'Us?' Maureen stared at her. 'Where would we get that sort of money? I've got fifteen pounds in the bank and I'm goin' to need most of it for the baby…'

'You keep your money, love. I've got the funds – I've got two hundred and fifty pounds in the bank as it happens, but I wasn't going to spend it all. We might need it for other things.'

'That's an awful lot of money, Gran…' Maureen was puzzled. 'I didn't think you had much in the bank?' Why was Gran always so careful with her money if she had savings?

'My grandfather left me this shop – and a cottage near the Docks,' Gran said. 'No one, not even my husband, ever knew about the cottage. I've been rentin' it out for six shillings a week to a lovely family for years. They're always on time with the rent and I keep it in good repair for them – and I've never spent a penny on anythin' else but the upkeep. I manage without it and it was always my little nest egg in case you needed help, my love.'

'Oh, Gran,' Maureen's eyes stung as she looked at the elderly woman she loved so much. 'I wish you would spend some of it on you – but if we can buy the stock from Violet we can keep the shop goin' with Tom's help and that would be wonderful. People in the lane were upset by the thought it might close.'

'We'll leave this here for Violet,' Gran took a letter from her bag and placed it on the table. 'It offers to buy the stock for a hundred and fifty pounds in my lawyer's name. He'll pay her and see it's all legal and she'll never know where the money came from. I knew if I offered her a hundred she would ask for more – so I have three letters. I wasn't going to two hundred, because we can buy what we need from the wholesaler but it would take time to arrange, and I want this shop open for business within a week.'

'You clever thing,' Maureen said and smiled as they went out, locking the door behind them. 'I do hope Violet will accept and sign your agreement...'

'You mean everything she said was true?' Violet stared at the lawyer, angry tears building inside her. 'All I get is the furniture – the money in the bank, those war bonds, and the stock at the time of Henry's death?'

'Yes, I am afraid that is correct, Mrs Jackson. The property was never your husband's to leave to anyone... but three hundred and fifty-five pounds altogether, with the money from the bank and the stock, plus the furniture is quite a nice little nest egg, and of course there's fifty pounds in war bonds, though you won't get anything for them for years.'

'The cheatin' bastard,' Violet said, bringing a shocked look from the lawyer. 'He let me think he'd got property and money – and what do I get when it's all over...?'

'Unfortunately, there's nothing you can do since the property was never his. Had he owned it and left it away from you, we could've tried to overturn the will, but your husband very properly left you what he had. I'm sorry, Mrs Jackson. I'm afraid you will just have to accept it.'

'It's her fault, his daughter – the conniving little bitch, turning him against me. I bet anythin' I've got, he's hidden money somewhere. He must have had more tucked away. That shop was always busy…'

'If you can find a secret bank account, you would have a legal claim to it,' the lawyer confirmed, 'but otherwise…' He spread his hands. 'Forgive me, Mrs Jackson, but I have other clients waiting.'

Violet gave him a look that was meant to slay and grabbed the documents from the desk before storming out. She'd been cheated. Henry's business had earned more than that, she would bet her life on it. Either his bitch of a daughter had salted some of it away for herself or Henry had hidden it in a bank – or perhaps somewhere in the house.

If her son hadn't taken all her money and demanded more, she wouldn't have been as upset. Three hundred and fifty-five pounds was enough to keep her going for a while, and the war bonds might be worth something one day – but that was nothing when her son wanted a thousand pounds.

Oh, hell! What was Bryan going to say now? He was her son and a mother always felt obliged to help her child, but she had to keep something for herself – and there was fifty pounds to pay for the funeral, plus more for the do she'd put on afterwards. Maybe she would clear off and leave the bitch to pay for the funeral!

Violet's brain felt as if a storm of bees had invaded it. Bryan was waiting for her now, confidently expecting her to tell him she had at least five hundred to give him. She couldn't meet him and tell him that she had hardly enough to start up her business elsewhere, because she knew just what he would say. He was a carbon copy of his father – a brute who'd knocked her about and taken every penny she'd earned until he dropped down dead in his favourite pub, where he spent what little he had, at the age of forty-three.

At least Henry had always been considerate. He'd let her believe he owned the shop – but perhaps he'd expected that his mother would leave him the premises, and she ought to have done. She was a nasty old woman and her granddaughter was an evil bitch. Together they'd planned to rob Violet of what she was entitled to. She'd bet that old hag was rolling in money. Probably had loads of cash tucked away in her house somewhere...

Violet stopped abruptly, causing a woman with a pram to almost bump into her and forcing her to walk round her. If she had nothing to give Bryan, he would be furious...

Chapter 18

Ellie was dressing when Peter entered the bedroom that morning. She was standing in the light of the window wearing only a thin petticoat and he frowned as he noticed the slight curve of her stomach. He'd noticed she'd put on a little weight and her breasts were fuller, but he hadn't thought any more of it until now. His anger rose like a swirling tide as the penny dropped.

'Who the bloody hell was he?' Peter demanded and strode towards her, grabbing her by the arms and giving her a violent shake. 'You rotten little whore! You're just like all the other bloody bitches... after another bloke as soon as their men are off fightin' for king and country...'

Ellie's heart sank. He'd only had a few days of his leave so far; she'd hoped he would go away again and never have to know the truth, but he'd guessed and there was no point in trying to hide it. She was going to have to tell him she'd been raped.

'It wasn't my fault...' she said, a sob in her voice. 'He raped me... I fought him as hard as I could and 'e beat me until I couldn't do anythin' but let him get on with it. It only happened the once…' Her head came up in defiance. 'It's this bloody war. If you'd been 'ere, it would never have 'appened. I never gave him any encouragement…'

'Liar!' Peter yelled at her and slapped her ear hard, making her recoil in pain. 'Were you goin' to foist yer bastard on me as mine then, Ellie? Did you think I wouldn't notice and you could switch the dates round so that I'd never know…?'

Tears dripped slowly down her cheeks as she looked at him helplessly. It was of course exactly what she'd hoped, but the way he said it made her realise how wicked she'd been and she hung her head. She was the victim, but Peter didn't see it that way, and his expression made her feel very afraid.

'I didn't know what to do after it 'appened,' she said in a low, shamed voice. 'I was goin' to go right away and have it – give it away and then come back… but then you came home and I thought if you never knew, I could just keep the baby…'

'I ought to beat the bastard out of you!' Peter said and shook her hard. 'You bloody cheatin' bitch! How many men have you had?'

He was yelling now as he shook her and then hit her across the face making her head snap back. Her mouth was bleeding and she could taste the blood. He was furious, beside himself with anger. Although Peter had a temper, he'd never been like this with her before and the coldness she sensed in him made her shake with terror. She looked at him in dumb silence and that made him even angrier.

'Answer me, Ellie!' he yelled, and his fingers dug hard into her upper arms. 'If you don't tell me the truth, I'll bloody kill you… How many other men did you have while I was tryin' to stay alive to get back to you?' He brought his fist close to her face, threatening her. 'I'm warnin' yer…'

'Stop that, Peter,' Mrs Tandy spoke from the doorway. 'Ellie is tellin' you the truth. She was raped and beaten. She was too terrified to go to the police, because he told her he would come back and kill her if she did – and besides, the police wouldn't have believed her; they always blame the woman. She isn't a bad girl, whatever you might think. I give you my word that Ellie is a good girl and she stays home with me at night now…'

'What the hell is it to do with you?' Peter glared at her.

'You both live in my home,' Mrs Tandy said quietly. 'I know you are angry, Peter. Angry and very hurt, but I saw Ellie after her ordeal. You didn't. It was unfortunate that a child should be the result of that brutal attack, but we can deal with that – Ellie can still go away to have the child and the Sally Army will find a home for the baby…'

'No…' Ellie sobbed and crossed her arms over her belly, suddenly protective of her unborn child. She hated the man who had raped her, but somehow the thought of giving it away to a stranger now appalled her. Ellie had never known a mother's love and she didn't want that to happen to her child, even though it was a child of rape. If Peter had been more understanding, she might have clung to him, done what he wanted, but he seemed like a stranger to her now and he'd shown a side of himself that she didn't like. She'd thought he was kind and generous, but he wasn't – not once he was angered 'I want my baby. I thought I could give it away, but I can't… it's a part of me.' She'd been hoping he wouldn't notice and she'd be able to keep the baby and the idea of letting it go now upset her more than she'd thought it would.

'I know yer don't want it, Peter, but yer won't want me either now – so I'll just go away somewhere I'm not known and have my baby. You needn't send me any money and you can divorce me if yer want…'

'No!' Mrs Tandy and Peter spoke at once.

'You'll stay here with me so that I can look after you,' Mrs Tandy said.

'I don't want a divorce…' Peter looked at Ellie. There were red marks on her arms and her face. 'I'm sorry, Ellie. I never meant to harm you, but I thought you were lyin' – you should've told me the truth straight away.'

'I thought you would hate me – and you do…' Ellie's salty tears trickled down her face and into her mouth. 'I thought I could keep you and the child…'

Peter stared at her. The emotions worked in his face and then, he held out a hand to her. 'We may be able to work it out, Ellie,' he said in a softer tone, though the look in his eyes told Ellie that it was just an act because she'd said she was leaving. 'You have to tell me everythin' – and tell me the man's name…'

'He's a deserter from the Army, a looter and a bully,' Mrs Tandy said. 'The police had him in custody, but I heard he got away…' Ellie started and looked at her fearfully. 'I didn't tell you, love, because I hoped it wasn't true – but he won't come back here after you, Ellie…'

'If he does while I'm home, I'll kill him,' Peter said and his eyes were hard. 'Now tell me his name, Ellie – and what he looks like…'

'I'll go,' Mrs Tandy said and looked at him. 'You won't hit her again, Peter? If you do, I'll be ringin' the police…'

'I shan't hit Ellie. I lost my temper because I thought…' He shook his head. 'Come here, Ellie, and tell me everythin'. That bastard isn't goin' to get away with what he's done to you, believe me.'

'Don't do anythin' silly,' Ellie said in a subdued voice as she went to his arms and he held her close to his chest. 'I don't want them hangin' you for murder.'

'That won't happen...' Peter promised and kissed the top of her head, but the look in his eyes was murderous. He might be able to forgive Ellie for her part in this mess, and even allow her to keep the child if she really wanted it – but the man who had harmed her would pay. His mouth hardened and his eyes turned to ice. The bugger who had attacked his wife had to pay – and he wasn't talking about money.

Peter still had several days' leave left; that might not be enough to track the man down and make sure he couldn't hurt Ellie or any other woman again, but Peter had friends – men he knew who wouldn't think twice about sticking a knife in the bugger's back. He would rather deal with it himself if he'd had time, but this man was destined for an early grave one way or the other...

Peggy looked at the picture of Pip's girlfriend. He'd sent it in a letter and said they hoped to come up for a visit in the summer, but weren't able to manage it just yet. She put the photo on the bed and bent down to retrieve a stocking she'd dropped and gasped as the pain struck her in the back. It was so violent that for a moment she felt as if someone had stabbed her with a knife and she swayed, sitting down on the edge of the bed as her legs went weak.

Surely, it couldn't be the baby coming just yet? They were only in the first week of March and Peggy's calculations told her the birth wasn't due for another two, or three weeks. She panted as the pain increased, ebbed and then came again, realising that she was definitely in the first stages of contractions. Immediately, she felt a wave of sheer panic. Able's baby mustn't come yet, because it might struggle to live and she couldn't bear to lose it as well as him.

Tears stung her eyes and she struggled to her feet and went along the hall very slowly and then down the stairs. She mustn't panic yet. Sometimes there were false contractions, which went away until the birth came at its proper time. She had to keep positive because either way she needed to be strong. At her age she ought to be in hospital to have the baby, and her bed was booked for three weeks' time in the London's maternity ward... but at this rate, she wasn't going to keep that appointment or even be able to get there before it happened.

Janet looked at her as she entered the kitchen. Mike was eating toast and marmalade at the table and Janet was brewing tea.

'I've made...' she began and then realised something was very wrong. 'Mum, what's the matter... it isn't the baby? Oh, my God, it's comin' now, isn't it?'

'I had a lot of pain just now,' Peggy said. 'The contractions are comin' too quickly. I don't think I have time to call a taxi and get to the hospital...'

'I'll telephone the doctor,' Mike said and pushed back his chair, 'unless you'd rather try for the hospital, Peggy?'

Peggy felt another strong pain and an urge to push. She shook her head and clutched at the back of a chair. 'I think it's going to be too late. I don't want my baby born in the back of a taxi...'

'Help your mum get back upstairs, Janet?' Mike said and

suddenly seemed in control. 'I'm going to telephone for the doctor – and you need to get undressed, into a nightie and in bed, Peggy. If the baby is comin' that quickly we may have to deliver it ourselves.'

Peggy smiled through the pain at the young man who had so recently been a patient himself. She thought it must be his naval training coming to the fore as he organised Janet into helping her up the stairs. 'I should've stayed upstairs, but I thought the pain might go off because it's early...'

'Well, it still might,' Janet said and Peggy understood she was trying to reassure her, but they both knew things were moving too fast for it to be a false alarm.

'Oh...' Peggy gave a little cry as they reached the top of the stairs. 'I've wet myself.' She met Janet's eyes. 'No, I haven't – My waters have broken so that's it – we're on our own, Jan.'

'No, you ain't,' Nellie's voice was cheerful as she walked down the hall towards them. 'I thought you might surprise us, Peggy love – I've delivered a few babies in my time. We never had the money fer doctors where I lived. I used to help all the young mothers, especially them what went into a quick labour.'

Peggy tried to smile, but she knew Janet was anxious and she couldn't help being nervous herself. Having given birth twice, Peggy was able to cope with the pain and the stress, but she'd had a midwife in attendance both times and she'd been much younger. Her doctor had stressed the importance of her having a hospital confinement, but there was no use thinking about that now. Peggy bent double as she watched Nellie and Janet strip the bed and replace the sheets with old ones, placing towels underneath to save the mattress. Peggy had made provision for the baby, but she hadn't thought about what they might need for a home birth.

Nellie had no such worries. 'You get down to the kitchen and start the kettles boilin', and you'll need a clean bowl, plenty of soft towels and things for the baby,' she told Janet. 'I'm going to tie a tablecloth or somethin' to the bed rails so that you can 'ang on to it, Peggy. It 'elps to 'ave somethin' to pull on when you feel the pain and the need to push, but don't start pushin' just yet. Let me 'elp you into this nightdress and Janet can take them wet things out of the way…'

'Have you really helped several mothers give birth?' Peggy asked as Janet left to collect everything Nellie had instructed her to.

'I've not had any formal trainin', but the midwife down our way was a drunken slut and the mothers trusted me more than her.' Nellie smiled at her. 'Breathe deeply, Peggy love. Now pant, as hard as you can… that's it…'

'I could do with some gas and air…'

'You'll have to make do with the bed rope until the doctor gets here,' Nellie said. 'I hope someone has rung for him?'

'Mike was goin' to do that,' Peggy said.

'That's all right then.' Nellie grabbed her hand as she gave a cry of pain. 'I know it 'urts bad, love, but don't worry about not being in 'ospital. If the child is coming now, 'e or she is ready and you 'ave to accept it. You're strong. You will come through.'

Peggy's eyes stung with tears. 'But what about my baby? I want this child, Nellie. I'm frightened it might not survive if…'

'Of course it will,' Nellie said. 'His father was young and strong – 'e or she will be a survivor, you'll see…'

'Can I come in?' Maureen's voice asked from the doorway and they looked at her in surprise. 'I was passing and something made me call in. Janet has her hands full downstairs with Maggie. I brought the bowl and towels up, and here's a tablecloth for you, Nellie. Janet says the kettles are on ready for when we need them.'

'You can sit with Peggy while I go and scrub me 'ands,' Nellie said. 'We've sent for the doctor, because Peggy ought to be in the hospital, but I don't think he'll get 'ere in time. I know fer a fact the local midwife's pretty busy, because I saw her out on her rounds when I went out fer a paper earlier – and that means you and me are goin' ter 'ave to bring the child into the world. I know what I'm doin' but I'll need 'elp as Janet is busy downstairs... Besides, you were a nurse, so you'll be even better.'

'Of course I'll help,' Maureen said and smiled at Peggy. 'Grab my hand if you need to, love. I have helped with a few deliveries since I've been at the London...'

'Thank goodness you came,' Peggy said. 'Were you goin' anywhere special?'

'No, not really. Violet wanted to see both Gran and me, but Gran's gone on ahead and she has Tom with her, so she'll be fine. I can stop as long as you need me...'

'Thank you,' Peggy smiled at her and then gave a shout of pain. 'Oh, hell! That was bloody awful...'

'I'm just goin' to take a look, Peggy – can you lie back with your knees up for me like you do at the clinic? Let me see what's happenin'. Yes, that's all fine... it looks as if you're nearly there, love. You can start to push soon, but for now I just want you to breathe deeply, and when Nellie gets back, I'll pop to the bathroom and scrub my hands too...'

★

'I wanted to speak to both of you together,' Violet said, glaring at Hilda and Tom. 'Where is Maureen and what did you bring him for? This is nothin' to do with him…'

'Tom is 'ere for my sake, and I can deal with any business, Violet. What have you decided?'

'I'm 'andin' the shop and flat back to you on Saturday night,' Violet said. 'I don't want to run the shop and I've found somewhere I like better for a cheaper rent. I'll be movin' my furniture on Friday or Saturday.'

'Please yourself,' Hilda Jackson looked at her daughter-in-law with something between pity and contempt. 'What do you want to do about the stock?'

'I've signed that agreement the solicitor sent. That stuff is no good to me – and the sooner I'm out of this bloody place the better. If I'd known the truth, I'd never have come 'ere. I 'ad a good little business where I was, but Henry said we'd do better together, now I've got nothin'…'

'He didn't leave you penniless,' Hilda said and Violet looked away from her piercing look. 'A lot of people would think two hundred odd pounds in the bank plus the stock was a lot of money – and you've got your own savings. I'm certain Henry didn't touch those…'

'That's none of your business…' Violet muttered but looked uncomfortable. 'He wasn't all bad and I'm sorry he went the way he did… but you and that daughter of his never liked me.'

'Henry married you and he was my son. I'd have helped you if you'd been a better wife to him and kept a civil tongue in your head towards Maureen and me, but that's it then – you'll be on your way by the weekend and let me 'ave the key through the door.'

'You'll have the bloody locks changed anyway…'

'Yes, I shall,' Hilda said. 'As I told you the other day, Violet – I don't trust you and you've only got yourself to blame. However, I don't think either of us has been unfair to you.'

'You're so bloody superior,' Violet said. 'Don't think I'm payin' any rent for the time I've been 'ere, because I won't.'

'I wouldn't expect it.' Gran picked up her basket. 'Tom has an inventory of all the stuff. I wouldn't advise you to try takin' what doesn't belong to you, Violet. I think you would discover that the person you've sold it to would come after you with the law. Your money will be at the lawyer's office by this afternoon. You can collect it when you like.'

'You bitch,' Violet said. 'You're so bloody smug. I'll bet it's you who's buyin' that bloody stock. I hope you fall over and break your damned neck.'

Hilda looked straight at her. 'I shan't wish you luck, Violet. Folk make their own luck in this world and I dare say you'll get what you deserve...'

She left the sitting room, Tom following behind to guard her back. At the foot of the stairs, he looked at her. 'Shall I lock the stockroom door, Mrs Jackson? Mr Jackson had a new lock put on when Dad came here to work and I've got the only keys.'

'Good thinkin',' Hilda said and gave him an approving smile. 'Better leave what money there is in the till though, because its hers by right. I don't want anything Henry left her – but she'll take more than she's entitled to if she can.'

'I'll lock the door and keep the key,' Tom said. 'We can't stop her takin' stuff from the shelves though.'

'If she does, that's too bad,' Hilda said. 'I know she'll get her hands on anythin' she can – but I think we've stopped her from cheatin' us too badly...'

'Right,' Tom pocketed the keys. 'I can be here first thing on Sunday if you need me, Mrs Jackson. Is there anythin' you want me to do in the meantime?'

'Just please keep out of Violet's way. She would do you harm if she could, Tom. We'll all just stay away until she's gone…'

'Oh, Maureen… Nellie, thank you so much…' Peggy said, looking at the babies in her arms. 'I can't believe they're both here and all right… twins. I know the doctor at the clinic said I needed to go in for the birth, but I didn't pay much attention, because they make too much fuss up there – but he didn't say he thought it was twins.'

'Didn't it cross your mind?' Nellie asked. 'You got quite big quick, Peggy love. That's why I wasn't surprised when you went into labour early – I've known it to 'appen before with twins.'

'I did wonder, but I was too busy to dwell on the idea. They are all right, aren't they?'

'They're perfect,' Maureen said and touched the little boy's head. He seemed the weaker of the two to her mind, but was really beautiful, with fine pale curls on his head and blue eyes, whereas the girl had darker straight hair. 'I know you said you wanted to stay home now they're born, Peggy, but if the doctor says you should go to hospital you must, for the sake of the twins.'

'I'm feeling weary but all right,' Peggy said and yawned. She let Maureen take the babies and put them in the cot. There was only one so it was a snug fit, but the twins seemed to like being together and the little boy curled against his sister, as if seeking comfort from her presence. 'But if you think I should go in for the twin's safety...' She looked a bit anxiously at Maureen.

'We'll see what the doctor says when he gets here,' Maureen heard something and went out into the hall to look. 'Janet is bringin' him up now, Peggy. He will be surprised to discover it's all over.'

'Well now, Mrs Ashley,' the doctor said as he entered the bedroom. 'I'm sorry to be so long coming – but it seems you managed perfectly well without me.'

'Only because Nellie and Maureen were here,' Peggy admitted, smiling at the man who had often attended her family in the past. 'Maureen is a nurse and Nellie has some experience of bringin' babies into the world...'

'Right, well I'd better examine you – perhaps everyone would leave, except you, Nurse Hart.'

Maureen nodded. 'I haven't taken my midwifery yet, Doctor Martin, but I helped with a few births at the London. Peggy's delivery was quick and straightforward, but the boy was born last... fifteen minutes or so after his sister...'

Doctor Martin gave Maureen a significant look and proceeded to examine Peggy, nodding his approval. 'A very small amount of bleeding, I see, but we'll keep an eye on that – and I'll call back later this evening to check your progress.' He turned to look at the babies in their cot, pulling the blanket back to examine them. 'They look fine, all their fingers and toes... but the boy is a little smaller and seems to have some difficulty with his breathing.'

'I thought he looked all right...' Peggy sat forward anxiously. 'You said they were both perfect...?' Her gaze went to Maureen.

'Perfectly formed,' the doctor agreed, 'but the girl has obviously dominated in the womb and the boy is a little weaker. Nothing to worry about, Mrs Ashley, but he may need help with his breathing, if I'm not mistaken.' He warmed his stethoscope by breathing on it and placed it on the child's tiny chest. 'Yes, it looks as if there is an irregular beat... I think we need to have this little one under observation for a while, do a few tests. I'm going to arrange for an ambulance – and I think we'll take all of you in, just to be on the safe side.'

'Yes, yes, if you think we should.' Peggy reached for Maureen's hand, her eyes brimming with tears. 'I couldn't bear to lose him...'

'I don't think you will lose the baby,' Doctor Martin told her with a brisk nod. 'However, he is showing some weakness and so we'll keep him under observation for a few days, and you can stay with him and his sister. We'll see how things progress, but hopefully, it should only be a couple of days at the most.' He glanced at Maureen. 'If you would just walk to the top of the stairs with me, please?'

'I'll be back in a minute, Peggy,' Maureen told her and followed the doctor from the room.

'You'd noticed the signs?' he asked as she accompanied him to the head of the stairs.

'I thought he seemed a little weaker and he was a bit blue at first, but he responded to a slap and started breathin' immediately.'

'We must hope there is no internal damage,' he said and nodded. 'No point in speculating, but it's unfortunate – an older mother, twins and a home birth. As you know, Nurse Hart, some babies are born with a little hole in the heart, which closes later of its own accord, but they do need a little extra looking after until we're sure there's no permanent damage. It's a mercy that you were there, nurse.'

'Nellie has more experience as a midwife than me, but it might have been better if we'd got her to hospital.'

'She would probably have given birth in the taxi. No, I have no fault to find with the delivery, Mrs Hart. I just hope the child pulls through.'

Maureen nodded, thanked him and returned to the bedroom. Peggy was leaning over the cot, stroking the boy's forehead, tears on her cheeks.

'Get back in bed, love,' Maureen said. 'You shouldn't be up yet. Try not to worry too much; we don't want you to start haemorrhaging. It happens that babies born second like that sometimes need a bit of help, but it isn't often necessary to do more than observe and perhaps give oxygen. Hospital really is the best place for him, Peggy.'

'I can't lose him, Maureen. I want both my babies... I feel guilty, as if I should've known sooner and got to a hospital for the birth – perhaps not done quite as much...'

'It probably wouldn't have been any different,' Maureen told her. 'I suspect that his sister hogged most of the room inside you and he's smaller, not quite as strong. We can't know if there's any damage, but it certainly isn't your fault, love. Besides, sometimes everythin' is fine after a few hours. I remember hearin' about it in a lecture, but don't know too much about it because I didn't get to do my midwifery course, though I did study the books and I've assisted with an emergency birth twice at the London, but it often isn't serious or life-threatenin'.' She crossed her fingers behind her back, because the condition could be serious but she wanted to save her friend anguish over the little boy. 'I'm sure he'll be fine once they give him some oxygen.'

'Thank goodness you were here,' Peggy said. 'I hadn't

noticed anythin' – and I don't think Nellie had either. She thought they were both perfect.'

'They are perfect,' Maureen said and squeezed her hand. 'You just rest for a while now, love, and then try to feed them. Jan will bring you a cup of tea – she's longing to see her new sister and brother – and the ambulance should be here by the time you've finished. Once the hospital doctors have a look at Freddie, they'll soon sort him out...'

Maureen stayed with Peggy until the ambulance came and then went to the hospital with her. She didn't leave until Peggy was settled in bed with a cot beside her, in which Fay was sleeping peacefully. Freddie had been taken to an intensive care ward for children and was being given oxygen. Peggy had shed a few tears as he was carried away, but then the nurse had given her a gentle sedative and Maureen had left her sleeping.

It was past five in the evening when Maureen finally got back to Gran's. She didn't notice at first, but as she got close, she noticed that lights were on all over the house and a policeman was standing outside. Maureen ran the last few steps to the house.

'Shirley and my grandmother – are they all right?'

'A little bit shocked, love,' the young policeman said, 'but fortunately the bugger had gone when she got back... Left a mess for her though. My boss is talkin' to her now.'

Maureen went inside and knew immediately that the house had been ransacked. The coats in the hall had been thrown down, drawers in an old chest pulled open and the contents pulled out.

Maureen went swiftly into the kitchen, where Gran was talking to a police inspector. He had his notebook out and was writing something in it.

'Are you all right, Gran?'

'Yes, I'm fine, love – how is Peggy?' Maureen didn't need to ask how she knew; news spread fast in the lanes and everyone would know by now about Peggy's twins.

'She's in hospital. One of the twins needed a little treatment,' Maureen said, glancing round at the mess. 'We've been burgled...'

'You are Mrs Maureen Hart?' the police inspector asked and she nodded. 'I'm Inspector Mark Baxter. Your grandmother thinks you may be the worst victim of the robbery. Your room has been turned over and she believes some items of silver and jewellery may be missing.'

'Oh no, most of that is my mum's stuff. She left me all her bits and pieces and they were in the wardrobe upstairs...' Maureen stared at him in distress. 'How did they know we weren't here? We seldom leave the house empty all day...' She glanced round. 'Where is Shirley?'

'I got back at three-thirty to be here for Shirley, but when I saw the mess I asked Anne to take her home with 'er and give 'er some tea, and then I went down the corner and rang the police...' Gran said and shook her head. 'I couldn't believe it...'

'It must have been such a shock for you, but I'm glad Anne is takin' care of Shirley. I don't want her to see this mess...' Maureen managed a smile. 'As long as no one was hurt, nothin' else matters. I'm sorry about Mum's things, but I don't think anythin' was very valuable. It's just upsettin'. We don't leave much cash in the house – you didn't, Gran?'

'No, I never have more than what's in my purse and I had that with me. I keep my valuables and the money in the bank – and as it happens, I had the bank book in my handbag too. So apart from a little silver and garnet brooch that my mother gave me, I don't think I've lost much. The silver candlesticks in the front room have gone, and the brass carriage clock that was a weddin' present, and a silver teapot, but I suppose we might be insured for those…'

'Oh, Gran, I'm so sorry,' Maureen said and gave her a little hug.

'I'm not bothered much,' Gran sniffed. 'It's a pity about yer mother's bits though. I suppose that's what he took.'

'I'll go up and look,' Maureen said. 'I'll make a list for you, inspector…'

'Yes, please, miss…'

Maureen ran upstairs and gasped in horror as she saw the mess. Whoever had done it had been in a hurry or meant to cause distress. Several little pieces of dressing-table glass had been smashed and a china ornament. Maureen saw the little jewel case in which her mother's small bits and pieces were stored had been thrown down and was empty of its contents. She went to the wardrobe and discovered immediately that the box containing a pair of silver Corinthian-column candlesticks, a silver tea and coffee set, and a set of silver coffee spoons, had also gone. Gran had told her to save them for her home and so she'd left them wrapped up, together with a pretty china tea-service.

Remembering that she'd worn her favourite brooch the last time she'd had her best dress on, Maureen looked and saw it was still there. The thief had been in too much of a hurry to look at all her clothes and had gone for the obvious. Tears of relief stung her eyes, because it was really the only thing that meant much to her; her mother had loved it, too, and so it meant more than all the rest.

She went back to the kitchen and told them which articles were missing: a heavy silver cross and chain and a thin silver bangle, a gold locket and chain and some gold earrings, also the silver candlesticks and other silver items, and her best china tea-service.

'What do you estimate the stolen goods are worth, Mrs Hart?'

'The thief missed my best brooch, which was pinned to a dress – the rest might be worth a hundred and fifty pounds altogether, perhaps two hundred at most. It's the sentimental value that's more important and the idea that someone would do this.'

'We've never had this happen round here before,' Gran said. 'When I was first married we never locked our doors, even if we went to the pub…'

'I'm afraid there are always a few bad ones about,' the inspector said. 'Well, thank you for your help – I think we're lookin' at about three to four hundred pounds havin' gone missin' in total, which is actually quite a large crime, Mrs Hart – Mrs Jackson. I'll make my report and we'll see what we can do, but the sort of things they've taken aren't easy to trace.'

'This is the second break-in round here recently,' Maureen said, 'but they arrested the other man…'

'You're talkin' of the break-in at Mulberry Lane…' Inspector Baxter said and frowned. 'We did have the man in custody, but you ought to have been told – he made a break for it when he was being transferred to a military base outside London and we haven't managed to track him down. He may well return to his old haunts, but I doubt this was his work. Knocker James will be in hiding. He's a deserter and if the Army get him now, I don't think much of his chances.' He glanced at his watch. 'I think this was someone else – and I don't believe it was a random theft. I believe this was planned. Is there anyone who knew you would both be out of the house?'

Maureen and Gran looked at each other. 'We were asked to visit someone this mornin' at half-past nine...'

'Who is the person who asked you to visit?'

'Mrs Violet Jackson – my father's second wife,' Maureen said, looking thoughtful.

'Violet couldn't have done this...' Gran said.

'Violet always thought she was entitled to Mum's things when she married Dad...' Maureen hesitated and then raised her eyes to the inspector. 'We have a dispute with her, because she thought my father owned the shop in Mulberry Lane, but it always belonged to Gran...'

'And she resents that?' the inspector nodded and made another note. 'It is unlikely that she did this herself – but she may have got someone to do it for her...'

'I don't think she knows anyone who would do this...' Gran said.

'Alice told me she has been meetin' a man – at a café on Commercial Road. It's that posh place where they sell coffee and cake... and she met him there more than once.' Maureen shook her head. 'It's hard to believe that she would agree to this, however disgruntled she was over the shop.'

Inspector Baxter made more notes, asked some questions about Alice and then took his leave. Gran and Maureen looked at each other and sighed.

'You'd better get the locks changed on the shop inside as soon as possible and then outside once Violet has gone for good,' Maureen said, 'and make sure the stock is intact before your lawyer pays her the cheque.'

'Surely, Violet couldn't be behind this?'

'Maybe she didn't plan it, but I'll bet she knows who did,' Maureen said. 'Whoever did this went for Mum's bits and pieces, but they were lookin' for money too. It's just as well you never kept anythin' much in the house.'

'I've just remembered,' Gran said. 'I'd put the money for the gas in a jar in the pantry…' She went bustling off to look and came back shaking her head. 'It was only five pounds in change, but it has gone.'

'Oh well, I suppose that just shows you need to put your money somewhere safe. I never dreamed anyone would do this…'

'Only an outsider would,' Gran said and scowled. 'It has to be Violet behind it – I'll be glad to see the back of her, and I'll tell my solicitor to wait until I'm sure she hasn't pinched the stock before I pay her…'

Chapter 19

'I'm so sorry this happened to you,' Anne said when she brought Shirley back at about six that evening. 'Can I help you clear up?'

'We've got some of it straight,' Maureen said. 'I did Shirley's room first. Luckily, they didn't take anythin' of hers. Gran tidied the kitchen and we've just shut the door on the livin' room until the insurance people come – though the police say they will take their report as gospel. I hope Gran gets her money back, but I wasn't insured for Mum's things. I'm not bothered about their value – just that they were hers.'

'It's awful when something like this happens,' Anne said. 'I've just got a few things of my mum's and some of my aunt's bits and pieces but I'd hate to lose them.'

'Well, it's done now and at least no one was hurt.'

'Do you have any idea who did it?'

'No, not really,' Maureen said, because she and Gran had decided it was best not to comment until the police caught the thief – if they ever did. 'We'll have the locks repaired and move on. I'm glad I didn't leave the money for the baby in the house. I banked it last week because I thought that was sensible – even a few pounds are a big loss when you're savin' for a baby. Gran had put five pounds away for the gas, and of course that has gone too.'

'Rotten devils!' Anne said. 'If either of you are short, I can let you have a few quid…' She moved forward and hugged Maureen. 'I really am sorry, love.'

'Thanks, but we're all right,' Maureen said and returned Anne's hug. 'Gran has got a little bit in the bank and I get Gordon's wage every few weeks, so I'll manage. Thankfully, Shirley's little bit of money is in the Post Office and her book was tucked away in a drawer, but the thief didn't go through her things.'

'Well, I'd better get to the pub,' Anne said. 'Janet asked if I would look after things this evening while she visits her mum. It's wonderful news that Peggy had twins – but a shame that the little boy isn't quite right.'

'The hospital will do a few tests, but he'll probably be fine in a few days…' Maureen said hopefully.

'Might just be the weaker twin,' Anne nodded. 'I've got twins in my class at school. One of them is as bright as a button and the other one is just that little bit slower…'

'Yes, it happens sometimes if the second birth is delayed…' Maureen sighed. 'We'll just have to pray he gets better soon' She shook her head sadly. 'We can't do anythin' except be there when she needs us, Anne.'

'And pray for them all,' Anne said and a little sigh escaped her. 'Peggy is lucky to have them. I was hoping I might have fallen for a baby, but I haven't…'

'That's a pity,' Maureen said, because Anne looked so sad at that moment. 'But Kirk will come home when he can and perhaps next time…'

'Yes, let's hope so,' Anne said. 'As I said, I'd better go – take care, Maureen, and don't do too much.'

Maureen went to the door with her friend and then returned to the kitchen. It was time for Shirley to have her milk, after which she was allowed to read one of her books for an hour or so in bed. Maureen would take her up and talk to her for a while to make sure she was not anxious or upset, and then finish clearing up her own room, which was much the worst, as though the thief had had it in for her.

Anne was thoughtful as she walked through the lanes to the pub. There wasn't much artificial light about, because if a warden saw a light showing he'd bang on the door and threaten the householder with a large fine, but a sliver of a moon made it easy enough to see your way if you knew where you were going. She was pleased that Peggy had come through the birth of her twins all right but she was concerned for the little boy, who had something wrong with his breathing. Peggy had done so much for everyone in the lanes and she didn't deserve to lose one of her babies.

Anne had been disappointed when she realised that she wasn't having Kirk's child. She'd hoped so much that she might have fallen pregnant on that wonderful honeymoon and it made her wonder if she was able to have a child... But no, that was silly. A lot of women were married for ages before they conceived and she'd only had a few days with her husband.

Although, Peggy hadn't had much longer with her American lover, so the amount of time didn't always matter. Maureen had been with Rory for longer, but she'd fallen for a child she hadn't really wanted at the start. Now she was looking forward to it, as she should, and she was lucky after all because Gordon had offered her marriage.

Why did children come so easily for some and not for others? Anne's aunt had never given birth, though she'd miscarried several times.

'I'm just not made for childbirth,' she told Anne when she'd grown up. 'We wanted them, but we weren't lucky – but then we had you, and you've been a blessing to us, Anne.'

Anne knew she'd been lucky that her mother's sister and her husband had taken her in as a young girl after her parents' deaths. Yet now she wondered if infertility might run in the family. Her mother had only managed to give birth once, though she might have had more had she not died so tragically.

Anne had hoped she might be lucky and conceive Kirk's child on honeymoon but perhaps that was foolish. They'd only been together for a short time, but still Anne had hoped. She was just too impatient! Seeing her friends preparing for the births of their babies had made Anne more conscious of her situation, and of course it would be such a comfort in these perilous times to have her husband's child. She wanted a big family and she knew that Kirk's uncle was hoping for good news, but it hadn't happened.

Sighing, Anne walked round the back of the pub. She just had to be patient. As Maureen said, Kirk would come back one day and perhaps they would be lucky then…

Peggy was sitting up in bed when Janet walked into the ward. She smiled and held her hands out to her daughter.

'Thank you for comin' to see me, darling,' she said. 'Is everythin' all right at home?'

'Yes, of course, Mum,' Janet said, reaching down to kiss her cheek. 'Anne is helpin' Helen in the bar this evenin' and Nellie is on hand if needed. I wanted to see how you're gettin' on – and the twins…'

'Fay is perfect, sleeping peacefully, as you can see,' Peggy said. 'Freddie is still in intensive care; they're giving him oxygen and there's no real news, except that he's holdin' his own so far.'

'You've made up your mind about the names then?'

'Yes, well, it was just up to me this time and I wanted somethin' different.' Peggy smiled. 'I think Fay is goin' to be a very determined young lady, and Freddie is a dear, so I thought he needed a friendly name… it's also Able's middle name, at least Frederick is, but I couldn't call a baby that…'

'Oh, Mum…' Janet's sympathy made Peggy's eyes water.

'Frederick doesn't sound right, does it?' she said, determined not to break down now.

'Of course not.' Janet smiled, recognising her mother's determination. 'If you'd called him Frederick everyone would say Freddie while he's a boy and Fred when he gets older. Fay can't be changed really, can it?'

'That's what I thought,' Peggy said. 'Everyone always changes children's names. You're Jan, and Philip is Pip, and Laurence is Laurie – and I was once Margaret…'

'I know and that's why I called Maggie by a name everyone could use easily. If I'd said Margaret she might have been Meg or Peggy, but I like Maggie best so I decided to put it on the birth certificate.'

'Well, meet Fay,' Peggy said as the baby gave a little wail. 'I imagine she wants a feed. Give her up to me, will you, love?'

'Yes, of course,' Janet said and lifted the baby from the cot, giving her to Peggy. 'Hello, sister: Little Fay. What sort of a person will you be then?'

As if in answer, Fay let out a long wail that went on and on, until she settled in Peggy's arms and began to nuzzle. She sucked contentedly and looked up at her mother with the bluest eyes imaginable, her cluster of dark curls half covering her head. Apart from the colour of her hair, she was very obviously Peggy's child, but when she was fed and Janet took her mother to the intensive care ward in a wheelchair, Fay sleeping in her mother's arms, she saw Fay's twin brother and the differences were clear. Freddie had fair hair and his eyes were a softer shade of blue. He was also smaller and seemed a little frail to Janet, whose heart immediately went out to him.

She placed a hand on her mother's shoulder as Peggy reached out to touch the baby inside the oxygen cabinet. Seeing his eyelids flicker, Janet smiled.

'He knows your touch, Mum. He'll be all right – he's a fighter just like you.'

'Yes, he's a fighter,' Peggy said. 'The doctor told me they're not sure why his heart didn't close as it should straight away, but he thinks Freddie will pull through, because he has a strong spirit. Like Able. You didn't really know him, Jan, but I know that life hadn't always treated him well. I think he'd had to struggle against somethin' – though he never told me what. We were only just gettin' to know each other...'

'He had a lovely smile and I liked the way he looked at you,' Janet said and smiled. 'Able loved you, Mum. He really did and I wish he was here with you now.'

'Thank you, darling, but even if he was alive he would probably be fightin' somewhere,' Peggy said with a sigh.

'Able wanted his country in the war. He would be glad that it happened – although not the way it did. That was a terrible and cowardly thing to do at Pearl Harbor.'

'Yes, it was, too many lives lost – but perhaps it will shorten the war and save countless others... that's what Mike thinks anyway.'

Peggy looked up at her from the chair. 'Has Mike started to remember the past?' She'd hoped it might happen once he was out of hospital and living with them.

'Not really, but he's accepted his life; we walked down to the Docks and visited the yard where he worked on the ships. Several men came up and spoke to him, and he talked to them, listened and seemed really intent. I think he feels that is where he belongs once he goes back to work...'

'Will he have to return to the navy?'

'No, I don't think so. He'll go for a medical, probably in the summer, but expects to be honourably discharged,' Janet said. 'Look, Freddie has his eyes open. He's looking at us. I think he knows us, Mum... and he's seen Fay.' The twins were looking at each other now, both wide awake.

'Yes, how could he fail to feel the love flowin' towards him,' Peggy said and looked at the nurse who had come to adjust something on the little cabinet that was helping her son to breathe. 'He looks better this evening, nurse.'

'Yes, he does,' the nurse agreed. 'Doctor will be round first thing in the morning and he'll let you know what progress your son has made, Mrs Ashley. I think you should return to bed now.'

'Yes, but my daughter wanted to see her brother – and I was anxious about Freddie.'

'Lovely name,' the nurse said, smiling at them. 'Well, I'm pretty sure there's not much to worry about in his case,

Mrs Ashley. We'll let you know tomorrow when you can take him home.'

'I know they're tryin' to take care of me,' Peggy said as Janet wheeled her back to the ward. 'But I'd rather be at home – the way you were, with your friend lookin' after you when I came down...'

Jan nodded. 'I was just thinkin' about Rosemary Jamieson this mornin'. She wrote and asked both Mike and I to go and stay with her at her home in Devon in the summer.'

'You should go – if Mike wants to,' Peggy said. 'Perhaps some contact with people associated with the navy base at Portsmouth might trigger his memory.'

'I'm not sure that's a good idea,' Janet said thoughtfully. 'He had a bad dream last night, Mum. He kicked and cried out, but when I woke him he couldn't remember what it was about...' She paused. 'I'm pretty sure he's on the verge of rememberin' somethin' awful but he's fightin' it,' Janet sighed. 'I'm not sure which is worst – that he should never remember me and our love or that he should remember all the horror of the attack...'

'Are you happy the way things are now?'

'Pretty much,' Janet said. 'Some things could be better – but I don't want him to be haunted by whatever was in that dream the other night. He was sweatin', callin' out and fightin'. It might be worse for him if he remembers it all.'

Peggy got back into bed and looked at her daughter sadly. 'I don't know what to hope for, love. I just want you to be happy.'

'I know I'm lucky, Mum. I've got Mike home and he's almost back to normal physically, and I've got Maggie. So many people have lost everythin'. I'll keep my fingers crossed and pray things don't go wrong – and I'll be prayin' for

Freddie tonight. He needs our prayers more than I do at the moment.'

'Yes, he does,' Peggy agreed, but then smiled at her daughter. 'I've got a feelin' he'll pull through, and so will you, however bad things get. All my children are strong. You write to your friend and tell her you'll go down. The best thing for both of you is to get on with your lives, Jan. Enjoy each day and fit in as much as you can.'

'Yes, I shall,' Janet said and bent to kiss her mother's cheek. 'We might go down in May or June perhaps. That gives Mike a little longer to recover – and you'll be back on your feet by then, Mum.'

'I'm lucky to have so many friends and helpers,' Peggy said. 'Helen, Maureen, Nellie, Anne and you are wonderful – all of you have done so much to make things possible. I think I must try and find someone to work in the bar on a permanent basis, though. Maureen won't be able to help much longer, and Helen is only a temporary guest, even though she says she is never going back to her husband.'

'Are you lookin' for a young woman or an older man?' Janet asked. 'Men are useful when it comes to humping heavy barrels about...'

'Yes, I know,' Peggy agreed. 'I think I'd rather have a woman about your age or a bit older, Jan. Older men can be very stubborn and set in their ways... and Tom will always give me a hand. He'll be able to manage the barrels, once his shoulder is better.'

'He came over this afternoon and offered to do anythin' I needed. I asked him to bring some wine up from the cellar and to put a new barrel on the tap. He soon had it up and runnin' – and he wouldn't accept payment. He said it was the least he could do, because you'd done so much for him.' Janet looked thoughtful. 'He seems to think Hilda Jackson is goin' to open the shop again next Monday and he'll be runnin' it.'

'Good. Everyone will be glad of it,' Peggy said, nodded and yawned. 'You get off now, love. I'm goin' to get some sleep.'

'All right, Mum. I'm glad you're better. It gave us all a bit of a fright when the babies came early and you were in such pain.'

'The nurse here told me it probably made things easier for me – but I shall always wish my pregnancy had gone full term and saved poor little Freddie from havin' to fight for his life...'

'We're all prayin' for him, Mum,' Janet said and bent to kiss her mother again.

She was thoughtful as she left the hospital, shivering at the drop in temperature.

Mike had promised that he would try to help in the bar while Janet was out. He was getting better at meeting strangers and accepting that some of them had been good friends once. Janet had been trying to find another place for them to live, but so far she'd been offered two smelly and damp rooms, which she'd turned down. Besides, Mike liked living over the pub and perhaps he would be content to go on as they were for the time being. It would make things easier all round – at least until her father came home.

Janet had telephoned Pip at his base and told him about the twins. He'd said all the right things, but she thought he was still a bit miffed over the whole situation; she'd also sent a letter to her father at the address he'd given them. She didn't know whether he would even bother to come home. The twins weren't his, so perhaps he wouldn't feel it was necessary, though he'd promised Peggy he would come when he could. Yet perhaps it was better he didn't, because he was sure to resent the twins and would probably take it out on his wife.

She was glad that there was no prospect of her father living at home for the time being, because it might be awkward. She wasn't sure that she could trust him not to distress Mike, because they hadn't got on well together in the past.

Janet wasn't ready to move out of the pub yet. It was easy just to help out in the bar, and there was always someone around to keep an eye on Maggie, and now the twins. Her mother would need help with them; one day she and Mike would need to look for a new home – but perhaps not until this wretched war was over…

Chapter 20

'Five bloody quid in coins, some rubbish jewellery and a few silver bits. I went to all that trouble and I'll be lucky if I get fifty quid from the pawnbroker,' Bryan said as he stood in her parlour and glared at Violet. 'I thought you told me she'd got a lot of valuables?'

'Her father said she'd taken all the silver and jewellery with her. I thought it was worth a lot, the way he went on about it – but I'm beginning to realise he misled me on everythin'...' Violet looked at him gloomily because there was no satisfying him. She'd already given him most of the money she'd saved over the years and he was demanding more. Despite her resentment towards her mother-in-law and Maureen, she felt a bit guilty that he'd got the idea to rob them from her. She was the one who had told him that they had money and jewellery. 'I haven't got any more for you anyway...'

'You mean Henry changed his will?' Bryan looked suspicious.

'No – but he didn't own the shop. That belongs to Hilda and she's given it to the bitch. They wanted a pound a week rent if I stayed here and kept the shop, so I've told them I'm leavin'. I've found a little place in Bermondsey and I'm movin' there at the weekend'

'Sod it!' Bryan glared at her as if he hated her. 'So there's no money? No property to sell?'

'Just me furniture and forty quid,' Violet lied, because it was the most she was prepared to give him. 'I'm sorry, son, I thought for sure the shop and house would be mine once he'd gone...'

'You bloody silly woman,' Bryan said and raised his arm, striking her across the side of her face and making her lip bleed. 'You led me to believe I would be able to pay my debts by next week. Do you know what they'll do to me if I don't come up with the cash?' Fear and anger were in his eyes but his expression settled into contempt as he looked at her.

Violet put a hand to her face. He'd hurt her and at that moment, she hated him. She'd been so pleased when he'd written to her and asked her to meet him, but all he'd wanted was money. He was a thief, a coward who had avoided the Army draft, by pretending to have a weak chest – and now he wanted her last penny. Well, he wasn't going to get it. 'I'll give you forty pounds to get you away from London – but that's every last penny you'll get from me...'

'You cheatin' bitch...' Bryan yelled and grabbed her by the throat. 'You're lyin' to me. I know you've got thousands tucked away. Stands to reason with a shop like this and your own business... You'd better hand it over now or you'll be sorry...'

'I've told you,' Violet said, standing up to him even though she was feeling afraid. 'I can only give you forty pounds... if you want anythin' more you can break the inner lock and get into the shop and pinch them fags and whatever else you can carry.' Her defiance might be foolish, but she'd reached the end of her tether and there was only one way to treat a bully; she'd learned that from his father. Unless you stood firm they just kept on hitting you. 'And if you...'

Violet didn't get any further because the blow he struck sent her flying. She made contact with the sideboard and felt the pain in her back. Then he was at her again, his hand about her throat, squeezing tightly. She clawed at his hands, trying to pull them away as she struggled to breathe. The room was going dark around her and she felt pain in her chest and her head as the blackness closed in and then he suddenly let her go and thrust her away. Violet's head struck the corner of the sideboard before she fell like a log to the floor.

'Wake up, you bitch...' Bryan bent over her and pulled her up by the shoulders. Her head lolled to one side and a thin dribble of saliva came from the corner of her mouth. 'Where did you put the money?'

Leaving her lying there, vaguely conscious of pain and of his ranting, Bryan began searching the flat, pulling open drawers and tipping everything onto the floor. He went into the bedrooms, emptying the wardrobes and throwing everything about. He found a few items of his mother's jewellery and pocketed them, but there was no cash anywhere. At last, in his mother's handbag, he found a post office book in her name with fifty pounds recorded. He scowled as he thrust it into his jacket pocket. He would've preferred cash because he would need a woman to pretend to be his mother to fetch the cash for him, but he wasn't finished yet. He would come back another day and make her give him whatever remained, but in the meantime, he might as well grab the fags and anything else of value downstairs...

'I'm going to pop into the hospital and take Peggy a card and a few flowers tomorrow afternoon,' Anne said to Helen that evening before she left to walk the short distance to Mavis's house. 'Would you like me to put your name on them as well?'

'Thanks, but I'll get a card and a box of chocs and pop up there in the morning,' Helen said. 'Peggy has been very good to me so I'd like to visit her. I'll go early and be back before the lunchtime rush…'

'I'm sure she'll be pleased,' Anne said. 'Goodnight then. It's been a busy night. I shall be glad to get home and find my bed.'

'Yes. I'm going to have a word with Janet and go up myself.'

Anne went out into the chilly night air. She hoped Peggy was all right and the twins. Her friend was an older mother and that didn't always turn out well and it made Anne worry about her own chances. She was several years younger but Peggy had already given birth twice; it would be Anne's first – if she ever became pregnant.

Her throat caught as she tried to hold back the foolish tears, but she missed Kirk so much and she worried about him. If only she was carrying his child… As she crossed the road, Anne saw someone leave the side passage next to Jackson's grocery shop. She didn't think it was Tom, it was definitely a man, but she supposed Violet Jackson was entitled to have who she liked to her flat. It wasn't Anne's business so she didn't think any more about it as she reached her lodgings.

She walked into Mavis's house and paused to take off her coat. The elderly lady came into the hall and smiled at her.

'You're home, dear. I stayed up to tell you that I took your letters up to your room and put them on the bed. Your dear husband has sent you three letters all at once…'

'Oh, thank you, Mavis.' Anne smiled, feeling pleasure at the treat awaiting her. 'I expect they've been delayed in the post. It's always happening…'

Her heart beating faster with anticipation, she ran up the stairs not even hearing Mavis when she asked if she wanted a cup of cocoa…

Tom had just put the kettle on when he heard the knock at the door, but before he could get there, it opened and a man walked in. He felt ice prickles at his nape, because for the last couple of days he'd sensed he was being watched, and he was about to grab a poker to arm himself when he saw who it was.

'Dad!' he cried and rushed towards him gladly. 'What are you doin' here? You haven't gone AWOL, have you?'

Jack Barton chuckled and then grinned as he tousled his son's hair. 'No, son – as if I would! The Army is the best thing that ever happened to me, apart from you and Sam. I love it. I may stop in when this is all over…'

'It's good to see you,' Tom said and gave him a fervent hug. 'How long have you got then?'

'A week,' Jack answered. 'We've finished our basic trainin' and after this, we're being sent all over the place. I've put in for keepin' the Army movin' – gettin' stores and supplies to wherever they're goin'. I'm gettin' on a bit for front line duty, but I'm good at organising stuff. It will probably mean I'm based over here for the next few months, until I know what I'm doin', and then they'll send me out to wherever I'm needed.'

'Does that mean you won't have to fight?' Tom asked hopefully.

'Don't know about that side of things,' Jack said. 'Wherever our boys are, they rely on chaps like me to get what they need where they need it. I'm doin' firearms trainin' because whatever I do, I may have to use it once I'm out there. I've taken me drivin' test and passed with flyin' colours – and that means I'll be fit for more kinds of work when the war is over. Then with this other stuff... well, who knows.'

'I reckon the Army is a good career,' Tom agreed. 'If I was old enough I'd be in now, but they won't take me yet.'

'I should think not either,' Jack said. 'You stop and look after Mr Jackson and Maureen...' Tom's smile vanished and Jack stared at him. 'Somethin' wrong?'

'Mr Jackson died,' Tom said. 'He fell down the stairs at the shop and I found him. The doctor said he probably had another stroke just before he fell.'

'I'm sorry to hear that,' Jack said and shook his head. 'Will Violet Jackson be keepin' the shop on?'

'Don't think so,' Tom glanced over his shoulder, even though he knew no one was there. 'She's been a bit of a so-and-so to Maureen and Mrs Jackson... I don't know it all, Dad, but I think Hilda Jackson is takin' the shop on, with Maureen and me lookin' after it for the moment – same as before in a way, but no one livin' over the shop, unless she gets a tenant...' He poured boiling water into the large brown teapot. 'Hilda had me there while the locksmith put extra locks on the shop door and the stockroom. I think Violet has gone, because I didn't see any lights upstairs last night or the night before come to think of it – but she hasn't taken her furniture yet... leastwise, I ain't seen the van.'

'When are you goin' back there?'

'I thought I might go round Hilda's this mornin' and ask her if she wants me to go in and do a bit of clearin' up before we open. She told me to stop away, but we're supposed to open up tomorrow – so maybe she'd like me to go in, even though it is Sunday. I reckon Violet must've done a flit. Although she wouldn't get a van out on a Saturday to move her stuff, unless it's her fancy man...' Tom grinned. 'Alice reckons she's got one and he's years younger than her...'

'Alice says more than she should at times,' Jack said. 'This bloke she's meetin' is probably her son by her first husband', he remarked guessing correctly.

'Yes, Alice did say it might be,' Tom said and cleared his throat, then looked into his father's eyes. 'Alice is all right, Dad. She took me in when this place was done over. I've cleared up what I can, but it's a good thing Mum is still in the infirmary, because I can't afford to get the suite covered yet...'

'That was her pride and joy,' Jack shook his head, looking round as he noticed the damage Tom couldn't repair. 'I couldn't believe it when you wrote and told me about them diamonds you found and what Peggy did for yer. They must 'ave been somethin' special, I reckon, to make that Knocker go to such lengths to get 'em. The coppers got him, didn't they, son?'

'Yeah, they got him, but the bugger tricked the police officer into lettin' him out for a pee on a country road and he legged it across some fields. He's a deserter, Dad, but they know he's worn his uniform round here to make out he's doin' his bit. If the Army get him now, I reckon they'll shoot him for sure.'

'Have they got any idea where he is now?' Jack frowned. 'I don't like to think of you alone here at night if that devil is on the loose, Tom.'

'I only found out last night. Maureen came to tell me. The inspector told her when they investigated the break-in at her gran's…'

'Do they think he did it?'

'Maureen doesn't…' Tom said thoughtfully. 'I think it's to do with the shop, Dad – and all that stuff with Violet Jackson. It couldn't have been her, because Hilda was with her durin' the time the break-in 'appened but perhaps it was someone she knows…'

'I wish I was here to look after you, Tom.'

Tom grinned and shook his head. 'I've got big sticks and a poker 'andy in the house, Dad – and Doctor Blake gave me a police whistle. He said I was to use it if Knocker came after me again in the lane. The doc reckons it would scare the life out of him.'

'He's probably right,' Jack said, 'but I still feel bad about you bein' 'ere all alone – but unless your ma chooses to come 'ome I can't do much about it…'

'I was thinkin'…' Tom frowned as he marshalled his thoughts. 'Supposin' Ma doesn't come 'ome ever? Is it worth keepin' the 'ouse on? I mean, I could probably find a room – or even live over the shop. If you're goin' ter stay in the Army after the war…'

'I might do that,' Jack admitted. 'Your ma didn't want me home. I shall always remain close to you and often be in touch, son – as long as we both live – but if you want an Army life too…'

Tom nodded. 'I ain't sure yet, Dad. I might work up my job at the shop and perhaps take on odd jobs in me spare time, though it might be fun to try the Army for a while.'

'You've got my permission to make up your own mind about the 'ouse – if your mother won't come 'ome it's a waste for one. A lot of people could do with a 'ouse like this…'

'That's what I thought. I know a lot of people are lookin' for 'omes – so you don't mind what I do?'

'This will never be 'ome for me again, Tom. I secured it for you and yer ma, but if Tilly prefers to stay in the nursin' 'ome…'

'It's a horrible place,' Tom said. 'It's the old workhouse, so Nellie says. She went to visit a friend of hers there once and hated it. I asked to see Ma but they told me she didn't want visitors yet – so I 'aven't visited again. Do yer think I should?'

'If yer can stand it,' Jack said. 'I'll go and take her some of her clothes and a few sweets, but she probably won't want to see me either.'

'Dad…' Tom began, but there was a loud knocking at the door behind them and then it was flung open and Hilda Jackson rushed in looking as white as a sheet. 'Mrs Jackson – what's wrong? It isn't Maureen…?'

'No, she's all right, but I'm glad I didn't let her go to the shop alone this mornin'. You haven't been over today?'

'No – has somethin' 'appened?' Tom's spine tingled as he saw her eyes; she looked horrified.

'We've been burgled, but that's not the worst…' Hilda sat down suddenly in a chair. 'It's Violet. She's been attacked and there's blood all over her. Maureen is downstairs telephonin' the police, but I told her not to go up. Can you come, Tom, and tell us what you think is missin' from the shop?'

'Yes, of course I'll go over and help Maureen,' Tom said. 'Why don't you sit down and have a cup of hot sweet tea, Mrs Jackson? Dad will look after you – and he'll bring you over so you can talk to the police.'

'Yes, Hilda, do as the lad says,' Jack endorsed his son's advice. 'Sit down and get your breath. I'll get you a cup of sweet tea for the shock. It must 'ave been awful for you – finding 'er like that...'

'I've never liked her much,' Hilda said, 'but I never wanted this...'

'O' course you didn't,' Jack said. 'Get over there with Maureen, son, and make sure she doesn't go upstairs. A shock like that in 'er condition could cause a miscarriage.'

Tom grabbed his jacket and ran. He discovered Maureen in the back kitchen making a cup of Camp coffee, into which she poured some Carnation milk. The room was cold and smelled a bit damp, as if the fires had been out for a few days. When he went to take the tin of milk from her, he noticed that her hands were shaking and that she was staring at him in bewilderment.

'Take yer time,' Tom said in a voice gentle and wise beyond his years. 'You've had a shock.'

'I rang immediately and the ambulance is on its way, also the police,' she said and gave a little sob. 'She's lyin' on the floor in the sittin' room, Tom. Whoever it was cleared the shelves of cigarettes and took some chocolate, but there wasn't much else of value taken...' Maureen sipped her coffee. 'Did you want one...?'

'I've just had a cup of tea,' Tom said. 'Dad came home this mornin' on a week's leave. He's lookin' after Hilda, givin' her sweet tea.'

'Violet didn't bring the key last night as she promised, but we'd got one ourselves so we came round to take a look. Gran went upstairs alone when she saw the inner door was open. Someone had broken the new locks we'd put on that door, Tom – but he was already inside the house, because the back door to the outside hasn't been damaged. That means Violet knew whoever it was that killed her…'

'Do you think she might be dead then?'

'I don't know. Gran gave a little cry and came down the stairs faster than I've seen her move for years, but she wouldn't let me go up…' Maureen broke off as they heard someone enter the shop. She went through and Tom followed her. He saw the police constable who was busily making notes in a little black book and listened in silence as Maureen gave her explanation.

'You didn't find your father's wife yourself then, madam?'

'No, my grandmother went up because she noticed the lock on the inner door, between the shop and the stairs to the flat, had been broken and I stopped to see what had been taken from the shelves – and then when she came down she told me not to go up, because of my condition.'

'Very wise…' the officer looked at Tom suspiciously. 'Who might you be?'

'I work for Maureen and Mrs Jackson,' Tom said. 'I haven't been up, but Maureen told me Mrs Violet Jackson is in the sittin' room – would you like me to show you the way?'

'Is what he says true, madam?'

'Yes, Tom works in the shop and he helped look after my father until he died recently. Ah, here is my grandmother and Tom's father…'

'I'll take a look upstairs first and then I'll do statements…' the officer said, nodding to the newcomers. 'It's been busy round here lately. Makes me wonder what's goin' on…'

Tom led the way upstairs. He could see instantly that someone had been looking for something; the room had been thoroughly searched and everything had been thrown on the floor. Violet was lying near the fireplace. The police officer went to her and knelt down beside her, applying two fingers to her neck and then taking her wrist and checking again. He looked up at Tom.

'Mrs Jackson is alive – only a faint pulse. She isn't dead yet, despite the cold in here. Has an ambulance been sent for?'

'Yes, Maureen told me she did that first…'

'Good.' The police officer looked about him. 'Someone was after money by the looks of it or something of value…'

'It looks nearly as bad as when our house was ransacked,' Tom said. 'Maureen and Mrs Hilda Jackson's house was burgled too…'

'Sounds as if you've got a nasty character on the loose,' the police officer said. 'So when were you last here then? Tom is it?'

'Yes, sir. I was here with Mrs Hilda on Tuesday for a meetin' with Mrs Violet, because she wasn't very nice and Maureen asked me to make sure she didn't have a go at her gran. I've got all the keys, but I ain't been here since. Mrs Hilda told me to keep away until we open again…'

'You've no idea when this happened then?'

'There has been a light up here every night until two nights ago. I told Dad when he came home for a visit this mornin' that I thought Mrs Violet had done a bunk…'

'Your father had been away?'

'He's in the army, sir. Just finished basic trainin',' Tom said proudly. 'He's goin' into logistics…'

'You'd make a good witness,' the officer said and then heard voices below and went to the top of the stairs. 'Up here, doctor. The lady is still alive – barely, but still breathin'.'

Two men came upstairs and went immediately to Violet's side, bending over her and checking her pulse, just as the officer had done. They nodded and then examined her gently, before lifting her onto the stretcher.

'I'm Constable Jenkins and I was sent to investigate this incident – a break-in was reported and what was thought to be a murder. So what are the lady's chances?' the police officer asked.

'We shan't know until we get her to the hospital,' one of the ambulance men said. 'She seems to have been half-strangled… see the bruisin' around her throat, and then thrust back with some force, hittin' her head as she fell. I think your people will find blood somewhere here on this mantle or fender…'

'Yes, I imagine so,' Constable Jenkins agreed. 'I'll get a team in to go over the whole place. You will keep us informed when you know what is happenin' with Mrs Violet Jackson please?'

'Yes, of course, constable.'

The stretcher was carried away. Tom saw an object lying on the floor and bent as if to pick it up, but Constable Jenkins called out to stop him.

'Don't touch anythin' now, Tom. Obviously, your prints will be found here, because you've been a visitor in the past, and by the look of this place it hasn't been thoroughly cleaned for a while. We need all the evidence to be intact… What have you seen?'

'I think that's a fountain pen,' Tom said, pointing to a rather smart-looking pen lying on the ground. 'You should ask Maureen and Mrs Hilda Jackson – but I don't think Mr Jackson had one and it doesn't look like a lady's pen, does it.'

Constable Jenkins walked over and looked down at the fountain pen lying on the ground. It was black with a gold band around it, obviously a good make but not the design a woman would necessarily choose.

'Well spotted,' Constable Jenkins said. 'I'll make a note of its position – and leave it for my team to find, but that pen rings a bell somewhere…' He looked up as he heard a step on the stairs, and a moment or two later Maureen walked in. 'Ah, just the person we need – do you happen to know if your father had a pen like this, Mrs Hart – or your stepmother come to that…'

Maureen came over to join them and looked down at the pen lying on the floor. 'I've never seen it before. Dad wouldn't have a fountain pen; he didn't get on with them, preferred a pencil and only used a pen if he was forced to fill in a form, but for years he left that to me – but Violet may have owned it or given it to him.'

'Yes, that is perfectly possible,' the constable said. 'It may be evidence, though, so don't touch it or anythin' else up here, please. It's best if you both go down and leave me to look round… or better still, I'd like to use your telephone. I need some specialised help here.'

'Yes, of course, officer,' Maureen said. 'Come on, Tom. I need you to check the stock for me. I shall need to claim our losses on the insurance. Hopefully, my father had kept up the premiums.' She caught her breath, holding back a sob. 'We'll clear this up another day, when the police have finished with it…'

'You can leave it to me,' Tom told her. 'You should go home, Maureen. You've had enough worry and upset for now. I'll stay here and lock up after the police have finished.'

Maureen nodded and went down the stairs, going through to the kitchen where her grandmother and Jack were sitting talking. She drew a deep breath.

'Tom has offered to hang on here and look after things,' she said. 'I think we should go home, Gran. We can't touch anythin' until the police have finished their work and it will be a few days before they let us clear up in the flat. It's obvious someone was lookin' for money. They didn't take much, from what I could see...'

'Henry didn't have much worth takin',' Gran said. 'I never understood what he did with his money. He hardly paid you a penny for years and he only went for a drink a couple of times a week. This place was a little goldmine when my husband ran it... made at least twenty pounds' profit a week.'

'Dad would never spend a penny if he could get away with a farthin',' Maureen said and smiled oddly. 'You're obviously not the only one who thought he had money hidden somewhere. Someone was intent on findin' it and if it was up there, they must have got it...'

Gran nodded. 'Violet is lucky to be alive after lyin' there for hours – a day and two nights by the sound of it. Whoever left her must be an evil devil. Surely he could have telephoned for an ambulance?'

'And risk gettin' caught?' Maureen said. 'He probably thought she was already dead. He must have attacked her first and then ransacked the place, so he obviously felt secure enough to believe he wouldn't be disturbed.'

'Don't forget the back door was opened from inside,' Gran said. 'Violet let whoever did this in – and then they must have quarrelled over somethin'...'

'He wanted money and she wouldn't give it to him. She thought she would come into a fortune when Dad died, but she didn't,' Maureen said and frowned. 'She must have led this person to expect she would have money and when she didn't give him anythin', he got angry...'

'Sounds as if they knew each other well...' Jack said, entering the conversation for the first time. 'Almost family...'

'Dad told me once she had a son but he went off years ago and that she hadn't heard of him since...' Maureen said.

'Her fancy man!' Tom exclaimed, having followed her down. 'Alice saw her meetin' a man she thought looked young enough to be her son... well, supposin' he was. He might have been in trouble and had come back to ask for money...'

'This is all speculation,' Maureen said as the constable came to the kitchen door and looked at them. 'But we think Violet had a son – and she was seen meetin' a younger man in a café in Commercial Road recently...'

The little black book came out again; the constable licked his pencil and began to write as Maureen told him what they knew, which wasn't very much.

'Violet thought she was due my late mother's few bits of jewellery and silver. Four days ago, they were stolen from my home together with some things of Gran's – and now this. Don't you think it all seems to tie together?'

'That's not for me to decide – or you, Mrs Hart, if you don't mind my saying so.' He took his helmet off and ran long fingers through his short hair. 'There are blokes at our place paid to work that sort of stuff out. I'm just here to report back, and keep the peace best I can – but I'll report all you say.'

Gran shook her head. 'Poor Violet. I had my differences with my son but he would never have raised a hand to me.'

'It's a sad thing, but there's a good lot who do,' Constable Jenkins said. 'You would be surprised at how much crime there is within families – and how many sons steal from their mothers, violent abuse too. We get called to all sorts and, believe me, some of them would strangle their granny for a half crown.'

'Come on, Gran,' Maureen said as she saw her grandmother's face go pale again. 'Let's get you home. Tom will see to things here – let me know if there's anythin' more we can do to help, officer.'

'Yes, Mrs Hart. You've all been very helpful. Now, I'd prefer it if you all left apart from young Tom here. He has a good memory this lad and I'm goin' to let him make me a cup of tea and tell me what he thinks about life in the lanes...'

'Do you want me to stop too, officer?' Jack asked.

'No, Private, you get off. I'm sure you've got things you would rather do on your leave. Tom will be all right with me – give you my word.'

'All right, Tom?'

'Yeah, I'm fine, Dad,' Tom said and went to fill the kettle at the sink. He turned when everyone else had left. 'What did you want to know, constable?'

'Tell me what folk are like round here,' Constable Jenkins invited. 'You're an observant lad. I want a picture of everyday life – it helps to know if there are local villains on the patch, who has fallen out with whom... you know the kind of thing.'

'Yes,' Tom said and smiled inwardly. The constable thought he'd picked on the youngest and therefore the easiest to influence, but Tom knew just what he was after. He thought he'd get Tom to dish the dirt on his neighbours, but that wasn't going to happen. 'Trouble is, we don't have many of them in this lane – of course there was that chap from Artillery Lane who half-murdered his brother-in-law in a fight over who owned their radio after they were bombed...'

'And how long ago was this?' Constable Jenkins's pencil hovered eagerly.

'Oh, just over a year. They're the best of friends again now, because in the end, it didn't work and they took it to the mender and he wanted ten bob for mendin' it and neither of them were willin' to pay...' Tom took a deep breath as he brought the pot to the table. 'The biggest rogue round here was that Knocker – the bloke what got the boys to dig on the bombsites for valuables and was recently arrested for theft. He then escaped. Now if it turned out to be him, you'd kill two birds with one stone...'

'What makes you think it might be him?'

'He had been hanging around here a bit...' Tom shrugged, not wanting to get too involved in case they thought he'd been selling stolen stuff himself. 'I don't know who did it, constable. I was just sayin' because I can't think of anyone else with a grudge against Maureen and her gran. Everyone likes them. Do anythin' for you, Maureen would, and Mrs Hilda grumbles a bit, but she ain't that bad – so only a stranger would do this. Stands to reason... you ain't goin' to find the culprit from the lanes...'

Jack entered the kitchen carrying a packet of fish and chips. He went to the cupboard and got two plates out, putting them in the oven to warm for a moment as he fetched knives and forks.

Tom had been washing his hands at the sink. He glanced up as his father brought the kettle over to fill it.

'I've had loads of tea today keepin' that lot goin',' Tom said. 'How about we have a bottle of beer – I'll have lemonade in mine...'

'Well, why not? You behave like a man, so why shouldn't you have a man's drink?' his father smiled. 'Did Constable Jenkins get what he wanted out of you, son?'

'He thinks he did,' Tom said. 'I told him a few bits and

pieces that made him prick his ears up but nothin' that isn't common knowledge. He didn't want to accept the obvious, Dad. Violet knew the man that hurt her – and she let him into the house but we can't prove it – unless she comes round and tells the police.'

'Let's hope she does, poor woman,' Jack said. 'I know she had a sharp tongue on her, but she wasn't all bad.'

'No, course not. She didn't treat Maureen well, but…' Tom shrugged. 'I like Maureen and Hilda. They've been all right to me – and Peggy. Did I tell you she had twins?'

'Not sure if you did,' Jack smiled. 'I think I heard it from Alice. I popped in to see Peggy this afternoon… after I'd been to see your mum.'

'How was Mum?' Tom asked. 'Did she speak to you?'

Jack shook his head. 'The nurse told me she was gettin' better and might be able to come 'ome soon, but I thought she seemed worse. She dribbled down 'er chin and 'er eyes were so vacant. It worried me, Tom – it worried me that she might be a lot of trouble to you if she came 'ere. We'll just have to wait and see,' his father said and sighed, then his eyes lit up. 'Peggy asked about you, son, and let me hold the little girl. The boy is still in that oxygen thing, but the nurse told her 'e is breathin' better and they think 'e's on the mend. She 'ad a few tears, Tom, and so did I – she's a lovely lady that Peggy Ashley.'

'Yeah, we're lucky to have her so near,' Tom said and grinned as he turned away to take the plates from the oven.

'I told her you might give up the 'ouse if your mum never comes 'ome. She said you can stay with her when you like.'

'Yeah, I know.' Tom's grin got bigger. 'I must be popular. I got the same offer from Alice, and Maureen told me that if I wanted to live over the shop I could – rent-free…' He looked thoughtful. 'If I was sure Mum wasn't comin' home, I might take her up on that… plenty of room for you to stay.'

'Give it some thought, lad.'

''Course, I could stay with Alice if I wanted, just for a bit…'

'Real ladies' man you are,' his father said. 'Just watch yer 'ead doesn't get too big for yer boots!'

'No fear of that – I've got your boots,' Tom said and looked down at his size elevens. They were too big for him, but he wore three pairs of socks inside.

'When I said you could have them, I meant when you grow into them,' Jack said and laughed. 'I'll get you a new pair, Tom.'

'Bob Hall promised me a pair in my size,' Tom said. ''E's got some size nine boots on his shelf that he repaired five years ago and were never collected. I've only got to pay four shillings for the repair and I can 'ave them.'

'I'll get them for you in the mornin',' his father said. 'You can't walk around in them damn great things…'

'I'm goin to start paintin' the kitchen for Peggy while she's away,' Tom said. 'I saw Janet after I left the shop and she asked me if I could get it done – what about you givin' me a 'and after supper?'

'O' course I will,' Jack said. 'I can work on it tomorrow as well if you're in the shop – we'll make it nice and fresh for Peggy to come home to when she leaves hospital…'

'It will be a nice surprise for 'er,' Tom said. 'If we both work nights and you put in a few hours in the day, it will be ready when she comes 'ome…'

Chapter 21

'I love this bright colour,' Peggy said as she walked into the kitchen carrying Freddie in her arms. Janet had Fay and she smiled as she saw her mother's pleasure in the surprise. 'How did you manage this then?'

'Tom and his father did it for you,' Janet replied. 'They found the yellow paint out in the shed. I think Dad bought it just before the war; he was goin' to paint the kitchen for you, but never got round to it – but Tom and Jack made a wonderful job, don't you think?'

'Yes, I do – did you ask them to do this?' Janet nodded and her mother smiled lovingly. 'I thought as much.'

'Tom was happy to do it and his father – and they wouldn't take any money. Said they would have a piece of pie when you were up to makin' them again.'

Peggy put Freddie into the cot, which Janet had placed near the fire but just far enough away not to make the twins too hot, but to keep them warm. Freddie especially needed to be protected from chills, according to the nurse who had released Peggy that morning, though there was no long-term problem for the child.

'He isn't in danger now so there's no real need to worry,' she'd told them, 'but he may be a little weaker than his twin for some time to come – so you'll need to keep an eye on him more. Try not to let him catch cold or any other childhood illnesses, for as long as you can. Freddie is a special little boy and he needs a lot of care.'

'I know he's special,' Janet had said to the nurse. 'But why does he need more care – is there somethin' wrong with him that they haven't told us?'

'No, Mrs Rowan, nothing in particular – but sometimes babies born early the way Freddie was are a little more susceptible to chills and other illnesses.'

Janet had nodded, but she hadn't been able to get the nurse's warning and her look out of her head. If Freddie wasn't actually suffering from a weak chest or anything else, why worry his mother? Peggy was concerned about the little boy, even though she hadn't made a fuss or asked lots of questions at the hospital. Janet was worried because she knew that it was hard enough not to fret about young children when they were perfectly healthy.

'Mum-mum...' Maggie came rushing at Janet as Nellie brought her into the kitchen. She clawed at Janet's skirts and Janet had to give Fay to Nellie and pick the little girl up. 'Where 'ou bin?' Maggie demanded in her baby talk. 'Maggie want 'ou, Mum-mum...'

'I've been fetchin' your cousins from the hospital,' Janet said and then realised they were actually her daughter's aunt and uncle, but that was too difficult to explain to a little girl. Maggie was only just getting confident on her feet and beginning to put words together. One day she would learn about their complicated relationship but not now. 'Come and meet Fay and Freddie…'

Janet took her daughter by the hand and led her to the cot where Peggy had now placed the twins side by side, having taken Fay from Nellie. Only a little bit of their faces was showing under the woolly bonnets, one pink, one blue, and the blanket was pulled up to their chins. Janet held Maggie up so that she could look into the cot.

'Dollies…' Maggie said and struggled to get to them.

'Not dollies, darling; a little baby boy, and a little baby girl – friends for you to play with when they grow up.'

'No!' Maggie said and punched her fists against her mother's shoulder. 'No babies – Maggie's cot…'

'It's not your cot now, darling,' Janet said and kissed her cheek. 'It belongs to Freddie and Fay – they are Granny's babies, your friends…'

'Not Mum-mum's babies?' Maggie demanded truculently, her mouth pouting and a look of jealousy in her eyes.

Janet laughed and nuzzled her neck, thinking it amusing. 'No, my darling girl, I promise you, not Mummy's babies. Granny Peggy's babies… friends for Maggie.'

Maggie stared at her, her eyes wide and then she nodded and the fierce look faded from her face. She giggled as Janet kissed her and tickled her tummy, before letting her down. For a moment, Maggie stared at the cot, but then she ran to Nellie and looked up at her.

'Cake for Maggie…'

'Yes, I told yer there was a glass of milk and a slice of cake for yer, didn't I, darlin'?' Nellie laughed and took Maggie's hand, leading her to the table and putting her in her special high chair. She lifted her into it and then went to fetch the milk and a cake that had been made earlier that morning.

'Maggie was upset when she saw the twins,' Peggy murmured and Janet nodded. 'She'll get over it. You were just the same when you saw Pip for the first time,' Peggy said.

'I think she was really jealous until I told her they were your babies not mine.' Janet was thoughtful. 'She's had us all to herself...'

At that moment, Mike entered the kitchen carrying some envelopes. 'These just arrived,' he said. 'I was in the yard and Reg stopped for a chat and gave me these. He told me there are jobs goin' at the Post Office – they need people to deliver the letters apparently.'

'Most of the men who can be, are in the Army,' Janet said. She looked through the letters Mike had put on the kitchen table, saw one for herself and slipped it into her jacket pocket. 'The girls seem to prefer workin' in the factory or shops – carryin' a heavy bag over your shoulder and walkin' miles in all weathers isn't exactly a great job.'

'Oh, I don't know, I wouldn't mind takin' it on part-time. That's about all I'm fit for at the moment...'

'You haven't been discharged yet,' Janet objected. 'You still have to go back to the hospital for further checks.'

'They're just routine,' Mike said. 'I think I could manage a round of postin' letters though people's doors...'

'I must say you do look better, Mike,' Peggy said and smiled at him. 'If you felt like it you could work in the bar...'

'I'm feelin' all right, though I couldn't go back to my old job yet – too tirin' workin' on the ships. It takes a lot of skill rivetin' and fittin'...' Mike broke off and stared at Janet. 'Just for a moment, I remembered what it was like, Jan – I remembered the smell and the heat when the metal melts...'

'Oh, Mike...' Janet could hardly breathe as she saw the look of wonder in his eyes. 'Has anythin' else come back?'

'A few bits and pieces recently,' he admitted. 'I haven't been sure whether it was somethin' from before or the recent past – but that smell and the heat… it was from my days as a ship's fitter. I wasn't a riveter, but I worked with them in the yard I know…'

'Yes, darling, it must have been a memory from that time.' Janet went to him, looking up into his eyes. 'It's somethin' – it might mean nothin', but it is a sliver of light…'

'Yes, Jan, it might mean I'm startin' to remember,' Mike said and put his arms around her. He was about to kiss her when Maggie, having finished her cake and been let down from her high chair, ran to them, pushing between them and demanding to be taken up. Her hands were sticky and her mouth had a smear of jam round it, but Mike swept her up and buried his face in her neck playfully, making her giggle; he inhaled the sweet smell of her. 'My little girl…' he said, looking at Janet over her head. 'She's ours, Jan… I know it now.'

Janet felt the tears sting her eyes but she blinked them away. Maggie was kissing her father with sticky, wet kisses all over his cheek and patting at him with her hands.

'Daddy not cry,' she said. 'Daddy not be sad…' Her eyes seemed to go accusingly to her mother, as if she were to blame for making her daddy cry.

'No, darling baby, your daddy is happy,' he said and kissed her. 'I've got you and Mummy and perhaps one day…' Janet shook her head at him and he looked puzzled but she put a finger to her lips. 'Run away and play now, darling…'

As Maggie ran off, Mike looked at the cot where the twins were still sleeping soundly. 'I thought you would like more babies?'

'Yes,' Janet agreed, 'but Maggie is a little jealous of the twins. I want her to get used to them before we have a brother or sister for her.'

'If we ever do...' Mike's smile faded and the shadows returned to his eyes. 'I'm sure we shall one day,' Janet said and kissed him, then rubbed at his cheek. 'You taste of strawberry jam.'

Mike laughed, but his attention was taken by the headlines in the paper. 'Well, that's one bit of good news,' he said. 'They've finally got a vital convoy of ships through to Malta. It was a bit of a fight by the sound of it, but those people were desperate.' 'Yes, I know. They've been goin' through hell there,' Janet said, reading the article over his shoulder. 'Two of the ships reached Valletta, but were sunk as the cargo was being unloaded, and another two were sunk within sight of the port.'

Helen came to the door of the kitchen, hovering uncertainly. 'I'm sorry to interrupt but could someone come to the bar please? We're rather busy...'

'Yes, of course, I'll come,' Janet said at once, but Mike placed a hand on her arm.

'I'll go, Jan. It's time I did somethin' to earn my keep round here. I've got to start so it may as well be now...' 'If you're sure...' she looked at him doubtfully.

'Enjoy yourself for a little while,' Mike said, 'and maybe you'll get time to read your letter...' Janet's gaze followed him as he went through to the bar. He hadn't appeared to take much notice of the letters he'd placed on the table, but did he know who hers was from? She'd recognised the writing immediately, but surely Mike didn't know anything about Ryan – how could he?

★

Janet read the letter through and frowned, before folding it and placing it in the drawer with other letters she'd kept. Ryan was returning to London after a spell abroad and wondered if they could meet. He'd written her just a few lines, but they tugged at her heartstrings:

> *I know I said I wouldn't ask for anything but I've thought about you so much, darling Jan. I shan't come if you tell me everything is wonderful, but if you're still unhappy, I'll be in town next week and we can meet. You can telephone my office and leave a message. If I don't hear I shall worry.*
>
> *I love you so much, Ryan. X*

She would have to telephone his office when she could be sure Mike was busy. Janet didn't want to risk the tentative happiness they were finding together now that her husband was feeling better. Once, she'd thought she might be falling in love with Ryan, but now she was so glad she'd resisted the temptation to take him to her bed the night he'd turned up at the pub in such terrible distress; the night he'd lost his wife, children and his home in a horrific air raid.

Ryan said he loved her, but would he have been willing to leave his family for her if they hadn't all died in the bomb blast? Janet doubted it. Ryan was alone and lonely now and that made him want her more, but she had a family to think of: Mike, her daughter, her mother and the twins. Janet couldn't go off with Ryan even if she'd been desperate to, and thank goodness she wasn't. Her love for Mike and her daughter came first. Janet nodded, acknowledging to herself that despite her feelings for Ryan, she had made the right choice.

She would always like him and think him attractive, but her love for Mike had come flooding back once he was home and they were close again. He'd kissed her and held her, even though the passionate loving she'd always enjoyed had not happened yet. Mike had apologised, but she'd told him not to worry.

'It will happen when your body is ready,' she'd told him. 'I love you, Mike, and havin' you here makes me happy. I can wait for things to be perfect – and I'm sure they will one day.'

Janet smiled as she remembered the look in Mike's eyes when he'd remembered his former work days. If he could only be really well again, she would have everything she could ever want. No, she would definitely not meet Ryan. Making up her mind, she took all Ryan's letters from the drawer in her bedside chest and put them in her skirt pocket. She had the number for his office in her book. She would burn the letters and ring the office with a message that she was happy and hoped that he was well. He'd been a good friend and she didn't want to hurt him, but her love for Mike came first…

Walking down to the kitchen, she put Ryan's letters into the kitchen range and watched them turn brown and then burst into flames. She'd just put the last of them in when the door opened and Mike entered carrying the biggest bunch of flowers she'd ever seen.

'Are they for me?' she asked very surprised.

'No, for Peggy,' Mike said. 'They just arrived, but I ought to buy you flowers and something nice. I wasn't able to buy you a birthday present last year, Jan, so I want to make up for it. What would you like?'

'I'd love to go dancing again,' Janet said wistfully. 'I can't ask Mum to look after Maggie for a night yet, but if Maureen would – could we go up West to that lovely hotel and spend the night, as we did before we were married?'

'Yes, of course, but you'll have to tell me the name of the hotel,' Mike said and put the flowers into the sink before coming to take her in his arms and kiss her. 'I do love you, Jan, very much – and I'm sorry if you were hurt when I was in the hospital and I wouldn't see you. I was going through hell and couldn't cope with the news that I had a wife and child. I was lost in a sea of fog.'

'That's all forgotten,' she said, looking up at him lovingly. She kissed him and smiled. 'I wonder who sent Mum those lovely flowers...'

'Your father perhaps?'

'I doubt it.' Janet shook her head. 'They're not the best of friends these days. Somehow I don't think they're from him.'

'If you're so curious, put them in water and open the card...'

'No, I mustn't spoil the surprise for Mum,' Janet said and laughed. 'It is intriguing though...'

'One of her customers perhaps?'

'Yes, perhaps – but I'm not sure that any of them could afford somethin' like this. She had some cards and a few small bunches of flowers at the hospital – but these came from a high-class florist and cost a lot of money.'

'Yes.' Mike laughed and raised his eyebrows. 'Clearly your mother has an admirer – are you surprised? I'm not. She's a very attractive lady and...' He broke off as Peggy walked into the kitchen. She was looking a little tired and Mike realised that she was probably feeling the strain of the past few days, the birth and then the ambulance trip to the hospital and all the trauma of not knowing whether Freddie would be all right. 'Can I get you a cup of tea, Peggy?'

'How kind of you,' she said on her way to the sink with a bundle of the twins' washing. 'I was just thinkin'... Where did those flowers come from?'

'They're for you,' Janet said with a wicked look at Mike. 'I think you have a secret admirer, Mum.'

'Not so secret if he has sent a card,' Peggy said and sent her daughter a repressive look. She opened the card and looked surprised. 'Good grief – they're from Michael Blake... I must telephone and thank him. What a nice thought. I mean, I hardly know him...'

'Doctor Blake?' Janet said, shocked. She'd wondered if Jack Barton had splashed out, but she hadn't considered they had come from the doctor. 'Well, that is a surprise.'

'He calls in for a drink now and then,' Peggy said a faint flush in her cheeks. 'We became friendly when Tilly was ill – and then he helped when Tom was attacked by that awful man...'

'Yes, I was meanin' to ask you about that, Jan,' Mike said thoughtfully. 'The man who attacked Tom – didn't I hear you say somethin' about him havin' a scar at his temple and his nose being a bit bent?'

Janet felt a cold chill at her nape. 'Why do you ask?'

'It was in the early hours of this mornin',' Mike said. 'I woke up and you were sound asleep, so I came downstairs and made myself a cup of tea. When I looked out of the landing window, I noticed this bloke standin' under the lamp post opposite. He was lighting a cigarette and I saw his face clearly for a moment. Then he looked up at the window and must have seen me move so he walked off...'

'Do you think he's come back for revenge for the trick they played on him?' Janet asked feeling a shiver of fear. 'He probably blames you and Tom, Mum...'

'It was Michael's detective friend who came up with the idea – he said if they caught him with the diamonds on him, they could get him to confess and he'd go away for years, but he will blame us, of course...' Peggy frowned. 'I wouldn't have thought he would dare to return to the lanes though, because they'll be lookin' for him everywhere – and they're sure to keep an eye on this area.'

'Perhaps it wasn't him,' Mike said, 'but I shall be watching from now on, and if I were you, Peggy, I'd let the police know he may have been in the lane this mornin' – at about two thirty.'

'Yes, I shall – or rather I'll tell Doctor Blake and he can inform his friend at the station.'

'We should let Tom and his father know about this, too,' Janet said. 'I hope you were wrong, Mike, because this man is a nasty character...'

Peggy bent to sniff the lovely flowers Michael Blake had sent for her and sighed. She guessed that he liked her quite a lot, but even though he was a good friend, she didn't want to get involved romantically with him.

She'd written to Laurie after the twins were born, telling him about Freddie, and he'd sent her a brief letter, politely saying that he hoped both she and the child were better. He was busy and didn't expect to be home anytime soon, but would send her a postal order to buy something for the twins.

She frowned. Laurie was doing his best to be civilised over the situation, but she hoped he wouldn't come home for a while, because she knew it was going to be awkward when he did. The twins were not his, they were Able's and she wished every moment of every day that their father was still alive and would come back at the end of the war...

Peggy had accepted the money he'd left for her with his solicitor, but asked him to hold on to it for her; it belonged to the twins and invested properly would bring in a little nest egg for them when they were older. She was determined not to use the money unless she was forced, even though she knew Able had intended it for her.

'Oh, Able,' she whispered. 'I do love you… so very much…'

Chapter 22

It was Tuesday afternoon when the police finally gave Tom the keys to the shop back and told him he could go over and clear up.

'Our chaps have made even more mess,' the young officer told him, 'but we had to be thorough. We've got some fingerprints and we need to eliminate the family – and you. Would you be prepared to give them?'

'Yes, I would, but my dad might not,' Tom said. 'Don't go jumpin' to conclusions, but he was in prison for robbin' a post office up West before he got a pardon and joined the Army.'

'He's been ruled out,' the young constable said. 'We knew his record of course and the first thing we did was check him out, but his alibi puts him in the clear so you needn't worry – we've got his prints.'

'Will mine be kept?'

'No – we just use them for elimination purposes and then destroy them,' the constable said. 'So I'll tell them at the station you'll come down later – yes?'

'All right,' Tom said. 'What about Mrs Violet Jackson? Have you heard how she is?'

'I think she's still alive, because this hasn't become a murder investigation yet – but I understand she's poorly…'

'She'll be lucky if she comes through,' Tom said. 'I didn't like her much, but now I feel sorry for her. I suppose you haven't found the bloke that did it?'

'Well, there has been a development but I can't tell you about that,' the constable said and winked. 'If things go well we might get lucky – and that's the difference between solving a crime and not, if you ask me.'

Tom thanked him for the keys and went back into the kitchen as his father came downstairs. 'The police just gave me the keys to the shop back,' he said and then looked at his father, who had washed and changed into a clean shirt and his suit. 'Where are you off to?'

'I got a letter this mornin',' Jack said. 'The infirmary have asked me to go in and talk about your mother's future. I haven't got time to talk now, but we'll sort things out this evenin'. If you need a hand with the clearin' up, I'll 'elp you when I get back.'

'I'm sure I can manage,' Tom said. 'My shoulder still aches now and then, but it isn't as stiff now.'

'Good. Don't work too hard, son.'

Tom nodded but didn't listen. When there was a job to be done, he got on with it, and pain in his shoulder wasn't going to stop him. He was just about to leave for the shop when someone knocked at the back door. He went to answer it and saw it was Janet's husband.

'Were you just leavin'?' Mike asked.

'Yeah, goin' to clear up the mess in the shop so we can open it this week,' Tom said, 'but I've got a minute if you need somethin'?'

'We thought you should know, Tom – there's a chance that Knocker is back in the lanes. I'm pretty sure I saw him this mornin' at about half-past two – or three. He was your side of the lane and stopped to light a cigarette. When he became aware of me he walked off…'

'Are you sure it was him?'

'I can't be certain, but I thought it might be, because Janet told me about the scar here…' Mike touched his temple. 'And his nose was a bit bent, as if it had been broken at some time.'

'Sounds like him,' Tom agreed. 'I've been expectin' him to come. We set him up for that arrest and he'll want to get even. You need to look out for Peggy and Janet – and the twins.'

'Yes, I'll do that; we've always got people around, but you're more vulnerable, Tom. Peggy has telephoned Doctor Blake and he has let the police know, so they will be lookin' for him…'

'He won't come here while my dad is here,' Tom said. 'I reckon he'll wait until he's gone back to the army… but thanks for lettin' me know. I'll be on the lookout.'

'Good.' Mike smiled. 'I shan't keep you. I expect you've got a lot to do before you can open the shop again.'

'Yeah, and the police want my fingerprints for elimination purposes.'

'I suppose they do that,' Mike said. 'Let's hope they catch whoever it was that harmed Mrs Jackson – we don't want that sort of stuff goin' on round here, do we?'

'No, we don't,' said Tom.

'Nice talkin' to you, Tom. Come over and see Peggy when you've got time. I know she thinks a lot of you.'

'Peggy is a great person,' Tom said and pulled the door shut firmly behind him before locking it. 'Ma never locked the door before the war. She started then in case the Germans invaded, but it's not Germans I need to keep out.'

Mike nodded grimly. The two men parted, Mike walking back up the street and stopping to talk to Bob Hall and Ted Jones from three doors up. Ted was a widower and lived alone, but his married daughter, Vera came three times a week to clean up and leave him some baking.

Tom waited for a baker's van to go by and then crossed the street. He inserted the key and went in, feeling the chill strike. It all seemed cold and bleak, and that meant the first thing he needed to do was to get the range going upstairs. He would clear up as much of the mess there as he could, though there were certain things that Maureen would want to do herself.

Tom had almost finished clearing the worst of the mess in the flat, when he heard Maureen's voice calling to him from the bottom of the stairs.

'Are you there, Tom?'

'Yes,' he said, going to the head of the stairs. 'The police returned the keys to me so I got the range goin' and I've cleaned up as much as I can. I thought you would rather go through personal things yourself, so I haven't put anythin' away, just washed off all the powder the police use to dust for fingerprints and straightened up as much as I could.'

Maureen looked about her appreciatively. 'You've done a lot, Tom. I asked about Violet at the hospital. The nurse said she came to her senses for a while last night and spoke to a police officer, but she got upset and they gave her a sedative to calm her and she's still sleepin'.'

'If she gets better, she'll want to pack up a lot of this stuff...' Tom said, glancing around the bedroom that Violet had used for her corset work.

'I'm goin' to fold it all neatly on the bed. I'll sort my father's papers out and put them back in his desk. I'd like to go through them and see if there's anythin' personal to my mother or me before Violet takes anythin'. I think she will probably sell most of it, except for the bits she brought with her.'

'What he didn't take...' Tom said. 'I remember there was a small pair of silver candlesticks on the mantle and a fancy clock...'

'Yes, I remember those. They belonged to Violet; she brought them with her,' Maureen said thoughtfully. 'We'll have to see what she wants to do when she's well enough to leave hospital.'

'I wonder what else he took...' Tom mused.

'I don't suppose we'll ever know.' Maureen sighed. 'You can start on the shop now, Tom. I popped to the wholesaler and bought some cigarettes this mornin'. Not as many as we had, but I filled in a couple of forms and they let me have what they could spare and were very understandin'.'

'Right, I'll go and finish in the shop,' Tom said. He considered telling her what Mike had passed on about Knocker but decided she didn't need to know. Maureen had enough to cope with without worrying about him...

Anne stopped to look in the shop window. She would like a nice new dress but the recent laws meant that there was nothing fresh or different in the shops. Hemlines had to be shorter than they'd been before the war and the styles were plain and utilitarian to save on material. It was just the same as rationing bathwater and toilet soap, only one bar a month – how was that supposed to last? Anne had one lipstick left, which she was saving for special occasions, but most women used beetroot these days to make their lips a bit redder, and good cosmetics were impossible to find – just like silk stockings.

Feeling down in the dumps, Anne decided to visit Maureen. She envied her friend because she was having her first child. If only Anne had fallen for Kirk's child, she might have felt she had something to look forward to. Living in lodgings wasn't much fun either, even though Mavis was sweet to her.

Anne sighed. She wasn't the only one feeling depressed. A lot of women were fed up with the strict austerity imposed by the shortages and rationing. Even if you could afford to buy a new pair of shoes, it wasn't likely you could find something you liked in the shops.

Anne's attention was drawn to a young woman pushing a pram. There were two children in it and the woman was pregnant and had a slightly older child clinging to her skirt. She stopped, looking tired and miserable as she stared at the cake shop window.

'Can I 'ave a bun, Mum?' the young boy asked, tugging at his mother's skirts. 'I'm 'ungry'.

'Yer always 'ungry, Siddie,' the woman said. 'Leave, orf. I ain't got no money fer cake.'

Driven by her compassion, Anne acted on impulse. She took half a crown from her purse and went up to them, pushing it into the woman's hand.

'Buy your son a bun,' she said. 'I can afford it and I'd like to help…'

'Who the bleedin' 'ell asked fer yer 'elp?' the woman said, looking at her as if she'd just offered to murder her. 'Clear orf and take yer bleedin' money wiv yer.' She threw the money on the ground. Her son dived on it, scooped it up and ran into the baker's shop. 'Nah see what yer've done?' the woman looked accusingly at Anne. 'Teachin' him to pinch. I'll never do nuthin' wiv 'im nah.'

'Sorry…' Anne held up her hands and walked off quickly. It had been an impulse, which she now regretted. Tears stung her eyes as she ran to catch a bus. She'd only been trying to help, because she felt lonely herself. That woman had more children than she could cope with and Anne had none. Her heart felt as if it would break, but hearts were resilient. Anne would go on living and bearing the pain of her need inside where no one could see or suspect it.

She knew she was missing Kirk because his letter was late again and that always made her tense. Anne had never expected to find love and she'd been gloriously happy for a few days, but now she was lonely and wishing this awful war was over so that her husband would come home. Yet, remembering Janet's ordeal after Mike went missing, Anne knew she was lucky. She had friends and a husband who loved her. She just had to get on with things.

Ellie was walking back from the market that afternoon. Peter had only one more day before he returned to his unit and she wanted to make him a lovely dinner that evening. She'd pooled all their rations and bought a nice joint of beef from the butcher up near the market and she had a selection of vegetables. She would make a Yorkshire pudding to go with it and that would please and surprise Peter, because he didn't know that she'd been learning to cook all the things he liked to eat.

A little shuddering sigh went through her. Peter hadn't hit her after Mrs Tandy warned him, but he hadn't made love to her since discovering she was pregnant and she'd seen a cold look in his eyes that sent shivers up and down her spine. He'd said he'd forgiven her and told her she could keep the baby if she wanted to, but she was sure that deep down he hadn't forgiven her. She was trying to behave normally, but inside she was fighting her misery, because she wasn't sure that she could live with a man who neither trusted nor loved her.

Ellie turned the corner of Mulberry Lane and then stopped and caught her breath. That man standing outside the pub... it was him... the man who had raped her and done so many other terrible things. Fear swept through her and she panicked. She took a step backwards, colliding with someone right behind her. He made an exclamation of pain and she turned to find herself looking into the eyes of Tom Barton's father.

'I'm so sorry,' she apologised. 'It was just... him... that man...' she lowered her voice. 'He's the one what broke into your house... Maureen said he caused the death of your son... and he...' her voice broke as she saw Jack Barton's jaw tighten. 'I shouldn't have told yer...'

'Yes, you should, Ellie,' Jack said. 'Wait 'ere while I deal with the bugger. I'll make 'im wish he'd never been born...'

'No...' Ellie cried, but Jack ignored her and set off in haste towards the man who had turned away and was walking down the lane. As she watched, Knocker looked over his shoulder and saw Jack in pursuit. He took off at a run and Jack went after him. Ellie ran round to the back of the pub and burst into Peggy's kitchen. She saw that Mike was there, together with Janet and their daughter. 'He's back...' she gasped. 'Knocker... Jack Barton's gone after him...'

'Which way did they go?' Mike asked and rushed past her as she gasped out the news that the two men were headed in the direction of Crispin Street.

'Mike – no...' Janet called, but Mike had already headed off at speed. Janet looked at Ellie. 'He isn't well enough to get embroiled in a fight...'

'I'm sorry,' Ellie said, 'but I thought I should tell Peggy and... someone needs to let the police know...'

'Know what?' Peggy asked, entering the kitchen at that moment. 'You look as white as a sheet, Ellie – and you, Janet. What's wrong?'

Ellie trembled as she said, 'Knocker was outside the pub. I told Jack Barton and he went after him and then I came round here to tell you and Mike went after them both... I'm sorry...' Ellie closed her eyes as she started to shake. 'I was just so frightened...'

'Yes, of course you were,' Peggy sympathised and touched her arm. 'We're all worried about that devil makin' more trouble...'

'Mike isn't well enough to get into a fight...' Janet said and gave Maggie a mug of milk. 'I've a good mind to go after them...'

'You'll stay where you are,' Peggy said. 'We don't interfere in men's business – do you hear me? What has been said in this kitchen stays here until we see what happens. We don't want the police, because if a few other blokes who live round here have any idea of what's goin' on I shouldn't want to be in Knocker's shoes. There's a lot of bad feelin' about deserters and looters – just wait until Mike gets back and hear what he has to say.'

'I'd better get home,' Ellie said and looked apologetically at Janet. 'I didn't expect he would go off like that...' She should have found Peter and told him – but Peter frightened her these days. There was coldness in him, a deep ice that he kept hidden most of the time, but she was aware of it sometimes when he looked at her. She hadn't gone to Peter because she was afraid of what he might do.

Mike caught up with them just as Jack Barton brought his prey down with a flying tackle. They were on the corner of Frying Pan Alley, and Mike bent over double, because it had been a long chase and he was out of breath. He leaned against the wall and watched as the two men struggled on the ground, Jack punching as hard as he could and Knocker trying to fend him off, but he was losing. Jack's recent army training had paid off and he was in better shape. He landed a stunner of a blow and Knocker gave a sigh and fell back, all the fight suddenly gone out of him. Jack grabbed his neck and was about to bang his head down on the cobbles when Mike leaned down and held his arm.

'That's enough, mate,' he said and Jack looked up at him. 'You've knocked the stuffin' out of him. Let it go at that – the Army will deal with this little toad.'

'Right...' Jack sat back on his heels and looked at the bruised face of the man lying on the ground. 'That's for what you did to my son, you rotten devil. Listen to this, you sod, I'd kill you as soon as look at you for what you've done to my family and to others I care about – but Mike is right. The Army will do what's needed...'

Jack got to his feet and hauled his exhausted victim upright, leaning him against a wall. Mike nodded as he saw the other man's limp stance.

'You may have done it already,' he said, looking anxiously at Knocker's pale face. 'We should get him somewhere – to a doctor or the police…'

'Yeah, he wants handin' over,' Jack said. 'The police are very anxious to talk to you, mate… and I can guess what the Army has in store for yer…'

Suddenly, Knocker's head came up; he shoved Jack back into Mike making them both stumble against the wall, causing Mike to bang his forehead hard, and giving Knocker a chance to take off. Jack started to go after him and might easily have caught him, but Mike grabbed his arm and held him back.

'Let him go,' Mike said. 'I can't see him comin' back in a hurry after the thrashin' you gave him. We'll go now and tell the police that he's been seen hangin' around the lane – and we'll set up a vigilante group. There are several men and lads in the lanes that will join in. If he comes back we'll know and so will he…'

Jack looked him in the eyes. 'There's more to you than meets the eye, Mike Rowan. I'll take your advice, 'cos I don't need trouble with the police.'

'I want him behind bars or in the hands of the military police,' Mike said, 'not lying dead in some alley and you back in prison…'

'Thanks. I'm glad you were here,' Jack admitted. 'I saw red when Ellie told me he was the one that hurt my lads…'

'Any other red-blooded man would have done the same in your place,' Mike said and smiled. 'Come on, we need to speak to the cops – and let me tell the story?'

'Yeah…' Jack grinned. 'Nice to have you in the lane, Mike. You're one of us…'

★

'I wish you'd come and told me,' Peter said when Ellie explained what had happened on her way home from the market. 'If I'd got to him, I'd have bashed his head in...'

'I went into the pub because it was the first place I thought of after Jack took off after him,' Ellie said and her eyes filled with tears. 'I didn't want you to kill 'im and be hanged...'

'They'd give me a medal more like,' Peter said. 'Do you know what our Army lads would do with a bugger like that?' Ellie shook her head. 'If I told yer, it would give yer nightmares. 'E'll get his comeuppance one way or the other, don't you worry.'

'Peter, you mustn't...' Ellie said and clawed at his jacket. 'Please...'

He smiled at her. 'I'm glad you care what happens to me, love, and don't worry, I shan't be involved – but if the police don't grab him first that devil will end up in the canal...'

Ellie stared at him and then turned away. She breathed deeply. There was a remoteness in Peter now that she didn't recognise. He'd changed from the generous man she'd married, perhaps because of what had happened to her, or perhaps it was just the war. Ellie didn't know, but she'd recognised that he was different, and he frightened her. Oh, he was fine with her most of the time, but something in his eyes told her that if he should ever come in contact with Knocker he would not hesitate to kill him...

Knocker turned as he heard the slow, heavy footsteps behind him; they'd been dogging him for a while now. He was feeling sore all over from the beating he'd taken earlier that day and there was no strength left in him to make a run for it. His head was swimming and he couldn't think straight, but as he looked into the face of the man behind him he gasped. Those eyes were the coldest he'd ever seen in his life.

'What do yer want?' he muttered hazily. 'Get out of me bleedin' face…'

'You're a nasty little shite,' the man said. 'Did yer think yer could get away with yer crimes? Murder, lootin', desertin', thievin'… and rape. Yeah…' A smile entered those cold eyes, but there was no humour behind it. 'Well, that's the end of the road fer you, Knocker… May yer rot in hell…'

Knocker felt the serrated edge of the knife go all the way in, turn sharply upward, and then the agonising pain as it was ripped out, tearing through his flesh. He clutched at his stomach as his guts tumbled out into his hands, the blood spurting everywhere. His eyes glazed as he saw the smile on the face of his killer and for a moment he wondered – what had he done?

He should never have legged it from the cops. At least the Army would have given him a clean death, and he might just have been sent back to the Front to take his chances with the others. As his knees crumbled and he collapsed on the pavement, his last thought was why… what had he done to set the knifeman after him?

As Knocker's eyes closed with his question unanswered, the killer turned and walked away, a smile on his lips. Job done and no trace, just as he'd been told.

Chapter 23

Ellie clung to Peter as they stood in the hall and kissed. His kitbag was packed and ready and he had to leave immediately to catch his train.

'I wish you didn't have to go,' she said, tears in her eyes. 'I do love you, Pete – and I'll never do anythin' to make you angry with me again, I promise. I hate that man and I – wish I'd never met him.'

'I know that, love,' Peter said and it was the man she'd married back again, his expression warm and loving. 'Everythin' will be fine now. You decide what you need to do about the kid. I'll stand by yer if you keep it – but it's up to you…'

Ellie nodded and smiled through her tears. 'Have you forgiven me now?'

'You should know,' he said and grinned. 'Didn't I take you dancin' and then make love to you last night? It's goin' to be just as it was, love. So forget it ever happened.'

Ellie hesitated, uncertain that she could trust him. One minute he was the loving man she'd thought she'd married and the next he was a violent stranger – a stranger who might be capable of anything.

'It would be best if I give the baby away, wouldn't it? You'd always resent it... I know you say I can keep it, but I want us to be happy.'

'Your choice,' he said and kissed her. 'But I'd like to have our own kids, Ellie – and after what that bugger did to you...'

'Yes, you're right,' she said. 'I keep thinkin' it's my flesh and blood – but it would remind us both. I'll do what Mrs Tandy suggested.'

'Good girl,' Peter said and kissed the top of her head, holding her pressed against him. 'It's all over now, love. You're quite safe. That bugger won't bother yer again, believe me. Just put it out of yer 'ead. I'll be back when this war is over unless they let me come 'ome on leave again – just be a good girl for me...' His hands pressed into her upper arms a little too hard. 'Promise...'

'Promise,' Ellie said. 'I didn't want it to 'appen, Pete – and I'll never let anyone near me again.'

'That's my baby,' he said and caressed her bottom with his hands, pressing her against him so that she could feel his erection. 'You belong to me, Ellie – and you might not like me if I got really angry. Now, behave and everythin' will be fine...' His eyes seemed to dominate her, sending chills down her spine. He'd said he'd stand by her and her decision, but she was certain he didn't mean it. A premonition of a future doing exactly what Peter told her sent cold shivers down her spine.

Peter picked up his kitbag and left. Ellie stared at the closed door. He'd refused her offer to go to the station with him, claiming that he didn't like long goodbyes, but she had the feeling he wanted to go somewhere first, before he caught his train. Suddenly, she shivered, feeling icy all over. Why did she feel as if she were a prisoner all of a sudden? That was ridiculous. Peter had told her she could keep the baby if she chose – but he wouldn't like it if she did. Perhaps it might be best to do what she'd planned with Mrs Tandy and let the Sally Army give it to a childless couple.

Pressing her hands to her belly, she apologised to the child growing inside her. 'I'm sorry. I could love you... I do love you, but he would hate you... he would hate us both...'

Ellie closed her eyes, feeling weak and nauseous. Something inside her told her that Peter wasn't the same man she'd married – he wasn't the man who had given her a whirlwind courtship and bought her a lovely ring and pretty clothes. It was something in his eyes, a coldness deep inside him. Perhaps it was the war. He'd changed and she wasn't sure she wanted to be married to him even though her heart cried out at the thought of losing him. How could she love him and yet fear him? It didn't make sense, but that's how she felt.

Sighing, she turned to walk up the stairs, but just as she neared the top, the dizziness swept over her and she could feel the sickness rising in her throat. She cried out and grabbed at the bannister for help, but her hands couldn't grasp hold of it and she tumbled all the way down to the bottom and then lay still...

'So, you did it?' Peter asked, nodding as the man answered in the affirmative. 'I owe you one, mate. Can't do much about it yet, but I'll see you right when the bloody war is over.'

'You've done me a few favours in the past.' The man stroked a purple scar down the side of his face; it ran from above his right cyc to the corner of his mouth. 'He squealed like a pig – they always do. The bullies are the worst cowards.'

'Yeah, I reckon,' Peter laughed, but it was mirthless. 'Anyone touches my property pays for it. You'll look out for Ellie while I'm gone – let me know if there's anythin' I should know?'

'Of course, mate. You and me go back a long way, and after the war we're goin' places together. Take care out there; keep yer head down, 'cos I want yer back in one piece. I can't do wivout me main man... ain't never known anyone wiv quite yer talent fer makin' the punters pay up, Pete, all wiv a smile on yer mug.' He chuckled deep in his throat. 'Stick it to a few of them bloody Germans fer me, mate.'

'Yeah, I will,' Peter replied. 'Got ter go now or I'll miss me train... see yer and thanks fer yer help.'

'Got ter stick by yer mates, ain't yer?' The man with the scar grinned. ''Sides, I enjoyed it... so long then...'

Peter turned and walked away. Scarface had murdered the devil who'd raped Ellie. He'd had it coming to him. Peter doubted that a single man in the lanes wouldn't have cheered at the news. They might have done it themselves if they had the guts or the contacts. Peter had both, but this way he was in the clear, and Scarface knew that he'd do the same for him if necessary.

He thought about Ellie's promise to get rid of the child once it was born. She'd better keep her word, because if she didn't, he would make her life a misery...

'Have you heard the latest news?' Alice said as she came up to Janet at the bar. 'Ellie collapsed at the top of the stairs and tumbled all the way down – Mrs Tandy found her and sent for an ambulance and they took her off to the hospital...'

'Oh, poor girl,' Janet said, thinking that Ellie might lose the child. Though perhaps she wouldn't mind that? 'I hope she's all right.'

'Mrs Tandy asked Maureen to go in the shop for her and she's sittin' up the hospital with Ellie now,' Alice said. 'She thinks the world of that girl, so I hope she comes through all right.'

'Yes, of course,' Janet agreed as her mother brought a plate of plain scones through to the bar and a dish of jam and another of what looked like margarine. 'Had you heard, Mum? Ellie had a fall down the stairs and they took her into the hospital.'

'Oh dear,' Peggy said. 'Has her husband left for his unit?'

'Mrs Tandy says he'd gone just before she heard the cry. She couldn't see him in the lane to call him back, but she'll let his base know that Ellie had an accident. I doubt the Army will give him more time off now though; he's just had a good long leave.' Alice sipped the milk stout Janet had poured for her.

'Compassionate leave perhaps?' Peggy suggested as Janet went off to serve a customer. She was about to turn away when Janet came back to them.

'This gentleman wants to see you, Mum – somethin' you'll be interested in he says...'

'He's a copper,' Alice said, gaze narrowed. 'Might not be in uniform but you can always tell – what does he want?'

Janet shook her head.

The man spoke to Peggy for a few minutes in a soft tone that neither Janet nor Alice could hear and then he nodded and went out. Peggy looked thoughtful as she joined them further up the bar.

'They've found the man that attacked Tom…' she said. 'His real name was Marnie James and he was a private in the army and a deserter. He was also wanted for several crimes – but none of that matters now…'

'Why?' Janet asked, a tingling sensation at her nape.

'He was found dead last night a few streets away from here – up past the market square. He'd been knifed and it was a particularly nasty affair by the sound of it.'

'He's dead?' Janet felt sick and clutched at the counter. 'Do they know when it happened?'

'They have a first estimate of about two-thirty this morning,' Peggy said. 'It's all right, Jan. Mike was in bed with you – and I'm quite certain Jack was at home in his bed. He left for his unit this morning so he would have needed his rest… Besides, it couldn't have been either of them.'

'How do you know?'

'I was told it was a professional job. Apparently, there was bruising consistent with a beating, which had happened earlier – but the killing was done by a professional hitman. That's what the police think… they're not lookin' for anyone local anyway. The inspector didn't quite say he wanted to give whoever did it a medal, but reading between the lines that's what he thought… Anyway, there were a lot of people after Knocker James. He raped a girl and left her for dead over in Bermondsey last summer. The police have a positive ID from the girl and her father. The father might have been capable of the killin', because he's a butcher and a special gutting knife for boning meat was used – but the butcher was in the hospital havin' an ingrowing toenail treated, so he's in the clear…'

'Lucky him…' Janet said. 'I wish Mike was…'

'What do you mean?' Peggy glanced at Alice, who was all ears.

'Don't mind me, love.' Alice grinned at them. 'I'm as deaf as a post when me friends are concerned – but I know what Jan means. I saw Mike walkin' down the lane at three this mornin'…'

'You saw him?' Janet gasped. 'He does sometimes go for a little walk in the early hours if he can't sleep, and he was very restless last night.'

'So might you be if you'd gone through what he has,' Alice said. 'Don't worry, love. I never saw a thing – and I didn't see Jack Barton with him neither…'

'Oh, Alice…' Janet looked at her mother, feeling as if she might faint. 'Mike said it was over… that they'd given him a thrashing and were leaving it to the military police.'

'I'm sure they did,' Peggy said stoutly. 'Just because they were both restless and couldn't sleep doesn't make either of them a murderer – especially the kind I've just been told about. I know Jack and Mike; they're not that sort, Jan. In anger they might be capable of killin', but not a cold-blooded assassination – and whoever did this knew where to find their victim. Neither of our men knew where he lived or where to look for him. It sounds more like a professional hitman to me.'

Janet breathed more easily. 'You're right, I was being silly. It's just that I wouldn't want Mike to be mixed up in anythin' nasty – or Jack.'

'I don't believe either of 'em would,' Alice said and nodded as she finished her stout. 'They're both of them good lads, Jan. Knock his block off, I shouldn't wonder, but stick a knife in, no.'

'Yes, you're right,' Janet said and felt easier. 'I'm being daft...' She indicated Alice's empty glass, 'Would you like another one – on me?'

'Not now, love. I'll pop in tonight,' Alice said. 'I've got ter cook me dinner and if I have another drop I shall put sugar in me gravy and salt in me custard...'

She got up off her stool and tottered off, giving a little sideways skip, just to show she was messing about.

'Alice!' Janet said and looked at her mother. 'She's got a wicked tongue on her sometimes, but she wouldn't do us any harm.'

'No, of course not. Alice wouldn't talk even if the police questioned her, but I don't think they will bother us. Knocker came from Bermondsey and I think they may centre their inquiries there – in case he'd upset one of the criminal gangs. Apparently, because a professional killer was used, they think it may have been a fall-out between thieves.'

'It seems a lot of people wanted him dead, and they think its poetic justice that he died here in the lanes,' Janet said and sighed. 'It's an awful thing to say, but I can't be sorry he's gone – I was a bit worried he might come after you, Mum.'

'I think the police have had someone watchin' the pub at night,' Peggy said. 'Knocker might well have tried somethin' if whoever it was that killed him hadn't got in first... The killer has done a lot of people a favour really, though it's a terrible sin to take a life.' She sighed as she heard a loud wailing from the kitchen. 'That's Fay. Freddie hardly ever makes a fuss. You'd think she was the one that wasn't right when she was born, not him...'

'Go and look after her,' Helen said, bringing in a dish of shepherd's pie and a plum tart with a jug of custard. 'I've finished my cooking, Peggy, and Nellie is washing up. I'll help Janet in the bar now.'

'Thanks,' Peggy said as the wails became louder. 'I'd better run – don't work too hard either of you...'

Janet glanced round the room, which was empty. 'Unless it perks up with the lunchtime girls, we'll be eatin' this food ourselves,' she said. 'If you're all right, Helen, I'll pop through and see if Maggie is still napping...'

'Of course. I can manage,' Helen said as one of the girls from the factory entered, hair tied up in a turban and a cigarette in her mouth. There was a smile on Helen's face as if she was enjoying herself. Janet thought she was gradually coming to life, as if she'd been half-asleep for years, under her husband's domination and was now beginning to believe that life could be good. 'I'll shout if I need help...'

'Glass of lemonade and a scone,' the factory girl told Helen as Janet followed her mother through the hall.

Ellie opened her eyes and then closed them again. Her head was sore and she could smell disinfectant and carbolic soap. Where was she? She was conscious of a deep ache in her side and felt as if she'd been kicked and punched all over.

A nurse went past and Ellie realised that she was lying in bed in a hospital ward, and beyond the shadows of shaded lamps were other beds with other patients. What had happened to her? It took her a moment or two to remember the attack of nausea and dizziness that had caused her to tumble down the stairs, and then another second to think of her child. Her child... had she lost her baby? Ellie's hands went to her belly but she could still feel the small bump that was all she had yet and felt reassured. If the fall had been meant to cause her to lose the baby, it had failed...

Where had that thought come from? Ellie was suddenly wide awake and tingling all over. Peter wouldn't have tried to make her ill in the hope that she might lose her child, of course he wouldn't! Yet she remembered him stopping by the jellied eel stall on the way home the previous night and buying her a dish, even though she'd protested she didn't like them and they made her feel sick. He'd almost forced her to eat some of hers – yet he'd eaten his own and finished hers and he hadn't felt unwell. Later, after they'd made love in bed, he'd fetched them both a cup of cocoa... unusual for him, and Ellie had noticed he hardly touched his. Could there have been something in the drink that would make her turn sick and faint a few hours later?

It was all nonsense, of course, and very disloyal of her. If Peter wanted her to get rid of the child he should just have said she had to, not leave it up to her. Ellie sighed. One thing she knew for sure, if her baby was still living and survived the full term, she wasn't going to give it away to parents she would never know, who might mistreat it, despite her promise. This baby was hers and if Peter didn't like it, he could do his worst. Peter had gone now and it might be years before he came home – if he ever did. There was a chance that he would be killed and she would never see him again...

No! She didn't want that, of course she didn't. Ellie remembered how his mother had tried to control her, warning her that Peter would be angry if he knew how she was carrying on. She hadn't given it much thought then, but now she'd seen the other side of him. A shudder went through her as she wondered just what kind of man she'd married and what it would be like to live with him if he did come back at the end of the war – and Peter was the sort who would. Ellie had known somehow that he was a survivor and even when she didn't hear for months, she never really thought he was dead.

Ellie closed her eyes as the nurse came to the bed and shone a torch on her face.

'Are you awake, Mrs Morris?' she asked, but Ellie didn't answer.

She didn't feel like answering questions yet. All she wanted was to be allowed out of here as soon as possible.

'Please tell me you didn't have anythin' to do with that murder,' Janet said as she and Mike were undressing that evening. 'Alice saw you in the lane – and she saw Jack Barton.'

'Did you think we went back to finish him off?' Mike grinned at her. 'Imagination, Jan. I think Jack would've finished him when he caught him, but I stopped him. We would've handed him in to the cops if he hadn't run off. I told Jack to let him go, because he probably could have caught him if he'd tried. Knocker would probably have still been alive if he had…'

'Thank goodness you didn't kill him,' Janet said and reached up to kiss him. 'I want you here with us, Mike, not banged up in a police cell…'

'I've no intention of leavin' you again,' he said and leaned over to kiss her. His arms tightened about her. 'Are you tired?' he whispered against her ear and she looked into his face, her heart jerking with excitement as she saw the look that had been missing for months. 'Only, I'd rather like to make love to you, darling…'

'Mike... I love you so much...' Janet went to his arms, giving herself up to his kiss as they fell back against the pillows together. Her hands crept into the back of his hair, caressing his neck and moving against him as the old clamour started inside her and she felt his mouth on her breast, nibbling and licking at the nipples in a way that made her cry out in sensual pleasure. His touch had lost none of its power to arouse her and she was soon panting with desire, melting inside for love of him. When Mike entered her at last, she felt her body cry out with pleasure and welcome him back. She'd needed this so much and the tears trickled silently down her cheeks as they lay together afterwards in silent content.

It was after they'd made love for the second time that Mike told her, 'I've begun to remember, Jan,' he murmured and stroked the silky skin of her back as she lay close. 'It isn't perfect yet, but this mornin' I remembered you in a blue dress outside the Docks. I used to walk you to work – and I remember thinkin' you were the loveliest girl I'd ever known...'

'Oh, Mike,' Janet said and pressed her lips to his shoulder, tasting the salt of his sweat. 'We were so much in love then... and I want it to be like that again, but I know there must be some things you don't want to remember.'

'I have had brief flashes of the attack on the ship for a while now,' Mike confessed. 'I remember the explosion and the water rushing in through a hole in the skin of the ship – and then the stink of hot oil and fire...'

Janet stroked his cheek, feeling a twist of pain inside because she knew this was the stuff of nightmares and the reason he cried out in sleep sometimes and at other times couldn't sleep at all.

'You're here with us now, darling. It's over...'

'It will never be over, Jan. I had good friends on that ship, many of them are dead, and it's a wonder that I survived – though I don't remember anythin' after I was blown off my feet and somethin' hit my head. I have no memory of being in the water. Either I got myself there in a daze or someone else did, but I was lucky I didn't go down in the engine room.'

'Did you work there?'

'No, I was probably sent there on an errand, but I think that's where I was when the torpedo hit us... and I'm very lucky to be alive, because a lot of the men aren't.'

Janet had no words. All she could do was press her face into his shoulder and kiss him, her hand stroking his arm. Nothing she could do or say would remove the pain of what had happened that terrible night at sea. It was possible Mike would remember more in time, because things were coming back to him little by little. She wanted to take all the sorrow and hurt from him, absorb it into herself, but she knew there was nothing she could do – except be there when he needed her.

'I love you, darling,' she said and kissed him on the mouth. 'Would you like me to make you a hot drink and bring it up for you?'

'No, just stop here in my arms,' Mike said. 'I think I might just be able to sleep now. I've faced the worst, Jan, and I've got you and Maggie, so I'm lucky – much luckier than most men in my shoes...'

Janet smiled and nestled into him, feeling the tension leave his body. She was lucky to have him back... much more so than she'd hoped. Mike was nearly his old self again and she loved him. She gave a little sigh of happiness as she curled into his body and drifted into a peaceful sleep.

Peggy was just about to start on the pastry making the next morning when she heard the wailing cry. At first she thought it was Fay, but it had come from upstairs and her youngest daughter was nestled in her cot in the kitchen, snuffling a little but sound asleep. Hearing another cry, she realised it was a woman and then she heard hurried feet and voices exclaiming. Her heart was racing as she went up the stairs and saw that all the commotion was coming from Janet's room. Helen had come halfway down the hall but hesitated uncertainly. Peggy shook her head at her and walked quickly towards her daughter's room. A sense of terror grabbed at Peggy's heart as she approached the open doorway. *No, don't let it be Mike. Please, don't let anything terrible have happened to him or Maggie…* But it had to be something awful for Janet to weep so uncontrollably.

Janet was in her petticoat as if she'd started to dress before realising something was wrong. She was screaming and crying, and Nellie was trying to calm her. Peggy entered the room and saw Janet kneeling on the bed. She was holding Mike's limp body in her arms and Peggy went cold as she saw blood on his pillow – not floods of it, but just a tiny trickle from his mouth as he lay sleeping.

'Mum…' Janet looked up at her as she walked towards her and her eyes were filled with horror. 'Mike's dead… I thought he was sleeping when I woke, so I got up and started to dress and then turned my head to look at him – and I saw the blood. He was better last night… more like himself than he'd been since…' Tears poured down her cheeks as Maggie started to wail from her cot.

'Nellie, will you take Maggie down and give her breakfast?' Peggy said quietly. The child knew something was wrong but didn't understand. Peggy was shocked and stunned herself, but had to be strong for her daughter. She took Janet in her arms, kissing the top of her head and holding her as the storm of grief took her and she sobbed bitterly. 'I know, my darling. I know how much it hurts and I'm so sorry... so very sorry. Yesterday Mike was like a new man, like the person you married, and this is a terrible shock for you. I don't understand it, Jan, but perhaps the doctors will...'

Janet gulped, pushed herself back and looked at her mother. 'Mike knew it could happen just like that,' she said, swiping a hand across her cheeks. 'He told me when he was still in the hospital that there was a tiny fragment of metal in his brain that might kill him if it moved... but I thought he was gettin' better and so did he.'

'He was much better,' Peggy said. 'I know this only makes it worse for you, but he was happy. Mike was happy here with you and Maggie. He loved you both – and I think he believed he was lucky to have you.'

'Why?' Jan said and now her grief and hysteria was under control, only a sob bursting through as she tried to speak. 'Why now, Mum? Was it because he went after that rotten devil and Jack... Did he get hurt in the struggle? Did he bang his head? I don't understand it, Mum.' Another sob left her although the tears had dried. 'I need to know why he died...'

'You've just told me, darling, Mike knew it could happen. Whatever he did or didn't do that fragment might have moved – even if he'd still been lying in a hospital bed. You mustn't blame yourself, Jan – or anyone else. It was the fault of this bloody war and that's the same for everyone who has lost a loved one.'

'I accepted it when he was in the hospital and didn't know me – but then he wanted me and he said he loved me... and it's like losin' him all over again. I lost him once and then he came back to me...' Janet covered her face with her hands, her shoulders heaving even though she wasn't crying. It was as if the pain now was too sharp for tears. 'I loved him so much, Mum. I don't know what I'm goin' to do without him – and Maggie loves him too...'

'Yes, darling, I know,' Peggy said and kissed her head. She felt like weeping herself but held her emotions in check. 'It hurts terribly to lose people you love. I had come to trust and feel real affection for Mike, Jan. He was a decent man and I wish it could be different.'

Jan brought her head up, and now she was calm, calm but cold as she looked into Peggy's face. 'We shall have to ring the doctor. I know what happened, but I suppose...' she shook her head. 'A funeral – I have to arrange...' her face crumpled and she flung herself down on Mike again. 'No, I can't... Come back to me, my love... please come back...'

Peggy took hold of her shoulders and pulled her upright, holding her as tightly as she could until the deep shudders stopped. 'Listen to me, Jan. You still have Maggie. You have to live for her. Mothers go on for their children however much things hurt...'

Janet nodded and pulled away; she was in control now, but her eyes looked dead. 'I'm goin' to ring for the doctor and hear what he has to say and then I suppose...'

'You're not alone, my love,' Peggy said. 'I've done this before for my parents and my stepfather. When we get the certificate we'll decide what to do for the best...'

'Yes, thanks, Mum,' Janet said. 'I know you've had your share of grief – but...' She shook her head, rose from her sitting position on the bed and walked to the door. 'I'll be all right, don't worry...'

Peggy continued to sit on the edge of the bed staring after her until a wail from Fay brought her to her feet. Her heart felt as if it had broken in several pieces for Janet's sake, but life had to go on. Peggy could help her daughter in practical ways. Janet had a home with her and they would help each other with the children, but no one could take away Janet's pain or even share it. That was a burden she must carry alone.

Why? Peggy echoed her daughter's question in her head. Janet had endured the months of her husband being missing and thought dead, she'd put up with being told to stay away when Mike was in hospital because he didn't remember her and her visits upset him, and then, when she finally had him home – when it seemed he was getting back to normal, this happened.

There simply was no justice!

Chapter 24

Maureen opened her front door to the young police officer. He greeted her with a smile, asked if he could come in and then told her the news: Violet's attacker had been caught trying to sell some of the things he'd stolen to a pawnbroker.

'We got lucky, Mrs Hart,' the officer told her. 'We circulated some leaflets to pawnbrokers throughout London's East End and one of them noticed somethin' unusual in the collection of silver and jewellery a man brought in. He asked him to leave it all for appraisal and rang us – we identified some of it as being Mrs Jackson's property, and perhaps some of yours. Mrs Violet Jackson's son has been arrested and we're hoping for a confession, but we've got him for theft if nothing more. A fountain pen was found at the scene – and our officer recognised it as having come from another burglary. So yours wasn't the first he'd done by a long way. We shall be asking you to come down to the station when you have time to pick out anything you recognise.'

Maureen had agreed and was about to put on her coat and leave the house when someone knocked at the door. Anne was standing there and Maureen invited her in, a chill at her nape as Anne started to speak in a halting, tear-laden voice.

'Oh no, not Mike,' Maureen said as Anne finished, and her throat closed with emotion. 'Whatever must poor Jan be feelin'? She was so happy to have him home and she told me only two days ago that he was much better and thinkin' of findin' a job.'

'Alice came and told me as soon as she heard,' Anne said. 'I went round to see if I could do anything. I don't have to work today as it's Saturday, but Peggy said the best thing I could do was to let our friends know.'

'It's so very sad...' Maureen said and felt tears on her cheeks. 'I'm aware she isn't the only one to lose her husband – but it's the way it happened. All those months of not knowin' if he was alive or dead, and then he was in the hospital and didn't know her... And then he came home and she looked happy when I last saw her. He did too. He was a different man to the one I saw in the kitchen on my weddin' day – what happened?'

'Peggy told me there was a tiny piece of metal in his head from the time when he was knocked unconscious in the explosion on his ship – and it must've moved. The doctor says that is the most probable cause and because of the hospital reports they're not going to do an autopsy.'

'At least that's somethin',' Maureen said, 'but it's still rotten for Jan – and the whole family. Maggie was just gettin' used to havin' her father home and now...'

'Yes, I know...' Anne brushed a hand over her eyes. 'I've been crying all the way here. There's just nothing I can do or say to Jan to help her through it. She must be devastated. I was feeling sorry for myself because Kirk was away – but Janet is going through hell...'

'And Peggy too,' Maureen said. 'Oh, Anne, it has all been so awful lately, what with the war and all the tragedy we've had round here. You hear one tiny piece of good news and then somethin' terrible happens...'

'Shall I make you a cup of tea?' Anne asked, looking round.

'No thanks, I've only just had one – and I have to pop out shortly...'

'All right. Where are your grandmother and Shirley?'

'Gran took her down the market. They've gone to look for some new shoes for Shirley – thank goodness she isn't here. It upset her when the house was ransacked. I don't want her witnessin' more grief.'

'Yes, poor kid,' Anne said. 'The children are suffering enough with their fathers away at the war without the kind of thing that has been happenin' here lately.'

'I thought when that awful man who attacked Ellie was killed – and now they've arrested Violet's son for attackin' her and robbery – that we might have come through the worst of it...'

'They've arrested Violet's son?' Anne was surprised. 'Did she give them some information?'

'All I know is that the police recovered some stolen goods from a vigilant pawnbroker and made an arrest. I'm just on my way to look at the stuff they've recovered and see if I can identify anythin'...' Maureen frowned. 'Do you think I should go round to Peggy's and see if there's anythin' I can do first?'

'Leave it until later. There was quite a lot going on when I went over,' Anne said. 'We'll both be there for Peggy and Jan when they're ready, but just at the moment I think Jan is too sensitive.'

'Yes, of course she would be,' Maureen said and placed her

hands on her stomach. 'Oh, he kicked. He's started doin' that quite often recently…'

Anne smiled. 'It shows he's – or she's – all right then,' she said. 'At least you've got something to smile about, Maureen. Having a baby is the most wonderful thing that can happen to any woman, whether it's a girl or a boy.'

'I feel it's a boy.' Maureen caught the wistful note in Anne's voice and reached for her hand. 'It didn't happen for you then?' she said softly. 'It will when Kirk comes home next time. You'll see…'

'Yes, I'm sure of it,' Anne agreed and lifted her head. 'And for now I'm taking pleasure in my friend's children. Did you know how well Shirley is doing at school? She's good at spelling and arithmetic and art… She's a very bright child, and she sings to herself in the playground. It just shows you've given her a real home, Maureen, a place where her talent can blossom.'

'Yes, I know she can draw well,' Maureen said and smiled. 'She's turned out to be a lovely child now, Anne. When we first met I thought her a little horror – but she couldn't be sweeter to me these days. She looks after me and fetches things for me and asks if I'm all right…'

'She calls you her mum and that's what you are,' Anne said. 'Lock up then, Maureen, and I'll walk down to the police station with you. It's on my way. I'm looking for a birthday present for Mavis and I saw some nice scarves in a shop in Commercial Road. If they've got one in blue or navy I shall buy it for her.'

'She will like that,' Maureen said. 'I think it must be a long time since she had anyone to buy her a lovely present… she's been a widow for some years.'

'Yes, I'm afraid it might be a while since she's had anyone

306

to share her birthday with,' Anne agreed. 'I think Mavis was lonely until I started lodging there and she was quite excited when I suggested we have a special tea for her birthday...'

Maureen nodded but didn't make any comment on the elderly widow. 'Have you seen your uncle recently?'

'I visited him three evenings ago,' Anne said and frowned. 'He was hopin' to come out of hospital and go home, but I don't think he will. The doctor asked me if there was any money to look after him. It's either the infirmary, which isn't much above the level of the old workhouse – or a home outside of London. I'm told it's nice there, but expensive. So it looks as if we shall have to try and sell his flat so he can be properly looked after...'

'It isn't easy to sell these days, because of the uncertainty of the war...' Maureen sighed. 'Nothin' is as it should be since Germany went mad and started marchin' into countries that didn't belong to them.'

'I know – but I have been asked if I would rent it out instead. I've got to see if we can balance the two, his fees and the rent a tenant would pay... if we can manage I'll hang on to it for a while.'

'It makes a lot of work and worry for you, Anne.'

'I don't mind it,' she said and smiled. 'He and my aunt gave me a home when my parents died, so I've got to do my best for him. Besides, it gives me something to do with myself. Stops me fretting about Kirk and wondering when I'll see him again.'

'I bet it doesn't,' Maureen said and linked arms with her friend. 'You might not think of him for a short period, but he's there in your head all the time – it's the same for all of us. I can't wait for the next letter from Gordon. If it's a few days too long I start thinkin' somethin' has happened – and I'd swear you're just the same.'

'Well, yes I am,' Anne agreed and laughed. 'I must have been mad to get married the way I did – but I couldn't help myself. If Kirk doesn't come home...' She stopped abruptly.

'He will,' Maureen said. 'We have to believe, Anne. I know a lot of men won't come back when this is all over, but we have to cling to the belief that we'll be some of the lucky ones...'

Violet opened her eyes and looked at the nurse bending over her. She tried to speak but her mouth felt dry.

'Would you like a sip of water, Mrs Jackson?' the nurse said. 'You'll start to feel better soon now. Doctor says you're over the worst.'

'What happened to me?'

'Don't you remember? You spoke to a policeman the other night and told him somethin' – about bein' attacked...'

'Bryan...' Violet said and a single tear trickled down her cheek as she remembered what he'd done to her, the threats he'd made – and then he'd just left her lying there, unable to move or get help. 'My son wanted...' she checked and shook her head. 'I fell and banged my head.' She felt the tears prick her eyes because even after what he'd done, Bryan was still her son.

'Yes, and you were very ill,' the nurse told her. 'Doctor said you can have water and perhaps later on somethin' light to eat – a little soup or jelly and ice cream...'

'Just water,' Violet croaked. She sipped eagerly at the glass, but it was taken away before she had swallowed anywhere near as much as she wanted. 'More please...'

'It will make you sick,' the nurse said. 'Just a sip now and then until you're over the sedation. We had to keep you quiet for a while because it was touch-and-go, Mrs Jackson – but you're very much better...'

Violet didn't feel better. Her head ached and she couldn't see properly for a start, though the mist was gradually clearing from her eyes. She felt exhausted, as if she'd run for miles or done strenuous work, and the weakness made her limbs feel heavy. It was too much effort to sit up and she closed her eyes again, but the pictures she saw were distressing and she gave a little cry.

Bryan was demanding money and the look in his eyes made her afraid. He was so angry because she wouldn't give him what little she had – and yet she knew he must have searched everywhere and he would've taken her post office book as well as any money in her purse. But luckily, she'd sent Henry's book back to be changed into her name, so he couldn't have got that and she hadn't fetched the money for the stock yet. If it was still waiting for her, she would need to collect it, but then what should she do? Violet didn't even know where she would go once she was discharged – she had no home, because the landlady wouldn't have kept the rooms she'd intended to rent when she didn't turn up...

Tears of self-pity welled in Violet's eyes. Surely, she didn't deserve this? She hadn't done anything wicked. Perhaps she might have been kinder to poor Henry – but he hadn't suffered, not really. She was the one who had suffered at the hands of her cruel son. She'd given him all her savings and still he'd demanded more. She was his mother but he didn't care whether she lived or died... he'd knocked her down and left her to die alone... and she would have died if her mother-in-law hadn't found her.

'Mrs Jackson,' the nurse was there again, breaking into her thoughts. 'You have a visitor. She says her name is Hilda Jackson and she's brought you some lovely flowers. I'll find a vase for you…' The nurse turned to the person standing behind her. 'Don't tire her too much, please – just five minutes…'

'Why are you here?' Violet asked weakly, her throat tight with emotion and fear. 'Have you come to tell me to quit your property as soon as I leave hospital?'

'No, as a matter of fact, I came to say the opposite,' Hilda said and gave her a straight look. 'You've not been fair with us, Violet. However, I'm a fair woman and Henry thought somethin' of yer, so I'm goin' to give you a chance. Besides, yer son didn't treat yer right. If yer behave yerself, you can stay on until you're on yer feet again. I'll pay you the money I promised for the stock and you can carry on with yer corsets upstairs…'

Violet felt tears wet her cheeks as she was overcome with emotion, sadness for her son and gratitude towards Hilda. 'I've been told they caught him…' she croaked. 'Have they recovered my stuff?'

'Yer post office book ain't been found yet, but yer son said it was in his room and the police were goin' to search. He talked, Violet, told the police everythin' – and he blamed you for a lot of it, but I told the police not to believe all he said. I know how men like that can be and I dare say he knew how to twist yer round his finger – sons are like that if you let 'em get away with it.'

'I gave him all me savings and he wanted more…' The weak tears spilled over.

'Well, he won't be troublin' you for a while,' Hilda said. 'We're not the only people he's robbed and he sung a pretty tune, I'm told; a list of offences as long as yer arm. The police told Maureen they think he wants to go to prison. Seems he's afraid of someone he wouldn't name...'

'He's in trouble for gamblin'. He owes the bookie money and they've been after him, threatenin' what they'll do if...' Violet clammed up as the nurse came back with a vase filled with spring flowers. 'Thanks for the flowers. I'm sorry for what happened...'

'So am I,' Hilda said grimly. 'But, like I said, I'm givin' you the benefit of the doubt – make sure you don't give me cause to change me mind...'

Hilda turned and walked off, not waiting for the nurse to tell her to leave. Violet closed her eyes. She could feel the tears on her cheeks but they were of weakness, nothing more. Hilda had offered an olive branch and Violet would take it and use it until she was ready to move on. If she'd still got the money in her post office account that might not be long, but for the moment it was a relief to know she still had a home to go to, even if it was only temporary.

'Gran, you're an old softie,' Maureen said and gave her a loving hug. 'I don't much like Violet, but I'm glad you did what you did... I do feel sorry for her after the way her son treated her. He knocked her down durin' the struggle and left her to die; no one deserves that. The police told us he claimed she tripped and fell and he panicked, but I don't think I believe him.'

'He's a rotten bugger,' Hilda said savagely. 'I don't hold with men treatin' their womenfolk like that and I hope they put the devil in jail and throw away the key.'

'If Violet won't accuse him of beatin' her, he'll probably be out in five years or less...'

'Maybe they'll stick him in the army and send him to the Front,' Hilda said. 'Henry wasn't much of a son to me and he didn't treat your mother or you as he ought – but he would never have done anythin' like that.'

'No, he wouldn't,' Maureen said and smiled. 'Dad wasn't so bad, Gran – he just took advantage of me and I let him. After I came home from nursin' he was nicer to me and I've forgiven all the rest…'

'Well, I've given Violet her chance. She can stay or go – I hope she won't cause you any bother.'

'I can cope with Violet on her own,' Maureen said. 'Her son was blackmailin' her, tryin' to get as much money from her as he could. I doubt she and I will ever be friends, but we can manage to be civil to each other if she stays.'

'She needed a place to come back to when she leaves the hospital,' Hilda muttered. 'I've been fair, Maureen, but don't let her take advantage of you – it's your business and she pays for anythin' she wants from the shop like anyone else, and the rent.'

'Yes, of course,' Maureen agreed, 'but it's your business, Gran. You bought the stock from her. I should've had to let the shop to someone because I hadn't got enough money to start up on my own.'

'I'm too old to bother with it,' Hilda said. 'I wanted you to have it all, love, and now you have. It will make sure you're all right – if anythin'… Well, we'll say no more.' She saw Maureen's smile dim. She didn't want to think about what would happen if Gordon died over there, but it had to be faced. Maureen had two children to think of and Gordon's wage would cease if he were killed; the army pension would be less than what she was getting now. Hilda had wanted to protect her, to make sure her girl would be all right whatever happened, though she prayed Gordon would come back safe. He was a decent bloke and both Maureen and Shirley loved him. 'Just get on with your life and be happy.'

'I'm lucky,' Maureen said sadly. 'Janet Rowan has been through so much and now she's lost her husband. I feel so upset for her.'

'Yes, of course you do – but don't let it overshadow your life. You've got yourself and the baby and Shirley to think of. You have to be strong for everyone's sake.'

'Yes, I know...' Maureen gasped as the baby kicked. 'He's goin' to be a fighter, Gran.' She smiled and put her hands to her bulging belly. She was getting so big now that she felt awkward and cumbersome, but so far she'd been well in herself, apart from the early nausea and faintness. Her ankles hadn't swollen and she didn't get a lot of backache. 'I'm goin' round to Peggy's this mornin' after I've taken Shirley to school. I know there's nothin' much I can do, but I want to offer my help.'

'You give her my love,' Hilda said. 'Jan is a mother, Maureen, and sooner or later she is goin' to remember how much that child means to her. Maggie will bring her out of it, you'll see. Mothers always respond to a child – and that Maggie has a strong will. She'll be demandin' attention and Peggy has enough to do with the twins.'

'Yes, that's what I thought. I might be able to take Maggie out to the park or somethin' – buy her an ice cream. Just to give them a rest...'

'You get on then, love...' Hilda said as Shirley came into the kitchen. 'Well, here she is then. Are you ready for school, love? Maureen is takin' you this mornin'.'

'Mummy,' Shirley said and went to put her arms around as much of her as she could, her head pressed to Maureen's stomach. She jumped back and looked up at her in wonder. 'He kicked me, Mummy – I felt him…'

'Yes, he's gettin' restless,' Maureen said. 'He'll be here with us in a few weeks, love. Are you lookin' forward to havin' a brother?'

'Yes,' Shirley nodded vigorously. 'Not a sister. I don't want a sister – but I'd like a brother…'

'Well, I think he's a boy, but I can't be sure.' Maureen smiled, because there was no rational reason to think she was carrying a boy, but she'd had an instinct for a while now.

'As long as she or he doesn't take my place…' Shirley said, a little jealous.

'That is never going to happen if I have half a dozen girls or boys,' Maureen said and Shirley giggled. 'Come on then,' Maureen said and held her hand out to her. 'We'll get you a few sweets on the way – what do you want?'

'A stick of barley sugar please.'

'We'll have to see what Tom has got then,' Maureen said and took her hand. 'He'll have somethin' nice for you, I'm sure…'

Chapter 25

'I wondered if there was anythin' I could do to help?' Maureen said when she saw Peggy a little later that morning. Peggy had been cooking and the twins were asleep in their cot in the kitchen. There was no sign of Janet or Maggie. 'I thought if Janet was too upset, I might take Maggie out for a while... give her a break.'

'She hardly lets the child out of her sight,' Peggy said and shook her head. 'She's always been an attentive mother but now – she is there the minute Maggie cries...' Peggy gave a strangled sob. 'I wrote to Laurie and told him about Mike. He hasn't written in months and I don't know whether he'll come back – but I had to tell him. Pip telephoned and spoke to Jan. He can't get leave but he talked to her for nearly an hour on the phone and she seemed a little better for a while. I'll be glad when Friday is over, Maureen. Perhaps once the funeral is done...' She swiped a hand over her eyes.

'It helps sometimes,' Maureen agreed, 'but I think the hurt goes too deep with Jan. She's been through so much, being told he was missin' and then all the rest... it's too much for anyone to bear.'

'I know.' Peggy looked at her in despair. 'She's like someone frozen, Maureen. She goes through the motions, does what she has to and answers me when I speak to her – but there's no emotion. I think she cries at night, but she won't let me in. She's just shut us all out, except Maggie...'

'I'm so sorry,' Maureen said and went to hug her. For a moment the two women clung to each other. 'I have no words of advice. What can you do when someone is hurtin' that badly?'

'It was such a cruel thing,' Peggy said. 'If he'd gone in the sea – but to come back to her and find each other again and now...' she broke off as the tears choked her. 'It's so much worse for her than it was for me. I lost Able, but I was older and we didn't have so long together...'

'I know you still hurt, Peggy, because you loved him,' Maureen said. 'But you have the twins – you have Able's children to love. I know Janet has Maggie, but it isn't quite the same.'

'No, because they were a family,' Peggy agreed. 'Mike had learned to love his daughter and he loved Jan. He was just beginnin' to show affection to her and Maggie and to act like the man she knew – and she's goin' to feel his loss so much. I know she'll cope, but I'm not sure what it's done to her. She isn't the Jan I know anymore...'

'Yes, she is,' Maureen said. 'The Janet you know and love has gone away for a while, but she'll come back. Her grief will take time to heal, but it will happen.'

'Thank you, Maureen. You're such a good friend...'

'I'm always here for you, Peggy; just as you are for me.'

'Yes, I know,' Peggy said and made an effort to pull herself together. 'Anyway, how are you gettin' on? Thank goodness they arrested Violet's son and he isn't likely to be around to terrorise us for a while – and that other one is dead. What does Tom have to say about that?'

'Nothin' much,' Maureen said. 'He just nodded when I told him what the police had said. He looked... satisfied, but he didn't say much. No doubt he was glad that Knocker wouldn't be around anymore, but you don't celebrate someone's death, however evil they are.'

'No, of course not.' Peggy bent to take some trays from the oven. 'How is Violet – have you heard?'

'Gran visited her at the hospital. She said she seemed tired but all right. The nurse told her Violet was on the mend – and she'll be comin' back to Mulberry Lane for a while when she leaves hospital. Gran told her she could stay on in the flat, but she's finished with the shop. Tom will be runnin' it, servin' the customers and I'll look after the stock.' Maureen sighed. 'What with Ellie falling downstairs and Violet being attacked – it's all hospitals and tears lately. My feet have hardly touched the ground what with visitin', helpin' Mrs Tandy – and the shop.'

'You're not doing too much?'

'No, not while I can manage...' Maureen smiled and touched her stomach. 'He will take up more of my time once he's here, but I'm sure I can manage to visit the wholesaler and do a few accounts. I can trust Tom for all the rest – and the profits will be mine, once we start to make a profit again... the war hasn't helped, and Dad never did make hundreds, though I was a bit surprised he hadn't got a bit put by.'

'Perhaps Violet had it and kept quiet about it?'

'No, I don't think so. Her son might have found it, though. Dad wasn't one for lettin' his right hand know what his left was doin'. He only banked what he needed to keep the business goin'. He used to have cash in his office and in the desk upstairs, but there wasn't any the last time I looked.'

'Perhaps he gave Violet a lot more than he ever gave you.'

'She says he didn't.' Maureen sighed. 'It's a mystery. If any money was found put away somewhere it would be Violet's, of course. Dad left her everythin' and she's his wife – but I doubt we'll find a secret hoard. I think it's just that the profits had dwindled since the war and more than ever after I left.'

'Well, it hardly matters to you,' Peggy said. 'As you say, you would only hand it over to Violet. I dare say she's had a good hunt for any money he might have left…'

'Probably,' Maureen said. 'Well, if you're sure there's nothin' I can do…?'

'You could go and give Helen a hand in the bar for half an hour or so…' Peggy glanced up at the clock on the wall. 'The lunchtime rush is about to start – though it isn't always much of a rush these days. Our profits are down by nearly half recently. As you say, it is due to the war and the shortages, and perhaps people don't have as much money to spare.'

'I'll go and see if I can help Helen,' Maureen said just as Fay woke up and began to wail. 'She's either wet or hungry…'

'Probably both,' Peggy said and looked tired. 'She wants twice as much attention as her brother.'

'Girls always need their mothers,' Maureen said. 'I'll stay to talk to Janet when she gets back – and then pop in and say goodbye before I leave…' She left Peggy and went into the bar where Helen had a little queue waiting.

'I'm glad you've come,' Helen said. 'I didn't want to ask Peggy after all the upset. Everyone is asking questions and it's taking ages to serve...'

'I'll give you a hand,' Maureen offered and approached the next customer. It was a good thing she'd come, because Janet couldn't be exposed to everyone's curiosity and Peggy was too upset to fend off the customers' questions. Maureen hadn't been sure it was a good thing taking in Sally's mother, but she'd turned out to be both helpful and friendly now that she'd escaped her overbearing husband. Maureen just wished Sally was here to see the remarkable change in her mother...

Peggy told Janet that Maureen had called to see her, but she shook her head and went straight up to her room. She knew that her friend wanted to show sympathy and to comfort her, but Janet couldn't bear that for the moment. Her father had written a sympathetic letter to her, saying he was truly sorry about Mike's death, but she tore it into shreds. He hadn't shown understanding when she needed it, and she didn't want it now.

She couldn't bear the sadness in her mother's eyes when she looked at her, or the unspoken sympathy Nellie conveyed every time they met. All of it made Janet want to scream and hit out at something or someone, because none of them understood that her overriding feeling was anger. She was furious with God and the world for cheating her. She'd been given a taste of happiness only to have it snatched away and it wasn't fair. Janet knew she wasn't the only woman suffering because of this dreadful war, but for the moment she could think only of herself and her beloved child. She felt as if she had to guard Maggie every second in case something should happen to her to and her mood was one of black despair as she waited the allotted days to watch them place Mike's body in the cold grave.

Tom put the latch on the door as he went through into the back kitchen to make a cup of tea. He'd brought his chicken paste sandwiches and he would eat them before he returned to the shop. People came to the door to try it even during closing hours, but if he was there and not out on a delivery, Tom always served them. He knew that Maureen could do with the trade and he wanted to help her make the business a success.

His tea finished, he decided to go into the stockroom and see if he could clear the last of the backlog of cardboard boxes from the far corner. They were all full of heavy stuff and he wasn't sure what was in them. Probably tins of some sort or washing soda, which was always heavy to shift. He opened the first box and saw bars of toilet soap and tins of tooth powder and nodded. Things like that were eagerly snatched from the shelf when they appeared because they had become scarce this past year. A lot of things were difficult to buy and people managed without them, substituting salt for their teeth and using the coarse domestic soap to wash their hands, which was more readily available.

He lifted the box and carried it into the shop, filling one of the lower shelves, out of sight. If he put this sort of stuff in plain sight everyone would buy it and it would be gone in two days. This way, he could make it last longer, but it helped to fill shelves that had looked a bit empty of late.

Returning to the stockroom, Tom opened the next box and discovered an assortment of shoelaces, writing paper and envelopes, greaseproof paper, knicker elastic, and other similar items. He moved it to one side and opened the last box, smiling as he discovered tins of pink salmon, pilchards, and a few of peaches. Now that was more like it!

He took the box through to the shop and filled the empty spaces on the shelves. Tom had no idea when the tins had been put in the stockroom, but they weren't damaged or rusty so he thought the food inside must be all right to eat; he would buy one himself and take it home for his tea. If it didn't kill him it wouldn't kill anyone, he reckoned, and grinned to himself as he went back to the stockroom. He had now opened all the backlog of boxes and most of the stuff he'd found was out on the shelves. There was a pile of old magazines in the corner and some empty boxes that had been stacked up right at the back. Cardboard and paper were all required for recycling by the government these days and Tom decided to sort them out another day; he would take them round to the scrap yard, because Bert was collecting the paper and cardboard in his shed until it was taken away to be reused.

Just as he turned away, something caught his eye in the corner. One of the floorboards had lifted a little and must have been kept down before by the heavy boxes that he'd now moved. He went to investigate, touching it with the toe of his boot. It was loose and that made him wonder. He knelt down and tried lifting it. As he'd thought, it came away easily and Tom peered into the dark space underneath – there was something there...

He was reaching for it when he heard the shop bell go. Replacing the floorboard, Tom went to serve the customer with a newspaper, ten Woodbines and two ounces of mint humbugs. He had no time before the next customer came in and was kept busy for an hour serving regular customers wanting some sugar or margarine and tins of Spam or corned beef.

He forgot about the hidey-hole under the floor when Peggy came in and asked him if he would come round after work.

'We've got a few jobs I can't manage,' she told him. 'Barrels need fetchin' up from the cellar and the tap needs changin' on the draught ale and...' she sighed. 'We're all upside down at the moment, Tom. With Janet so upset and the twins...'

'You must be at the end of your tether,' Tom sympathised. 'I'll always come when I'm needed, Peggy. You know that...'

After Peggy's visit Tom had a stream of labouring men; workers from the Docks and essential services who worked in protected jobs. They came in for cigarettes, sweets, packets of crisps and a newspaper and invariably stopped for a chat about the weather, the state of the war or their wives. The RAF had started a bombing campaign against the German arms' factories at the end of the last month and the papers were full of articles about the successes and the loss of life it was causing.

It was past six when Tom finished serving the last customer, popped a tin of salmon in his pocket, and put the 'Closed' sign in the door. He'd half thought Maureen would pop in and collect the stocklist he had ready for her. There were so many things they needed, from boxes of matches to white flour and the tins of condensed milk that so many people relied on these days. Tom knew she'd been helping Peggy, but it was unusual for her not to pop in at all.

It was only when he went through the back to pick up his jacket that he remembered the loose floorboard. Returning to the stockroom, he lifted it and shone his torch down the hole. Yes, he wasn't wrong – there was a box hidden away in the dusty hollow. Withdrawing it, Tom saw it was a metal cashbox.

He tried the lid but it was locked. Shaking it, he heard the sound of something inside but not coins; it might possibly be notes or something heavier. Tom couldn't be certain. Clearly it was of value or Henry Jackson wouldn't have gone to the trouble of hiding it under floorboards weighted down with heavy boxes.

Tom sat back on his heels and thought about it. Whatever was in the box it belonged to Henry's wife, because he'd left everything to her – and yet if he'd wanted her to have it, wouldn't he have told her or put it in the will?

If Tom gave the box to Maureen or Gran, he knew they would feel obliged to hand it over to Henry's widow. Tom didn't think that was fair or right. Maureen had worked for her dad for years for next to nothing. If there was anything of value here it ought to be hers – but she would give it to Violet.

Tom didn't have the right to decide, but if he hadn't been so industrious in clearing the stockroom the box might have remained undiscovered for years. Who knew what might happen in a few years?

Tom replaced the box where he'd found it, fitted the floorboard into place and then dragged the empty cardboard boxes over it. No one knew what he'd found – he didn't even know it was valuable, except that Henry Jackson wouldn't have gone to so much trouble to hide it if it wasn't.

Tom left the stockroom and switched off the light. He would think about what he'd found and what he ought to do about it. By rights it probably was Violet's, but she hadn't treated Henry decently and Tom thought Henry Jackson might want his daughter to have whatever the box contained. For the moment Maureen didn't need it, and she would just pass it on to Violet – but one day she might be in difficulty. Tom would keep his find to himself for the moment...

Janet looked so pale and ill. Maureen sat on the front bench in church with her, Peggy, Anne, and Pip, who had got leave for his brother-in-law's funeral, Alice, Nellie and Gran. Janet hadn't cried, though Peggy's cheeks had been wet and so were Maureen's. Now as they stood by the open grave, watching Mike's coffin being lowered into the earth, Maureen thought Janet would break, but she didn't. Her hands clenched at her sides as she stepped forward to throw a single red rose onto the coffin. She ignored the earth offered her, though Peggy, Maureen and Nellie took some and let it trickle into the grave.

Janet just stood there staring at the grave, frozen and seemingly unaware of what was going on. Maureen stepped forward and put an arm about her waist.

'Time to go home, love,' she whispered as everyone began to turn away. For a moment Janet's eyes flickered with some strong emotion – as though she was about to refuse and throw herself wildly into the grave with her dead husband. 'Maggie needs you…'

Maggie and the twins were being cared for by Anne's Uncle Bob and Mavis so that the family and close friends could all attend the funeral.

At the mention of her beloved daughter, Janet's eyes moved to hers. She inclined her head and moved away, Maureen ready to support her if she stumbled, but Janet kept her head high and ignored all those who looked at her with pity. She got into the car with her mother and brother and was driven away. Peggy had laid on a small reception at the pub, but Maureen wasn't sure she wanted to go. She wasn't sure she could bear more of Janet's heavy grief – and yet Peggy had to bear it and she'd particularly asked Maureen to come.

'Maureen...' the girl's voice broke into her thoughts. She turned and saw Ellie. The girl was wearing dark colours and looked pale. 'I wanted to come and see you one day...'

'Are you better now, Ellie? I'm sorry I only got to see you once in the hospital,' Maureen said and looked at her.

'You looked after Mrs Tandy's shop so she could come,' Ellie said and smiled at her. 'I know you have enough to do – it can't be long now until the baby is born...'

'A couple of weeks or so,' Maureen said. 'The sooner the better, as far as I'm concerned. I'm lucky though, I haven't had as rough a time as some women do.' She looked at Ellie in concern. 'What about you – the baby wasn't harmed when you fell?'

'No, thank goodness. The doctors think it was just some dizziness caused by something I ate and I'm fine now,' Ellie said and smiled. 'I've made up my mind, Maureen. I'm goin' to keep my baby. If I'd lost it that would've been the end of it, but it lived and that means I'm meant to keep it... I don't care if people talk and I don't care if Peter doesn't like it. This baby is mine and I love it, even if I hate the man who put it inside me.'

Maureen was silent for a moment and then she nodded. 'I think you're right to keep the baby, Ellie. None of us know what will happen in the future. Keep your baby – if you're sure you can manage?'

'I'm gettin' Peter's money now and I'm still workin'. They kept my job for me while I was in the 'ospital – no one else would work for my wages and not many want to try. Most girls want to work in the factories or join the services. I thought I might try joinin' the women's voluntary services. You belong to that don't you?'

'Come and see me in the mornin' and we'll talk about it. Are you goin' to Peggy's now?'

'We've got to get back to work...' Ellie glanced at Mrs Tandy. 'She's been ever so good to me, more like a mum than a landlady...'

'You're lucky to have her, Ellie.'

'Yes, I know,' Ellie said. 'I'll see you in the mornin' then – in my lunch hour...'

'I'll have the kettle boilin'...'

Gran joined her as Ellie walked off. 'Are you goin' to Peggy's, love?'

'I think we should. I'd rather go home and put my feet up, but Peggy needs us. Janet hardly speaks to her or anyone...'

'She's taken it bad,' Gran said, 'but I'm concerned about you, Maureen. You look tired and you mustn't overdo it. You could have the baby any time now.'

'Not for a few more weeks...' Maureen said, but she knew her grandmother was right. First babies could be early or late and she had a feeling hers might be in a hurry. She'd started to feel very tired lately and her instincts told her that she was very near to giving birth. 'We'll go just for a little while – and then I'll put my feet up when I get home...'

Maureen woke in the night with a start. At first she couldn't think what had woken her, but then she felt the pain in her back and cried out. She panted as it wrenched through her, making her feel as if she wanted to scream and hit out at something. Remembering her nursing training, Maureen got up and dressed in a loose makeshift maternity gown. She had a bag packed ready for this. Now all she had to do was phone the hospital and then get a taxi... except that she didn't feel capable of doing either. Where was Gordon when she needed him? Maureen felt a wave of self-pity that she had to cope alone, but quashed it. She wasn't alone. She had Gran and she had friends. She just needed to remain calm and everything would be fine.

'Are you all right?' Gran entered the kitchen wearing her dressing gown. 'Has it started?'

'Yes, I think so...' Maureen gasped as the pain struck again. 'I've got time to get to the hospital. I just need to pop out to the phone box and ring ahead to let them know and then get a taxi...' They'd always had a phone at the shop for business, but Gran had never thought it necessary at home when she could rely on her neighbours for anything she needed.

Gran walked to the sink and filled a kettle. 'Sit down there and I'll make a cup of tea when I get back...'

'Where are you goin'?'

'My neighbour's husband will ring the hospital and he'll get you a taxi. Just sit there and breathe deep when the pain comes. We'll have you there in plenty of time, so there's no need to worry...'

Maureen nodded. 'Thanks, I was just wonderin' who to ask for help!'

'Mick will oblige,' Gran said. 'He's too old for the Army but he trains with the Home Guard and he'll likely still be up...'

Maureen sat down and closed her eyes as Gran went out of the back door. She smiled at her own foolishness. Of course she wasn't alone. This was the East End of London and the folk in the lanes were like an extended family. She only had to ask for help and someone would be there...

*

Maureen opened her eyes as she heard a buzz of voices. The maternity ward was open for visitors and she was in the end bed, being the newest mum. Her son's cot was beside her and she leaned over to look at him sleeping peacefully, his hair a darkish red that clung to his head in tiny curls. His birth had caused her a lot of pain and he'd taken six hours to make his appearance, but he was worth everything, she thought. Maternal love flooded through her as she looked at the child she loved so much that it filled her with happiness. She'd wondered if she would slightly resent the baby for being Rory's and he definitely had his red hair, but it didn't matter. He was hers and she loved him with a fierce protectiveness that surprised her. She smiled, because she was a mother twice over now; Shirley was her little girl and she was glad she had a boy.

'Mrs Jackson, are you ready for visitors?' the nurse looked at her inquiringly. 'We have six people waiting to see you, but we allow just two at a time – and only if you feel up to it?'

'Oh yes, please – who are they?' Maureen asked.

'Mrs Peggy Ashley and Tom Barton,' the nurse said. 'Also Alice Carter, Mrs Tandy, your grandmother and Shirley. The little one can only come in for five minutes I'm afraid.'

'Ask Gran and Shirley in first,' Maureen said. 'Then Gran can take her home and get her to bed...'

Shirley lagged behind Gran, looking uncertain until Maureen held her arms out to her and then she laughed and ran to her. 'Have you got my little brother for me, Mummy?' she asked breathless with excitement.

'Yes, look at him; he's in the cot there,' Maureen told her and smiled. 'We knew he was goin' to be a boy just for you, didn't we, love? He's lovely, isn't he? Do you like him, Shirley?'

'I love him and I'm goin' to help you look after him,' Shirley said. 'Dad told me to take care of both of you – and I shall...'

'Thank you, darling. Be good for Gran, won't you? I'll be home in a couple of days, but I'll have to stay in bed for a week or so – you'll have to carry my drinks up and down, won't you?'

'Yes, and change his nappies,' Shirley said. 'I've been practisin' on my friend's little brother and I haven't stuck a pin in him once...'

She looked so proud of herself and so earnest that Maureen smiled, though she didn't allow herself to laugh. 'You're a lovely girl, my darling,' she said and Shirley climbed on the bed to kiss her.

'How are you, love?' Gran asked and jerked her head in the direction of the corridor. 'They're queuin' up to visit you. I think several people just popped in with flowers and have gone again...'

'I've got some here...' Maureen looked at a posy of violets by her bed. 'I like these, but I don't know who they came from...'

'Wasn't there a message?'

'None that I've seen...'

Gran bent her head to sniff. 'They do smell nice – they were your mum's favourite flowers, I think?'

'Yes, they were. Dad might have known that I love them, but I'm not sure...' Maureen glanced at the flowers and suddenly remembered. Rory had once asked her what flowers she liked best and she'd told him violets were one of her favourites... but it couldn't be him. Rory wouldn't send her flowers. He couldn't know she'd just had a baby – nor that he was the father...

'What's wrong, love?' Gran asked and Maureen shook her head, smiling at them. 'You looked sad...'

Maureen pushed the worrying thoughts from her mind. 'Everything is wonderful. I have a lovely son and daughter and I've got you – and one day Gordon will come back to me.'

'I've got a letter for you,' Gran said and produced it from her bag. 'I think it's from Gordon?'

Maureen tore open the envelope and read the brief letter, which had several thick blue lines through some sentences. She smiled and folded it again, slipping it under her pillow.

'Daddy sends his love,' she said to Shirley, 'and he's fine. He says it's like being at the seaside where he is and he's lookin' forward to takin' us to the sea when he gets home.'

'Is he comin' home soon?'

'Not for a while,' Maureen said. 'It won't be long though. A few months and he'll be due for leave again...' She hoped she was telling the child the truth, though she had no idea when her husband might come home. This terrible war seemed to drag on and on with no end in sight and the news was mixed, better at one moment and then terrible the next. 'We'll have such a lovely surprise for him when he comes though, won't we?'

'What are we goin' to call the baby, Mummy?'

'I'm not sure – what do you like?'

Shirley thought for a moment, then, 'Why don't we call him Robin? He has bright eyes and red feathers just like a robin...'

'Yes, his hair does look a bit like feathers,' Maureen agreed. She thought about it for a moment and then nodded. 'Yes, I like that name, Shirley. Robin is what we'll call him – Robin Hart; that sounds good.'

'The nurse is signalling to us,' Gran said. 'I'd better take Shirley home. Have a good rest, love. We'll be waitin' for you when you get back…'

'Thank you for comin', Gran, it's lovely to see you both.'

'Couldn't keep this one away.'

'Ask Peggy and Tom to come in next. I want to talk to them…'

Gran nodded and took Shirley by the hand, leading her from the ward. Shirley looked back at the door and waved, but didn't seem unhappy about leaving. Perhaps Gran had promised her a treat, Maureen thought.

She wondered about the unknown person who had sent the violets again and then dismissed the thought as Peggy and Tom came in. Peggy had a large bunch of flowers and Tom had brought her a bag of grapes and a newspaper. He looked a little uneasy but grinned when she smiled and thanked him for coming.

'I thought I'd best ask if you want me to go to the wholesaler's. I've got a bit of money in the till – I could spend what I've got on the most urgent stock and leave the rest until you're ready?'

'Thanks, Tom. I'll leave it up to you until I'm home,' Maureen said. 'I've decided I need a telephone at Gran's and that will make it easier to keep in touch with the shop and the wholesaler. If I'd had one the other night I wouldn't have had to get someone to telephone for me…'

'I wish I'd known,' Peggy said. 'I'd have been there in a shot. You saved my life when the twins were born, Maureen…'

'Nothin' that dramatic,' Maureen said and laughed. 'I'm a nurse, Peggy. It's my job to help people in need – and Robin wasn't in as much of a hurry as your two. I had plenty of time to get here.'

'Is that what you've decided to call him?' Peggy peeped in the cot. 'He's beautiful. Anne is goin' to visit tomorrow, and Helen sent her good wishes. I think she's got a little gift for you. She and Anne stayed in the pub so I could come this evenin' – but I've had people in and out all day asking for news. You're a popular girl, Maureen. Everyone wants to know about your baby.'

'Yeah, they've been in the shop an' all,' Tom said. 'I've got some presents for you from various customers, but I thought you'd have them when you get home.'

'Thank you both so much,' Maureen said. 'Everyone is so kind – just as they were when I got married.'

'We all care about you,' Peggy said. 'Janet sent her love and said she will get to visit you when you come home.'

'Is she any better?'

'I think perhaps a little,' Peggy said. 'The funeral was an ordeal for her but it's over and in time she will come to terms with her loss. She still has Maggie – and she isn't the only one to lose her husband. Too many of our men are gettin' killed, Maureen.'

'Yes, I know,' Maureen said. 'I had to give up work when it became too much for me, but once I'm fit again, I hope to work a few shifts at the hospital again. I'll need a babysitter, but it shouldn't be too difficult... There are a lot of women at home with children of their own and they might be glad of a bit of extra money.'

'You'll find plenty of takers, but surely you won't want to leave him?' Peggy looked at the child in the cot.

'Not at first, but when he's weaned I may think of it – just a few hours. I'm not goin' to work full-time. I couldn't – but the hospitals need all the nurses they can get...'

'Yes, I'm sure,' Peggy said, but looked doubtful. 'I'll see you when you get home. We'd better go, there are others waitin' to see you...'

Maureen kissed Peggy when she leaned over her. She closed her eyes as Peggy and Tom left the ward. Her eyelids felt a bit heavy and she was almost ready for another little sleep, but her friends had come out of their way to visit and she couldn't refuse, but she was a little tired.

Alice and Mrs Tandy had both brought little gifts. Mrs Tandy gave her a baby coat in white wool wrapped in tissue and Alice gave her a silver rattle with teeth marks in the handle.

'I've kept this for years,' she said. 'I wanted your little one to have it, Maureen. You've been good to me and to a lot of others, love, and I'm glad it all went well for you...'

'Yes, I echo Alice's sentiments,' Mrs Tandy said. 'Everyone has been talkin' about you in the shop today, sayin' how much they like you and how pleased they are you've settled in the lanes. Ellie sends her love. I know she wanted to talk to you about joinin' the voluntary services to do her bit, but she says it'll keep until you come home... Everyone wanted to send their good wishes. We know we've got you to thank for keepin' the corner shop open and that means a lot to all of us in Mulberry Lane.'

'That was mostly Gran...'

'She couldn't have done it without you,' Mrs Tandy said and Alice nodded. 'Besides, it's lovely to have some good news for once. I think we've all had enough of gloom and doom lately...'

'Yes, it has been a bad few months for local people,' Maureen admitted. 'I think it's mostly over now, though. They got the brute that ransacked Tom's house and hurt... others...' Maureen caught the warning look in Mrs Tandy's eyes. Alice didn't know about the rape and it would be better for Ellie if no one else guessed. 'And Violet's son is in a remand cell waitin' for his trial... so perhaps the worst of our troubles are over now.'

'Not until them bloody Germans are crushed, it ain't,' Alice reminded them. 'We're makin' the best of things in the lane, and we'll hang on for dear life, but them buggers are sure to come up with somethin' nasty. You mark my words. They ain't finished torturin' us yet...'

'We all know that, Alice,' Mrs Tandy said, looking cross. 'But we're not about to let bullies get us down. The more they throw at us, the more we'll fight back – it's the British Bulldog spirit. We're not done for by a long shot, whatever they do to us.'

Maureen lay back and closed her eyes as her friends quarrelled gently. Neither of them was in the wrong, but neither of them was ready to give in either. She couldn't help sighing with relief when the nurse came and asked them to leave.

'Mrs Hart is very tired,' she said. 'You've had your time. Please leave now and let Maureen rest...'

'I'll see you when you get home, Maureen love,' Alice said and kissed her cheek. Mrs Tandy did the same and Maureen drifted into a peaceful sleep.

She was smiling as she lay there, half-dreaming of a world that was no longer at war. Gordon would come home and they would be a family and everyone would be happy and smiling again, the pace of life in the lanes slow and steady as it had been when she was a young girl.

'Hello, Maureen,' a man's voice said, making her start awake. She saw him and a chill ran through her, scattering her feeling of peace and warmth. 'When were you goin' to tell me I had a kid?'

'Rory...' she breathed. 'What are you doin' here? Who told you I'd had a baby?'

'They gave me leave and I wanted to see you, Molly love. So I came back to London on a visit to my cousin – and news travels fast in the lanes.' His expression hardened again. 'I'm not without friends here, even if you hate me. Did you really think I wouldn't find out about the kid?'

'Why should you? He isn't yours. I'm married...'

'I know, but I can count,' Rory said and his smile made her shiver. 'That kid is no more Gordon Hart's than the man in the moon's...'

'He isn't yours and he never will be,' Maureen said and pushed herself up against the pillows. 'Go away. I don't want to see you ever again...'

Rory looked down at the cot. 'He even looks like me. How you goin' to explain that away, tell me that?'

'He's not yours,' Maureen said. 'Please go away or I shall scream for the nurses...'

Rory hesitated and then nodded. 'I didn't come here to upset yer or make a scene – but I know that's my kid and I want to see him. You can't stop me, Maureen. I'll find a way, no matter how much you try to hinder me, and you can deny it until you're blue in the face. I'll never believe you...'

Rory turned and walked away, leaving Maureen to stare after him. The tears trickled down her cheeks because she felt as if her happiness had shattered like brittle glass. She hadn't wanted Rory to find out because she'd known he would make trouble for them and she was right.

'Is something the matter, Mrs Hart?' the nurse asked her.

'That man – if he comes here again, don't let him near me or my son...'

'I thought he was your husband...' the nurse looked startled. 'He said he was...'

'No, he isn't – and I don't trust him. He might try to take my baby...'

'Surely not? He seemed such a charming man and so concerned about you... He brought you some lovely flowers... those violets were from him.'

'Give them to a patient who doesn't have any,' Maureen said. 'Please, don't let him come in again. I don't want his flowers or him anywhere near me.'

The nurse took the violets away and Maureen leaned over to look down at her son. Yes, his hair was red, but Gordon's had a hint of red in it. No one could know for certain and she would never admit that Robin was Rory's son.

A look of determination settled over her mouth. She would need to be on her guard where Rory was concerned in the future, but she wasn't going to let him bully her. Alice had talked about the bulldog spirit and she was right. The British people refused to let the Blitz crush them and they continued to stay strong and fight despite shortages, the bombing of strategic ports and towns, and the loss of so many fine young men. Maureen wasn't going to let Rory intimidate her. Robin was her son and she would decide who was allowed access to him. Only a very few people knew the truth and none of them would talk.

She smiled and allowed herself to drift into a peaceful sleep. She had everything she wanted. All she had to do was to stay strong in the coming months. Surely the war would be over soon. Gordon would come home and she and Robin would be safe. In the meantime, she was determined not to let Rory bully her. She had too many friends who would look out for her. Rory was an outsider and if she said he wasn't allowed near her son, he wouldn't get the chance.

Rory could only harm her if she let him. If he thought he could frighten and bully her, he'd soon discover he was wrong. Maureen had accepted emotional blackmail from her father for years, because she cared for him. Rory had cheated her and let her down too many times. She wouldn't let him destroy her happiness.

Maureen let go of her fear as she slept. She'd come through the birth of her beautiful baby with ease and had only a happy future ahead of her...